THE REBEL'S WRATH

⚜ a novel ⚜

CHRISTOPHER W. MORIN

The Rebel's Wrath

ISBN 13: 978-1-63381-068-6

Designed and produced by
Maine Authors Publishing
558 Main Street, Rockland, Maine 04841
www.maineauthorspublishing.com

Printed in the United States of America

To my parents, who first took me to Gettysburg, PA, in the summer of 1988. They opened up a whole new world of historical interest to me, fueled my passion for Civil War history, and inspired me in many ways.

✠

Author's Note

In creating this work of fiction, I made every attempt to be as historically accurate as possible. I tried to use as much descriptive detail and period language necessary to give the reader the best understanding of the strained political and social atmosphere of the time. There is racist language and contentious symbolism used in the story that is considered both offensive and controversial by today's standards. This is in no way meant to glorify or promote racist views/organizations or the old Confederacy and its symbols in general. The story and its content do not reflect any political views of the author whatsoever. It was my intention to create an interesting story composed of many fictitious elements using accurate language, political ideology, and symbolism common in that time.

CHAPTER 1

Little Round Top

Chamberlain stomped up and down the line ducking under tree branches and stepping over large stones and exposed roots lying haphazardly in his path. Crouched before him was a thick line of blue-uniformed soldiers hurriedly piling up rocks, stacking small logs, and seeking cover behind thick trees. Down the rocky hill and just out of sight, Chamberlain could hear the sounds of the advancing Rebels making their way up toward his regiment's position. Behind and to his left were the standard-bearers of the 20th Maine Volunteer Infantry Regiment. After issuing a few last-minute orders to his company commanders, Colonel Chamberlain drew his revolver and calmly lined up next to the rigid soldiers presenting the regimental flag and the Stars and Stripes. The colors hung limply in the oppressive July heat, but were bravely displayed in anticipation of the imminent fight.

++

Toward the extreme left of the line crouched a young Union soldier—a private. He meticulously watched Chamberlain's movements as mixed thoughts about his commanding officer, the approaching danger, and the war in general raced through his mind. All around him men were hastily jamming ramrods down the barrels of their .58-caliber Springfield muskets. The private—not remembering whether his musket was loaded or empty—instinctively reached for his leather cartridge box. But before he could put his fingers on a paper cartridge, he hesitated, then caught sight of Captain Spear waving his sword and shouting orders for G Company to move farther to the left. Instantly and automatically the private sprang up with the other soldiers of his unit and hastily redeployed left to the new position indicated by the highly animated sword-wielding Spear. In search of cover, the private resumed his crouch and pulled some downed tree branches, small stones, and handfuls of earth toward himself. He piled the rocks up high until his frightened, adrenaline-soaked mind was convinced the paltry little barrier was adequate protection against any Rebel musket fire sent up in his direction.

"Damn…this is it. I'm gonna be face to face with the Almighty before this day is through, I just know it. I can feel it down in my soon-to-be-liberated soul," muttered the now-trembling private amid the shouting and unruly commotion unfolding around him. He removed the rumpled blue kepi from atop his head and looked inside. Sewn into the interior with thick white thread was his name—Sherman Jackson. He stared at it for what seemed like an eternity and was certain he'd never again hear it called out.

From his new position, Sherman looked back and to his right. He could still see Chamberlain standing calmly before the colors and wondered how his regimental commander planned to defend this little rocky hill so hurriedly occupied by 3rd Brigade. Much closer to Sherman was Chamberlain's younger brother, Tom. G Company's First Lieutenant and his older brother's adjutant, the peculiarly whiskered Tom showed unbridled enthusiasm as he scrambled back and forth issuing orders to his platoon. In a broader voice, Spear continued barking out commands to the entire company.

"We're it, lads!" shouted Spear. "We're the end of the line! Keep it tight!"

Sherman, a bit stunned, quickly turned his head to the left. His heart was struck with a jagged lightning bolt of fear upon realizing that nobody was next to him. He was the last soldier in line.

"Where's the rest of the brigade?" shouted Sherman as he clutched his musket.

"The 16th Michigan, 44th New York, and 83rd Pennsylvania regiments are lined up to our right. The 20th Maine holds the extreme left of the line," answered a sergeant Sherman didn't recognize. At that moment, the fear-stricken private felt like the most vulnerable target in the entire Union Army of the Potomac. It wouldn't be long before every musket barrel of Lee's Confederate Army of Northern Virginia was trained directly on him—he was convinced of it.

I never should've enlisted, he thought. *Why'd I embrace such a foolish notion? To prove I'm loyal to my country and help preserve the Union?*

To destroy slavery? To inflate my own sense of worth and character? To impress my father? Matters little when you're dead.

Sherman had enlisted when the 20th Maine was mustered in Portland back in August of 1862. He was spared from the fighting when the regiment was held in reserve at Antietam and saw limited action assaulting Marye's Heights at Fredericksburg. An outbreak of smallpox kept the regiment out of combat at Chancellorsville, and the pursuit of Lee's army north into Pennsylvania yielded little action except for a few skirmishes, fought mostly by opposing cavalry. The imminent battle about to unfold on a small rocky hill on the outskirts of a town called Gettysburg would be where Private Sherman Jackson would experience his first major engagement of the Civil War.

The danger lurking downhill became apparent to the men of the 20th Maine, as the sounds of the advancing enemy, personified by boisterous whoops, howls, and authoritative shouts in peculiar-sounding southern accents grew in intensity. The commotion was accompanied by bursts of gunfire that forced many Union soldiers to duck for cover—but not Chamberlain. He stood tall, ready for anything Robert E. Lee could hurl against him this day.

"There!" followed by several sharp cries of "Here they come!" echoed up and down the Union line. Sherman jerked his head forward, straining to see the approaching danger. Suddenly a deep, ragged line of gray, tan, and butternut uniformed Confederates emerged through the trees. They looked lean and hungry, flaunting a reckless determination to get up the hill and smash through the Union defenses. Leading the formation was an old, heavyset Confederate with a long white beard. At first glance he seemed out of place among the younger and much thinner soldiers around him; moreover, to Sherman, his appearance strangely resembled a likeness he had seen of Santa Claus as drawn by Thomas Nast in a January publication of *Harper's Weekly*. His jolly appearance aside, what really made this man stand out was the fact that he wasn't dressed in a colorful suit, nor was he bringing gifts to the Union army. He was in fact bravely leading the attack carrying nothing save the Confederate battle flag. The Southern Cross, colored brightly in the Confederacy's own version of red, white, and blue, captured Sherman's attention for a moment. The enemy was upon him!

Stricken with an overwhelming sense of fear he had never experienced in his young life, Sherman hesitantly trained his musket on the approaching wall of Confederate soldiers. Unbeknownst to the young Federal private, the situation was more critical than he ever could have imagined. Since the beginning of the war in 1861, Robert E. Lee's Army of Northern Virginia had consistently outmaneuvered, outfought, and outwitted the Union Army of the Potomac by employing simple yet brilliantly unconventional battle strategies. Lee's unorthodox tactics and superior generalship kept the Union army constantly guessing and always on the defensive, unable to dictate the war on its own terms. Consequently, Washington replaced its top commanders as frequently as the sun rose and set. The revolving chaos at the highest peaks of the Federal command did not help the Union army's chances for overcoming its earlier defeats and embarrassments at the hands of Robert E. Lee and the late Stonewall Jackson.

Now it was 1863 and the soldiers of the Confederacy had an unrivaled confidence astride a sense of invincibility that was deeply encouraged by their leaders and now personified by their bold invasion of the North. It was truly a high-water mark for the southern states in rebellion and their armies. The Confederate push into Pennsylvania not only put the Federals on the defensive in their own territory, but it also showed Lee's aggressiveness and his potential to directly threaten Washington itself. A Confederate attack on the U.S. capital was conceivable by some Union officers but generally discredited by the majority. However, this day on the battlefield of Gettysburg, Pennsylvania, there were enough influential men wearing blue uniforms to appreciate the threat.

╪╪╪

"Hold the line," was the order cemented in Chamberlain's mind. He knew the dangers to his regiment and to the army in general. He also knew that he could not pull out under any circumstances. The 20th Maine had to hold, or the extreme left of the Union army could cave in and be flanked by rampaging Confederates. If that happened, the battle would certainly be lost; Meade's army would suffer a blow from which it couldn't recover—assuming it wasn't destroyed completely—and an open road leading straight to Washington and a Confederate siege of the city would be the end result. Such an outcome could force Lincoln to sue for peace, thus ensuring the creation of a separate and victorious Confederate States of America.

Private Sherman Jackson didn't share any of the deep concerns of his commanding officer. He was too scared and too concerned about his immediate situation to ponder what would happen to his country should the Union lose the day's battle. His mouth was dry and his stomach fluttered as he tried to steady his musket. He did his best to settle on a target but wasn't sure of the range. He didn't dare fire. Fear and uncertainty held him back until the first volley.

With a mighty thunder, the Federal line cut loose its fire first. A wall of hot lead crashed into the advancing Confederates below, knocking several off their feet, sending them tumbling backward to their deaths. Some cried out in agony while others simply crumpled forward and fell silent. The holes in the Rebel line were quickly filled and an equally devastating blow from dozens of Confederate Enfield muskets soon matched the Federals' fire. Stunned, Sherman watched as several Union soldiers on the right were hit. Many struggled to reload their muskets and were picked off by hidden Confederate sharpshooters.

The Rebels continued to lumber up the hill in waves, stopping only to reload and fire when the time was right. Several were cut down, but many were able to get off a successful shot and drop a Union soldier, thereby weakening the defenses. Sherman continued to observe the battle unfolding before him as if in a trance. His senses took in the action all around him but his body refused to react. Amid a thick cloud of smoke, and with the ground strewn with dead or dying men, the Rebels made a concentrated push to reach the Union line. They fell short of their goal in a hail of murderous gunfire that cut down many a soldier in gray. The southerners left standing limped back in hopes of regrouping for another charge.

Sherman watched as the Confederates retreated out of immediate danger. In his daze he failed to notice that the extreme left of the Union line hadn't been hit. Perhaps it was by design or just plain dumb luck that his position was spared the first wave of the Rebel assault. Whether he knew it or not, he was lucky to be alive. He kept a fixed gaze downhill and didn't move a muscle.

"Christ Almighty, Jackson, wake up," snapped the soldier to his right. He cuffed Sherman across the head, knocking off his kepi and revealing his disheveled dark brown hair. "I ain't gonna get my ass shot off on account of you sitting there doing nothing! Either you get in this fight or I'll shoot you myself." The soldier hurriedly aimed his weapon at the developing threat looming before him. "Open your eyes, Jackson! They're moving against the left!"

Sherman reached behind him and pulled his fallen kepi back on. His fear had subsided long enough for his mind to process what was now happening. Several dozen Rebel soldiers were moving laterally to the left at a quickened pace. Within minutes a mass of Rebel troops lined up directly in front of Sherman's position. He readied his weapon just as fire and smoke erupted from both sides, sending hot lead zooming in every direction. Several shots whizzed by Sherman's ears, forcing him out of his spell. The battle suddenly became all too real, and Sherman's brute instincts took over.

Feeling an unbelievable surge of adrenaline course throughout his body, he took a bead on the nearest gray uniform and squeezed the trigger. As the hammer dropped he waited for the flash of smoke and the hard kick of the gun into his braced right shoulder. To his surprise and horror, the gun did not discharge.

"Keep up your fire! I want no gun silent! Pour it into 'em, boys! Pour it into 'em good and heavy!" shouted Captain Spear, still madly waving his sword and bounding up and down the left of the line like a spooked rabbit with a ravenous fox on its heels.

Sherman dropped as low as he could just as Rebel fire slammed simultaneously into the faces of two men on his right. Each let out a piercing cry of agony, then collapsed backward. Blood splattered the right side of Sherman's neck and face. Unfazed, with his instincts for combat and survival at last in control of his actions, Sherman hurriedly retrieved a paper cartridge from his leather cartridge box. He ripped it open with his teeth and poured the black powder down the barrel of his musket. He methodically seated the Minié ball at the tip of the barrel and slid out the ramrod. Using the metal rod, he pushed the powder and projectile to the breech of the barrel. Countless hours of drill ensured he automatically replaced the ramrod back into the pipes under the barrel before reaching for his cap box so as not to misplace the precious loading implement. With the hammer half-cocked, he placed a copper percussion cap filled with fulminated mercury on the nipple, then brought the hammer back to full cock. This was it. He was now ready to fire.

Sherman summoned all the strength and courage he could muster. He positioned himself in a tight crouch, then swung his heavy musket into firing position. He again took aim at the closest gray uniform he could find. Without thinking, without speaking, and without any hesitation, Sherman squeezed the trigger. As the powder charge ignited, it sent the lead projectile hurtling toward its mark at incredible speed. However, in Sherman's eyes, the bullet moved as if it were in slow motion. He watched it as it left the barrel, sailed through the air, and struck its target.

The Rebel was hit in his upper right leg and he dropped instantly. Clutching the wound, the man's hands became soaked in blood. With little time to react and no knowledge of what to do, he couldn't stop the massive hemorrhaging. He cried out in pain with a tremendous howl but soon fell silent. Sherman saw the man spasm with a quick jerk, then nothing. It was his first kill.

"My God, I got one…I got me my first Reb," said Sherman, not knowing what to think. His mind had no time to ponder it as his bodily machinery took over again. Automatically Sherman reached for another paper cartridge and repeated the loading and firing process. He realized he had to fight and fight hard if he were to last this day. Survival now dominated his thoughts, pushing out all previous notions of being killed. A heavy sense of self-preservation overtook the young private and he became determined not to surrender to death. If death wanted him, it would have to beat him in this fight first.

As the battle progressed the Confederates were having a hard time getting up the hill. At first they formed firing lines and went muzzle to muzzle with the Union troops. Since the Federals had the high ground, they were in a better position to break up the Rebel formations. The southerners then charged valiantly with direct frontal assaults, only to suffer heavy losses, until eventually they had to fall back. Occasionally a dozen or so brave souls in gray would make it to the Union line and try to smash through using nothing more than bayonets, the butts of their rifles, or in some cases their fists. These mostly suicidal charges did little for the Rebels except force small breaks in the line and create some temporary disruption in the Federal ranks—at a horrific cost.

Time and again the Rebels pressed the attack, determined to dislodge the Union soldiers from the little rocky hill they were so vitally defending. The summer heat was unforgiving and the air became thick with hazy smoke that choked the breath out of many. The ground was littered with the bloodied dead and dying while the trees became scarred and disfigured by the multiple hits of musket fire they deflected or absorbed. There was no escaping the death and destruction all around. Soon, after another Confederate pullback, there was a brief yet merciful lull in the fighting.

To Sherman it was unclear which side was taking the most punishment, but he could see that the Union line was looking dangerously thin and the number of men in blue uniforms lying dead outnumbered those standing. To him the 20th Maine, particularly G Company, seemed to be taking the worst of it and he started to wonder just how long they could hold out. The left had been hit repeatedly and it was no secret that the Rebels were making an all-out attempt to flank their position.

Just then Sherman saw Chamberlain off in the distance. At the sound of a bugle, Spear and every other company commander converged on Chamberlain's location. Exhausted and painfully parched, Sherman and other soldiers of the regiment could only watch as the colonel and his standard-bearers became enveloped in a circle of captains.

After a very brief meeting the group disbanded and immediately began shouting orders. Sherman looked for Spear. The wiry captain soon emerged and hollered commands for his men to get to their feet and extend the line farther to the left. The worn-out warriors in blue hustled along at the prodding of their sergeants. Using his lieutenants as position-markers, Spear extended G Company and skillfully redeployed his men at sharp angles to match the Confederates' flanking maneuvers. The other companies fell into place and soon a new line was formed. The Federals now had the position they wanted, but did they have the manpower to hold it? The line was despairingly weak—just one man deep in many places. Suddenly, as if matters weren't bad enough, a far more serious problem revealed itself through the desperate voices of many Union soldiers.

"I don't have anything left," cried out a private, his hands frantically rummaging through his leather cartridge box.

"I got three shots. Only three!" replied another after checking his ammunition supply.

"The Rebs just keep coming. How can we stop 'em all? The whole damn Confederacy is trying to take this hill! We got nothin' but sticks and rocks to throw at 'em now," yelled another panicked soldier upon realizing his cartridge box was empty too.

Spear gave an order for his men to scavenge ammunition from the dead and wounded. Other officers followed suit and soon the soldiers holding the thin line were again ramming bullets down the muzzles of their muskets.

"Lord in Heaven please spare me an extra shot or two," implored Sherman as he searched every pocket he had in hopes of finding additional paper cartridges to supplement the five remaining in his dog-eared cartridge box. His search came up empty.

"Here they come again!"

Sherman looked up and saw a muddled formation of Rebel troops attempting to assemble into a firing line. At first they appeared to be a harmless menace, more like a disorganized rabble than a spirited fighting force, but as the sounds of drumbeats married up with authoritative voices of southern commanders, the soldiers in gray quickly transformed into a formidable threat. They had endured a solid hour of punishment and were as exhausted as their northern counterparts, but they still had a lot of fight left in them—and more importantly, plenty of ammunition.

The air was split with a piercing Rebel yell that sent eerie chills shooting through Sherman's body. It was an almost indescribable war cry that personified southern resolve and morale on the battlefield. Suddenly, amidst all their shrieking and howling, the Rebels charged. They raced forward with all the force and tenacity their hearts and souls could muster. It was as if the fate of the entire Confederacy rested on the success or failure of this one attack against the farmers, loggers, and fishermen of the 20th Maine regiment.

The Rebels stormed forward with untethered ferocity. Their attack was met with a torrent of fire from every 20th Maine musket fortunate enough to have a Minié ball tamped down the barrel. Some southerners were hit while others took cover and returned fire, inflicting more damage on the already tenuous Union position. Both sides exchanged a massive volume of lead, hoping to deliver the knockout blow that would decisively end the battle. The Confederates brutally hemorrhaged their manpower with repeated flanking assaults aimed at the Union left. The Federals continued to maneuver and match the Rebel movements in a desperate attempt to keep them in check, but the cost in blood was high and many Federal soldiers were cut down.

"Keep up your fire! Pour it on, boys! Pour it on!" shouted a sergeant before two Confederate balls slammed into his chest. He toppled over and into Sherman, knocking him out of his firing position. Two more volleys ricocheted off a rock near Sherman's head. Stunned, he got back into his crouch and fired off his last shot. As the gun discharged, the bearded and butternut-clad Rebel in its sight dropped and fell dead. Sherman could tell he was an officer and wondered how many Rebels he had killed today. Sadly he had lost count a long time ago. More distressingly, the young private was now out of ammunition. He pounced on the cartridge box of every corpse near him. The ground was littered with Union dead and he prayed he would not be joining his fallen comrades.

He reached into a mortally wounded sergeant's cartridge box and discovered one remaining paper cartridge. He bit open the paper with his black, powder-stained teeth and began reloading his gun. Suddenly a terrifying sight caught his eye. Through the thick haze of dirty black powder smoke, a line of thirty Confederates standing shoulder to shoulder appeared from behind some trees. They raised their muskets in unison and let off a murderous barrage of fire toward Sherman's position. His legs gave out in an involuntary act of self-preservation. As he dropped, several shots whizzed past. Bullets nicked his uniform at the shoulders and waist while another knocked his kepi clean off his head. Miraculously, however, no bullet tore into his flesh or shattered his bones.

As he hit the ground, the thin line of men around him seemed to evaporate. A gaping hole was effectively shot out of the Union line, and the Rebels exploited it without delay. With another ear-splitting Rebel yell emanating from their parched throats, the Confederates charged.

Their officers encouraged them forward by waving their swords and shouting, "Give 'em the cold steel, boys! That's the style!"

In an instant, Sherman found himself alone. He was the only man standing amidst a sea of blue-uniformed casualties. His nearest help was a disorganized mass of troops several yards to his right. To his left was nothing but a graveyard of fallen men. Blind instinct again took over as Sherman was overcome with a wave of adrenaline that willed him to fight and not flee. He reached for the bayonet dangling on his belt and quickly affixed it to his gun barrel just as the first Confederate reached him. He swung his musket like a club and caught the gray-clad Rebel with the butt end. The impact fractured his skull and sent him reeling backward just as another Rebel charged. Sherman thrust his bayonet forward, jamming the pointed blade into the chest of his attacker. He jerked it out and violently slashed at another Confederate trying to take him down. This time he slipped and hit the ground hard. His musket fell out of his hands and—more alarmingly—out of his reach.

"You rotten son of a bitch," Sherman madly shouted as a Rebel jumped on top of him and tried to strangle the life from his body. The two thrashed on the ground, kicking, scratching, and clawing at one another, each trying to get in a solid blow that would lead to the eventual kill. Sherman was able to break the Confederate's grip on his throat and land a punch squarely on the man's chin. As he broke free, another Rebel grabbed him from behind and went for his throat. Just then, shots rang out and men in gray dropped all around Sherman. Several Union soldiers rushed over and jumped into the melee, trying desperately to plug the holes in the line. The remainder from the last Rebel assault wave soon joined what few Confederates had made it to the top. An all-out bloody hand-to-hand brawl ensued. Men leaped at each other, hollering and screaming, trying desperately to kill one another with whatever weapon was handy. Guns fired at point-blank range while bayonets and Bowie knives plunged and slashed their way through forward-driving soldiers from both sides.

Sherman fought hand to hand, armed only with his fists. In the close-quartered confusion of the scuffle, many soldiers on both sides had unexpectedly dropped or lost their weapons. Sherman, tackled to the ground twice, was able to punch or kick his way free and force his attackers to retreat or be killed by a comrade in blue fortunate enough to have a loaded revolver or bayonet handy. Sherman choked the life out of another Confederate before a timely volley of Union fire compelled the shattered force of Rebels at the top of the hill either to evacuate downward to safety or throw up their hands and surrender. Before long, the Rebels had again completely withdrawn to a safe distance away from the Union 3rd Brigade.

Sherman picked up a discarded musket and looked around in disbelief. The 20th Maine was in shambles and he estimated that half of the regiment was either dead or wounded. He could only guess that the rest of 3rd Brigade was not any better off. All around him wounded and suffering men screamed out in agony, slowly dying and unable to defend themselves. Those who were lucky to still be standing were not much better off. Dazed, tired, afraid, and quickly losing the motivation to fight, they faced a far greater problem—their ammunition had finally run out.

The remaining soldiers of the 20th Maine began frantically looking for ammunition wherever they could. They scoured the ground for discarded muskets in hopes that they were still loaded. They ransacked the pockets and cartridge boxes of the dead, praying for just one shot to be found. Almost all were thrust into despair as they came up empty. Sherman was no better off. He grabbed a musket, attached the bayonet, and dolefully waited for the wickedness yet to stream back up the hill.

The Union men staggered back into some semblance of order, forming a pitiful line of defense. There were gaping holes everywhere and no chance to stave off another Rebel attack if the Confederates returned in force. Sherman looked around in despair as the sounds of the Rebels reforming echoed up the rocky hill. As his eyes scanned back and forth looking for an officer, Sherman waited for what he assumed would be his final orders. Glancing to the right, the young private once again caught sight of Colonel Chamberlain. His face and uniform were filthy, covered in sweat and dust from intense fighting. It was readily apparent he had not held back from the action. He hobbled along with his pistol in one hand and his sword in the other. He was injured, and winced in pain with each step he took using his sword more like a cane than a weapon. His bugler sounded the assembly, and every able officer surrounded the commander of the 20th Maine awaiting his orders.

Sherman observed the meeting with trepidation as the foreboding sounds of yet another Rebel drive grew in intensity. He looked to his right, then down the hill, then back to his right again. He convinced himself that the only reasonable course of action was retreat. He was sure the regiment and possibly the entire brigade would pull out. It was the only way to prevent its total destruction. They'd fall back to a rear position while fresh troops from units farther down the battlefield and not yet engaged in the fighting would replace them. It was logical and practical. The 20th Maine had done its job and held its position. It hadn't been flanked and had preserved the Union left at great cost. Now it was appallingly short on manpower and out of ammunition. What else could it do? Retreat was the only option aside from total obliteration. Chamberlain had to know this. Sherman impatiently waited for the bugler to blow retreat. What he witnessed next shocked him beyond all comprehension.

Captain Spear burst out of the meeting like a madman on the loose. He yelled at the top of his lungs, calling for what remained of the left to stand and get in formation. Sherman leapt to his feet and found himself shoulder to shoulder with what few troops in blue were left. He looked behind him and tried to identify the nearest escape route his regiment would employ for their hasty withdrawal march. Instead, he heard a mighty voice bellow out, "Bayonets forward!"

Instantly Sherman realized the order had come directly from Chamberlain. His sword was gallantly raised and pointed staunchly downhill. Spear drew his own sword and commanded, "Fix bayonets!" The brave soldiers realized what was about to happen, but didn't disobey the order. Every man reached for his bayonet and affixed it to his musket. Some started to pray out loud while others stood silent in a state of near shock. The Confederate line emerged from behind the bullet-riddled trees and through the smoke, stepping over scores of their own dead, poised to break the Federals and finally conquer the little rocky hill for which they had sacrificed so much and gained nothing. Their guns fired one by one as they advanced. It now seemed inevitable that they would win this bloody engagement. Just as all seemed lost, and while Sherman waited for the regiment to defy the commander's orders and break apart with a cowardly and chaotic scramble to escape, Spear gave the order that would change everything.

"Charge bayonets!"

The men assumed an aggressive attack stance with their bayonets sharply pointed at the approaching enemy. Spear followed his previous order with an audacious, "Right wheel! Charge!"

Just then the bugler blew charge and the extreme left of the Union line plunged forward like a hinged door opening outwardly. He didn't know what it was exactly, but something inside Sherman compelled him forward. Whether it was his sense of duty, his obligation to follow orders, or simply a brief moment of insanity, the young private let out a thundering war cry and charged to meet the Confederates head-on with an empty musket. Every shred of reason swirling in his mind told him to stop and move away from the danger—not collide with it. But reason wasn't in charge at this moment. Passion, aggression, recklessness, and sightless fury now fueled Sherman's every action. His adrenaline surged as the first Confederates came into view.

Stunned at what they were seeing, many Rebel soldiers stopped their advance. Before they could decide what to do, many were swept up in the wave of Union troops crashing into them and immediately surrendered. Others were able to fire off a hasty shot only to be clubbed by a musket butt or run through with a bayonet in return. Many Rebels simply turned and ran back down the hill, slipping and falling, crashing and tumbling through the rocky brush with the Federals in close pursuit. A few hand-to-hand fights broke out but were over quickly as the exhausted Confederates had had enough. Their shattered force was now scattered and in total disarray. What pockets of resistance remained were easily mopped up by the surging Federals of the 20th Maine. Officers in gray gave up their swords while their soldiers either dropped their muskets or held them straight up in the air by the barrel, signifying their submission.

Sherman charged for what seemed like forever. He chased down a few Rebels who eventually dropped to their knees and raised their hands. Sherman stuck his bayonet right in their faces until an officer with a revolver arrived and ordered him to continue the advance. Not knowing exactly how much farther he needed to go, Sherman cautiously moved forward. He came upon a thick tree and sidestepped around it. Without warning he was punched from behind and knocked to the ground, his musket wrenched from his hands. Sherman rolled over on his back as a Confederate soldier raised the gun and prepared to drive the bayonet straight through his heart. Sherman rolled onto his side just as the Rebel jabbed the bayonet deep into the ground, narrowly missing its intended mark. Sherman scrambled to his feet and tackled the Rebel. The men punched and kicked at each other until two Union sergeants arrived and pulled the combatants apart.

"That's enough, God damn it," hollered out one of the sergeants. The other stood the Rebel up and did a quick search to see if he was in possession of a concealed weapon. He found nothing. The Rebel just stood there and glared at Sherman as the young private got to his feet and brushed himself off.

"Private, take this prisoner up the hill. There's a collection point being organized near the top. Take him up and deposit him with the other Rebs," said the first sergeant as he handed Sherman his musket.

"Yes, sir," he replied with a weak salute. The two sergeants moved on and Sherman eyed his prisoner, who continued to beam a rotten glare at him. The Rebel was a young man, not much older than Sherman. He was about six feet tall and very lean. He too was a private, wearing a filthy gray uniform that was torn and frayed in several places. He wore a long, scraggly, black beard and under his slouch hat was a head of equally long black hair. His eyes were brown and set deeply back in his skull. There was an air of arrogance and deep-seated anger about him. Even unarmed he looked very dangerous and Sherman didn't want to take any chances with him.

"That way. Move," he ordered, gesturing with his bayonet. The man sneered and slowly started walking. Sherman, not wanting to tip off his prisoner to the fact that his gun wasn't loaded, cagily reached for a percussion cap and seated it on the nipple before bringing the hammer back to full cock. The seated cap and sound of the hammer clicking into firing position gave the illusion that the gun was loaded and ready to discharge should the need arise. Sherman hoped this would put the Rebel on guard and make him more cooperative.

"Goddamn Yankee," muttered the Rebel with a total lack of respect for Sherman's charade. "Kill every damn one of ya. You won nothin' here. Three fresh divisions are gonna swing around and crush ya before this battle is done…and it's gonna be you with a bayonet in his back, not me!"

"Shut up and keep moving," Sherman ordered. "That's enough of your damn lip, you southern trash."

The Rebel balled up his fists and seethed like a pot of hot water ready to boil over. He looked like he had plenty more to say but bit his tongue instead of expending his energy with fiery rhetoric in support of his cause.

Sherman prodded him along and the two trudged up the hill. Both men were drenched in sweat, thirsty, and physically spent. The emotional surge of energy produced during the battle was gone and there was little reserve left. Confusion was everywhere as the soldiers from the 20th Maine tried to organize and march off their Rebel prisoners before Confederate reinforcements arrived. Most cooperated, but some were being difficult and stubborn, which only added to the disorder.

Sherman's prisoner had apparently decided it was time to make his move. Unexpectedly he stopped in his tracks and simply sat down.

"On your feet, Reb," commanded Sherman, who badly longed to sit down too. "C'mon, move it! Get your ass up and get a move on!"

The Rebel sat there defiantly and stared at Sherman's bearded and bloodied face, as if scrutinizing his every physical feature. Just then a line of twenty Rebel prisoners under the guard of just one Federal soldier passed by. The soldier stopped and got the attention of a nearby lieutenant, who walked over. He saluted and said, "Sir, I've been pushing these Rebs along with an empty musket. Where can we get more ammun—"

"Hold your tongue, private," sternly whispered the lieutenant after pulling the private up close to him. "You'll start a riot if you're not careful. No one has any ammunition and if you keep announcing that fact then all these Rebs will have no problem jumping you, taking your musket, and escaping. Now be silent and brandish that bayonet like it was a roaring howitzer and get these prisoners clapped in irons and put into submission."

"Yes, sir," replied the private sheepishly, now fully aware of the fragile position of the 20th Maine. He kept his musket at the ready and used his bayonet to march his prisoners up the hill. Sherman prayed none of the prisoners had heard their conversation.

Sherman's own prisoner continued to remain seated, staring resentfully at his young captor.

"I said, on your feet, Reb," ordered Sherman. "I ain't gonna tell you again."

The Rebel looked to his left and then to his right, before slowly getting to his feet. Suddenly, in one swift action he grabbed a tree branch from the ground and swung it, taking Sherman by surprise and knocking the musket out of his hands.

"Stop, God damn it," yelled Sherman, picking up his gun and chasing after his fugitive, who was scrambling downhill. He caught up and grabbed him from behind. The Rebel wheeled around and punched Sherman in the gut. He doubled over and hit the ground in severe pain. The Rebel turned to run again only to stop at the sight of a Colt revolver pointed right at his head.

"Don't try it, Reb. I promise you, this one *is* loaded," said a confident Captain Spear. "On your feet, son," he added, addressing the struggling Sherman. "Can I rely on you to get him up top with the other prisoners?"

"Yes, sir. Bastard won't get away from me again," answered Sherman. "Son-of-a-bitchin' southern trash."

The Rebel took strong exception to Sherman's insulting remarks. "Y'all be dead soon," he snarled. "Bobby Lee gonna whup your asses all the way back to Washington. And my regiment is gonna lead the charge that takes the Executive Mansion out from under that braying ass, Lincoln. And when he's swinging from a tree, I'm personally gonna light the fire that will burn that white house of his to the ground! Ain't no sniveling little sack of shit from Maine gonna stop me, neither!"

The Rebel spit in Sherman's face, then aggressively lunged forward, knocking Spear hard to the ground and landing a solid punch right on Sherman's chin. He grabbed for the young private's musket. His combativeness was remarkable and he seemed utterly determined to fight on, no matter what the circumstances or how hopeless his situation appeared. Sherman was able to recover quickly and he wrenched the weapon free of the Rebel's grasp. He swung the butt upward, catching the irascible Confederate under the chin and knocking him flat on his back.

"You're going nowhere except straight to hell," brutally announced Sherman, still reeling from the last punch. He raised up his musket and with a mighty yell drove the bayonet deep into the Rebel's right shoulder. Blood gushed from the wound and the Rebel cried out in pain. Sherman jerked the bayonet free and prepared to plunge the weapon into his enemy's chest.

"Stop! That's enough, Private," ordered Captain Spear as he slowly pulled himself up. A trickle of blood flowed from his brow, as he had hit his head after being knocked down. "There's been enough blood spilled today. No more. This fight is over."

Just then two privates rushed over to help Spear. The woozy Captain ordered them to get the Rebel on his feet and take him to the top of the hill. As they stood him up, one tied his hands behind his back. Blood spilled from his wound and stained his gray uniform red. Before he was taken away he locked eyes with Sherman.

"I'll remember you," he snarled. "Mark my words, Yankee, I will remember you!" He spit at Sherman one last time and was then hauled off.

"Are you okay, sir?" said Sherman to Captain Spear.

"Yes, just a scratch. I'll be okay."

Both looked off in the distance and saw Colonel Chamberlain hobbling to meet Colonel Rice of the 44th New York regiment. Sherman looked to Spear and asked, "Beg pardon, sir, but I don't even know who we opposed today. Do you?"

Spear wiped the blood from his brow. "I heard some prisoners tell our men that they were from the 15th Alabama regiment. Some scattered Texans from the 4th too. These would be General Hood's boys. He's Longstreet's right arm, so I've heard."

"And this place, sir? Does it have a name? What do the locals call this place?"

"I'm unsure. But if it doesn't have a proper name now, it surely will in the days and weeks following today's action."

With that, Spear turned and walked in the direction of Chamberlain. Sherman stood motionless and watched the last few scattered remnants of the 15th Alabama being marched up the hill. His eyes then came to rest on a familiar figure. He watched two Union soldiers wrap bandages around the bloody arm and head of the old Confederate flag bearer who looked like Santa Claus. He was seated with his back against a tree. Sherman could tell he was badly hurt and in a lot of pain. Another Union trooper scooped up the Confederate battle flag and furled it before stuffing it in his haversack.

Sherman was exhausted and not sure of where to go or what to do. He didn't see one familiar face from G Company. After making up his mind and with no officers screaming orders at him, the private sat down under a tree and rested. He dearly wished he had a tall glass of beer, perfectly chilled with ice freshly harvested from the Kennebec River in January. For the moment, no other thought interested him.

CHAPTER 2

The Letter from Home

Sutherland Station in Dinwiddie, Virginia, was a hideous sight. The region was scarred and scorched with harsh reminders of the desperate fighting that had taken place there a month earlier. Wrecked remnants of battle implements and human carnage lay strewn across the landscape in twisted, unrecognizable piles of charred rubble and mangled earth. The roads were mostly impassable and every building constructed of wood and brick was severely damaged, burned out, or destroyed.

It was May 1, 1865. Lee had surrendered weeks earlier at Appomattox Court House, and the shattered Army of Northern Virginia was finally vanquished. Just days earlier, Joseph E. Johnston had surrendered the Army of Tennessee and all Confederate forces still active in the Carolinas, Georgia, and Florida. Some 89,000 haggard and starving troops surrendered. With every conquered soldier who lay down his arms and wearily staggered his way south died all the hopes and dreams of a new and separate American nation. The Stars and Stripes fluttered in the breeze over the decimated capital of Richmond while Jefferson Davis fled, determined to keep his beloved cause alive.

The South had been smashed. The Confederacy lay in ruins, beaten down by a relentless General Ulysses S. Grant in Virginia and ripped apart at its very core by the equally audacious General William T. Sherman. Chaos ensued as the ravaged South suffered from deprivation and lawlessness. The economic and political collapse of the aspiring nation touched all, from its wealthiest planter class to its poorest farmers. Stately mansions overlooking sprawling acres of cotton were looted and burned just as readily as the common man's shack. Little was spared. Soon every southerner looked the same. For the time being, class distinction ceased to exist. Everyone was now poor, hungry, filthy, and desperate. Despite the Confederacy's imminent demise, Rebel armies still carried on the fight in western regions of the Deep South and west of the Mississippi River. Large pockets of resistance still existed while Confederate generals Edmund Kirby Smith, Richard Taylor, and Nathan Bedford Forrest struggled on.

The North was not without its own major problems. Aside from trying to properly coordinate and administer the end of the war, it was reeling from the loss of its leader. President Lincoln had been struck down while attending a play at Ford's Theatre in Washington on April 14. He died early the next day, slain by an assassin's bullet. Secretary of War Stanton declared martial law throughout the district and an unprecedented search for the killer followed. The madness spilling over in both regions of the country threatened to destroy the reunification of the United States of America—possibly forever.

At Sutherland Station, a few miles from Petersburg, the 20th Maine was encamped. They had been sent there to guard the railroad and try to restore some semblance of order to the region, which had been utterly devastated by earlier battles and was now rife with fanatical Confederate marauders, looters, miscreants, and other assorted folk of low reputation and character. The regiment was present at Appomattox and had been shined up to formally acknowledge and accept Lee's surrender—a surrender personally received by now Brigadier General Joshua Chamberlain, commander of 1st Brigade, First Division, V Corps.

Outside a filthy tent on a stubby little stool sat a freshly shaven man, having his hair cut and reading a copy of the *Philadelphia Inquirer*. The newspaper rustled in his hands as he turned the pages. He tried to peruse different articles of interest, but kept returning to the front page and rereading the paper's main article.

"Says here a detachment of the 16th New York Cavalry cornered them in some tobacco barn in Port Royal, Virginia."

"Who, sir?" replied the scissors-wielding barber, busily snipping away at the reader's hair.

"That son-of-a-bitch Booth and his accomplice Herold, that's who. Says here that Herold surrendered but Booth remained defiant and wouldn't give himself up. The troops set the barn on fire to try to flush him out, then some trigger-happy sergeant named Boston Corbett shot him through an opening. According to this, Booth didn't die instantly, but didn't live much longer after they dragged him outta that barn."

"What kind of man goes by the name 'Boston'? Seems kinda odd to me, sir—you know, to be named after a city. I wouldn't care much for folks yelling out, 'Hey, Boston, come over here and cut my hair.' Feel like people would be constantly asking me if I was from Massachusetts or something. And that'd be strange, you know, 'cause…I ain't."

The barber's voice trailed off. The youthful ignorance in his voice, and the realization that he obviously didn't grasp the magnitude of the recent extraordinary events that had unfolded, prompted the newspaper-reading man to ask a question.

"Private, how old are you?"

"Nineteen, sir."

"And how long you been cutting hair?"

"Since I was ten, sir. My daddy's a barber and he showed me how."

"Well, do me a favor, Private. Promise me you'll just keep cutting hair and not get any silly notions about getting into law or politics," said the man sarcastically, adding under his breath, "We got enough fools up on Capitol Hill." He held up the newspaper. "Here. Take this and give it a good read. Learn something. It's a few days old, but it's hard getting your hands on news around here unless there are stars on your shoulders. Understand?"

"Yes, sir. There's just one thing," said the young barber. "I can't read or write. Never had time for schooling and Daddy only showed me how to cut hair and tend crops."

"Well, maybe you should just concentrate on becoming a barber, then, once this war is over and the army lets you go."

"Oh, no, sir. I want to stay in the army."

"Why's that?"

"So I can learn all about soldiering, get promoted, make all kinds of important decisions and be somebody for once, with a nice uniform… all decorated with medals and such. Make my daddy proud. Ought to be easy now that the war's done."

The man stood up and pulled off the barbering cloth. He watched the hair and whiskers slide down and disappear into the muddy ground. He turned to face the young barber and then placed the cloth and newspaper into his hands. He then spoke in hopes of imparting some wisdom.

"War ain't over yet, Private. All we've done is lop off the head of the serpent. He can't bite and poison us with his venom anymore, but his body is still thrashing around out there uncontrollably, still capable of causing damage before he finally succumbs. Proof of that is right there in that newspaper." He pointed to the article about John Wilkes Booth. "Do yourself a favor, Private. When they let you out of this army, you go. Go back home and make a living cutting hair, but learn to read and write. Get someone to teach you or get yourself some formal schooling. Once you can read and write you can learn about all kinds of other opportunities life has to offer. Me, I seen enough soldiering, war, and death. I don't want to see any more. Take my advice, Private. Get out of the army and go do some real living before the next war comes and you're forced to fight again."

The young barber looked down at the folded newspaper in his hands, then back up at the man. He said nothing but slowly shook his head. He gave a quick salute, then turned away and disappeared into his tent.

"I hope he listens. Lord knows I'm not the best at giving advice, but the last thing this country needs is another witless general in charge of its armies," muttered the man with the fresh haircut.

"Sergeant Jackson," called out an approaching voice. "Sergeant Sherman Jackson, stand tall and be seen."

"Here, sir," replied Sherman, running his fingers through his hair in an attempt to clean out any loose strands and make himself more presentable.

A lieutenant, whom Sherman recognized as one of the officers in charge of the V Corps mail wagon, approached him.

"Are you Sergeant Sherman Jackson, 20th Maine?"

"Yes, sir," replied the young sergeant with a quick salute, which the lieutenant acknowledged with one of his own.

"I have a letter here for you," he said, handing Sherman a rumpled envelope. "You should have gotten it sooner, but for some reason it got lost among all our other post. I found it at the bottom of an empty mail sack yesterday morning. Would have got it to you sooner, but we're overwhelmed with large volumes of letters now that the war's ending. Christ, we can't even keep up with the requests for distributing newspapers now that that lunatic Booth has been hunted down and shot. Anyway, that's all I have for you, sergeant."

"Thank you, sir," said Sherman as the lieutenant turned and walked away.

Sherman ducked into his tent for some privacy. He looked at the letter and could tell instantly from the handwriting on the envelope that it was from his father. It had been over a year since he had received a letter from home, and even longer since he had written one himself. Moreover, every letter he had received during the war had been written by his mother—never his father. This was most curious. Despite his usual lack of interest in corresponding with his parents, he found himself anxious to discover the contents of this particular letter. He tore open the envelope and unfolded the stationery within. It read:

> *Dear Son,*
>
> *I pray you're still alive. I hope this letter finds you fit and able and that you're not suffering from debilitating battle wounds in some army hospital far away from home. As you know, I've always been a man that insists on getting to the crux of a matter, so I'll tell you plainly that your mother is ill and her health has been failing steadily for the past few months. She was struck with fever early last winter and never fully recovered. For the past several weeks she's been bedridden and there's little the doctors can do to ease her suffering. I fear when you get this, she'll have left this world for the next.*
>
> *Mourn the loss of your mother, son, but do not let it interfere with your duties or hinder your ability to contribute to the preservation of the Union. I expect you to be a model soldier and to make me proud of your accomplishments during these dark and tempestuous times. I only pray that when you receive this you are of sound body and mind.*
>
> *Son, now that the war has unquestionably tipped in Mr. Lincoln's favor, I must conclude that an abrupt end to the hostilities in the field is near. News has spread that the Confederacy's collapse is imminent and that the Army of the Potomac—which you proudly serve—is poised to break the defenses ringing Richmond and Petersburg, thereby destroying General Lee's army in the process. It is my sincere hope that when Richmond falls, the war will finally be over.*
>
> *Though my primary thoughts revolve around the state of your mother and your own well being, I must confess a*

more wily and selfish reason for inscribing this letter. Though hardships and despair have touched everyone throughout this nation torn asunder, exceptionally arduous times have fallen upon our family home and business. In addition to the devilish disorder that has befallen your mother, I myself have become physically weakened with shortness of breath and chest pains trying to compensate for her inability to mind the household and help me run the store. Trying to manage our home, our possessions, our business, and the care of your mother has overwhelmed and exhausted me to the point I fear I may not ever fully recover. Business has been bad on account of the war and I haven't the means to hire additional help. I am not one to accept charity from neighbors, especially from those who are struggling themselves and can least afford to give, and our complete lack of relatives in the area gives me even fewer options to choose from in terms of reaching out for help—which I am uncomfortable asking for anyway. My mindset and the course of action I have undertaken leave me little alternative to remedy the situation.

Having now informed you of your family's plight, I implore you to return home as quickly as possible when the war ends and you are formally discharged from your military duties and obligations. I ask that whatever thoughts you have of furthering your education or starting a career be temporarily suspended so that you may help stabilize our home and business which has provided a means of shelter, clothing, food and currency to live by since long before you were born. I fear that if you don't come back soon, there will be nothing left to come back to at all. I will respect and honor whatever decision you make, but I hope you will weigh the needs of your own flesh and blood before anything else. I do hope and pray that you are still alive and without permanent infirmity. I will hold out as long as I can, and I eagerly await your return, Sherman. All my best.

Your Father,
Mr. Anders Jackson
March 25, 1865

Sherman slowly folded the letter and safely tucked it away with his other possessions. He sat quietly in thought as his ears filtered out all the noisy commotion coming from outside the tent. He was angry it had taken so long for the letter to reach him and he wanted to lash out at the first man he saw. However, he remained calm and his anger gradually turned to anguish at the thought of his ailing mother, who was most likely dead by now. Tears welled up in his eyes, but he refused to cry. He bit his lower lip and tried to wipe away all traces of sadness from his face. He felt an unmistakable yearning, followed by a growing sense of urgency, to return home to Maine for answers and for closure.

His family was from North Scarborough, Maine, and ran a general store next to their home. It was simply called Jackson's General Store, and his father had built it himself. The family had owned and operated it from as far back as he could remember. Sherman was an only child and grew up helping his mother around the house as well as his father in the store when he wasn't in school. He wasn't particularly fond of either responsibility but truly disliked working in the store. His father was a hard worker and a bit of a perfectionist who insisted that transactions go smoothly and that customers were never uncomfortable or inconvenienced when frequenting his small, rural establishment. As Sherman grew older, and his responsibilities increased, greater pressure was put on him to help keep the store running to his father's standards. Eventually he grew to despise the store work and became determined to get an education so he would never have to rely on working in the store a day in his adult life.

Upon completion of high school, Sherman gained acceptance at Bowdoin College in Brunswick where his father had graduated, and his future regimental commander, Joshua Chamberlain, had taught. Sherman completed only one year of school before enlisting and joining the 20th Maine regiment in 1862—for reasons still unclear to him today. He was now twenty-two years old and for the first time in several years he began to think seriously about his future when the war was over. He was alive and free of serious injury or disfigurement. During the long periods of waiting between battles, he had often considered returning to Bowdoin to complete his education. Once that was accomplished, he'd then decide what career path to follow. A fleeting thought of remaining in the army had once crossed his mind. He had been promoted twice since enlisting. His latest promotion—sergeant—gave him some authority and power over other men that he had never tasted before, yet gave him some gratification. Tempting as it was to rise through the ranks and become a commander of men, he'd had enough of war and the army in general.

Now with this disheartening letter in his possession, Sherman painfully grappled with the idea of returning home to aid his ailing family and rescue the family business before its virtual collapse and utter obliteration. The thought sickened him in more ways than one. He couldn't bear to see the heart and soul of his parents' very existence and livelihood disintegrate—and them with it—yet he also was repulsed by the idea of having to return home and become trapped in an occupation that he disliked and of which he wanted no part. He sat and contemplated his options.

"Maybe mother has recovered. Maybe she didn't die. Maybe she's able enough to help father now and relieve his physical burdens," whispered Sherman. Thoughts of both his parents in good health tending the store briefly flashed through his optimistic mind. "Maybe I just need to check on them. Yes…I can return home to ease their worries and show them I'm all right and have done my duty. Their spirits will be lifted and that will reinvigorate the store. I'll stay and help them…perhaps over the summer…and then return to school. Yes, that's how it will be. I'm sure of it," concluded Sherman with self-assurance. Though his thoughts dwelled on the most positive of outcomes concerning the current state of his family and their affairs, deep in the darker recesses of his mind lingered a far more unpleasant scenario—one he couldn't bear to face.

A bit perplexed, Sherman uncovered some paper he had and an old, dull pencil. He regretted not having a proper pen and inkwell, but the thought quickly passed. He began writing a letter home. He addressed it to his father but worded it as if his mother were going to read it too. In the letter he acknowledged that the war was winding down, yet made it clear that he was as of yet unaware of when his regiment would be mustered out and when he would be able to return home. He listed many obstacles and unknowns that could hinder his return and stated that it could be as long as a year until he was able to set foot in Maine again. He did not write these things to sound cruel or uncaring of his family's unfortunate position, but merely stated them as genuine facts that could not be ignored. Halfway through writing the letter, Sherman was startled by a voice from behind.

"Sergeant Jackson."

Sherman turned around to find his platoon's first lieutenant standing in his tent's entryway.

"Yes, sir." He stood and saluted.

"We just received orders that we'll be moving out tomorrow or the next day at the latest. Have your men ready to strike their tents and march at a moment's notice. The order to move out will likely come quickly and I want my platoon to set a shining example for preparedness. Understand, Sergeant?"

"Understood, sir. Does the lieutenant know our destination?"

"No, I don't know specifically yet, but as soon as I talk with the captain, I hope to have a better idea. The word among the officers is somewhere in the direction of Petersburg. Some are saying we're headed to Washington, where we'll be mustered out and sent home for good. I don't know about you, sergeant, but taking a walk up to Washington sounds awfully good to me. Last thing I want is for this regiment to get assigned some long-term garrison duty or be posted to another theater of operations where the fighting is still raging on. Damned Rebels ought to know when they're licked."

The lieutenant paused for a moment before exiting the tent. "Just make sure your boys are ready to move at a moment's notice, Sergeant."

Sherman sat in joyful disbelief at the thought that the war for him was coming to a close much sooner than he could have hoped. Thoughts of clean sheets and a nice comfortable bed followed by a decent, hearty meal and a thorough, cleansing bath sent shivers of excitement up and down his spine. He could be back in civilian life enjoying comfortable surroundings of his choosing in no time. Most importantly, he had survived the war and would now be able to pursue the life that he wanted. Glorious thoughts of good living ran through his mind until his eyes rested upon the half-written letter lying on his lap. Instantly his mind shifted away from happy reflections toward more gloomy prospects. He thought of his parents again. He decided he needed to return home as quickly as possible to determine the state of their health and affairs first and foremost. That's what mattered most, despite his ill feelings about the store and his own future. He convinced himself that his mother was not dead, nor would he believe she was until he personally viewed her grave. The same went for his father. Sherman crumpled up his letter and tossed it into the mud. For the moment, his mind shifted back to his military duties and responsibilities. He packed up his possessions, straightened his uniform, and prepared to address the men under his command in accordance with his superior officer's wishes. He knew the march ahead would be long and hard, and his safe return to Maine not guaranteed.

CHAPTER 3

Returning Home

Two sturdy horses side by side clomped along in unison up the hot and dusty dirt road baking under the noon sun. Behind the horses in tow was a four-wheeled calash carriage with a driver at the head and a single passenger in the rear seat. The heat was dry and there was no humidity in the air. The cool and clear azure skies were deceiving and provided little psychological relief from the mid-July heat. Despite this, the lone traveler insisted on riding with the carriage's folding top down. The narrow rural road was bereft of traffic and there were few sounds to be heard outside of the noise the horses and the rolling buggy made as they drove along toward their destination. The horses snorted and whickered occasionally as they plodded along, kicking up small clouds of dust with every hoof impact. The buggy swayed and creaked over the uneven and bumpy road, making the journey uncomfortable for the jostled passenger.

The driver said nothing save an occasional command directed at the horses. It was apparent he was well skilled at his profession as the buggy moved along steadily and always under control. At no time did the horses veer off the road or become rebellious. Behind the driver sat the sole passenger. He was hot, sweaty, dirty, and uncomfortable. His eyes were closed and his head tilted back in a vain attempt to sleep. Try as he would, he could not nod off. Frustrated, he gave up and opened his eyes wide. He looked in all directions at the rural countryside and was pleasantly surprised to see landmarks he recognized. He was in familiar territory now, which brightened his spirits.

"Driver, how much farther, do you reckon?"

"Oh, I'd say another twenty minutes or so, if we don't run into any unexpected delays."

"Good," replied the passenger. "I've been trying to sleep, so I haven't paid any attention to our location since we left Portland. I seem to recognize some of these hills and trees we're passing. Can you tell me exactly where we are? It looks like Scarborough—or at least the Scarborough I remember."

"Yes, sir, you are correct. We just entered the town limits and will reach your home in North Scarborough very soon," said the driver without once turning around to look at his passenger.

Having given up trying to sleep, the man sat back and gazed at the passing countryside. The farther they traveled along the road, the more familiar things became. Scattered houses, rock walls, old rickety barns, and sprawling farmland bursting with crops and livestock soon came into view. When the buggy crossed over a small bridge spanning a lively little brook, the man knew his home wasn't far away. The buggy reached a junction in the road and turned left.

"Is this Settler Road?" asked the passenger.

"Yes, we just turned onto it." The driver glanced at his silver pocket watch, then clicked it shut. "Should have you home no later than one o'clock."

After a few more minutes of travel, the buggy stopped in front of a house painted white with green trim. It was an impressive-looking home that looked almost as if two houses had been spliced together. The right half of the house had three stories and was the main section. The left half was only two stories tall and its most prominent feature was a long, covered porch. Three large brick chimneys were evident at first sight. The largest ran up the side of the three-story half while two smaller ones shot up through the roof centers of both the two-and three-story sections of the house. Large three-paneled vertical windows let plenty of light into the front rooms that protruded outward and flanked the main entrance—an interesting and aesthetically pleasing architectural design. The same window construction was repeated on the second story. Directly attached to the house via a sheltered walkway that originated from the two-story section was a very tall and imposing barn. At the front of the barn was an immense wooden door on well-oiled wheels that effortlessly slid it open. In front of the door was a ramp and small platform designed for easily unloading heavy goods from a horse-drawn wagon.

"Here we are, sir," said the buggy driver, finally turning to face his passenger. "That'll be two dollars."

The man climbed off the buggy, reaching back in to retrieve his bag—a soldier's haversack. Placing it on the ground, he dusted himself off the best he could. He was filthy, and the common blue suit and white shirt he wore looked dingy brown. He pulled a handkerchief from his pocket and tried to wipe away the sweat and grime from his face and neck. When finished he reached back into his pocket and produced two Seated Liberty silver-dollar coins, which he promptly handed over to the driver.

"Thank you, sir. I'll be getting along now," said the driver with a tip of his hat. Then, with a quick snap of the reins, the horses pulled away and the buggy was soon out of sight headed back down the same road from which it had just come.

"Oh my sweet Lord in Heaven! Sherman Jackson, is that you?"

The man turned around to face an elderly woman wearing a worn blue and white gingham-check hand-sewn cotton work dress that covered every inch of her body except her hands and her face. Atop her head was a rather large bonnet, and around her waist was a dirty white apron. Instantly the man knew exactly who had spotted him.

"Yes it is. Hello, Mrs. McClatchy," responded Sherman with a slight wave.

"Oh, I am so happy to see you well, my dear boy!" she exclaimed while embracing Sherman in a long, thoughtful hug. "I worried about you something awful. I was afraid you might have been injured or worse. I...I doubted that you'd ever return. I thought for sure your parents would receive a dreadful letter from the War Department confirming your demise. Oh, I'm so happy you're back! Your...your father will be most pleased to see you. That we can be sure of."

"It's good to see you too, Mrs. McClatchy. Are my parents in the house? I was going to walk over and check the store first, but it appears to be closed—that is, unless my eyes are deceiving me."

Adjacent to the Jackson home approximately twenty yards down the street was the family general store. It was a simple two-story structure, light brown in color, trimmed in white, with a pitched roof and a redbrick chimney in the center. At the front of the building was the main entrance, a single door with a window. To the right of the door was a much larger horizontal picture window that allowed customers to view the goods on display inside. Centered just above the door and picture window was a large white sign with red lettering outlined in black that read, "Jackson's General Store." Above the sign were two more vertical windows on the second floor. On the back of the building was a sliding door similar in design to the one on the barn but not nearly as big. It was through this door that the majority of the store's goods were brought in. Curiously, there was no activity to be seen near the store's entrance. Everything seemed dark, quiet, and serene, very unlike the normal hustle and bustle of activity Sherman was accustomed to witnessing at that time of day in years past. Indeed, the store was closed. This sent an uneasy jolt of concern down Sherman's spine.

"Yes, dear…the store is closed for the moment. Your father is resting in the house. He had an unfortunate spell earlier today and needed to get off his feet. I closed up the store an hour ago and was on my way to go check in on him when I saw you arrive," said Mrs. McClatchy.

"Is he seriously ill?" asked Sherman. "Should I wait to see him? Maybe he needs some rest before…."

"Goodness, no," interrupted Mrs. McClatchy. "Don't hesitate another minute. He'll be so happy to see you. I can't think of any better medicine for him than to see his only son back from the war all safe and sound. He'll be so proud of you, I just know it."

Sherman dipped his head and closed his eyes. He was terrified to ask the question that was silently gnawing on his brain.

"Mrs. McClatchy," Sherman uttered, pausing before painfully adding, "My mother…is she…inside as well? I had received word a while back that she was ill, too. Might she be inside resting…resting with my father?"

The old woman watched as Sherman's head rose up and his eyes, filled with dread and nervous concern, stared into hers. She hesitated a moment, then spoke.

"Go see your father, dear boy. Your *father* needs you now. All will be better now that you're here. I should be on my way. We'll talk again soon."

With that the old woman turned and started to slowly walk away. Her shoulders slumped and her head dipped. She moved with a mournful gait as Sherman watched until she was around a corner and out of sight. It was then he realized the terrible unpleasantness that awaited him inside his family home. He had repressed it long enough with thoughts of superficial matters and foolish notions of denial. But there was no denying it any further—his dear mother was most assuredly dead.

Picking up his bag, he willed his legs to move, though he did not want them to. Despair and indescribable dread poured into his soul with each step that brought him closer to the front door. He had been exposed to death and suffering for so long that he was convinced he had become immune to its horrors. Yet now he was having trouble holding back the flood of emotions overpowering him. He soldiered forward, bravely turning the doorknob and slowly entering his family home for the first time in several years.

The door creaked open. Once inside, Sherman closed it firmly behind him. He froze in place and let his senses take in the flood of familiar sights, sounds, and scents that had been absent from his life for so long. The first thing he noticed was silence, save the tick-tock sound of the slowly sweeping pendulum in the family's longcase clock. He listened closely for other sounds throughout the house but heard nothing. It was eerily calm. Sherman inhaled deeply. The unique scents of the domicile nestled in his nostrils. The familiar aromas deeply entrenched in the wood floors, the furniture and rugs, and the walls themselves reminded Sherman that he was indeed home.

His blue eyes rested first on the wooden staircase directly in front of him. It was stained a dark and rich brown color that gave it a shiny and stately appearance when waxed. Sherman remembered back to his days as a child, when he'd feared the grand-looking staircase that had seemed so tall and intimidating. He'd refused to climb them himself for fear of falling. He remembered his mother's calming words and how she used to hold his hand as they climbed the shiny steps together. Eventually, with his dear mother's help, his fears were conquered.

Sherman walked over to the longcase clock towering against the wall across from the base of the stairs. He retrieved the crank from a hidden drawer in the ornamental hood and opened the glass face. He inserted the crank in the first of two keyholes on either side of the dial and proceeded to wind the clock. When finished, he took out his own pocket watch and set the hands to match the time on the clock. Satisfied that the time was right, Sherman began to explore the rooms one by one.

The first front room on the right was the parlor. This was the largest room, where most of the family gatherings, celebrations, and entertaining were done. The room contained various comfortable upholstered chairs, small ornate mahogany end tables, and a plush carved-rosewood red velvet sofa. The walls were decorated with oil paintings and family portraits mostly depicting happy and tranquil scenes of the Jackson family at play along the rocky Maine coastline. On shelves and tabletops there were grainy, black-and-white framed daguerreotypes and tintypes featuring various family members long since passed, but preserved forever in picture.

The focal point of the room was the main fireplace, its ornate mantel, and hearth. Facing the fireplace at an angle on either side were two dark leather upholstered chairs. Between them was a small rectangular table. Sherman remembered how his father would sit in front of the fire for hours on cold nights sipping his whiskey and smoking cigars. He remembered the last time he'd sat in one of the leather chairs in front of the fire. He'd been with his father as the two quietly discussed the thought of Sherman enlisting in the army. Sherman remembered sharing a drink with his dad as he reluctantly gave his blessing for his only son to go off and help preserve the Union.

In the far corner of the parlor was an upright piano. Sherman's mother had learned to play as a young woman and would often entertain guests with her skillful renditions of Beethoven and Mozart. Sherman walked up to the piano and wiped a substantial layer of dust off the keys. Clearly it hadn't been played in some time now. This added to the building dread in the pit of Sherman's stomach. He moved on to the next room at the front of the house.

Adjacent and to the left of the front door was the study. Sherman's father used this room as his personal office and library. It contained a desk, chairs, and multiple bookcases housing many leather-bound books and an assortment of files and ledgers pertaining mainly to the store and its business. The wooden desktop was cluttered with a pile of letters strewn across it in no discernible order. Sherman glanced at the paperwork, concluding that it was mostly bills that appeared to be past due. He shook his head and moved on.

He walked down the hall that led to the dining room. The long dining table was still there, and all the dishes, glasses, and silverware were neatly stored in the hutch behind it. At a quick glance everything appeared to be just as Sherman remembered it. He spent but a brief moment of reflection in the dining room before moving on through an open door into the kitchen. It was there he felt a cold chill and a wave of uneasy sadness sweep over him. The kitchen was in disarray. Empty cabinets and drawers were open, a chair was knocked over, and a small wooden platter with decaying half-eaten vegetables and meat, resting on a small wooden table, filled the air with a foul odor. This was not Sherman's mother's kitchen. Her kitchen would never be left in such a miserable state. The untidy sight was a clear indication that something was terribly wrong. Deep in his soul he knew what it was, but still couldn't bring himself to acknowledge it. He still clung to a shred of hope as he looked out the kitchen window into the back fields where the vegetable gardens, livery, and outhouse facilities were. He opened the window and tossed out the rotting food, and with it several buzzing flies.

The gardens looked as if they badly needed tending, the livery appeared strangely dark and dormant, and the outhouse was clearly in disrepair. Sherman shook his head and became filled with an odd sense of urgency.

"Father," he called out while returning to the entryway at the base of the stairs. There was no reply. Without any hesitation or childhood fear, he charged up the staircase in search of his parents. He walked down the hall of the second floor without bothering to look inside his old bedroom, his mother's sewing room, or the guest bedroom. Instead he made a straight path for the master bedroom. The door was only partially closed. Sherman reached out and slowly pushed the door open. He felt a weak breeze trickle in from an open window. He saw that the unmade bed was empty. He turned his head in the direction of the window and saw a familiar figure slumped back in a large, comfortable chair.

"Father, it's Sherman."

There was no response. The old man's body sagged and slouched in the chair with his head cocked back at an odd angle, his eyes closed, and his mouth wide open. He was fully dressed but his suit was disheveled and it looked as if he had clothed himself in a great hurry. His hair was white and covered his entire head. The matching white whiskers on his face formed a distinct chin-curtain beard that he'd had for as long as Sherman could remember. His face was wrinkled and gaunt. He had lost a significant amount of weight since Sherman had last seen him. He did not look well, and Sherman feared he might be dead as there was no movement in his chest or any sound from his lungs. Gripped with dread, Sherman rushed over, took his father by the hand, and knelt by his side looking for any indication of life.

Suddenly, the old man took a breath and groggily tipped his head forward. With great effort, his weak legs slowly pushed his body back up squarely into the chair. He yawned a bit, then stretched his arms upward only to wince in pain and bring them back down firmly onto the armrests. Sherman closely observed in silence, waiting for the moment when his father would open his eyes and look upon him. The old man's eyelids, heavy and wrinkled as they were, gradually began to rise. The first sight the weary eyes focused on was that of the young man's expression. Sherman's father, stunned and surprised for a split second, soon realized he wasn't dreaming and a weak smile crept across his face.

"Lord be praised, my only boy is home," the old man said in a hoarse voice. He squeezed his son's hand with what little strength he had while a small tear ran down his cheek. "I'm glad to see you, my son. It's as if a great weight has just been lifted off my very being. I thank God for this moment."

"Father, are you terribly ill?" asked Sherman.

"Just tired and a bit dizzy, boy. Help me out of this chair and onto the bed. I reckon I'll be better off stretched out."

Sherman put his father's arm around his shoulders and slowly eased him up. The old man, still very groggy, shuffled over to the bed using his son as a crutch. Sherman helped him lie down. Upon his father's request he propped up pillows behind the old man's head so that he could sit up a bit and talk more comfortably.

"Ayuh, that's much better. Less pressure on my chest in this position. Helps when I can raise my legs up a bit, too."

Sherman tucked another pillow under his father's legs. He removed his shoes and rubbed his feet to help increase the blood circulation. When he was done he pulled up a small wooden stool and sat next to the bed close to his father.

"Thank you, son. That felt good. I had an awful dizzy spell earlier and had to get off my feet. I musta dozed off after sitting down. The widow McClatchy helped me up the stairs. My head's starting to clear up now. The spell's passed. In a few minutes I'll be able to get back on my feet. Enough about me, though…talk to me, boy. Please tell me you're well and free of injury. I pray God you're not feeble in any way."

"My body is sound, Father. The Lord was with me. In the many engagements I fought in, no Confederate bullet or blade ever struck my body. Either the light of God shielded me from all that brutal madness, or them southern boys just couldn't bring themselves to kill me. Must be 'cause I'm so handsome and smart," Sherman said with an impish smirk.

The old man weakly returned the grin. "Well, the jury's still out on that line of thought, son…but it does me good to see you well, with all your faculties and all your limbs intact."

"Father, I must ask, what is it that ails you? I don't ever recall seeing you weak like this before. While between battles or in camp, I would often tell my fellow soldiers about how resilient and ageless my father, Mr. Anders Jackson, was. When I left…."

"Was years ago, son," said Anders. "I'm not the hearty individual I was before you joined the fighting. The years of laboring in the store have caught up with me, I'm afraid. Something has gripped my heart and lungs like a vise. There is an unrelenting pressure on my chest that will not subside. It lessens with relaxation, but intensifies immensely when I exert myself. With the pain comes dizziness and numbness in my arms and legs. My breath runs short and I find myself gasping for air. It's at that point where I must find relief in the form of a chair or my bed. In time, and with limited exertion, the painful wickedness diminishes, so I'm able to function somewhat normally, but it doesn't last long."

"Have you seen a doctor, Father?"

"Ayuh, when this affliction first became unbearable, your mother sent word to a doctor in Portland. He arrived several days later. He produced all manner of scientific instruments to listen to my heart, measure my lung capabilities, and diagnose my malady. When he was through he told me I suffered from a 'weak chest' that was common in men my age. He prescribed a remedy of fresh air, reduced activity, and plenty of nourishing food such as fresh game or stock that was prepared immediately upon slaughter. He also recommended a stiff drink or two on occasion… to help with the pain."

"Did he offer up any other form of medication, Father?"

"Yes, he gave me a bottle of his own special tonic. He said it was an elixir of his own creation after I asked why there was no label on it describing the contents. My guess is that he acquired it from some medicine show out West near the frontier…or possibly it was something he was creating and peddling himself. When I asked what it was made from, he told me it consisted of a variety of natural cure-alls with the primary ingredient coming all the way from southeastern Europe. He said it was a wonderful medicine derived from a special species of poppy plant. He called it opium."

"Has it alleviated your suffering, Father?"

"I tried a teaspoon in the beginning. It was vile and rancid-tasting. I couldn't stomach it. Your mother tucked it away somewhere," he said, his voice dropping noticeably.

Anders's mention of his wife sent another chill up Sherman's spine. The next question would be the hardest one he would ever have to ask. This he was sure of. Prefaced with a mournful sigh, the words fell from his lips.

"Father, where is Mother?" he asked, knowing full well what the excruciating answer would be.

"Did you get my letter, Sherman?" the old man asked with a steeled tone.

"Yes, Father, I received your letter and read every word. I hoped…."

"That things would turn out better? That everything would be fine when you walked through the front door? That God would cure her sickness and heal our family's problems? Well, son, that isn't the case. Your mother, my dear sweet Julia, succumbed three weeks ago this very day. The sickness wouldn't leave her body no matter how hard she fought it. The winter fever was unremitting. I don't understand how she managed to stave off death for so long. I had multiple doctors try to help her, but none of them did anything to improve her condition. I'm sure that it was her own strong will and that of God's that gave her the strength to endure for as long as she did. I've never known a braver woman. We prayed every night. We prayed for her recovery, for my health to convalesce, and for your swift and safe return from this country's descent into madness and bloodshed disguised as civilized war…if there ever was such a thing! Your mother is eternally at rest now. Her mortal remains are buried in a family plot I had constructed in the meadow at the far edge of our property, near that little stream she loved to sit by and gaze up at the sky."

Sherman couldn't hold back his tears. The memories he had of accompanying his mother to that very spot as a little boy sent a surge of sadness through his mind that he couldn't contain. He tried to cover his face and hide his misery, but it was no use. He slipped off the stool and slumped into a sobbing heap on the floor.

"Now, we'll have none of that, son," said Anders sternly with a renewed sense of vigor in his voice, which now sounded more powerful and authoritative. Sherman recognized the voice his father used when he demanded something of someone. "I stated in my letter that she would most likely be gone before your return home. You've had plenty of time to mourn, son, as have I. The time for mourning is over. We have more pressing matters to attend to now. I'll take you to her grave and you can pay your last respects, but after that I don't want to see any more tears. She was a good wife and mother. We'll always remember and love her. But if this family is to survive, we must move on and move on swiftly, boy! I don't know how much longer I...."

Anders's voice trailed off and he turned his head away. Sherman pulled out a handkerchief, dried his eyes, and blew his nose. He got back up on the stool and did his best to compose himself.

"Father, how do you expect me just to shed a few tears and then forget my mother? I will mourn her loss for as long as necessary...for however long it takes to ease my suffering," he proclaimed.

"You will not, boy," roared back Anders. "You're a man now...and a soldier. The horrors you've undoubtedly seen on the battlefield must have hardened you in ways I could never understand. You need to harness that toughness now and focus your energies on more imminent and productive enterprises. To say it plainly, son, I don't know how much longer I can endure. The pains in my body seem to worsen with each passing day. I'm nearly to the point of total helplessness. Our store, our very means of existence, is in shambles. I can't tend to it properly now. I'm physically unable to do everything that needs to be done in order for our business to be successful. Times are hard enough. Everyone has been negatively affected and financially hurt by the war. It doesn't matter that we won. It will be a long, long time before this country heals and becomes prosperous again. If we are to survive, then I must ask of you... no, I implore you to stay and help revive our business, our home, and our community. You've done your duty on the battlefield for this country. Now do your duty for your home and for your family—what's left of it."

Sherman got up and began to pace. He put his hands on his hips and shook his head in agitation.

"Father, how long have you been sick?"

"I first felt these pains strike me about a year and a half ago. They were mild at first. I considered them nothing more than an annoyance at the time," he answered.

"And when did you first tell Mother about them?"

Anders hesitated, then answered, "Last Christmas, just before she was seriously stricken with fever."

"So you hid it from her for a long period of time. Why, Father? Did it ever occur to you that she could have done more to help you? She could have searched for a better doctor. The two of you could have traveled away from this place in ideal weather and found more competent help. Then, just maybe you'd have been cured and she never would have come down with the fever she caught while trapped here! And just maybe I'd be standing here now in this sweltering room with two healthy parents instead of a dead mother and a dying father!"

"I couldn't worry your mother about my ills," responded Anders. "She was a wreck while you were gone. She couldn't bear to hear news about the fighting or read newspapers filled with casualty lists for fear of seeing your name. I was concerned for her well-being. Besides, I had to mind the store and keep our business afloat. If I told your mother about my frailties she would have made me stop working, the store would have failed, the business I built with my bare hands would be gone forever… and then where'd we be?"

Sherman stopped pacing and stared his father right in the eyes.

"It's always been the store first and foremost, hasn't it, Father? Anything to keep that wretched store open, right? Well, that business of yours just possibly cost you your wife and me both my parents! Was it worth it, Father?"

"That store has clothed and fed you since the day you were born, Sherman. It is the reason you have had the decent, often privileged, and educated upbringing that you so obviously have never appreciated! How dare you imply that your mother's death was my fault! If I had the strength I'd stand up and make you sorry you ever uttered such nonsense. I'd show you who the real man in this room is. Get out of my sight, boy! Leave this bedchamber before you say something you'll end up truly regretting."

Sherman seethed with anger and frustration mixed with sorrow. He said nothing and grudgingly decided to obey his father's orders. He stomped out of the room and slammed the door shut behind him. He dashed down the stairs and out the front door. Once outside he again looked down the road at the family store. It filled him with anger. Oddly enough, as much as he hated the very sight of it at that moment, something compelled him to charge over.

The front window was filthy, layered with a thick film of dust and grime that made it nearly impossible to see through. Sherman tried to rub clean a small section with his coat sleeve, but found that the dirt was mostly on the inside! He tried to enter through the front door but couldn't, as it was locked and he didn't have the key. He walked around back and forcefully slid open the rusty sliding door. As he'd anticipated, Mrs. McClatchy had not bolted it from the inside. She had obviously forgotten, as Sherman had many times while tending the store in his youth. Despite the sunlight shining in from the open door, the back room was still quite dark and a strong, musty smell hung in the stale air. Sherman reached for a nearby candlestick and box of matches. The light produced by the lit candle pushed aside the darkness, revealing to Sherman a largely empty room, save a few barrels and some assorted small goods scattered on storage shelves. He had never seen this room so empty before. Normally it was filled with barrels, boxes, and crates labeled and filled with a variety of goods both manufactured and grown. Now there was hardly anything. Sherman pulled the lids off the barrels, only to find them as empty as the room.

He blew out the candle and pushed open the door that led into the store itself. After a few steps he found himself in a familiar spot behind the counter. He wiped the wooden countertop with one hand, only to discover it distressingly filthy and gritty to the touch. He turned to look behind him at the towering wall of shelving that was always fully stocked and meticulously merchandised with rows of essential canned and bottled goods. He was shocked to see this vital display space virtually empty, with only a stray can or two strewn about in a disorganized manner. Sherman walked over to the front door, unlocked it, and opened it to allow in more sunlight and some much-needed fresh air. His eyes then scanned the rest of the store.

The floor was covered with a fine layer of dirt and looked as if it hadn't been swept in months. The black kettle-shaped woodstove in the center of the selling floor looked to be in disrepair and was noticeably rusty and filled with leaden ash. Sherman examined it closely and found there to be several rusty holes in the stovepipe. Sure enough, faint rays of light poked through the ceiling where the stovepipe punched through and connected with the brick chimney on the roof. Sherman wondered just how much damaging rainwater had leaked down onto both the stove and the wooden floor.

His spirits dampened further upon looking at the tables and display bins where the family had always merchandised smoked meats and recently harvested crops. All that was present were a few rotting vegetables being consumed by a small family of mice. Disgusted, Sherman grabbed a broom and swatted at the rodents until they scurried across the floor and out the front entrance. He then used the broom to clean up several piles of droppings and rotting vegetable remains, which he disposed of outside. When finished he reentered the store and slammed the broom down hard onto the deck. He simply couldn't believe the sad state the store was in. It looked as if someone had ransacked the place. There was almost nothing in inventory, and what was there, he was uncertain whether it was marketable—or even safe for consumption.

Sherman looked over the empty shelves and floor space where the majority of the consumable product was normally kept. Barrels, boxes, glass jars, canisters, and tins that normally held coffee beans, dried beans, flour, sugar, spices, baking powder, molasses, oats and grains, honey, crackers, cheese, fresh eggs, milk, and churned butter were empty or contained just a trace of their original contents. He then glanced over to the shelves where his father merchandised bottles of patent medicines and various other items related to personal health and hygiene. There were a few bars of brown soap, a bottle or two of perfume, and some small corked vials of various medicines and elixirs, their bright labels guaranteeing that they would cure whatever ailed you. Last, Sherman took a quick mental inventory of the store's dry goods and general merchandise. There were a few bolts of colored cloth leaning against the wall and some pins, needles, buttons, ribbon, a pair of men's pants, and one set of suspenders scattered across the shelves. Sherman didn't see any hats, belts, or shoes, which were always high in demand.

There were no shovels or axes. The glass display case under the counter was barren of the rifles and pistols normally kept there. There were no gunpowder or cartridges to be seen either. Hanging on the walls were a few lanterns, some rope, and miscellaneous cooking pots and pans. There were some bundled candles and scattered boxes of matches, but the usual place where the cigars and other tobacco products were kept was barren. There was also no liquor to be found.

Sherman sighed and shook his head, wondering how anyone could shop there without becoming ill at the sight of things. Before leaving, Sherman walked over to the far corner where there was a narrow, partially hidden staircase that led up to the second story. He climbed the stairs. At the top was a room that contained a single bed, a desk, two wooden chairs, a small bookcase with a limited number of books, and a bureau with an attached mirror and chamber pot on the floor next to it. Covering a portion of the floor was an old moth-eaten patchwork rug that Sherman thought was older than time itself. It had been in that very spot for as long as he could remember. It was extremely hot up there, and Sherman felt beads of sweat start to form on his brow.

The room had been used for multiple purposes. Anders had used it as both a private office and his own personal quarters when the store was exceptionally busy and required extended hours of operation, or when he'd had a falling out with Julia and found himself unwelcome in their bed. Sherman determined that Anders had used the room quite recently, since the bed was not made, there were recently dated papers scattered across the desk, and the chamber pot reeked of urine. Disgusted to the point where he couldn't stomach any more, Sherman stomped down the stairs and out the front door, slamming it hard behind him. He wished the horses and buggy had not left. He'd climb aboard, slam two more dollars into the hand of the driver, and demand they race back to Portland as fast as the horses could deliver them.

He looked over at the house again. His anger toward his father throbbed uncontrollably inside him. He had no desire to confront his father—ailing or otherwise. Instead he wanted to be alone and seek out anything that would provide comfort to him. He felt very lost and emotionally confused. He looked away from his home and began walking down dusty Settler Road toward the nearby North Scarborough Community Church. It was located across the street and was only a short walk away. Upon arrival, Sherman noticed it hadn't really changed at all from the last time he'd seen it. It was painted a glowing white and had a formidable steeple with an impressive cross on the top. On Sundays the great church bell inside the steeple would ring out, signaling the beginning of services. Sherman's family was Protestant, as was most of the community. The church had been constructed not long after he was born, and he knew for a fact that his family had never missed a Sunday service up until the day he went off to Bowdoin. Sherman paused and wondered if his father's fragile state or the loss of his mother had forced Anders—a deeply religious man—to break that streak.

Just a bit farther down the road was the Old Liberty Grange Hall. Sherman continued his walk until he faced the much older and larger two-storied building used for community suppers, town meetings, and other social functions such as dances or festive holiday parties. The building suffered from overuse and was urgently in need of both structural and cosmetic repair. Its gentle green paint had peeled away, leaving exposed the weather-beaten wood that was dingy, washed out, and gray. The brick foundation was crumbling and the steps leading up to the entrance were buckled. Sherman also noticed a window or two with significant cracks in the glass and a shutter hanging loose from a broken hinge. It swayed back and forth in the warm breeze, letting out a subtle creak with each movement.

The heat was starting to get to Sherman as he squinted toward the sun and wiped the sweat from his brow and cheeks. He felt like the only man on Earth. Aside from his father and Mrs. McClatchy, he hadn't come across another soul since his arrival in North Scarborough. He looked way off down Settler Road toward the horizon. His eyes examined the rolling hills and meadows in the distance. He saw familiar houses and farms dotting the landscape, but no people or livestock. He quickly surmised that everyone was hunkered down in shady spots avoiding the heat. It actually pleased him that he was alone for the moment, as he was in no frame of mind to be polite or hospitable should he run into an old acquaintance.

Sherman turned around and walked in the other direction. He passed by his house without a glance and walked on until he came upon the last building he desired to see. It was the small one-room schoolhouse that had provided many a local child with an education. It was called the Budwin School, after Albert Budwin who financed its construction in 1836 and taught there with his wife Georgiana, until their unfortunate and untimely deaths in a horse-and-buggy accident during the winter of 1859. As an adolescent, Sherman had spent many years under the tutelage of the Budwins until Anders and Julia insisted he attend a larger school out of town.

The wooden schoolhouse was painted a faded red with white trim. Several windows lined both sides of the rectangular building and a black stovepipe shot up through the middle of the pitched roof. Just outside the front entrance steps was a towering yet barren flagpole. The building appeared to have been used very recently and Sherman wondered who had replaced the Budwins. However, there wasn't a soul around to ask. Sherman walked around the building once, then decided to head toward the spot where his mother was buried.

He moved with a slow and deliberate gait. He was in no hurry to reach his destination and tried to convince himself that the slower he walked, the less painful it would be. Each labored step seemed to prove him wrong. He walked around to the back of his house, not bothering to look for Anders. He meandered through the vegetable gardens and cursed at their apparent neglect.

"How could anyone live off these withered crops…let alone purvey any of them?" Sherman pulled up a clump of dry and decaying weeds. He tossed the useless vegetation onto the ground and proceeded over to the family livery for closer inspection. He entered the dark building and was astonished to find none of the four family horses present. There was no sign that they or any other creature had inhabited the livery for quite some time. The structure, like so many others, was empty and slowly deteriorating from disuse.

"What did he do? Sell 'em? Were they stolen? Did they run off or simply collapse and die from starvation or deprivation?" wondered Sherman aloud. "Damn him."

Sherman hastily exited the livery and made his way toward the far edge of the property, which was enclosed by a snaking split-rail fence. He crossed the meadow and soon heard the running stream that cut through a section of their land. A minute later he could see a headstone enclosed within a simple square picket fence shaded by a large oak tree. Once through the gate he knelt down next to the white marble headstone. A tear came to his eye as he read the engraving.

> *Here lies the most benevolent being God ever graced His fair Earth with. Blessed she was in life and also in death. God keep her, cherish her, and never allow us to forget her.*
>
> Mrs. Julia Anne Jackson
> *May 2, 1814–June 24, 1865*

Sherman bowed his head and wept openly for his deceased mother. He couldn't speak, he couldn't move, and he couldn't stop crying. As the minutes passed, his mind wandered and he couldn't recall the last time he had sobbed so uncontrollably. Not since he was a very young boy at the very least. He had been witness to death and frightened beyond all comprehension many times during the war, but he hadn't cried, even when his friends were cut down by enemy fire. The pain and suffering of losing a loved one was quite different than the losses he had experienced on the battlefield. Both cut deep, but the loss of his mother was indescribably agonizing. He sat on the ground in a heap with his head buried in his hands oblivious to all around him. He didn't stir for two hours until his ears picked up a faint noise. It was the sound of approaching footsteps. Sherman lifted his head when he felt a hand gently rest on his shoulder.

"Leave me be," Sherman said.

"No, son. Sitting out here next to this stone ain't doing you or me a bit of good, particularly on a hot day like today. Let her rest. Come back inside the house," said Anders firmly.

"What right have you to order me about?" Sherman got to his feet and brushed himself off. "I'm an adult now, Father, not some child resigned to do your bidding. I've served my country and given orders to men twice my age. Why should I listen to you?"

"Damnation, Sherman! It matters little to me what you've done, who you've served, or whether you're an adult or not. I'm still your father and I will be treated with the respect I deserve for bringing you into this world and raising you proper. Do you understand me, boy?"

Sherman hesitated. He wanted to lash out at his ailing father, but something inside stopped him. Perhaps it was his mother's virtues of cool-headedness, patience, and her uncanny knack of handling uneasy situations emerging within him. Perhaps it was the peace and serenity of standing in his mother's favorite spot that calmed and inspired him. Maybe it was her spirit guiding him. Whatever the cause, Sherman nodded his head, conceding that he would respect his father's wishes. Sensing that, Anders spoke again.

"We have many things we need to discuss, Sherman. I'm sorry we quarreled earlier and I'm sorry your mother has departed leaving you nothing but a crotchety old father with a broken chest and a failing business. But I say again, if we are to survive, I desperately need your help, and you must listen to me and trust that I know what's best. Together, we can turn around this sad state of affairs that not only afflicts our home but our community. Come, let's get up to the house before my waning strength is totally exhausted. You'll be none too happy if the energy that powers my legs drains completely. I doubt you'll desire to carry me on your back."

"Put your arm around my shoulder, Father. Use me as a crutch and I'll help you conserve your breath and hasten your step," said Sherman.

The two lumbered back to the house and sat down in the leather chairs facing the fireplace in the parlor. Earlier, Anders had placed a bottle of whiskey and two glasses on the table between them. After a moment of rest and silence, Anders poured himself a drink. Sherman did the same. The two sat quietly and imbibed, neither really wanting to speak or knowing exactly what to say. It was Anders who broke the silence.

"Your mother worried about you incessantly. I doubt she slept a full night since the day you left. Some nights she'd climb out of bed and just pace endlessly. I tried to calm her fears, but she was convinced you'd be killed or maimed in some horrible fashion. She tried to hide it, but I knew it constantly ate away at her very core."

Anders took a swig of whiskey and tilted his head back so the liquor would easily slide down his throat. He swallowed slowly, enjoying the rich, nicely aged flavor. After the last drop glided down his gullet, he spoke again.

"Seeing that she was so bothered by your service in the army, I didn't wish to further burden her mind or strain her heart with additional worries concerning my own health. I thought it best to fight through the pain and continue my daily duties as if nothing were ailing me. I wanted to exhibit strength and courage, and moreover, a sense of routine and normalcy to pass the days while you were gone and keep her from fretting about your hazardous endeavors—endeavors that are unsettling yet common with men who have taken up arms to defend their country."

Sherman said nothing and didn't look his father in the face. Instead he stared at the blackened hearth of the barren fireplace and slowly sipped his whiskey.

"I don't know what caused her fever, but be assured I did everything within my power to arrest the illness. Yes, maybe I could have done more…or done things differently. However, the fact remains, son, that she's no longer with us, and we can't continue to dwell on her absence if we are to survive. This community is dying. Our store is dying. Son, I am dying. I've fought hard my whole life to make a difference in this world through hard work and dedication to family and business. I'll not depart this mortal coil without knowing I did my best to better my life and those around me. I'll not give up—not yet. But I desperately need your help."

"What would you have me do, Father?" asked Sherman, still staring into the fireplace. "How can one man make a difference to such a complex problem? The store and this community were your dream…they were never mine. I wanted to go to school and explore law or even medicine. I wanted to travel abroad and see what life overseas had to offer. I had so many ideas. I didn't ask for South Carolina to fire on Fort Sumter. I didn't ask for my country to be torn apart, and I didn't expect to have to don a uniform and fight a war to preserve the Union and crush slavery. I'd never even seen a Negro until the army swept me up and dropped me in Maryland and Virginia with a musket in one hand and a flag in the other. That goddamned war interrupted my life irreparably…but I survived. And just when there was some glimmer of hope that I might be able to get my life back on track, I find myself here again, drowning in the loss of my mother and chained to the old existence I wanted to escape."

Sherman swallowed the last gulp of whiskey in his glass, then slammed it down hard onto the table causing Anders to flinch. Sherman buried his head in his hands and wished he were in another place at another time.

"Son, I have no right to dictate your life for you. You are the master of your own destiny. After all you've fought and suffered through, you've earned the right to set your own course. Would that I could convince you to stay. But I will not force you to choose one or the other. You make up your own mind and I will bless whatever decision you render. Regardless of how you feel about me, I say a thousand times over that I am proud of you and of your service to this country. You are a hero. You are my hero as well as my only son…and I am proud to be your father."

Sherman raised his head and finally looked Anders in the eye. He sensed the sincerity in his voice and it made a true impact on him.

"I'm sorry I didn't write home much more than I did. I should have written mother a letter every opportunity I had. It would have calmed her nerves and maybe she wouldn't have gotten sick. My God, maybe this whole situation is my fault," Sherman said as a stunned expression swept across his face.

"Nonsense!" exclaimed Anders. "Neither of us could have prevented her illness. It's useless to dwell upon, son. She's with God now and we must carry on like the good and responsible Christians we are. I refuse to allow you to think any of this tragedy is your fault."

Anders poured another glass of whiskey and motioned for Sherman to drink it down in hopes of settling his anxieties.

"I don't know how it got so bad so fast," said Anders while dolefully shaking his head. "Everything just seemed to steadily decline once the call to arms was made back in '61. When boys like you began enlisting, it seemed that the very lifeblood of this community and others like it was mercilessly drained away. Without young, strong men to work the fields and handle the heavy labor on the farms, the task fell to old men and women who were not up to it. Farms began to fall into disrepair, crops were not adequately planted or harvested, livestock was neglected, and the flow of much-needed raw materials and manufactured goods dried up. Sufficient support just wasn't available no matter how much we banded together and tried to help one another. North Scarborough has become a community drained of its inhabitants. Many abandoned their farms and left in hopes of finding a better living with relatives far away. Some went bankrupt and were forced to sell everything they had. Others, like your mother and I, fell ill but struggled on. It's only by the grace of God that we managed to hang on for as long as we did. The store is almost dead, but I've not lost it yet."

"What happened to our four horses, Father?" asked Sherman, remembering the empty livery. "Were you forced to sell them? Did they perish from neglect?"

"No. I lent them out to a friend in Gorham a few weeks ago. He needed them to cart away lumber he had cut down and was hoping to sell."

"Did he offer to pay you for use of the horses?"

Anders dipped his head and stared into his glass.

"He's my friend, son. Times are tough. I couldn't ask him for any money. I doubt he even has any. He lost two sons at Chancellorsville. He has nothing. He's a widower like me."

"Well, Father…our business is helpless without those four young horses. The store can't manage without them. We have to get them back immediately, regardless of your friend's plight."

Anders looked at his son with a glimmer of optimism in his eye. A faint sense of hope began brewing in the old man's ailing heart upon hearing the words "our business." He composed his thoughts carefully, then voiced his response.

"Yes, I agree, Sherman. They are indeed vital to the success of our business. I must arrange for their return posthaste. I pray they've been well cared for and not abused. It was foolish of me to think I could continue to conduct business without them…even for a short period of time."

Sherman rose to his feet and sipped his drink. He rested his eyes on what was hanging on the mantel above the fireplace.

"Father, where did you get this? I've only seen a few of them and regrettably I was never able to get my hands on one."

"Oh…well, that was your mother's notion."

"How do you mean?"

"It echoes what I was saying earlier, Sherman," said Anders. "She was so afraid of you getting hurt or killed that she wanted you to have every advantage on the battlefield. We were able to scrape up the money to buy it; however, we had a devilish time finding one…and when we eventually acquired it, we didn't know where to send it. You see…we hadn't heard from you for so long, we didn't know where you were, or even if you were still alive. She insisted that you and you alone have it, and if she didn't know for certain where you were or if you were still in action, then she wasn't going to allow me to send it. So we waited for a letter in hopes it would reveal your exact whereabouts. Unfortunately it never came. Then she grew ill…and my attentions turned elsewhere."

Sherman let out a small sigh, then ran his hand down the smooth barrel of the Henry repeating rifle mounted in front of him. He examined the gun thoroughly, admiring the unique brass-framed receiver that shined brilliantly as if it were crafted from a lustrous block of gold. He fingered the trigger and imagined himself working the lever action back and forth in the heat of battle. What a tremendous advantage—squandered.

"I'm filled with regret, father," said Sherman. "If only I hadn't been so lazy and thoughtless. If only I had the sense God gave a common mule I would have picked up a pencil and written a letter every day that I could. Why was I so ignorant in understanding the benefits reaped from such a simple undertaking? Now my heart grieves so fervently for my departed mother, who tried to care for me in so many ways. God forgive me!"

"I forgive you, son. What's important is that you're here now," said Anders. "You're alive. And God will forgive you. You have my personal blessing, son."

"And mother's?"

"Of course, Sherman. She's looking down upon you from the heavens and sending you her blessings with every breath you take. She's proud of you and loves you very much. Even though she's no longer with us bodily, she's with us in spirit, and she'll be by our sides guiding us until it's our time to join her."

Sherman nodded and wiped a small tear away from his eye. He sat down again and paused a moment before speaking.

"Father, the plot you made for mother is quite special and certainly worthy of her mortal remains. However, I'm puzzled as to why she wasn't buried in Pyne's Cemetery. If I recall correctly, you had set aside plots there for our entire family to be buried together when the time came."

Anders hesitated and drank more of his whiskey. With an agitated sigh he answered, "I couldn't bear the thought of placing her there after what happened."

"What do you mean, Father? What happened?"

"You remember Sam Lester, the undertaker?"

"Yes, I remember him," said Sherman. "Did something happen to him?"

A shiver went up Anders's spine and Sherman could tell he was uncomfortable, especially when the color drained from his face, leaving it with a gray pallor.

"Back in autumn of '62 he had some fool notion he was going off to join the fighting. He didn't enlist...he didn't even try. He knew he was too ignorant and disturbed in the head to be taken seriously by any recruiter. Instead he found himself a blue uniform, grabbed his musket, and rode south on his horse. He galloped away hollering all this nonsense at his wife and two girls. Nobody heard from him until summer of '64 when the army brought him back to his house clapped in irons.

He wasn't wearing a uniform anymore and he looked like he had been beaten and imprisoned in some madhouse. Why they brought him back is a mystery. His mind was gone and he babbled on nonsensically about the Devil, war, and death. Several people, including me, tried to help get his head right, but he was already too far lost. Well, one night these horrific cries were heard coming from his house by some who lived nearby. They pierced the darkness and echoed far and wide throughout the community like howling ghosts. A few of us men gathered at the church, and we braved our way up to Lester's house by torchlight. What we saw when we arrived was so indescribably wicked, that I shudder in fear even thinking of it now."

"What was it, Father?" asked Sherman, trying to be brave and sound reassuring.

"We went inside and saw everything in shambles. The house was very dark and reeked of a foul odor. All the oil lamps had been smashed. Furniture was broken and all the family's meager possessions were strewn and scattered in heaping piles as if they had been purposely launched into the air in a fit of rage. At first we thought the house had been burglarized. However, the more we looked around the more we speculated differently. A few of us started searching room by room, calling out Sam and Muriel's names. We called out for the children, too, but nobody answered. It wasn't until my old friend Ben Larson went up into the bedroom that we found out what had happened."

Anders paused again and looked away from Sherman. He was visibly shaken and appeared reluctant to divulge any more information. Sherman remained silent and didn't press him to continue. Anders took another sip of whiskey, then sighed deeply before looking up with a sullen and fearful expression that Sherman was not used to seeing from his father.

"Ben let out a holler and we all rushed into the bedroom. The floor was soaked in blood and Muriel Lester's body was draped over the bed. Her clothes were mostly ripped from her body...and...and...her head... had been hacked off. Lord have mercy! We found it under the bed! Her face was almost unrecognizable! Many of us got sick at the horrid sight. I could barely breathe. We were all terrified beyond comprehension...and the worst was yet to come. Ben rushed out of the room and tripped in the hallway. It was so dark he couldn't see what caused him to stumble. When we finally got some light on him, it became clear."

Anders's head dropped again and he started to tremble. Sherman knelt beside him and clutched his father's arm, hoping to steady him and calm his nerves. He wanted to hear the rest of the gruesome tale— whether he needed to or not.

"What was it, Father? What did you find?"

After another long pause, Anders reluctantly said, "It was the Lester girls…Winny and June. They had been murdered too! They were only twelve and fourteen years old if they were a day." Anders struggled to continue. His voice cracked and his breathing became erratic. He rubbed his chest vigorously and winced in pain.

"Those two lovely girls were dispatched in the same fashion as their mother. We couldn't understand how anyone could conceive of such a dastardly act of unmitigated violence. Panic set in and we all fled from the house. Once outside we gathered in the cemetery and tried to get our wits about us. We were scared because none of us were armed and we feared the murderer was still lingering close by. Even though there were four of us, not one man was up to the task of confronting so savage a person… an insane fiend clearly mad and capable of unspeakable brutality. We decided it was best to regroup at the store, compose and arm ourselves, then alert the proper authorities. So that's what we did. The next day we went to Gorham and found Sheriff Silas Ridgeway, and he came out to investigate. Reluctantly we went back to the scene of the crime. Ridgeway concluded that since there was no trace of Sam Lester anywhere, he must be considered as the prime suspect. We all figured he'd snapped and forced his demons upon his innocent family. Why he felt compelled to slaughter them, we'll never know. I guess that any man exposed to so much death could easily succumb to the evils of the Devil, driven mad and forced to do the unspeakable. Nobody around here has seen him since the day before his family was murdered. We don't know for sure that it was him, but nobody can think of any other plausible suspect. Since those dark days, nobody goes near his house or Pyne's Cemetery. Both have become unholy places and have fallen into disrepair…much like many other places around these parts. So you see, Sherman, that's why I deemed it necessary to bury your mother on our property, a place I hold more sanctified than that domain of wickedness just a mile away from here."

"I understand, Father. You made a sensible decision regarding mother. I don't envy your mental torment, no doubt lingering from the gruesome sight you regrettably encountered years ago. I myself have seen death manifested in so many different forms on the battlefield that it numbs me now…yet the true and horrible nature of killing never leaves a man once he's experienced it. It's a cold and unpleasant thing to carry around with you, and as hard as you try, you can never cleanse yourself of it…whether you've simply been witness to it or if you're the one who's executed it. Murder is murder, Father, whether it's done in a criminal manner or carried out on the battlefield masked behind flags, uniforms, shiny medals, and politics."

Anders and Sherman, both shaken by the unpleasant discussion, took a few minutes to sit quietly, sip whiskey, and calm their nerves. Anders felt the pain in his chest ebb and flow. He tried to focus silently on more engaging thoughts in hopes of clearing his mind of the horrible visions of the Lester murders, while also hoping to ease the wrenching pain in his chest and lungs. He found some relief as the minutes passed, but wasn't sure if it was due to his positive mental capabilities or simply the effects of the flow of alcohol entering his system.

"Son," said Anders, "Stay here tonight and for as long as you wish. I think we both have some healing to do and it might be beneficial if we help each other along the way. I have no desire to interrupt your future plans…whatever they may be. I will not interfere. If you stay, you have my blessings. If you go…you still have my blessings. North Scarborough is not what it used to be. We are a community that has a church, but no minster. We have a schoolhouse, but no educator to teach or students to learn. We have a grange hall that sits abandoned and does little except attract vagrants. And we have a store that is rapidly slipping away…on the verge of extinction, without caretaker or customer. Our farms are failing and our people are leaving. I would not blame you one bit if you chose to abandon this place of degradation and misery for greener pastures and the prospect of a more fruitful existence. I'm a survivor and I'll fight on until the life leaves my body permanently. That is all I have to say about that, son."

Sherman said nothing and the two men sat and drank in silence as the sun slowly began to dip toward the western horizon. Later in the evening the widow McClatchy stopped by and generously served a pot of hearty vegetable and beef stew, which the three thoroughly enjoyed. After dinner, the widow went home and Sherman went out to the family well. He lugged several buckets of water back to the house and filled the cast-iron bathtub. His father bathed, then Sherman helped him into bed, where he promptly fell into a deep sleep aided by a stomach full of hot food and a bloodstream soaked in alcohol. Sherman cleaned himself up as well and put on a fresh shirt and pants. He entered his old bedroom and discovered it was unchanged from the day he had last occupied it. All his old clothes and personal items were exactly where he had left them. It was an eerie yet comforting sight.

As the day came to an end, Sherman again found himself outside at his mother's grave. He listened to the babbling stream and gazed up at the sky much like his mother used to do. As the sun dipped below the horizon and the stars slowly began to emerge one by one, Sherman dwelled on his situation and contemplated his options—and ultimately his future. It was a future filled with hard decisions and uncertainty. As the darkness enveloped the countryside and the sky filled with bright, twinkling stars, Sherman rested his hand on the headstone and said very solemnly, "Goodbye, mother." He turned his back and slowly made his way toward Settler Road—haversack in hand.

CHAPTER 4

June 1873

The afternoon sun beamed through large banks of billowy clouds that lazily drifted through the blue sky resembling mountainous tufts of fluffy white cotton. Settler Road was lively with foot traffic as travelers, farmers, and other local residents made their way up and down the main thoroughfare of North Scarborough. A ramshackle wagon, heavily laden with large burlap sacks, wooden crates, and barrels of assorted supplies and dry goods, pulled by two bay Shire stallions with white stockings, noisily lumbered toward its destination. The driver was hunched forward and held the reins tightly. A scowl jutted across his face in angry defiance of the laborious work he had done and the job yet to be completed. Loading the wagon was strenuous and bothersome enough, but unloading it always seemed much worse.

The wagon came to a stop in front of the small platform and loading ramp of the Jackson barn. The driver dismounted the wagon and wiped the grimy sweat from his brow. He reached into his back pocket and retrieved a beat-up metal flask filled with a crude liquor that burned his throat and caused him to grimace with each quick nip. He was a young man, only twenty, and his dirty face was boyish with little trace of a beard, even though he hadn't shaved in days. His hair was a fine-colored brown and cut quite short. He was rough and wiry and made no effort to smile or engage in polite conversation when in the presence of others. He was young, arrogant, and felt a certain sense of entitlement he clearly had never earned over the course of his short life.

After securing the horses, the young man walked over to Jackson's General Store. He looked in the front window and saw nobody inside. Instinctively he headed back to the house. Halfway there, he saw a small figure off in the distance standing by the stream that cut through the meadow at the edge of the property behind the house. He walked toward the figure and watched it grow larger with each step. Finally he got within comfortable earshot and stopped. The figure's back was turned to him.

"Sir, I've returned with the store's supplies. Whaddya want done now?"

The figure—a man aged thirty—did not turn around. He stared at the stream and the large oak that shaded him. After a few seconds he put his hands on his hips and acknowledged the question put forth to him.

"You know what needs to be done now, Danny. I want the wagon's goods unloaded, inventoried, and properly secured in the barn. You're then to take your list and reference it to the store inventory list I compiled this morning. It's in its usual place on the counter…you'll easily find it. I want you to determine what stock needs to be replenished and begin transferring the goods we need from the barn to the store's stockroom. Once that's done I'll begin stocking, pricing, and displaying the newly arrived merchandise. Clear?"

Danny angrily sighed and rolled his eyes. He had foolishly thought his work for the day was done. He had no desire to unload and inventory the wagon after the work he had done loading and transporting the goods earlier.

"Sir, I thought I'd rest a bit from that long ride from Portland. Seeing that I loaded up the wagon all by myself, don't you think it's fair that you unload it? Also, you're better with lists and figures. I reckon the inventory figuring would best be gauged by you, not me."

"Danny…Mr. Ricker…you seem to be under the delusion that I work for you and not vice versa. You should be grateful that I'm a tolerant and patient man, and that your shortcomings have—to this point—*not* forced me to conclude that your duties as my employee are no longer required. I suggest you not test my patience any further and simply perform the tasks I've outlined for you without any additional delay."

"What about my pay, sir? You haven't paid me in two weeks! When can I expect to get the money I've earned?" insolently bellowed Danny.

The man, now swelling with ripe indignation, turned and confronted his rebellious young employee.

"Danny Ricker, you'll get your pay when I've determined you've performed your duties to my expectations! I'll also call attention to the fact that you've certainly not gone without! You have a roof over your head, which I provide, and several good meals served to you at no cost from the widow McClatchy. Why she pities and looks after you in the kindly manner she does is beyond my comprehension. You've got her fooled, but definitely not me!"

"What exactly are you driving at?" snapped Danny.

"You've managed to take advantage of my hospitality, my land, my store, and you've exploited my need for a young and hearty laborer. You live in my room above the store virtually rent-free…and when you feel audacious enough, you find opportune moments to steal from right under my nose."

"What are you talking about? I ain't stole shit from you!"

"Do you take me for a complete idiot, Danny? Am I that feeble in the brain that I can't see what you've done? I know you stole and devoured two of my chickens and I've found random holes in the topsoil of my garden where certain vegetables were carefully dug up."

Ricker said nothing. He stood firm and frozen in place. His eyes indicated he desired to launch into a defensive verbal tirade against his accuser, aggressively professing his innocence, yet something held him back and he wisely chose to remain silent.

"Danny, I would have been inclined to overlook the stolen chickens and vegetables had I not recently discovered more despicable and overt acts of thievery. I've noticed things have gone missing from around the store. Merchandise has subtly and mysteriously been removed from inventory, removed in a way meant to deceive anyone needing to keep accurate records—someone like me. I've estimated that you've pilfered upwards of fifty dollars worth of goods in the last month. I'll add that that amount doesn't include what you've taken directly off the supply wagon during your trips to Portland and back."

"You're a goddamned liar," violently and ignorantly erupted from Danny's lips. "You have no right to accuse me of anything, and more importantly, you have no proof I've stolen one single thing from you."

"I wouldn't be too eager to test that statement if I were you, Danny. But if you're willing, I'll send for Sheriff Ridgeway and he can help us sort out this matter and render judgment. And while he's here, I'm sure he wouldn't mind taking a few minutes to look around your room. I know I wouldn't mind that. Hell, it'd be my pleasure to show him around up there considering it is *my* dwelling that I so graciously allow you to stay in."

The two men stood in silence and stared at each other until Ricker finally backed off. His head dipped, then he slowly stepped back and turned away with balled-up fists. He seethed with fury but was unwilling to test his foe's patience any further.

"I think you know what to do now, Danny. I suggest you get to it without any further derogatory remarks aimed at me. One other thing—consider yourself on probation. If you perform the tasks I set out for you and do your job in the manner I expect, you can continue to live and work here. However, if I find just one more item out of place without a *very* damn good reason, well, let's just say that Sheriff Ridgeway will be a lot more lenient on you than I will! Now get to work!"

Danny, his face searing with a rebellious and contemptuous scowl, turned and said, "You got it all figured out, don't ya, boss? Yeah, I'll go back to work, but this business ain't over. You think you're a real tough man, Mr. Sherman Jackson. But I'd watch myself if I were you. Someday you might unexpectedly find out what happens to tough men who think they got all the answers. And I expect my pay sooner than later." Danny grumbled as he made his way back to the wagon and the unfinished work waiting for him.

Undaunted, Sherman turned away from his sour employee and looked down at his mother's headstone. He placed his right hand on it, then rested his left on an identical one adjacent to it.

"I need to get back to the store now," whispered Sherman. "I hope there's no further ugliness today, but I fear there might be. God, grant me the strength to overcome my daily burdens and the troubles with my unruly employee. I must go now. God bless you, Mother," he said looking down to his right. "And God bless you, too…Father," he added, glancing to his left. Sherman left the gravesite of his parents and returned to the store. He paid no attention to Danny Ricker and left him to unload the wagon without any additional directives or criticisms. He thought it best to allow his young employee to simmer a bit unmolested. He had no desire to further jab the hornet's nest, lest he get stung severely—perhaps permanently.

Sherman attended his inventory list and daily sales ledger. He meticulously went over the figures until his eyeballs grew weary behind his round reading eyeglasses and the temples of his head throbbed. Finally, he pushed the paperwork aside, took off his spectacles, and rested his eyes on his immediate surroundings, which he found to be much more pleasing. The store was cleanly swept and free of unpleasant odor or unwelcome vermin infestation. The windows were new and the glass spotless, allowing the store to be bathed in vibrant sunshine. The stove had been replaced and the roof repaired long ago. The shelves, barrels, and bins were all overflowing with a vast assortment of new and fresh goods all neatly stocked, stacked, priced, organized, and suitably merchandised.

The store was brimming with fresh-picked and prepared perishable items that Sherman felt could feed a small army. Fruits and vegetables of all sorts, including baskets of rich green asparagus, broccoli, cabbage, peas, celery, and crisp orange carrots; barrels of earthy robust potatoes; and buckets of luscious bright-red strawberries and dark red cherries all perfectly ripened and ready for purchase, lined the walls and deck of the sales floor alongside everyday staples such as coffee beans, flour, and sugar. There was also a limited supply of fresh milk, butter, cheese, and salt pork.

An impressive display of dry goods and general merchandise including an assortment of colorful cloth, leather shoes and boots, fashionable hats, sewing implements, tools, nails, lanterns, crockery, cooking utensils, knives, rope, small farming implements, a saddle, brooms, shovels, axes, black powder, and other useful goods were all neatly displayed, cleverly utilizing every square inch of space the small store could spare. There was also plenty of soap, brushes, bottles of tonic, and perfumes, all properly stacked on their own shelf.

The glass display case under the counter now contained a new Spencer 1865 Carbine .50-caliber rifle and a .41-caliber Colt House Revolver displayed in its own presentation box. Other items featured in the locked case included two large, ornate, leather-sheathed Bowie knives, a box of cartridges for the Spencer, a steel-jawed bear trap, and a neatly coiled leather-braided bullwhip. These items were of special interest to Sherman. Only he had the sole key that unlocked the case, and he maintained it on his person at all times. He kept these items locked up not only because they were valuable and commanded a high retail price, but also because they were potentially dangerous in an untrained or malicious hand. Such thoughts led Sherman to dwell on his current troubles with Danny Ricker. An absent head of lettuce or a stolen bar of soap was harmless in the hands of a disgruntled employee. However, should a firearm or large-bladed knife go missing, only to appear in the possession of a known thief, there was no telling what harm could be done.

Sherman didn't wish to dwell on the unpleasant idea any further. What he *was* pleased about was the condition of his store. It had profited very handsomely as of late and Sherman was proud at how he had resurrected the once-failing business into a successful and useful local enterprise. It had taken several years of hard work and determination, but he had succeeded and in the process helped breathe new life into the North Scarborough community.

Sherman flipped through his sales ledger. As he swiftly turned the pages, a small piece of loose paper flew out and gently floated down to the floor. Sherman walked from behind the counter and squatted to retrieve the stray document. He unfolded it to discover that it was a list of supplies recently ordered by Edwin and Reba McPhee, who owned and operated the Old Liberty Grange Hall just down the road. The list included items such as twine, writing paper, candles, scissors, small metal hooks, and hangers, plus an assortment of special-ordered multicolored cloth and lace. Realizing that the order had been placed two weeks ago, Sherman concluded that it must be in today's shipment from Portland. He stuck his head out the front door and called over to Danny, who was still unloading the wagon.

"Danny!"

The young man stopped what he was doing and looked in Sherman's direction.

"Did that McPhee order arrive today?"

Danny scratched his head and jumped up on the wagon. He moved some crates aside and immediately found what he was searching for.

"Yeah, it's here," he shouted back to Sherman.

"Well, bring it inside. I want to enter it into the sales ledger and then deliver it today. I'm sure the McPhees are wondering where it is, and I need to get paid."

"Yeah, so do I, you cheap son-of-a-bitch," muttered Danny, his back turned to his boss. Ricker picked up the small crate and brought it inside the store. After depositing it on the counter, he went to the rain barrel outside the door and scooped himself a dipper of water. After quenching his thirst, he went back inside and sat on the floor mopping his brow and neck with a dirty handkerchief.

"It's powerful hot today. I just need a minute. Don't want to drop from heat exhaustion. I ain't no field hand who spends all day in the sun, you know. I ain't used to it," Ricker said with a hint of defiance.

Sherman scowled and said nothing. He didn't wish to inflame the situation any further. He marked his ledger and examined the McPhee crate of goods, checking for any damage to the exterior. There was none. Danny continued to wipe his face and neck while staring intently at the floor as if in an annoyed trance. Sherman observed him for a minute or two, then decided his employee's improvised break was over.

He cleared his throat to get Ricker's attention, and just as he did, the door swung open and through it entered a tall, broad-shouldered man, age fifty-two, with a thick moustache. A black bowler hat was atop his head and a brown leather vest with a star-shaped sheriff's badge hugged his white-shirted torso. Tan trousers and spurred leather boots finished off his ensemble.

"Afternoon, Silas. Didn't hear you ride up," said Sherman while leaning to gaze out the front door to view the sheriff's tied-up horse.

"Phew, it's hotter than hell out there. That afternoon sun is just relentless today. Reminds me of First Bull Run. That was a bitch of a day, boys. I don't mind telling you that there ain't nothing I want to remember on that date, including the goddamned heat!"

"It's funny, Silas, Danny and I were just talking about you a little earlier. What a coincidence that you happened to show up just now. Help yourself to a dipper of water from the barrel outside. Folks around here generally just help themselves without even asking," said Sherman with a hint of cynicism aimed at his loafing employee.

"Don't mind if I do," said Silas. He drank his fill, then went back into the store.

"Haven't seen you in a while, Sheriff. What brings you out this afternoon?"

"Well, I'm on my way to Gorham. There've been some thefts out there that need investigating. A couple of barns were broken into and some livestock stolen, according to various reports that come across my desk. You heard anything about that, Sherman? Any rumors circulating around here? Has anything gone missing from your store?"

Sherman hesitated a moment, then glanced in Danny's direction. Ricker slowly stood up and looked at Sherman with a pitiful expression chiseled on his face.

"No, Silas, there've been no rumors or trouble around here far as I know," Sherman pronounced.

"Good," replied the sheriff. "Now, what I really could use is a cheese sandwich and a pickle."

"I can help you there, Sheriff. Danny, go fix Sheriff Ridgeway his sandwich and fetch him a pickle from the barrel."

Ricker nodded and was all too happy to be put to work and excluded from the conversation.

"Sherman, I'm also in need of a good rifle. I got an old-model 1866 Winchester Yellow Boy that's seen better days. She don't fire straight anymore and the lever's about ready to fall off. I'm riding naked right now and I don't like the thought of runnin' up against something or someone of a nefarious nature without being properly armed, if you get my meaning."

"Ayuh, I sure do. I think I can fix your problem there, Silas." Sherman reached deep into his pocket to retrieve his key to the counter display case. Quick as a flash he unlocked it, pulled out the Spencer, and placed it on top of the counter.

"Sheriff, this is a brand-new Spencer 1865 Carbine .50-caliber rifle. Never fired before. She's a little older than your Winchester but she's new and can pack quite a wallop."

Silas picked up the gun and worked the lever. He peered down the barrel and rubbed the stock, feeling for any imperfections, then nodded.

"Oh, yeah. I remember these. I seen some of the cavalry boys use 'em back during the war. Always wanted to get my hands on one but never could."

"Well, you got your hands on one now, Sheriff. Whaddya think?"

"Ahhh…she feels good, Sherman. Got cartridges?"

"Right here." Sherman placed the box of bullets on the counter.

"How much you looking to get for this thing?" asked Silas.

"She's priced at fifty dollars."

"Fifty dollars! Jesus, Sherman…the county's not made of money and neither am I. I can't pay fifty dollars. I was hoping for something in the fifteen-to twenty-dollar range."

"Silas, that's the only rifle I have in my inventory. It's brand new and retails for fifty bucks. Any less than that and I don't make hardly any profit."

"Can't come down any more than fifty? Even for a lawman in need of protection? How about I buy it on credit?"

"No. I can't risk credit on an item like this. Tell you what, Silas. If you buy the gun for cash I'll throw in the box of cartridges for free."

"I thought they were included already! Christ almighty, Sherman, you're gonna bankrupt the Sheriff's Office and me with it. Eventually the whole county is gonna be indebted to you."

"Best I can do, Silas. Sorry."

"Okay, Sherman, lemme make you a credit counteroffer. I'll give you ten dollars outta my own pocket as a down payment. I'll come back every week and pay you five dollars until the debt is paid in full. If I miss a week, then you can tack on some interest. But I get to take the gun now. If she gets bent or broken before the debt's paid off, I'll still make good on the payments and throw in an extra ten dollars on top of what I owe. I get the box of cartridges for free, though. Is that reasonable to you?"

Sherman thought for a minute, then nodded. He then extended his hand and said, "Well, if I can't trust a lawman's credit, whom can I trust? Just don't make me regret this, Silas. My list of debtors who have abused their credit line with me is getting far too long. Deal."

The two men shook before Sheriff Ridgeway reached into his pocket and counted out ten one-dollar coins.

"Here's your sandwich and pickle, Sheriff." Danny placed a plate on the counter.

"Are you sure it isn't *you* that's been doing all that purloining out in Gorham?" asked Sherman slyly with his eyes firmly locked on Danny Ricker. "Because I feel like I'm getting robbed right now with this gun deal…Sheriff."

"That's funny, Sherman," replied Silas as he bit into his food. "Hopefully now I'll be better prepared to face and capture the scum that is doing all the stealing out that way. I plan on finding him and bringing him to justice. Rest assured of that."

"Yeah, any man who steals from another man, woman, or child is definitely scum, Silas. I'll agree with you on that point," said Sherman without taking his eyes off Danny.

Feeling the mounting tension, Danny spoke up to divert any inference of thievery away from himself. "Sheriff Ridgeway, you were in the war, right? What outfit were you with?"

Silas swallowed the last of his pickle, then answered, "I was a lieutenant in the 2nd Maine. I served from 1861 through 1863. I was living in Bangor at the time I enlisted. We fought in eleven different engagements and I was wounded twice, but not seriously, thank God."

"I bet you saw a lot of gruesome things in those days," said Danny.

"We *both* did," chimed in Sherman.

"That's right, Sherman, I forget you fought too. You were with the 20th, right?"

"Yes, and I had a real baptism by fire at a little battle called Gettysburg. Even you have heard of Gettysburg, right Danny?"

"Yeah, I know about Gettysburg," Danny snarled. "I ain't stupid, you know. Now, if you'll both excuse me, I got a wagon to unload." Danny walked out and returned to his earlier task, but not before shooting an angry look at Sherman.

Sheriff Ridgeway finished his sandwich and paid Sherman the ten dollars he owed him for the Spencer plus an additional twenty-five cents for lunch. Sherman felt the desire to discuss further the thefts in Gorham and how they might have involved his angry employee; however, he had no proof or direct knowledge as to what had happened, and decided it was best to hold his tongue—for now.

Sherman followed Ridgeway out to his horse and handed him up the rifle after he had climbed into the saddle. The sheriff pulled out the magazine tube from the butt stock before dropping in seven cartridges. He reinserted the tube and placed the now-loaded gun in a leather rifle case strapped to the saddle.

"Thanks, Sherman. I'll be around more regularly now that I owe you money," said Silas wryly.

"Ayuh. Take care of yourself, Silas. Go catch them crooks before they decide to venture into North Scarborough and rob me!"

"Don't you worry about that, Sherman. But send word to me if you see or hear anything suspicious."

With that, Sheriff Ridgeway rode off up Settler Road in the direction of South Gorham. Sherman looked toward his supply wagon and Danny, who was taking his time unloading it between nips of liquor from his flask. With better things to do besides fight with an angry young drunk, Sherman grabbed the McPhees' crate and headed toward the Old Liberty Grange Hall.

"Danny," Sherman called out, "Watch the store until I get back. And look after the horses. Make sure they get watered and fed. God knows I can't afford to lose them to this ungodly heat."

Ricker said nothing but did acknowledge his boss's request with a dismissive wave. Sherman expected nothing more than that, and continued down the road to his destination. He passed the North Scarborough Community Church and waved to the kindly pastor, Thaddeus Morrell, and his corpulent wife Erin. Both were tending the flower garden near the entrance that contained freshly planted red, white, and pink geraniums. As Sherman waved, he couldn't help but notice a strikingly attractive figure appear in the open doorway of the church at the top of the steps. A young woman, in a lovely white dress with little pink roses and a matching hat with long-flowing pink ribbons, stepped out into the unforgiving heat. She had long strawberry-blonde curls and a pleasing little figure that refused to permit Sherman to divert his transfixed gaze, almost causing him to stumble over his own feet. She was most definitely new in town, as Sherman was certain he had never laid eyes on her before. However, she disappeared almost as quickly as she had appeared. In the blink of an eye she was gone. Sherman didn't know if she was real and had just retreated back into the church, or if he was succumbing to the high temperature and suffering from heat-induced hallucinations. *No matter*, he thought. He was only a short distance from the grange hall.

The Old Liberty Grange, like most of North Scarborough, had gone through a positive transformation in recent years. It had been purchased and taken over by Edwin and Reba McPhee, who were an amiable and energetic couple in their fifties. They were originally from Rockland and had moved to Scarborough in 1868. They were hoping for a fresh start in life, in a new place, as both were deeply saddened and troubled by the loss of their only son—yet another unfortunate war casualty.

Edwin McPhee was never at a loss for words when talking about his son Charles. He frequently recalled how courageously the twenty-two-year-old had enlisted with the 4th Maine Volunteer Infantry Regiment back in May of 1861, and how proud he was of his "brave boy." Edwin frequently read aloud to people old letters Charles had mailed home describing army life, battles he had fought in, and the war in general. Edwin always made it a point to explain that Charles never criticized or complained about the hardships of soldiering or the ugly politics associated with war. He always spoke of his comrades and commanders in a positive manner and never failed to mention his undying allegiance to the country he loved and to the destruction of the institution he despised—slavery. Though the McPhees were always overjoyed to receive letters from Charles, the last letter they received—from the War Department—had changed their lives forever. Charles had fallen in combat during the battle of Cold Harbor on or around June 3, 1864. As Edwin had read the cold-worded missive to his sobbing wife, his only relief had been that the fate of his son was known and that the body would be properly buried at the site of a new national military cemetery in Arlington, Virginia.

Though still grief-stricken, both Edwin and his wife Reba dealt with the loss of their son in a positive way that not only honored his memory, but also honored the men he fought with, while providing information of historical importance to the community. Back in 1868, shortly after their arrival, the McPhees had hired a small army of laborers to transform the old grange hall into a useful structure. They renovated the dilapidated building from the brick foundation all the way up to the roof. They covered it in a fresh coat of blue paint that resembled the shade of blue in an old Union soldier's uniform. The trim was painted white and the windows were adorned in pleated, fan-shaped, patriotic red, white, and blue bunting.

The two-storied grange hall still served as a meetinghouse and place for community gatherings including popular bean suppers, dances, and holiday parties; however, it now also served as a military museum housing information and artifacts of local interest from those who had fought bravely in wars past. The McPhees spent years gathering uniforms, hats, muskets, swords, pistols, journals, letters, books, musical instruments, regimental flags, paintings, pictures, and other personal effects that told an interesting story about soldiers' time in the service of their country. A small but very special portion of the museum was reserved exclusively in honor of the McPhees' fallen son Charles. They displayed his letters, a uniform, and several tintypes of himself with the 4th Maine regiment. The second story of the grange hall served as the museum while the first was reserved for special occasions or functions.

Holding the small crate with both arms, Sherman lumbered up the steps and rapped on the front door with his right foot. He waited a moment in silence, wondering if anybody was there or if the McPhees were home at their farm. Sherman grumbled at the thought. Their farm was at least two miles away and would require him to return to the store and saddle up one of his horses to make the delivery. He didn't want to walk the distance and back in the heat of the afternoon sun. He had marched many miles in temperatures and conditions worse than this, but he was wiser now and no longer wore a uniform or took orders. He appreciated the privilege and convenience a horse offered and took advantage of it whenever he could. His days of uncomfortable marches in unforgiving weather were thankfully now over. Such were his thoughts.

Another minute passed, causing Sherman to gently kick the door again. The crate, although not terribly heavy, was burdensome and he wanted it taken off his hands quickly. Just as he was about to give up and head back, Sherman heard faint footsteps growing in intensity as they approached the door. To his relief, the door swung open and there stood Reba McPhee with a pleasant smile on her face.

"Oh my goodness, it's you, Mr. Jackson. And I see you have a package for me. How delightful," said Reba.

"Indeed," replied Sherman, adding, "I'm so glad I caught you here. I was afraid you might be at home and that I would have missed you. Your package arrived today and I always want my customers' goods delivered in a timely manner. I never wish to have them inconvenienced by having to travel to my store in person to pick up their supplies, particularly on such a hot day as today."

Sherman looked away from Reba and tried not to grin. He had caught himself in a fib and he knew it all too well. In reality he preferred not making personal deliveries at all. He'd rather customers come directly into his store and pick up their goods. It saved him time, labor, and the hassle of leaving the store unattended, and it kept the goods in his possession until the buyer paid for them. He had more control when the goods were in the store. All too often he had delivered them to a customer's residence only to hear, "I don't have all the money at this time, but I can come by the store later and pay you in full. Is that acceptable?" Sherman often found himself chasing those who owed him money, a task he did not enjoy. He hoped it wasn't about to happen again.

"Oh, what wonderful service, Mr. Jackson," gushed Mrs. McPhee. "How much do I owe you, sir?"

"Well, let me see. The bill came to a dollar and forty-seven cents if I recall correctly, Mrs. McPhee."

"Just one moment, Mr. Jackson. I must fetch your money from upstairs. Do please come in while you wait. I shall only be a minute. Please excuse me. I'll be right back."

Sherman stepped inside and closed the door behind him as Reba scurried upstairs. He was happy this delivery would result in payment on time. As he waited, he looked around the largely empty room. His footsteps echoed on the hardwood floors. Sunlight poured in through the many brightly decorated windows that lined the walls, giving the room a heavenly glow. Dozens of wooden chairs were stacked up high in the corners while a grand piano occupied a prominent position atop a small stage at the head of the room. There were also some open crates filled with decorative banners, streamers, and flags spilling out over the sides. It appeared the McPhees were planning an Independence Day celebration.

"Mr. Jackson, would you mind assisting me upstairs for a moment? I'm afraid I'm in need of your youthful muscles," called out Reba.

"Certainly, Mrs. McPhee. I'll be right there," answered Sherman.

He climbed the stairs and found Reba sitting at a table wildly fanning herself. Sherman noticed how considerably hotter it was on the stuffy second story of the grange. He stood in awe for a moment at all the exhibits and the artifacts and information they showcased. Apparently the McPhees had been busy adding to their collection, as there were many things Sherman was certain he had not seen since his last visit.

"Mr. Jackson, could you please just push that old cedar chest against the wall for me? I'm afraid Mr. McPhee has stored far too many weighty items in there and I can't budge it to save my life. It's in the way at the moment and I'd like to have it moved aside before someone trips and hurts themselves—in all likelihood, me!"

"I would be happy to oblige, ma'am," said Sherman before shoving the heavy chest against the wall with a mighty heave.

"Thank you, Mr. Jackson. I do appreciate your help. And here is the money I owe you, plus a little extra for your time and thoughtfulness."

Reba handed Sherman two one-dollar greenbacks, which he accepted and graciously thanked her.

"Mrs. McPhee, I must say you've done a marvelous job with the museum. I'm very impressed with the exhibits. The items on display are well represented and displayed in a very respectful, tasteful, and patriotic manner. I must admit that I recognize many of the war-related items in your collection. I used a great many of them myself during my time in the army," Sherman said with a chuckle.

"Oh, yes…and I'm so glad you came home without injury. I wish the same could be said about my beloved son, Charles. Unfortunately the war took him from us forever," Reba said with a sniffle. "But we honor his memory and those of other brave soldiers like you who fought for the Union. I must say, Mr. Jackson, we don't possess any personal items of yours from the war. We certainly insist on honoring your brave exploits and telling your tales, which have gone unsung. Would you be interested in making a donation and perhaps regaling Mr. McPhee with an oral history, which he can then record and display for our visitors? I don't believe we have many artifacts or stories detailing the heroic achievements of the 20th Maine."

Sherman paused a minute, then exhaled deeply.

"Honestly, Mrs. McPhee, I don't have a lot I can contribute. I didn't bring back much and what I did is precious to me—not meant for a museum. I try not to talk much about the war. I left most of it in Virginia and that's where it should stay, in my opinion. The country still isn't completely unified and has a long way to go before it's healed, despite what President Grant may think or say to the American people. The South's bitter and will have to be closely governed and garrisoned for a long time to come."

Reba stood silent and slowly nodded, wondering if she shouldn't have brought up the subject.

"That, of course, is just my own opinion on the matter, you understand," said Sherman. "However, if I ever feel the need to discuss my military days, I will certainly give Mr. McPhee first preference."

"I understand, Mr. Jackson. Oh, my, do look at the time," said Reba, spying her pendulum clock hanging on the wall. "I mustn't detain you any longer and I have so much more work to get accomplished before this day is done. We're preparing for a special Independence Day gathering on the fourth. I've been planning it for weeks. Now it's time to start decorating. Edwin and I have so much to do. Your delivery today was timely and the contents of that small crate will be of great help. I do thank you kindly, Mr. Jackson."

"It's my pleasure, Mrs. McPhee. And might I say that it's a truly wonderful and historically important thing you've done with this old grange hall. I salute you and your husband. My deepest regrets for the loss of your son. As a former soldier, no one can understand that kind of loss better than me. Good day to you, ma'am. Please stop by the store and visit any time."

With that, Sherman offered a gentlemanly bow to Reba and then made his exit from the Old Liberty Grange. He hurried back to the store, fearing disgruntled customers needing service and also dreading what Danny Ricker had been doing, or more specifically *not* doing, in his absence. On his way back, though, he couldn't help but pause for a moment in front of the church. The pastor and his wife had apparently finished their gardening and were now nowhere to be seen. The church looked quiet and very still, with no sign of any activity inside. Sherman had hoped he might have a friendly word with the pastor; however, he wasn't interested in discussing passages from the Bible. He had a more personal motive. He wanted to find out more about the lovely young woman he'd seen earlier. He thought about going up to the entrance and knocking on the door. His feet started to carry him in that direction, but then he stopped abruptly. It was getting late and he had much to do at the store. After one last hopeful glance at the church, Sherman hustled down the road.

Inside the store, Sherman found Danny lazily sweeping the floor. He peered out the back doorway and around the corner. To his pleasant surprise, the wagon was fully unloaded and it appeared the Shire stallions had been tended to properly. Regardless, Sherman felt the need to ask.

"I see you finished unloading the wagon; thank you. Did you feed and water the horses?" asked Sherman, trying his best to be civil.

Danny stopped sweeping and replied, "Both Phineas and Lucky are all taken care of. They have full bellies of oats washed down with plenty of water."

"Good. Let 'em digest for a while, then unhook 'em and get 'em settled for the night in the livery."

"You the boss," said Danny aloofly while turning his back and resuming his idle sweeping.

"Did you take care of the Morgans, too?" reluctantly asked Sherman.

Again Danny stopped his sweeping and slowly turned to face his employer.

"What?" he asked indifferently.

"Did you feed and water Skipper and Budley after taking care of Phineas and Lucky?" asked Sherman in hopes that Danny hadn't neglected his two prized Morgan stallions stabled out back.

"No, I didn't get around to that," Danny said sharply. "They're shaded in the livery, and they ain't exposed to the heat as badly as the others. They can wait until later."

Sherman sighed and did his best to control his temper. He wanted to be authoritative and shout out instructions, as if he was a sergeant back in the army issuing an order to an unruly private. The one thing Sherman missed about the war was military discipline and the privileges of rank when assigning tasks and duties. Orders were followed without question, with serious repercussions heaped on those who were disobedient. Sherman wondered why the same principles couldn't be applied to his employee now. Moreover, he wondered why all attempts at enforcing discipline, responsibility, and strong work ethics on Danny seemed useless. Against his better judgment, he decided to tread lightly.

"Danny, those horses are of great value to me. They help sustain my business, they perform laborious tasks I wouldn't be able to accomplish without them, and they provide recreation and companionship. The least I can do in return is offer them adequate food, water, and shelter. I can't in good conscience rent them out to people in need if they're in poor health due to neglect. Now, please go attend to their basic requirements before you sweep up another scrid of dirt from this floor."

"Mr. Jackson, I told you they're fine now. I been around and cared for horses my whole life. I know when they need tending and when they don't. I'll check on the Morgans when I get ready to leave tonight."

With that, Danny turned his back on Sherman and continued sweeping. What little restraint Sherman had was now gone. He wasn't about to be told what to do in his own store by some insolent kid.

"You'll do what I goddamn tell you to do and you'll do it now, without question or hesitation, Danny!" yelled Sherman as he pounded his fist on the counter.

Danny slammed the broom down hard, upending a basket of vegetables and sending the produce sprawling across the floor.

"Pick that up, now!" ordered Sherman.

"Naw, you can pick that up your damn self!" fired back Danny. "I just decided I ain't gonna do one more fucking thing around here until you pay me all the money you owe me. And I do mean now!"

Danny glared at Sherman, who carefully watched him reach into his pocket and pull out a knife. He quickly unfolded the blade and pointed it at his boss. The pocketknife was small but still deadly if wielded by skilled hands.

"Put down that knife and get out of here now, you goddamned thief!" hollered Sherman, after recognizing the knife was stolen from his own inventory.

"I ain't going anywhere until I get what you owe me," belched out Danny.

Sherman could smell the liquor on the angry young man's breath and could tell that he was slightly drunk, which made him all the more dangerous.

"Give me my money now! Better still, give me all the money you got hid under the counter!"

"You're nothing but walking trash, Danny Ricker. I shoulda handed you over to the sheriff when I had the chance. I'll bet you're responsible for those thefts out in Gorham, ain't ya? Been stealing from folks all over, not just me—right, Danny?"

"Shut your goddamned mouth, Jackson! I ain't listening to you no more and I sure as hell ain't taking any more orders from you. But I am taking what's mine, and a little extra. Now hand over the money! I will not hesitate to kill you if I have to!"

Sherman froze in place as the deranged Ricker slowly edged toward him, holding the knife up high with clear intention of going for his throat.

"You'll have to kill me, Danny, 'cause I ain't giving you a damn thing," said Sherman bravely if not a bit foolishly.

"Have it your way, you fucking son-of-a-bitch!" Danny lunged toward Sherman. In his semi-drunken state, Danny tripped and fell face-first onto the floor. Sherman jumped on top of him and managed to knock the knife out of his hand. The two grappled, punched, and kicked violently at one another. Displays of items for sale were knocked about and spilled all over the floor, creating a morass of damaged and inedible merchandise.

"I'll kill ya, you bastard!" screamed Danny, using both hands to try to choke the life out of Sherman. Taller, stronger, and more experienced with hand-to-hand combat, Sherman wrestled free from his attacker and landed a blow squarely on Danny's chin, sending him reeling back toward the counter. Danny's head hit hard against the wood and he crumpled into a sitting position with his legs fully extended and his arms hanging limply from his shoulders. His dazed head hung low as he tried to recover. Sherman reached out and got his hands on the knife before Danny realized what had happened. Sherman pulled an axe off the wall, pointing the sharpened metal head at Ricker's chest. Danny's mind cleared enough to realize he was beaten.

Sherman's adrenaline surged in a way he had not experienced since the war. Wildly violent and dangerous emotions that had been suppressed for a long time were now creeping to the surface and working their way down to the axe poised to strike deep into the defenseless man. In his mind he knew he didn't want to kill Ricker, but some unimaginable instinct deep within his soul was willing him to. Sherman, breathing heavily and dripping with sweat, got control of himself and allowed Danny to slowly stand up. He wasn't sure what to say or do next.

Ricker, still slightly dazed and unarmed, cautiously stepped toward the door. When it became clear that Sherman was done fighting and wasn't going after his assailant, Danny spoke with hatred and surging defiance.

"I'm not through with you, Sherman Jackson! You'll be seeing me again! You won't know when and you won't know where—but believe me, I will get what's coming to me and more! And if you think that son-of-a-bitchin' sheriff, or anyone else in this fucking shithole of a town, will protect you…well…I pray you're not that stupid! I hope you saved room for another marble headstone in that shitty little family plot of yours out back! You'll need one…soon!"

Before Sherman could say another word, Ricker burst out the door and ran up the road. He vanished into the woods without a trace. Sherman took a few deep breaths as he glared up Settler Road. A few curious passersby paused to look upon the disheveled figure standing in the store's doorway holding an axe. Realizing there could be trouble, they quietly moved on. Sherman paid them no attention and eventually retreated back inside. He slammed the door and hung a "Closed" sign in the window before grabbing a broom to start cleaning up the mess. As he swept and straightened up, he pondered how big a problem he had created, and how horrific a monster he had just unleashed upon himself and possibly the town. He wondered just how much genuine danger he was in. His thoughts began to dwell on the Henry rifle above the mantel and the exact whereabouts of the bullets—if there were any.

CHAPTER 5

A Stranger in Town

Sheriff Ridgeway would return in a short time—a week at the latest. If he was serious about honoring his debt for the Spencer, then he'd be back. Sherman's mind was suddenly preoccupied with the sheriff and his own safety. He barely slept during the night, nodding off at random times only to be awakened by every little unusual sound echoing through the house. He had taken every precaution he could think of. He'd bolted the doors and locked all the windows before locking himself in his bedroom. The sealed house was now unbearably hot and extremely uncomfortable, but at least it was secure from everything except a forced entry.

Sherman started the day much earlier than normal. Apart from the fears of his own safety, he feared for his property—mainly his horses and the store. The livery was vulnerable and could easily be broken into. All four of Sherman's horses could be led away in the dead of night or just as effortlessly slaughtered where they slept. His wagon could be taken or destroyed, his crops pilfered, his chickens stolen, and both his house and store set ablaze and decimated with little or no warning. Thankfully all was safe and secure upon inspection at dawn. Sherman tended his horses and kept all four sheltered in the livery. His supply wagon was untouched and his crops and chickens were all intact. Most importantly, his house and store hadn't been vandalized or burgled during the night. He entered the store and opened for business on time and with a watchful eye.

Sherman went about his morning duties. He checked his inventory lists over and over to try to pinpoint exactly what Danny had stolen. Midmorning he thoroughly searched the room above the store where Danny had been staying in hopes of finding missing items that were hidden, or any evidence that would suggest criminal activities he could report to Sheriff Ridgeway. He found nothing out of the ordinary except a messy bed and random clutter, which consisted mostly of Danny's wardrobe, scattered on the floor. Sherman deduced that Danny perhaps had a hiding place somewhere outside where he hid stolen items. He obviously was smart enough not to leave any evidence lying around his room. Sherman straightened up and bagged the clothes before returning downstairs. Though everything seemed normal, he still worried.

"Just how dangerous is this kid?" he muttered. "Was his threat serious or was he just liquored up and trying to act all hard and callous? He's gotta know I'll warn the sheriff. Maybe that's got him scared and he's run off for good now. Maybe he was just jawing and has no real intention of doing me harm. Maybe after he's sobered up and spent the night in a field he will've understood his error in threatening me and come back to turn himself in. Hmmm…not likely."

Sherman started listing options in his head. As a former soldier he understood the hazard of ignoring a problem such as this and also knew it was best to prepare oneself rather than be caught off-guard. He had searched the house thoroughly looking for ammunition for the Henry. He looked in every conceivable place his father might've hidden it, but came up with nothing. The thought occurred to him that it was indeed possible that his parents had never purchased ammunition for the gun. His mother and father were naive about firearms, and the fact that a recently purchased rifle actually required bullets to function properly was a subtle yet vital detail that could have easily slipped their well-intentioned minds. Sherman didn't carry .44-caliber rim-fire cartridges in the store; he would most likely have to order them from one of his suppliers in Portland.

"Why don't I just saddle up Skipper and ride to Portland now?" he mumbled. "I could get cartridges for the Henry and then ride directly to Sheriff Ridgeway's office. What if he's not there though? What if he spent the night in Gorham and plans to stay there for a few days to conduct his investigation?"

The weight of frustration began to press heavily on Sherman's mind. The more he tried to develop a plan to help resolve his situation, the more of a conundrum the problem became. Standing alone behind the counter, the troubled man continued to mutter to himself.

"Even if I do leave and successfully find the sheriff, my house, store, and all my possessions will be at risk. He could come in the night while I'm away and pilfer everything I have, then burn my life to the ground.

I could have someone watch the house for me—someone like Hiram Lovell, or Edwin McPhee, or even Pastor Morrell. They would certainly be obliged to offer assistance after all I've done for them over the years. But what could I tell them? I couldn't in good faith put them in harm's way…and I certainly couldn't lie to them and pretend nothing was amiss. God would never forgive me if Danny Ricker hurt any of them. I'd never forgive myself. Hiram has a wife and two children. Edwin has already suffered more misery than he and Reba deserve, and Thaddeus is a man of God. How could I in good conscience put him in potential danger?"

Sherman's heart began to race and his head began to pound. He hadn't faced anything as serious as this since the last battle he fought for the Union. It was easier to contemplate death when a man was in an army uniform. It was a brutal business, but it all seemed much simpler. Orders were given, battles were fought, soldiers were expected to die in the face of the enemy, and civilians were unfortunately caught in the middle… and subsequently, many were killed. However, Sherman no longer wore a uniform. Moreover, he wasn't sanctioned by his government to eliminate his enemies. Killing a man was no longer a necessary evil to benefit the greater good of the nation. Killing now—whether for the cause of righteousness or simple self-defense—was nothing more than an act of murder. And murder had tremendous legal consequences, many of which led to horrific ends for the accused. Sherman had to weigh the potential costs of his actions and the harm they could inflict upon the innocent individuals who might get caught up in them—a very unsettling thought.

He tried to convince himself that he was overreacting and that he had blown the situation out of proportion. Over and over he rationalized that Danny was a hard talker but ultimately a coward when it came time to act. He would never have the courage to attempt something as serious as the destruction of property—or murder. He may have been a petty thief bathed in youthful arrogance and rebellion, but a hardened criminal with intention to enact revenge resulting in a person's death? It just didn't seem fathomable.

"He's curled up in some thicket somewhere wondering where to go and from whom he'll bum his next meal…that's it. He'll probably sneak back over to the widow McClatchy and prey on her aged ignorance and generosity. He'll eat his fill, then creep off again like a cagey fox. He'll bide his time leaching off others until he feels he's in no danger from the law.

Then he'll worm his way into someone else's business in a town far from Scarborough and I'll never have to see or deal with him again. Yes, that's how it is, I'm sure of it. I don't even need to inform Silas of yesterday's scuffle. Ricker won't be back to bother me or anybody else in this town—and if he was responsible for those thefts in Gorham, Silas will track him down and bring him to justice. When he does, that's when I'll seek compensation for my losses here. That's how this business will unfold and that's where it will end. Yes…I'm sure of it."

Sherman breathed an audible sigh of relief. He had successfully persuaded himself he wasn't in any danger and that life would proceed normally—that is, until he glanced down at the display case lock under the counter. Sherman examined the keyhole and discovered to his horror that the lock had been forced open! The keyhole appeared deformed and the wood encircling it had been chipped away. Instantly, and without using his key, Sherman threw open the case to discover that the Colt House Revolver and one Bowie knife were missing!

"Jesus," said Sherman, "How did he get them, and when?" He thought feverishly, trying to determine if the items had been stolen during the night. "They had to have been. I saw them in the case after I returned from the grange hall."

Sherman quickly checked the front-door lock and the sliding door on the rear storage-room entrance. The front door lock hadn't been tampered with and the rear door was bolted shut from the inside. Sherman looked for any sign of broken glass or forced entry via the front windows. After running out front and examining both floors, he quickly saw that all were intact and secure. Just then a sinking thought entered his head. He raced back inside and upstairs. To his horror, he found the room's single rear-facing window open. He stuck his head out and noticed a rickety wooden ladder resting on the ground in an odd position, as if someone had hurriedly scurried down and simply kicked it away, giving no thought to how or where it landed.

Sherman sat on the bed and buried his head in his hands. How could he have been so careless? One unlocked window was enough to bring on a torrent of dangers from which there was uncertain defense. If only he had made sure it was locked, then Ricker would have had to force his way in, thereby exposing himself amidst the sounds of broken glass or wood. Sherman could have been easily alerted and taken action…

and just maybe have been able to restrain Ricker long enough for help to arrive. The problem would have ended there. However, that wasn't the case now.

Just then Sherman heard the door open downstairs and the sounds of several sets of footsteps entering the store. He quickly stood up, composed himself, and adjusted his suit so he appeared presentable. He then walked downstairs.

"Ah, good morning, Mrs. Morrell," said Sherman upon seeing the pastor's wife and two sons looking around.

"Well, a very good morning to you, Mr. Jackson," said the portly woman in a yellow dress that more resembled a small circus tent than an article of women's clothing. Erin Morrell was a kind woman but not exceptionally bright. She was known as a sweet and caring individual devoted to her family and God, but sorely lacking in education and common sense. Her two ill-behaved sons, who were more inclined to partake in mischievous activities rather than follow the teachings of the Lord or obey what their parents dictated, easily and often outwitted her. Erin had a round face and curly brown hair that wasn't very long. She wore a large bonnet and often carried a Bible in her bag. She frequented the store in the morning in hopes of finding fresh-baked pies for sale cooling on the windowsill—the delicious results of the widow McClatchy's talent for creating luscious culinary delights. Sherman would often sell the pies and split the profits with the widow. Unfortunately there were none to be had this morning. It mattered little because Erin Morrell was visiting on another matter.

"Mr. Jackson, I must put forth my sincerest apologies and ask for your forgiveness."

"Madam?" asked Sherman quizzically.

"It has come to mine and the pastor's attention that our two sons may have roamed a bit too freely on your property and been tempted to either damage or outright take and consume some of the vegetables from your garden. We've found evidence of these deeds in the boys' possession and the pastor himself was able to wheedle a confession from Olin here."

Olin Morrell was fifteen and in recent years had felt the urge to rebel against his church upbringing. Pastor Morrell was a devout man of God but hardly a disciplinarian. He didn't believe in harsh punishments for any of his children's wrongdoings and thus preferred a more gentle and forgiving approach to addressing misconduct. Olin, often referred to by his nickname, Ollie, took full advantage of his father's overt kindness and used it to his advantage when engaging in less-than-desirable activities. Sherman saw the beginnings of another Danny Ricker when he looked at Olin Morrell. He hoped he would eventually be steered down the right path.

"Wilbur, step forward and be seen," said Erin to her youngest son. Wilbur was eyeing the assortment of medicines and elixirs on a nearby shelf toward the back of the store. He reluctantly obeyed his mother and stepped forward. All three now stood in a line before Sherman. The thirteen-year-old Wilbur jammed his hands in his pockets and kept his head down. He stared at the floor not wanting to say anything. Wilbur was known as Willy to most who befriended him. He was a bit different from his older brother. Wilbur was always more inclined to follow the rules and listen to adults; however, he was under the spell of his brother's miscreant nature and often found himself guilty by association. He also easily succumbed to pressure from his brother, who more often than not coerced him to commit the crime himself, thus giving the older sibling deniability if caught.

"Well, Olin, what do you have to say to Mr. Jackson?" Erin's voice, struggling to sound stern, was almost laughable.

Olin looked at Sherman and spoke in a monotonous tone that seemed to lack even the tiniest shred of sincerity. "Mr. Jackson, I regret that the Devil's influence has led me astray from the Lord's path of righteousness as of late. His seductive calling has entangled me in a web of deceit and disrespect causing me to unwillingly engage in unsavory activities at the expense of my fellow Christians and neighbors. I humbly ask that you have faith in the Lord's ability to guide me through these troubled times, and that you can find forgiveness in your heart and soul for any suffering, financial or otherwise, I may have caused you. I swear on my honor that nothing like this shall ever happen again so help me God."

Sherman listened to Olin finish his speech. He wished he could take it to heart, but deep down he knew it was just well-scripted words written by a genuine God-fearing pastor, simply memorized and mechanically regurgitated by an insincere schemer with no earnest intentions other than appeasing those who might punish or prosecute him.

"Well…thank you for the apology, Olin. I hope you're a man of your word. I don't want to hear about something like this happening from you again. A boy your age ought not get mixed up in matters that would ordinarily involve the law. From now on I expect you to respect my property and not cause any more mischief. Is that understood?"

Olin nodded and said nothing. Sherman looked at Wilbur, who hadn't moved or breathed a single word.

"What about you, Willy? Are you going to set a good example and stay out of trouble?" Sherman asked, placing his hand on the boy's shoulder.

"Yes, sir," he replied sheepishly. "I don't want to cause any trouble for folks."

"Splendid! I'm glad this is settled," beamed Erin. "Boys, I want you to run along now and make sure you're home early for supper. Why don't you ask around town and see if there's any work that needs to be done. You can do the Lord's bidding by helping others in need."

The two boys looked at each other, then bolted out the front door. Erin Morrell smiled foolishly, undoubtedly under the impression her boys were off to help turn a field or repair a barn. Sherman said nothing, but could tell from their direction that they were headed straight for the Stroudwater River and a day of lazy swimming.

"Mr. Jackson, I didn't want to do this in front of the boys and make them feel any worse than they obviously do now, but I wanted to give you some compensation for those few vegetables my boys stole…uh…that is to say…*relieved* you of. Will a dollar be adequate payment?" Erin thrust a dollar coin into Sherman's hand.

"Ah, yes, Mrs. Morrell, that will be fine. Is there anything else I can help you with this morning? Any supplies for the church? I'm afraid I don't have any pies at this time."

"Well, maybe I'll just browse for a little bit. I'm always in need of something, you know," she said cheerily.

"Please, take your time and just call out if you need any assistance," said Sherman, retreating behind the counter. He glanced out the front window and secretly wondered just how many people in North Scarborough were stealing from him. More importantly, why? It occurred to him that maybe it hadn't been Ricker who had stolen some of his vegetables and chickens. Maybe, in truth, it was the Morrell boys. Maybe Sherman had needlessly and wrongly escalated his earlier confrontation with Ricker by falsely accusing him of a crime he didn't actually commit. Maybe Danny Ricker hadn't stolen anything. Maybe it was the Morrell boys who were the root cause of everything that had gone missing recently.

"No, impossible," muttered Sherman inaudibly.

He knew that too much had disappeared from inside the store and off the supply wagon for Danny to be totally innocent. Regardless of the severity of his earlier crimes, his recent verbal threats and supposed theft of the Bowie knife and Colt revolver were certainly more than enough reasons for Sherman to alert Sheriff Ridgeway. He continued to stare out the front window as Mrs. Morrell lazily perused the store's clothing inventory, particularly women's hats. Just then, a sight through the window remarkably shifted Sherman's thoughts away from his recent troubles. A nervous twinge shot up through his gut and caused him to shudder in a strangely excitable way he hadn't felt for many years.

The door delicately swung open and Sherman found himself at a loss for words. Even the simplest of greetings would not escape his lips. He stood there foolishly until Mrs. Morrell interrupted the awkward silence.

"Ah, hello, my dear. I didn't realize you were out this way. I thought you'd still be out at the farm. Did you meet up with the pastor at the church or did you have some other pressing duty to perform at the schoolhouse?"

Standing before Sherman and Erin Morrell was the lovely young woman Sherman had spied briefly standing in the church entrance yesterday afternoon. She was dressed in the same garb as yesterday and thus easily recognized. The young woman smiled and addressed her portly acquaintance.

"Hello, Erin. Yes, I'm on my way to the schoolhouse. I have so much to do and so little time to do it in, it seems. I thought I'd get an early start today. I saw Ollie and Willy a few minutes ago and they said you were in here. I thought I'd stop in and say hello before continuing on to the school. I also assumed it would be a good opportunity to pick up some necessary supplies."

"Oh, what a splendid idea! I was just doing a little browsing myself."

The young lady turned and looked at Sherman, who smiled but couldn't muster up anything to say. It was as if the wires connecting his brain to his vocal cords had been cut. He knew what he wanted to enunciate but couldn't get his mouth to translate his thoughts into words.

"Oh my! Where have my manners gone?" blurted the pastor's wife as she threw her hands up in the air and waddled forward. "My dear, may I present the owner of this fine establishment, Mr. Sherman Jackson. Mr. Jackson, this is the latest blessing to enter the Morrell family's lives and our glorious household. It is my pleasure to introduce to you Miss Sophie Curtis. She is the new summer-session teacher at the Budwin School."

"I'm delighted to make your acquaintance," Sophie said softly with a pearly smile and an extended hand.

Finally, Sherman's brain and vocal cords cooperated and kicked into action.

"The pleasure is all mine, Miss Curtis," Sherman replied with a slight bow and gentle handshake. "Am I to assume that the Budwin School will reopen permanently? If I recall correctly, it's been a solid three years since old Mr. Phibbert taught his last lesson there and closed up the building. He left town discreetly. I wasn't sure the school would ever be reopened again."

"My desire is to have the school opened permanently and for it to be a beacon of knowledge and education for this community's youth. It was my understanding that the school had been closed due to lack of support and interest from this and surrounding towns. As fortune would have it, my superiors have deemed it essential to reestablish academic ties to this area and help educate the area's youth. I was fortunate enough to be selected for this important task."

"Well, may I extend my warmest congratulations and welcome you to North Scarborough," said Sherman. "May I ask, are you originally from around these parts?"

"Goodness, no, I'm afraid," replied Sophie. "I'm a stranger to this area and this town in particular. I'm originally from Boston, Massachusetts. My mother and father still reside there. I unfortunately had to leave them to take advantage of this wonderful opportunity. However, I've been blessed to have met the Morrells, who have shown me unparalleled kindness."

"Miss Curtis has been staying with us since her arrival several days ago," said Erin Morrell. "Pastor Morrell and I have enthusiastically welcomed her into our home as our guest until she gets settled and is able to collect wages for her work. Her presence is a blessing in both our home and our church. We couldn't be happier with this lovely young angel sent to us straight from Heaven."

Sophie turned away and blushed from embarrassment. She tried not to giggle at Erin's gushing. Quickly she changed the subject.

"Mr. Jackson?"

"Please, Miss Curtis, call me Sherman. I insist."

"Very well…Sherman, I noticed the schoolhouse was not in possession of a decent United States flag. I'm afraid Mr. Phibbert didn't leave much when he shuttered the building years ago. It needs lots of interior work, but I thought running a new American flag up the flagpole would be a decent and patriotic first step, considering that Independence Day is nearly upon us. Would you happen to have one in your inventory?"

"You're in luck, Miss Curtis," said Sherman cheerfully. "I happen to have a brand-new supply of them that arrived yesterday from Portland in preparation for celebrating Independence Day. You may have first pick."

Sherman retrieved a crate from the back storage room and presented Sophie with an array of American flags in different shapes and sizes. Vibrant colors of red, white, and blue burst from the drab crate, evoking a burgeoning sense of pride and patriotism for those who laid eyes on them.

"I would propose this one, Miss Curtis," suggested Sherman after digging a particular flag out of the crate. "It's specifically designed for displaying from a flagpole and I believe it's a proper size that will suit your needs. What do you think?"

"It's lovely. What's your opinion, Erin?"

"Yes, it's quite nice, my dear. And I insist on paying for it."

"Oh no, Erin. I've got a little money. Surely I can part with a few pennies and nickels to buy a flag."

"Nonsense, my dear. I won't hear any more of it. You are our guest and the Lord will provide. How much for the flag, Mr. Jackson?" asked Erin, digging around in her purse.

"Seventy-five cents will be sufficient Mrs. Morrell, and thank you."

Sophie's eyes lit up as she examined the flag. She counted the thirteen red and white stripes and the thirty-seven white stars organized perfectly upon a sea of blue. She then folded the flag neatly and tucked it under her arm.

"I do thank you very much for this, Sherman. It was a pleasure meeting you and I do hope we can talk further at another time," said Sophie. "Unfortunately I must hurry to the school and start making preparations for the upcoming summer session. There just never seems to be enough time. Good day to you, sir, and I will see you later tonight, Erin."

With that, Sophie made her exit. Sherman watched her from the window until she was well down the road and out of sight.

"You know, Mr. Jackson," said Erin Morrell slyly, "She's twenty-three years of age and unmarried. She's very lovely and would benefit greatly from some gentlemanly companionship, if you ask me. I would certainly advocate for a fine, upstanding young man such as yourself to call on her on occasion…that is to say, if she's agreeable. Are you?"

Sherman let out an uncomfortable little chuckle and replied, "I must admit that she has some intriguing and very pleasant qualities, Mrs. Morrell. She is quite nice and very attractive. I would be remiss if I didn't seriously consider your assistance concerning Miss Curtis. You play the part of matchmaker with earnest sincerity, which I can appreciate. I would be honored and grateful for your subtle aid in helping me get to know Miss Curtis on a more personal level."

"Splendid," cried out Erin. "My course has been set and I shall endeavor to help grow your acquaintance with Sophie through God's good grace. Now I must take my leave of your fine store, Mr. Jackson. However, I shall return and post you of my progress," she said with a wide smile across her rounded face. "Good day."

"Good day, Mrs. Morrell," said Sherman as the obese woman waddled out the front door.

Sherman was smitten for the first time since before the war. He hadn't been with a woman since his days at Bowdoin, and even then it was simply lust he was experiencing and not true love. He had gone without the touch of a woman the entire time he was in the army—for obvious reasons, and some not so obvious. Realistically there was virtually no time for sex during the war, and when the rare opportunity did present itself, in the form of prostitution, Sherman never could bring himself to part with money for sexual favors. No matter how much he craved the company of a woman, he felt that prostitution was sinful and could only lead to immoral degradation. He was also aware of social diseases that were widespread among certain groups of individuals including prostitutes. The fear of contracting one of these sicknesses was enough to keep him out of the brothels and away from the loose ladies who found themselves visiting Union Army camps on occasion.

Since his return home in 1865, up until the present, he hadn't thought much of women. Oh, there were cravings and desires of the sort that affect all men, but Sherman often found himself too busy or too heavily engaged in other pressing matters involving his livelihood to think much of courting women. He was now thirty years old and had occasionally thought of life as a husband and father, but the blunt reality was that there were hardly any young ladies around North Scarborough. The overwhelming majority of women Sherman was acquainted with were either too advanced in age for his liking or married. The young storeowner couldn't honestly remember the last time a beautiful young woman had stepped into his life. The feeling was invigorating, like a cleansing breath of fresh air or a long draft of icy water from a pure-flowing stream. The thought of seeing Sophie again was so pleasantly intoxicating and all-consuming that for a while, Sherman had totally forgotten about his problems with the Morrell boys—and even Danny Ricker.

For the rest of the day Sherman went about his duties with vim, vigor, and a positive attitude. His step had an animated bounce to it and he didn't grumble about the added work thrust upon him by the absence of his disgruntled employee. By the end of the day he was very pleased and looking forward to a hearty dinner and a peaceful rest. Business was good overall. Traffic in the store had picked up and sales were on the rise. He took the money brought in throughout the day and entered it into his sales ledger. Once the numbers matched up accordingly, he pocketed the cash and began to lock up the store. It was only then that his jovial mood turned sour again at the thought of Danny Ricker and the potential problems he represented. Sherman double-checked all the windows to ensure they were locked and properly secured. He brought anything of value merchandised outside into the storage room. He hid potentially dangerous items in new locations that were not easily found at quick glance. He went out back and retrieved the old wooden ladder, which he brought inside the storage room. He bolted the rear door and exited through the front entrance, making sure it was locked. He looked in all directions and then made a short inspection of his property. He walked to the livery and tended his horses, which, to his relief, were safe and secure. He checked his barn, vegetable garden, and chicken coop. All seemed in order.

Once inside his stuffy house, Sherman carefully inspected every room, making sure the windows were closed and locked. He looked for anything out of the ordinary or out of place. Fortunately, all seemed fine. Throughout the house, he closed doors and locked them behind him. Before retreating to the kitchen to prepare a meal, Sherman first slumped down into his favorite chair facing the fireplace in the parlor. He opened one window to let in some much-needed air and then poured himself a glass of whiskey. He sat there quietly trying to think about Sophie, but instead found himself staring at the mounted Henry rifle and concentrating on Danny Ricker.

"Give it a few days…then see what happens and go from there," he muttered between sips.

As hard as he tried not to think of it, he couldn't help but wonder if it was indeed Danny Ricker who stole the knife and revolver. It was proven via direct confession that the Morrell boys had stolen from him in the past, and either one could have climbed the ladder, opened the unlocked window, crept down into the store, and cracked into the display case. Olin could have effortlessly coerced Willy to do the deed and both could have hurried off into the night without any thought of trying to cover their tracks or conceal their crime. If Ricker was in fact the culprit, why did he leave all his extra clothes lying on the floor? Why did he just take the knife and gun when he certainly could have stolen and escaped with much more—especially much-needed food?

Sherman was now truly perplexed. The theft of the knife and gun was either perpetrated by an angry and possibly disturbed young man bent on personal revenge against his former boss, or by two rebellious, thrill-seeking teenagers with a taste for unlawful adventure and danger. Both posed a risk to Sherman, but the first was definitely more perilous than the second. He wanted to take action, but didn't know the best course to follow.

Just then there was a knock on the door. Taken by surprise, Sherman nearly spilled his drink. He got up, and with his heart pounding he furtively went to the window to see who was at his front door. At an instant he exhaled a sigh of relief, walked to the door, and opened it without hesitation.

"Good evening, Sherman," said Mrs. McClatchy, who stood before him with a large black pot in her wrinkled hands.

"Hello, Mrs. McClatchy. What brings you around this evening?" asked Sherman.

"I made a scrumptious vegetable soup today and I wanted to share it with you and Danny. I stopped at the store first and discovered it was all locked up with no signs of him to be seen or heard. Is he here with you? Or perhaps he's away this evening on some other business?"

Sherman remained speechless for a few seconds, then motioned for the old woman to step inside.

"Please come in, Mrs. McClatchy. Let me relieve you of that heavy pot and we'll sit and enjoy the soup together in the kitchen," said Sherman.

The two sat down at the kitchen table after Sherman ladled up two large bowls of the widow's creation. He also provided a pitcher of water and two glasses. After each consumed several spoonfuls of soup in awkward reticence, Sherman cleared his throat and finally spoke.

"Mr. Ricker is no longer an employee of mine and he no longer resides in the spare room above my store, Mrs. McClatchy. Yesterday I had to terminate his employment due to difficulties and differences between us that were unable to be resolved."

"Oh, goodness me," exclaimed the widow, "I had no idea there were problems with you two. Where on earth has the dear boy gone off to?"

"I don't know, and frankly I don't care," said Sherman, speaking in half-truths. "Danny was not performing his duties to my satisfaction, nor was he being honest with me concerning many store-related matters. He was costing me money and in the end I felt he wasn't trustworthy. I had no choice but to let him go. There was nothing more I could do for him."

"But he's just a boy, a mere twenty years of age. Where will he go and what will he do? He has no family that I'm aware of and his education was quite limited," stated Mrs. McClatchy.

"I'm afraid I can't offer any further insight. He didn't provide me with any details of his intentions or future plans."

"Are you sure your reasons for declaring his termination were of sound judgment? Was there no clear route of probation you could have pursued with him that would have allowed him to keep his job and a roof over his head?" implored Mrs. McClatchy.

Starting to get agitated, Sherman pushed his soup bowl away and fidgeted in his chair. Trying to contain his growing tension, he took a breath and exhaled deeply before answering.

"Milly," said Sherman, unaware he had never addressed the widow McClatchy solely by her first name, "I was very patient with Danny and tried to address his faults in the most helpful and beneficial way I know how. He was unwilling to embrace my guidance and showed me a lot of disrespect that I could not tolerate. He took advantage of my hospitality and showed no initiative or means of ever even thinking to repay my kindness. I simply cannot have a person of such low standards in my employ."

"I see," said the widow tersely as she stood up from the table and wiped her chin with a linen napkin. "I'm not sure that I agree with your assessment of Danny's qualities. I always found him to be pleasant and courteous when in my company. But I will not judge your business acumen and simply accept your position as it regards the success of your store."

Sherman sat with elbows on the table and his fingers rubbing his temples. He could tell that the old widow was displeased and blissfully ignorant of Danny Ricker's true nature. Maybe it was her openly kind and generous nature, her motherly instincts, or simply her advanced age—she was nearly eighty—that willed her to be protective of a man who clearly had fooled her. It was useless to argue further, and Sherman was in no mood to defend his actions or reveal any more facts about Danny that he had omitted or purposely avoided earlier in the conversation.

"Shall I escort you home, Mrs. McClatchy?"

"No, I can manage quite well on my own, young sir. I'll leave the pot here and will collect it once it's drained and when I next visit the store to drop off more pies. To be honest, Sherman, I'm not sure when that will be. Suddenly I'm not in much of a baking mood."

The old widow shuffled her way to the door with Sherman lagging behind. She let herself out, then turned back to the young man who stood in the open doorway. "At the very least I expect you to think long and hard about your recent actions concerning Danny. I also expect to see you in church Sunday to offer a prayer or two on his behalf. You should feel responsible for his well-being. I pray he returns to us in good health and cheerful bent of mind. Good evening to you, Sherman. I shall pray on your behalf as well."

The old lady wandered off and out of sight. Her house was not far away and Sherman was unconcerned with her ability to make it home safely. The young man closed the door and retreated back to his favorite chair in the parlor. With drink in hand, he again stared at the Henry and deeply pondered whether he should make an immediate run to Portland to find .44-caliber rim-fire cartridges. He swallowed the last of his whiskey, then climbed the stairs to his parents' old master bedroom, which he now claimed as his own. He barricaded himself inside, then undressed and climbed into bed. He knew he would have trouble slumbering, as it was still unbearably hot. Yet somehow he managed to close his eyes and drift off to sleep, allowing his mind to focus on just one thing—Sophie Curtis.

When morning arrived, Sherman again went through the same rigorous routine of rising extra early and checking over everything of importance to him to see if anything was missing, damaged, or dead. Fortunately there were no signs of thievery or foul play. Once in the store and open for business, Sherman decided he would assume a defensive posture and not actively seek out or incite trouble. He wasn't exactly sure when or how he came to decide on this course of action, but he was tired of dwelling on what *could* happen and instead decided to wait and see what *did* happen. He relied on the fact that Sheriff Ridgeway would return soon and that together they would determine what needed to be done. Sherman looked at the calendar hanging on the wall by the door. Today was Friday, June 27. Independence Day was forthcoming.

Sherman spent most of the morning tending his animals, harvesting ripe vegetables from his garden, and moving heavy supplies from his barn to the storage room, where they would eventually be unpacked and put on display. It was laborious work and kept Sherman unusually busy and not readily available to tend to his customers. On three separate occasions impatient shoppers sought him out and pulled him back into the store to finalize their purchases. It was quickly becoming apparent to the young storeowner that he was stretched too thin and the store couldn't function properly or efficiently without the help of an additional laborer or clerk. In all his years he had never known his father to run the place entirely solo. He always had his son and wife to rely on. Occasionally,

Anders hired a laborer to pitch in temporarily when things were really busy or he needed help with the harvest. Sherman, in the years since his father's death, had a string of hired help assist him, primarily in the summer and autumn months. The help was never consistent or lasting, but it was always enough to get him by on a tight budget. It wasn't until a few months ago that Sherman found a permanent worker to help him run the store. To his undying regret, though, it was Danny Ricker.

The day moved forward and soon it was early in the afternoon. Sherman scratched away at his ledgers with a dull pencil until he couldn't read his own writing. Finally he gave up. He took off his glasses, put the pencil down, and slammed the ledgers shut. The store was empty and Sherman took a moment to relax and stare out the window. He watched as folks on horseback, in horse-drawn carriages, and on foot passed by the store traveling up and down Settler Road. As the traffic cleared, he caught sight of someone who immediately grabbed his attention. Walking along in a simple blue dress and bonnet toward the Budwin School was the lovely Sophie Curtis. Sherman watched until she was out of sight. He paused a moment, then made a decision. He took off his work apron, straightened his brown vest and black floppy bow tie, smoothed out his trousers, and put on a new brown bowler hat. Making sure his clothing was free from any undesirable odors, he put the "Closed" sign in the window and rushed out the door, almost forgetting to lock it behind him.

Sherman briskly walked up Settler Road until the Budwin School was in sight. He paused to catch his breath and compose himself. He wiped away the sweat from his brow and quickly tried to concoct a plausible reason for an unexpected and unscheduled visit with Sophie. He swiftly devised an introductory topic of conversation, and then proceeded to the front door. He gently knocked twice. To his delight, the door opened and there stood Sophie with a smile that lit up his heart.

"Hello, Mr. Jackson…ah, I mean, Sherman. It's nice to see you again. What can I do for you?" she asked pleasantly.

"Good afternoon, Miss Curtis. I just happened to be passing by and I wanted to know how your new flag was faring," said Sherman as he looked up at the Stars and Stripes atop the school's white flagpole.

"Very well indeed," replied Sophie, adding, "It's the perfect size and shape. It's quite attractive and I think it gives our school a charming patriotic and historical character that all can be proud of."

"I believe you're correct, Miss Curtis. What an encouraging and insightful way of putting it," said Sherman energetically. "I'm delighted I could help you out. I certainly hope that if there are any other items or supplies you find yourself needing, you won't hesitate to call on me. I'd be honored to have you come by the store again. It would be my pleasure to help you find whatever your heart desires."

"Well, that's awfully kind of you, Sherman. Please step inside," said Sophie. "I'm afraid it isn't any cooler in here, but at least we'll be out of the sun and perhaps we'll benefit from a cool breeze through the windows. Also, please call me Sophie…not Miss Curtis."

"Thank you, Sophie," Sherman said with a smile as he stepped inside the schoolhouse and removed his hat.

The two went to the front of the classroom. Sophie pulled out the wooden chair from behind her desk and placed it next to another that was facing a row of student desks. She motioned for Sherman to take a seat and the two sat down together.

"I haven't been in this school for many years now, but I can say with certainty that it hasn't changed much from what I remember," Sherman said. "The desks, chairs, and even the old potbelly stove look exactly the same."

"So you were a student here, Sherman? I take it you must have grown up in this area."

"Yes, I was born here. My parents owned and operated Jackson's General Store before I took it over. My father built it before I was born and it's been a part of my family ever since. I grew up in the house next to it and that's where I live now. Regrettably both my mother and father have passed on."

"Oh no, I'm so sorry to hear that," said Sophie with genuine sorrow. "What were their names?"

"My father's name was Anders and my mother's was Julia. I don't have any siblings and I never knew my grandparents. I was told they all expired at various times during my infant and early childhood years. I have some kinfolk scattered across the state—aunts, uncles, a cousin or two and such—but none that I am well acquainted with or see on a regular basis."

"I see. If you don't mind my asking, Sherman, how did you lose your parents?" timidly asked Sophie.

"Well, my father died in 1867. His body just wore out after too many years of laborious work in the store. It was his life, I'm afraid. He put the success of his business before all else and it just ground him down physically to the point where his body became too frail to handle even the smallest of tasks. He had pressure on his chest that became too much for him to overcome. My mother died early in the summer of 1865 a few weeks before I returned home. She was stricken with fever the previous winter and never recovered. She was strong-willed and had a tremendous heart, but she eventually succumbed. I never got a chance to say goodbye to her."

"I'm truly sorry, Sherman," said Sophie. "You said you 'returned' in 1865. Were you a soldier in the war?"

"Yes, I was a sergeant in the 20th Maine Volunteer Infantry Regiment. I served from 1862 to 1865. Just before my regiment was formally deactivated, I received a letter from my father stating that my mother was ill and that the store was failing. He beseeched me to return home. Upon my arrival I discovered him in poor health and the unpleasant details concerning the recent death of my dear mother."

"That must have been an extremely arduous time for you," said Sophie. "However, I'm sure it wasn't a difficult decision for you to stay, aid your father, and lend much needed help to the store."

"Actually, it was," said Sherman. "It was probably the hardest decision of my life. You see, Sophie, I never wanted any part of my father's business. It was his dream, not mine. I was at Bowdoin College in Brunswick before the war broke out. I had so many possibilities and courses of study to choose from. I was interested in law and medicine as well as the wonders of travel abroad. I wanted to learn about and experience life in a whole new way. I was excited and happy that for once I could set my own path. Then the war came and changed everything. I fought through that bloody mess and saw things no man should ever witness. I thought I was going to die on many occasions, but I always survived. I made it, though, remarkably unscathed—Lord knows why. And just when I thought I was going to get my life back on track, the news of my parents and the fate of the store cruelly intervened. I was drawn back into a former existence I was looking to escape. I was angry and bitter, resentful toward my father and the decisions he had made. We fought the day I came home and he pushed me to the point where I wanted to leave and never return. It very nearly came to that. That night I slung my haversack over my shoulders and made plans to walk to Portland and never set foot in North Scarborough again. Something stopped me, however. I guess I felt that if I left not only would I be abandoning my dying father but also all the memories and everything that my mother once was. I couldn't bear that. Deep in my heart I knew she would have been very disappointed in my decision and in me. I knew that running away wouldn't solve anything, and deep down I knew I couldn't just leave my father to die alone. So I made the decision to stay until things got better. That was eight years ago and I'm still here."

"Do you regret your decision to stay?" Sophie asked gently.

"There are plenty of days when I wonder about what *could* have been. Ultimately I wish my life had allowed me to steer a different course. Life can be mysterious and dangerously fickle in all its unique twists and turns. Sometimes I believe our destiny is set and there's no way to change what lies ahead of us. Other days I feel rebellious and unpredictable. I feel like packing my bags, mounting my horse, and just riding off into the sunset to wherever life takes me. Then I regain my senses," said Sherman with a practical little smile.

"Well, I must say that your story is a bit tragic, Sherman. I'm sorry to hear of all your earlier misfortunes. I hope you don't find me too intrusive?" asked Sophie, wondering if she had crossed the line of decency with some of her questions.

"No, not at all, actually. It's been a while since I've thought about any of that. I think it's good for one's soul to talk about one's troubles from time to time. However, I think that's enough about me. I'd really like to know a little more about you, if that's agreeable?"

"Yes," said Sophie. "I suppose that's only fitting. I'm afraid there's not much of interest to tell. I was born and raised in Boston. My mother was an Irish immigrant from Dublin and my father a professor at Harvard. He grew up in Cambridge, the son of a textile mill owner. He was well educated and he teaches rhetoric and Latin. I have an older sister who is married to a fisherman. Her name is Sharyn and his is Stephen. She and her husband have two girls and live in Gloucester. I attended Elmira College for women in New York and received a degree in education. I wanted to be a teacher like my father; only I wanted to teach children and not college students. After I received my degree, I stayed in

New York for a short time, then eventually traveled home. I looked for teaching jobs in and around Boston, but there weren't many, and I would routinely lose out to an older and more-qualified candidate. By a sheer stroke of luck, I heard about the opportunity here in Maine and I leapt at the chance. I started out a bit foolishly, not really knowing anything about where I was going or where I would live. Fortunately, upon my arrival here I stopped at the church and met Pastor Morrell. He and his lovely family took me in with open arms. Now I have a place to stay and friends to look after me while in an unfamiliar town. I'm going to teach the summer session as soon as I can get everything in order and round up enough students."

"Well, I'm delighted you're here," said Sherman. "It sounds like you've worked hard to achieve your goals and now you can begin to enjoy the fruits of your passion—that is to say, teaching. I must give you fair warning, though. Some of the adolescents around here can be a handful. I don't wish to gossip or spread disagreeable rumors, but in case you haven't noticed yet, the Morrell boys are quite spirited and not inclined to behave in an appropriate manner."

Sophie giggled softly. "Oh yes, Sherman. I have noticed that they have the knack for 'misleading' their parents. They might have them fooled, but certainly not me. They will learn respect in my classroom, I assure you."

"That's good. I'm very glad to hear you say that. As for the other children around here, there's only two more I can think of. A man named Hiram Lovell and his wife Gertrude have a successful dairy farm not too far from here. He's one of the wealthier individuals in North Scarborough. They have two kids—Josephine, who's thirteen, and Alexander, who's eleven. They're quite different from the Morrell boys and should be enjoyable to have in your classroom. Both are very polite and eager to learn, from my observations of them in my store. Besides those four kids, I don't know of any others unless you're looking to draw students from South Gorham or other parts of Scarborough such as Oak Hill or Dunstan."

"Oh, I'm positive there will be more children attending my classes. I'm hoping for some younger ones. I've always enjoyed working with littler children. The older ones always think they have everything already figured out," quipped Sophie with a gentle and distinct giggle that Sherman was quickly falling in love with.

The two continued their discussion. Sherman explained his business and how he ran Jackson's General Store, while Sophie enlightened him concerning her ideas for fixing up the schoolhouse and how she intended to execute her planned curriculum. The topics changed as time passed but both were thoroughly enjoying each other's company and neither wanted the conversation to end. There was a natural feeling of comfort between the two that developed into a mutual trust with each exchange of meaningful words and genuine sentiments. Sherman was stricken by the young Sophie's outward beauty, but he was even more smitten by her obvious intelligence, immensely sweet and caring personality, and her apparent work ethic punctuated with a desire to pursue her passion of teaching. All these attractive inner qualities were matched or exceeded by her stunning yet wholesome appearance. Her luscious strawberry-blonde curls fell slightly past her shoulders. Her eyes were deep pools of blue that were warmhearted and engaging without a trace of dishonesty or insincerity. Her cheeks were slender and her lips full. When she smiled, not only did her teeth resemble a perfectly placed row of pearls, but her lips and mouth seemed to form a heart shape that was distinctly feminine yet uniquely her. She was not exceptionally tall but certainly not petite either. Sherman estimated she was approximately five-foot-six. Beneath her lovely blue dress was an hourglass figure accentuated by an ample bosom and a well-rounded bottom that caused Sherman's eyes to inappropriately wander and his mind to conjure up lusty thoughts. She was by no means what Sherman had envisioned or expected an ordinary teacher to resemble. She was certainly nothing like her predecessor, old man Phibbert. He had been quite advanced in age with a crotchety and embittered temperament. He was tall and skinny with long, white, stringy hair that hung down the back of a mostly bald skull. His nose was exceptionally pronounced, awkwardly supporting a pair of bent-framed bifocals that made his appearance both comical and creepy.

Sophie laughed along with Sherman as he described Mr. Phibbert. Once he finished and both paused to compose themselves, Sophie looked out the window and commented on how dark the skies had gotten. Sherman clicked open his pocket watch and was stunned at the time. They had been talking for hours! It was past suppertime.

"My goodness, it looks like it's going to storm," said Sophie, looking out the window at the ominously blackened skies.

"I'm terribly sorry, Sophie," said Sherman. "I didn't mean to detain you from your duties for so long. I'm afraid the afternoon has left us behind. I didn't realize it had gotten so late. The skies certainly do look angry."

"Oh, it's my fault, Sherman. I should have kept track of the time. Unfortunately there's not much I can accomplish today, and I should hurry home before the heavens open up. I hope I can make it. I don't have an umbrella or parasol."

The two stepped out of the school after Sophie secured the windows. She closed and locked the door behind her. Both looked up at the sky that was now exceedingly dark and stormy. Cracks of thunder echoed off in the distance while the wind started to pick up indicating that the calm before the storm was coming to an abrupt end. Suddenly, streaks of lightning filled the sky, causing Sophie to tremble.

"You'll never make it back to the Morrell farm in time on foot," said Sherman. "I have an idea. Come with me." He extended his arm in hopes of providing some gentlemanly comfort to the frightened young lady. Sophie took Sherman's arm while he hurriedly escorted her to his livery.

"This is Skipper. He's my fastest horse and he's going to take us out to the Morrell farm. There's no time to saddle him up, so you'll just have to hold onto me tight. We'll go as fast as we safely can." Sherman grabbed a stool and used it to climb aboard Skipper. Once mounted and with the reins in hand he said, "Just untie him and I'll help you up."

Sophie freed the horse and stepped up onto the stool. With Sherman's help, she climbed aboard the sleek Morgan.

"Here we go. Hold on tight," he said, giving Skipper a gentle kick in the sides with both feet. The horse snorted and whinnied a bit, but immediately trotted out of the livery and down Settler Road. Sherman could sense that Skipper was not happy with the extra weight, but he plodded forward without protest. The wind picked up even more and Sophie was forced to shield her head behind Sherman's back. Every unnerving crack of thunder was accompanied by a hard squeeze from Sophie, who had wrapped her arms snugly around Sherman's waist. The lightning lit up the sky with miraculous displays of raw and frightening energy that spooked Skipper and struck Sherman with awe at such godlike power. As much as he wanted to stop and observe the awesome spectacle of light and energy rampaging across the skies above him, he knew he had to keep Skipper calm and focused on the road and get Sophie home safe without further delay.

"Not to worry. We'll be fine," said Sherman while giving Skipper a little more incentive to pick up the pace. It was now really windy and the blackened skies gave the impression it was night rather than the early evening hours. Sherman was beginning to have a hard time navigating the road. He actually welcomed the large bolts of lightning as they helped illuminate his route. Sophie looked upward and wondered just when the skies would open and let loose a torrent of wind and rain that would sweep the unsuspecting travelers away in a flood worthy of Noah. The downpour hadn't come yet, and Sherman was determined to outrun it. Soon Skipper turned off the main road and onto a well-worn trail that led directly to the Morrell farm. After a few intense moments, Sherman cried, "There! I see the farm."

Sophie looked up and relaxed her grasp around Sherman's waist. A sigh of relief was released from her tense body. Sherman directed Skipper off the trail and into the Morrells' meadow, which was the most direct route to the house. He could see faint lights from oil lamps in the window and a portly shape on the porch. He spurred Skipper yet again and soon the pair was finally at the house, greeted by an anxious Erin Morrell who had been standing on the porch on the lookout for Sophie's safe return.

"Oh thank God you're here," exclaimed Erin as Sherman helped Sophie dismount Skipper. "We were just about to go after you. We thought you'd get caught up in this storm and lost for sure. Come inside quickly, my dear."

Sophie turned and looked longingly at Sherman. For a moment it appeared as if she didn't want to leave him.

"Thank you, Sherman, for looking after me. I enjoyed our talk and hope we can get better acquainted under more suitable circumstances," she said, smiling and making reference to the untimely weather. Just then the first raindrops started to fall and splatter heavily against the ground.

"It was my pleasure, Sophie. I should like to call on you soon and perhaps we may have lunch together at an agreeable time and place?"

Sophie smiled widely and nodded, but before she could respond, Erin spoke up and said, "Land sakes alive, you two! There'll be enough time for exchanging pleasantries and making social engagements later.

Now get in this house this instant, young lady." Sophie waved at Sherman, then retreated inside as another bolt of lightning fractured the sky.

"You better come inside too, Mr. Jackson," said Erin Morrell. "We'll put you up for the night if necessary. Don't know how long the good Lord intends this storm to last. You can bunk with the pastor."

"My deepest thanks, Mrs. Morrell, but I must get back and tend to things at my house and store. It's not a long ride, and Skipper and I'll be fine. A little rain never hurt anyone, ma'am." Sherman tipped his hat and pointed Skipper back in the direction of Settler Road.

"Be careful, Mr. Jackson...and Godspeed," said Erin before retreating inside the house herself. Sherman gave a salute, then spurred his horse. Skipper took off like a shot and the two galloped away. He was unaware that Sophie was watching from the window, where she remained until he was well out of sight.

Suddenly the skies opened. A deluge of pounding rain, driven hard by an unrelenting wind, mercilessly pummeled Sherman and his horse as they trudged forward, headfirst into the devilish tempest of weather. Settler Road was quickly becoming a morass of thick mud beneath the heavy barrage of rainwater, forcing the now-drenched young man to slow the horse's pace and struggle to keep him pointed in the right direction. The thunder and lightning intensified, brutally reminding Sherman of the horrific times his regiment had fallen under Confederate artillery fire. He tensed up and buried his head deep in his shoulders after every thunder crack. After several grueling minutes of punishment and skillful horsemanship, Sherman estimated he was over halfway home. He had to keep his head lowered and continually shield his face from the driving rain and wind in order to keep it from blowing away his saturated bowler hat, and possibly he himself! This problem, coupled with the darkness, made it extremely hard to navigate. He pressed forward—it was all he could do.

Eventually Sherman reached the main thoroughfare of Settler Road. To his tremendous relief, he could vaguely see the Old Liberty Grange Hall and knew his house was not much farther. He pushed his worn-out and aggravated horse a little harder with gentle kicks to the sides and some motivational words shouted over the wind. Just as it seemed Skipper would quit and go no farther, the besieged horse finally arrived at the front of Jackson's General Store. Sherman hopped off the horse's back just as a bolt of lightning struck a nearby tree, splitting it clean down the middle. Sherman held the reins tight as Skipper lurched forward out of fear, nearly slamming his owner to the ground. Sherman wrestled with his frightened horse for a minute and was finally able to pull him into the livery and calm him down. He tended to Skipper first, then checked on his three other horses. Once his animals were sheltered and secured, Sherman hustled over to the store. Once inside he closed the door and lit an oil lamp to provide some much-needed light.

Soaked to the bone, the young storeowner went upstairs, stripped off his drenched suit, and proceeded to dry himself. His pocket watch and billfold were damp but not ruined. He placed them on the bureau and sat down on Danny's messy old bed. Once he felt dry enough, he dug into the clothes bag and dressed himself with some of Ricker's abandoned work clothes. He looked around the store to see if anything was amiss or if the windows were open. All was safe and secure. Under the dim lamplight Sherman took some time to compose himself after his adventurous ride. Eventually he checked the time and saw that it was past eight o'clock. The intense thunderstorm had subsided a bit, but outdoors it was still fairly dark and the sun was setting fast. Sherman decided to finish some recordkeeping paperwork before locking up and going home for the night. He stood behind the counter working away when suddenly there was a knock at the door. Startled, he looked through the front window and saw the dark figure of a man huddled outside. He couldn't recognize who it was and feared just opening the door in light of the recent problems he'd had.

"Who is it?" shouted Sherman with authority through the door. "We're closed," he added, wondering what good, if any, that extra statement would render.

"Yes, sir, I understand that," said the dark, unidentified man. "I'm not from around here. I was passing through when I got caught in the storm. I'm alone and on foot and the weather's spun me around so many times that I ain't sure what direction I need to be heading in now. I'm tired and wet. I saw your light and was hoping I could come in out of the rain…just 'till I can get my bearings…or maybe find a place to bed down for the night?"

Sherman strained to get a better glimpse of the mysterious figure outside his door. His sunken head was hidden under a dark, sopping wet, wide-brimmed felt hat while the rest of his body appeared swallowed up by an equally saturated thick-collared overcoat. Sherman reached for the doorknob, then pulled his hand back. He knew nothing of the potential danger within the man lurking on the other side of the door; moreover, he wasn't keen about unleashing it.

"Sir, I can appreciate your hesitation, and I'm sure that you're not accustomed to opening your door to outsiders after business hours, but I can assure you that I'm completely harmless, unarmed, and in desperate need of shelter from this weather. Could you find it in your heart to help a God-fearing Christian?" pleaded the man.

Instantly the skies lit up with multiple bolts of lightning ripping through the heavens, accompanied by ear-splitting cracks of thunder. Sherman stood in silence, wondering at the divine suggestion cleverly disguised as an aggressive weather pattern.

"Perhaps the Almighty is sending me his approval to let this drenched soul into my life," quipped Sherman in an inaudible voice. "Who am I to challenge such a ringing endorsement?"

Going against his instincts, he unlocked and opened the door, closing it quickly once the man was inside.

"Bless you, sir," said the gentleman, lifting his head and removing his sodden hat. He combed his wet hair back and out of his eyes with his fingers and then tried to wipe the excess water from his face. His cheeks and neck were clean-shaven; however, he sported a very soggy-looking Van Dyke–style beard. His hair, moustache, and chin whiskers were black with lots of gray hairs interspersed throughout. He wore a small pair of spectacles perched atop his nose. But most curiously, the man had one defining feature that stood out after he unwrapped himself from the thick overcoat. Sherman looked on as the coat hit the floor—the man's right arm and shoulder were missing.

"Excuse me, sir," the stranger said, embarrassed, adding, "I don't do well with wet, heavy coats. I put it on earlier to help protect me from the rain. All it did was make me sweat profusely—so you can say that I got soaked from both the inside and the outside."

"That's quite all right, sir," replied Sherman as he picked up the smelly coat and hung it on a wooden peg jutting out from the wall. He noticed the man had a bulging blanket slung and tied around his upper torso. It hung from his left shoulder down to his opposing hip like a sash. He struggled to pull it off, as it was heavy and wet. Sherman stepped up and kindly relieved the man of the burden and hung it on the same peg as the coat.

"Thank you," the man said. "Could I trouble you for a chair? I'm afraid I might collapse if I stand for another minute."

"Certainly," said Sherman. "Why don't we *both* sit?" With that, Sherman produced two wooden stools from the storage room and offered the man a seat. Once he appeared comfortable, Sherman sat down beside him.

"Thank you again for your kindness, sir. My name is Jeffrey Parlin," said the man as he extended his left hand to shake.

"Sherman Jackson," replied Sherman as he shook hands. "I own this store."

"Good to meet you, Sherman. My old boss was named Sherman too…only he went by William Tecumseh Sherman."

"Oh, I see…you fought under Uncle Billy?"

"Yeah, I was with Uncle Billy throughout his famous march to the sea. It was a helluva success that cost many a good boy his life, but only cost me one arm. I left it in Bentonville, North Carolina, after a scrap with some of Joe Johnston's boys," Jeff said with an offhanded chuckle. "Recently I've thought about writing to the provisional governor and asking for it back! Might have a helluva time finding it though, at least in one piece. A chunk of artillery shrapnel tore most of it off. Some army butcher in a bloody apron claiming to be a doctor surgically removed what remained. I don't remember much. I was unconscious through most of the whole, painful ordeal. Did you fight?"

"Yes. I was with the Army of the Potomac under Grant. Well, actually, the commanding general was George Meade…but since Grant was his boss and his headquarters were located with the Army of the Potomac, then I guess you can say I was under Grant the same way you were under Sherman. What unit did you fight with?"

"I was a part of the Army of the Tennessee under General Oliver O. Howard. Sherman was his boss like you said Grant was Meade's. I was part of the XV Corps, 1st Division, 3rd Brigade. I fought with the 32nd Missouri Infantry Regiment."

"Oh, I see," replied Sherman. "I fought with the 20th Maine Volunteer Infantry Regiment. We were attached to the Army of the Potomac's V Corps."

"Well, it's good to meet a fellow soldier, Sherman. I do thank you for letting me in and out of this storm. It's good to dry off a bit," said Jeff.

"It's no trouble, Mr. Parlin. Would you like a cup of coffee?"

"Yes, I sure could use a cup or two," Jeff said enthusiastically.

"Just sit right there and I'll see about brewing us up a couple cups," Sherman replied. "Do you take sugar?"

"No, sir…black is just fine."

Sherman got up and went over to a shelf that contained small sacks of ground coffee. He lit the stove and heated some water. Soon the coffee was ready.

Jeff drank his quickly, trying not to appear desperate for another cup. Sherman sipped his, not really wanting it. Jeff rose from his seat and tried to hasten the drying of his clothes by standing close to the stove. Water continued to drip down his frame. Sherman looked outside and noticed the worst of the storm had moved off. It was raining lightly now, but it was dark, as the sun had completely set. It was also getting very late and Sherman was eager to get to bed.

"If you don't mind my asking, sir, where are you headed this evening? What's your destination?" Sherman inquired.

"Overall? I really don't have one, for absolute certain," Jeff replied. "I'm a drifter…have been for many years now. Since the end of the war, really. Bushwhackers led by William Quantrill destroyed my family's home in Independence, Missouri. His raiders killed my mother and father during the summer of 1862. For a time, the Rebs had a dominant presence in the area around both Independence and Kansas City. Goddamn murdering guerrillas like Quantrill roamed freely along the border, killing Jayhawkers and terrorizing anyone sympathetic to the Union or who was against slavery. My family was both pro-Union and anti-slavery. They didn't stand a chance."

Sherman listened with a sympathetic ear as his guest continued to talk. In his own travels with the army, the young storeowner had been privy to many different accents and regional dialects, particularly in the South. He was also keenly aware of his own Maine Yankee parlance, which had been teasingly brought to his attention on many occasions by visitors from away. Try as he could, however, he was unable to place his guest's accent. It had a subtle yet distinct southern ring about it, but also sounded deeply immersed in a northern inflection that he was much more familiar with. To Sherman, it simply sounded foreign and strange. He readily dismissed it, however, as it hardly seemed important. He'd never been to Missouri, and he logically deduced that the old wartime border state could have easily produced such an accent due to the inundation of both northern and southern influences. He continued to listen to Parlin's oratory.

"There was nothing left for me in Missouri, so I lit out after the war. Moved around from state to state working my way north and following whatever path brought me a little money and kindness from others. I'm a 'jack of all trades,' and I travel to wherever I can find work…that is, when I have the means. Recently I've been working my way northeast because I've had an itch to see the ocean again, possibly work my way aboard a ship, try my hand at whaling. I thought about heading to Portland, but I lost my way. The storm hit while I was walking and…well, here I am. What town is this? Where am I, exactly?"

"You're in Scarborough—North Scarborough, to be precise. Portland is several miles to the northeast," said Sherman. He added, "You'd never find it tonight, striking out on your own in the dark, especially on foot. It's several hours' walking journey from here."

Though it was the truth, Sherman instantly regretted making his last statement, for he knew what the next few questions from his one-armed guest would be and he selfishly dreaded them.

"Oh, I see," said Jeff. "Well, no sense in going for it tonight. I'm so exhausted I don't think I could take another step. Is there a hotel or lodging house nearby?"

A great sigh reverberated through Sherman's mind. Knowing full well what was coming next, Sherman answered honestly.

"No, nothing like that close by. You'd have to walk a few miles before finding a hotel."

Sherman briefly flirted with the idea of saddling up Skipper and Budley and leading Parlin to the nearest hotel in Gorham, but he quickly frowned on the idea as he was exhausted himself, wasn't interested in fighting his way through the darkness and rain on a tired horse who had already been through too much, and wasn't keen on leaving his property unattended at night with a stranger he hardly knew. Unpleasant thoughts of Danny Ricker paying a dangerously unwelcome visit once again put him on guard…and he knew what was coming next.

Parlin said sheepishly, "Sherman…Mr. Jackson, I don't presume I could impose on your hospitality a bit further and humbly ask that you allow me to spend the night here? I would be fine right there on the floor next to the stove. I've slept on many a wood floor and it don't bother me none. I promise I won't be no trouble. All I need is to dry out my clothes and get some rest. Then I'll be on my way in the morning…that is, if you wouldn't mind pointing me in the right direction." Parlin tactfully added, "From one soldier to another, I sure would appreciate any help you could spare."

Sherman hesitated. Deep down he had little interest in accommodating this vagabond—even for one night—who had inexplicably appeared at his door. His head was filled with other unresolved problems and issues that required his full attention. The last thing he needed was yet another indeterminate distraction in his life. With all the problems and threats he had endured recently, *trust* was not a virtue he could easily extend to others—especially strangers. Regardless, the thought of forcing a tired, one-armed man out into the rainy night with no place to go and no clear knowledge of the area was inexcusable.

"Look, Mr. Parlin…."

"Call me Jeff," he interrupted.

"Okay, Jeff. You're not an animal and I would never force a man to sleep on my floor next to the stove like a dog. Having said that, it's late, I'm tired, and I'm going to give it to you straight. This is *my* store. Recently I've had a lot of problems with people trying to *take* what rightfully belongs to me. I don't care who you are or where you came from. I do care that you respect my property and don't give me any trouble. Upstairs is a small room with a bed. You're welcome to spend the night up there. I'm not going to deny a man shelter on a night like this, but I'm not in the habit of providing unlimited charity either. Recently I've learned what kindness can reap from those who aren't pure of heart. You can stay the night, but that's all. And let me make one more thing perfectly clear. If I find anything out of sorts or missing from here in the morning, I won't hesitate to get the law on you as fast as humanly possible. I don't care who you've served with in the past or what you suffered through. You steal from me and I'm going to make you pay. Do you understand?"

Parlin looked at Sherman and saw the sincerity in his eyes. He wasn't entirely sure if he was just talking tough or if he was a man who actually backed up his threats with action. It was too early to judge.

"Well, it's good to know where a man stands," said Parlin. "I give you my word, you'll have no trouble from me. I'm a man who believes in earning what he gets. It is my full intention to pay back your hospitality. Rest assured of that, Mr. Jackson."

Having said that, Jeff Parlin stood up and extended his hand in friendship. Sherman took it and the two shook.

"Follow me," Sherman said after grabbing and lighting a candle. The two climbed the stairs and the weary storeowner showed his guest the messy bed that once belonged to Danny Ricker. Parlin took the candle and used it to light two others so he could see better.

"I'm going to lock you in from the outside. The chamber pot is in the corner. There are towels and extra blankets in the bureau if you need them. Feel free to use the stove to dry out your clothes," said Sherman. "My house is next door. I'll be back early in the morning to check on you. We'll discuss the best route to Portland then. Sleep well, but remember what I said."

With that, Sherman bid goodnight to his curious guest. He doused the oil lamp and locked up the store before hustling over to his house in the rain. He was very tired and went straight up to his bedroom. After getting ready for bed, he couldn't help but go down the hall and into his mother's old sewing room, which had a window facing the store. He looked hard through the drizzle and could see the dim candlelight emanating from the store's guest room. He watched for several minutes until the light finally went out and all was dark. He pondered who this stranger was and whether he had made the right decision by allowing him to spend the night. Soon fatigue overpowered him and he retreated to his bedroom. He locked the door and crawled into bed.

"A one-armed whaler? I just can't envision that," he whispered. A moment later, he was sound asleep.

CHAPTER 6

The Business Proposition

Sherman awoke early Saturday morning the twenty-eighth and spared no time dressing and getting ready to start the day. For once his thoughts weren't squarely on Danny Ricker, the Morrell boys, or even the lovely Sophie Curtis. Instead, they were on the store and Jeff Parlin. The sun had returned and it was shaping up to be another hot day. Realizing he had left his billfold and pocket watch on the bureau in the spare room, Sherman immediately made his way over to the store. He unlocked the door and paused after stepping inside. He intentionally looked around, searching for anything missing or out of place. Everything seemed in order except a makeshift drying rack next to the stove. Parlin had draped his wet clothes over the two stools he and Sherman had sat on the night before and moved them close to the stove in order to dry them out more quickly. Parlin's coat and rolled-up blanket still hung from the wooden peg on the wall.

Sherman listened hard, but heard no commotion upstairs. He picked up Parlin's dry clothes and quietly crept up to the spare room. He looked in. Still in bed and buried under the covers was his guest—sound asleep. Sherman walked over and watched Parlin's chest gently rise and fall with each slumbering breath. He slept soundly without a hint of a snore. Sherman didn't wake the sleeping drifter. Instead he retrieved his billfold and watch, which were in exactly the same place he had left them. He then sloppily folded Parlin's clothes and left them on the bureau. Convinced his guest had kept his word, Sherman rewarded him by allowing him to sleep for as long as he needed. He exited the room and quietly went about his duties to prepare for the day's business.

Several hours later, Parlin emerged from his deep slumber. He came down the stairs fully dressed and cleaned up. Sherman was behind the counter entering numbers into his ledger. In contrast to Parlin's neat and reenergized appearance, Sherman looked dirty and a bit haggard.

He had spent the morning moving and unloading heavy inventory, tending his animals, and working in his garden to ensure fresh produce was available to his customers. With Ricker gone, all these extra duties now fell upon him.

"Good morning to you, sir," said Parlin. "Thank you for bringing up my clothes and letting me sleep. I was powerful tired and appreciate your not disturbing me."

"Do you want some coffee and eggs?" asked Sherman. "I brewed up a pot earlier and fried some eggs just a little while ago. Normally I eat my breakfast in the house, but this morning I had so much to do that I was forced to make it here. I have some ground oats and fruit as well, if that's to your liking."

"Yes, much obliged," replied Parlin, trying to hide his enormous hunger.

Sherman fixed up a plate for his guest and offered him a seat. Each drank some coffee and ate. It wasn't long before Jeff's plate was all but licked clean.

"So, Sherman, do you run this store all by yourself?" asked Parlin.

"At the moment I do," answered Sherman. "I've had inconsistent help, unfortunately. My last employee was unreliable and I had to let him go."

"That's too bad. What kind of work did he do around here?"

"I needed him mostly for labor. He would load, unload, and stock heavy inventory, help tend my animals, particularly my horses, and do other chores around the store like sweeping up and keeping the mice from infesting the place. Things like that."

"And you ran the place while he was laboring?"

"Ayuh, I focused on the bookkeeping, ordering, local deliveries, merchandising, and customer service."

"And now you got to do everything yourself, right?"

"Yeah, you could say that."

"How do you manage all that work?"

"I do what needs to be done. It's that simple."

"I reckon you could use some help around here," said Parlin as he surveyed his surroundings. "Look, Sherman, I got an idea. Last night I said I was gonna pay you back for your hospitality. Now, I ain't got no money, but I can do everything you said your last employee did. Why not hire me? I can work off what I owe you first, then you can pay me a steady wage as you see fit. You can even pay me the bare minimum in exchange for room, board, and meals. I can take the room upstairs and be completely outta your way. I promise not to intrude into your home. I'll stay in my place here. Whaddya say?"

"What about going to Portland and working your passage onto a whaler?" asked Sherman.

Parlin replied, "It's like I said, I don't have any money, and lately I've come to accept the fact that a crippled man such as myself doesn't get the same chance as a man with two perfectly good arms. A man in my position in life needs to grasp opportunities as they present themselves. He needs to act swiftly and seize what's laid out in front of him. Now, I see an opportunity that would benefit both of us. I need a job and a place to stay. You need a laborer and help runnin' this place. It's true I got just one arm, but I make up for it by finding ways to accomplish things more efficiently. I use my head to solve problems in unique ways that compensate for the loss of a limb. I know I could be very useful around here if given a chance."

"I don't know." Sherman hesitated. "That arrangement is exactly like the one I had previously with my former employee. Needless to say, it didn't work out. In the end he stole from me and I couldn't trust him at all. And I knew him better than I know you. I'm afraid the same thing might happen all over again. Give me a reason why I should trust you."

"Sherman, you'll just have to take me on my honor," said Parlin. "I'm a decent, hardworking soul just trying to make an honest living by playing the cards I was dealt. I don't whine and complain about being crippled and I insist on pulling my weight in life. I served my country faithfully, as did you, and I've sacrificed a lot. I have nothing except what you see here before you. All I ask for is a chance to prove myself. I'll even sweeten the deal if it makes things easier. I'll forgo any form of payment for my work—for the time being—and just accept room, board, and meals. That's all I need for now. In time I know you'll be impressed enough with my work that you'll insist on paying me an honest wage. From one soldier to another, you have my word I'll be an asset to this store. In time I'll move on and pursue my other interests...once I get some money in my pocket, that is. Whaddya say? Do we have a deal?"

Sherman sighed and scratched his head. He knew he had to decide which option he considered the lesser of two evils. He needed and wanted a laborer badly, but he had to weigh the cost and potential risk of hiring an individual that could turn out to be another Danny Ricker. He knew virtually nothing about this one-armed stranger named Jeff Parlin, and to bring him into his store and his life was a gamble. Parlin was waiting for an answer.

"Your timing is uncanny, but also convenient, sir. I only envision things getting harder around here in the future and I honestly don't know if I can handle everything myself. In fact, I know I can't. I have to put my good faith in you and your abilities, Jeff. Don't make me regret this decision. What I said last night still stands. If anything goes missing or I suspect you of thievery, then I will have you brought up on charges and prosecuted to the full extent of the law. That said, you're welcome to stay in the quarters upstairs and be fed three meals a day at my expense for however long you work here. In return I expect you to satisfactorily accomplish all tasks I set out for you. Failure to do so will make our contract null and void and will result in your immediate termination. In time, once you've proven your worth, I will pay you fair wages for your work. Are these terms of employment acceptable to you?"

"I think we got ourselves a deal, Sherman," said Jeff as he shook hands with his new boss. "You won't regret this."

"Let's hope not," said Sherman. "Go get settled upstairs. When you come back down, I'll explain what I need done around here and we'll get you started."

"Thanks, Sherman. I appreciate this. Sincerely I do."

For the rest of the day, Sherman assigned menial duties for Jeff to accomplish while he waited on his customers. When time allowed, Sherman showed Jeff around his property with emphasis on the livery, the vegetable garden, and the chicken coop. He also gave him a quick tour of his barn and the storage room where all the supplies and surplus inventory were kept. Cleverly, he managed to avoid bringing him into his house. Jeff needed to earn his trust before he was comfortable allowing him into his home. By the end of the day, Sherman was pleased with Parlin's work ethic. He appeared to be a fast learner and discharged his duties in both an effective and timely manner. He accomplished every little task and did so without hesitation, question, or complaint, as had been typical of Danny Ricker.

When the evening hours were upon them, Sherman prepared a meal of roast chicken and fresh vegetables, which he served and ate with

Jeff in the store. The two consumed their food and talked for hours in an effort to become better acquainted. Sherman shared stories about his past as a boy growing up in Maine. Jeff responded with tales of his life as a young farmer and his learning of various skills while on his way to becoming a general tradesman. He also spoke highly and in great detail about the beauty of his home in Missouri—before the war.

Both men purposely steered clear of discussing politics—each had an idea on where the other stood from previous discussions and personal disclosures—or the destructive conflict that raged for four long years, forcing them to detour their lives into the army. It seemed more appropriate and pleasing to discuss earlier stretches in their youth when things weren't so complicated and life was less harsh. The conversation rolled on until it became very late and fatigue started to overtake both men.

"Jeff, I'm starting to feel awful tired. This hot weather is miserable for trying to sleep. I haven't had a decent night's rest in weeks, it seems. I think I'm gonna go to bed now. I hope it's not too hot up there for you." Sherman looked up in the direction of the spare room.

"Are you serious? This weather ain't too hot for me. Where I come from, this is what it feels like in the winter," Jeff said with a quick laugh. "You folks from the North don't know what hot is. I'm fine. I don't need a thing."

"Good," said Sherman. He pulled a piece of paper from his pocket and shared it with Jeff.

"This is a list of chores and duties I need accomplished tomorrow. I wrote down what you'll need and where to find it. Study it tonight and be prepared to start right after church tomorrow. You do plan on attending church, right?"

"Oh yes, I'm a man of God and his teachings," Jeff said. "I'm happy to join your congregation. Y'all ain't Catholic…are ya?"

"No," said Sherman. "We're a Protestant congregation in this community."

"Well, praise the Lord. Consider me a part of your assembly then," said Jeff.

"I'm sure Pastor Morrell will welcome you with open arms. He's always looking to expand his flock," remarked Sherman. "I can lend you one of my Sunday suits if you like. We appear to be roughly the same size and build. I have a nice blue one that should fit you."

"Do you have one in gray?" Jeff inquired. "You see, I prefer *gray* over blue…if you don't mind."

Sherman pondered a moment, then said, "As a matter of fact, I do have a gray suit. It belonged to my father. I think it would fit you fine. He wasn't any taller or fatter than me."

"Excellent. Well, I'm good and full. If you don't mind, I'd like to go for a walk before I retire for the evening. We still got a few minutes of daylight left."

"Certainly. Feel free. I'm going to leave the door unlocked, run up to the house, find that suit, and bring it back here for you. If you're not back by then, just lock the door from the inside and leave this on the counter before you go to bed."

Sherman reached into his pocket and pulled out the long metal key that controlled access in and out the front door of Jackson's General Store. He dangled it precariously before Jeff, who rightly sensed that Sherman was not yet entirely comfortable entrusting him with it—even temporarily. However, the young storeowner decided to take a small leap of faith and test the waters of trust with his new employee. This was to be the first step.

"Thank you," said Jeff as he slowly reached out and took the key. "I don't suspect I'll be gone too long."

"Don't lose it. It's my only one, and I'm not going to wait for you if you're not back. I'm tired and just gonna go to bed."

Sherman followed Jeff out the door. Once outside, the two men walked off in opposite directions. Sherman headed over to his house while Jeff decided to walk down Settler Road. It was getting dark quickly and Sherman found himself needing to light several candles and an oil lamp in order to see properly once inside his home. He carried a candle to light his way upstairs until he reached his bedroom. He lit the oil lamp beside his bed and brought it over to the closet. He started to dig through piles of clothing looking for the gray suit. Over the years Sherman had done nothing with his parents' clothing. He couldn't bring himself to get rid of any of it—especially his mother's. Anders had felt the same way. When he closed his eyes and brought one of Julia's dresses up close to his nose, he could still detect the unique scent of her when he inhaled deeply. This gave him a warm feeling inside and left him with the impression that she was—in a sense—still with him.

For nearly twenty minutes Sherman dug deeply in the closet and through the two wooden trunks on the floor below the hanging clothes. He eventually found his father's gray suit in one of the trunks and pulled it out. He looked it over well. Satisfied the moths hadn't feasted on it, he brushed it off and smoothed it out the best he could before bringing it downstairs.

It was dark now and Sherman needed a candle to light his way back to the store. The dull lamplight coming through the house windows was insufficient, and heavy clouds obscured the stars. With suit in one hand and candlestick in the other, he walked slowly across the yard, trying to protect the flickering flame from burning out amidst a very dark night. He got halfway and suddenly stopped. The curious sound of twigs crunching underfoot and the abrupt interruption of the buzzing crickets in the darkness caught his attention. He held the candle up high and looked off in the distance toward the rear of his property, thinking the sound may have come from one of his horses in the livery. He couldn't see anything because the candle was too dim and the darkness too thick. There was another crunch.

"Jeff? Is that you?" called out Sherman, straining to see through the blackness. He turned his head to the right in the direction of the store just before the sounds of rushing footsteps in front of him filled his ears. Before he could react, a lowered shoulder crashed into his chest, knocking him flat on his back. The candle flew from his hand and was instantly snuffed out. Sherman gasped for air as the impact knocked the breath out of him. Suddenly he felt a knee jammed firmly into his chest. Before he could react and raise his arms to defend himself, the next thing Sherman sensed was the cold, razor-sharp blade of a large knife being pressed against his throat! He was helpless, immersed in the dark, and didn't dare move, speak, or even blink.

"You think you're safe, but you're not," said the mysterious attacker in a nearly inaudible whisper hissed directly into Sherman's ear. "You think I've forgotten what's happened, but I haven't. You think you're going to get away with what you did to me, but you're not. You think you don't have to pay for what you've done, but you do. Believe me when I say, I will get what's coming to me and you will get everything that you deserve. And the best part is, you won't know when or where or how, but I will promise you that you'll suffer—and I will have satisfaction. I guarantee you that."

Sherman felt the knife blade slide off his throat. In an instant, the attacker leapt to his feet and ran off without a trace. Sherman slowly sat up and coughed loudly as he desperately sucked air into his lungs. His breathing soon returned to normal and he stood up. He fumbled around until his hands found the candlestick within arm's reach of where he was knocked down. He promptly relit the wick, retrieved the suit, and staggered over to the store.

"Goddammit," he uttered as he let himself in and slammed the door shut behind him. He put the candlestick and suit on the counter, then leaned against it to help compose himself. His breathing deepened and intensified as the sheer horror of what had just happened finally began to sink in. His mind began to wander again with thoughts of the Henry rifle. He would get ammunition for it immediately and perhaps find a pistol to accompany it. It now became a priority. A few minutes passed before the door swung open. Sherman wheeled around abruptly, catching the entrant off-guard.

"Sherman? You okay?"

The disheveled storeowner held up the candlestick. Standing before him was Jeff, who looked at him with concern.

"No," said Sherman. "I was just assaulted on my way back here."

"Jesus—what happened? Who was it?"

"I don't know. He knocked me down in the dark. I never got a look at him...but I got a damn good idea who it was."

"What happened? Did he rob or injure you?" asked Jeff, as he looked out the front window in a vain attempt to locate the attacker.

"Naw, I'm fine. He just knocked the breath out of me. He didn't take anything."

"Well, what'd he want, then?"

Sherman sighed and locked the front door. He pulled up the two stools and placed the dim candle on the floor between them. Both men sat down in the eerie glow while Sherman prepared to reveal his big problem.

"You remember the employee I told you about? The one I fired because he was stealing from me? Well, he didn't leave amicably. In fact, he threatened me and we got into a scuffle when I refused to pay him. When it was over he took off, vowing to take revenge on me and 'get what was coming to him.' Christ, he's just a twenty-year-old kid—not well educated, likes to drink excessively, full of piss and vinegar. Got nothing and nobody and no place to call home. There's no telling what harm he's capable of. I thought he was just full of wind, but after tonight, I think he's serious. If he comes around here again, it could jeopardize both our lives, I'm afraid. Jeff, I hate to say it…but you need to leave this place and move on. I don't want to put your life in danger. He might mistake you for me some dark night and slit your throat. I just couldn't live with myself if someone got hurt on account of a man's quarrel with me."

"What's the law got to say about this?" asked Jeff.

"Law don't know about it yet," glumly replied Sherman. "I was hoping it wouldn't come to that. I was hoping Danny would just take off and leave without giving me or anyone else any trouble. I guess I was hoping for too much."

"Danny?"

"Yeah, his name is Danny Ricker. He's the troublemaker."

"What kinda law enforcement you got around here to deal with someone like this Danny Ricker character?" asked Jeff.

"Well, let's just say it ain't the U.S. Cavalry. We got a sheriff who's around from time to time, but his duties frequently take him to other towns and he's based out of Portland. Needless to say, we don't see much of him around here. But we have some ongoing business that should bring him back in just a few days—Wednesday at the latest, I'm guessing. Anyway, I plan on riding out to Portland on Monday. I need to pick up some…uh…supplies. Hopefully I'll find the sheriff in town and in his office. Meantime, I really believe you should think about moving on, Jeff. It's just not safe around here."

"Like hell," Jeff responded. "I may have just one arm, but that doesn't make me any less of a man in the bravery department. I ain't afraid of some cracked kid. I been around violence and terror my whole life. Early on I saw it ruthlessly charge into Missouri dressed as bandits on horseback, and later I watched it unfold before me in a sea of gray on the battlefields of Tennessee, Georgia, and the Carolinas. I didn't run from it then and I don't plan on runnin' from it now. I got a good thing going here and I won't let some unwelcome lunatic of a kid mess it up for me. As far as I see it, we're in this together. I'll help you protect your property—that is, of course, if the sheriff can't do nothing to help us."

"I can't ignore this any further. I have to report it," Sherman said dourly. "We have to put this matter in the hands of the law. As of now, you're the only other soul I've told about this. I don't want to create any kind of worry or panic among our neighbors, so I reckon it's best if we don't mention this business to anyone until the sheriff is informed. Then he can break the news to folks as he sees fit."

"Sounds sensible to me," said Jeff. "Whadda we do in the meantime?"

"We stay on guard and alert like the soldiers we are. We take turns watching over the store and my property. We'll patrol the grounds regularly and we'll always make sure doors and windows are locked. There isn't much harm he can cause in the daytime, particularly if one of us is around. I doubt he's foolish enough to commit a violent act in broad daylight, especially when people are out and about. Nighttime is a different story, though. That's when we're vulnerable. He could easily steal my horses, break into the store, set fire to the house, or God knows what else."

"Well, ya know, Sherman…I always been the nocturnal type. Never did get much sleep at night during the war. I could make it a habit of working early in the morning, finishing up in the early afternoon, then go to bed real early so I can wake up by nightfall and secretly keep an eye out for any trouble. You'd be asleep and I'd be watching both the store and your house. I could silently observe from the window in my room. I could also do a little late-night reconnoitering. Back in the army I used to do a lot of nighttime scouting of enemy positions. I was real good at it, too. They never suspected a thing until our artillery started raining lead down on 'em the next morning! Maybe, if we're lucky, we can catch this little son of a bitch in the act, tie him up, and deliver him to justice."

"You'd do all that for me, Jeff? I mean, we hardly know each other."

"I know enough to know that you're a good man, Sherman. You extended me both trust and a means of supporting myself. You gave me an opportunity when choices were scarce. You've fed me and put a roof over my head. Not many people are sympathetic to a cripple like me. Most people think I'm useless and just wanting sympathy and a handout. That ain't so. Besides, we both fought and suffered for the same cause. Soldiering brings men closer together and forms special bonds among strangers. Hell, I felt closer to the men I served with than my own family at times. You've extended me help, so I'm gonna help you in return."

Sherman stood silent for a moment, then extended his hand out to Jeff. The two shook and the young storeowner was confident he had struck up a good partnership with a new friend. For the first time since meeting Jeff Parlin, Sherman sensed a bond of faith between the two.

"I like the way you think, Jeff," said Sherman. "I'm not one to resort to violence, but I got a Henry rifle in the house and I'm not afraid to use it if the time comes. If I feel threatened enough, I'll go to that rifle and let justice be meted out by the bullet that rips fire from the barrel."

"That leads me to my next question. I see you've got some gunpowder stored here, and a few pocketknives on display—plus that bear trap and whip in the case—but I don't see any other firearms. Do you have any guns locked away somewhere?" asked Jeff as his head swiveled around, scanning the store.

"No," answered Sherman. "I had a rifle and pistol, but the sheriff bought the rifle. And the pistol…it was stolen."

Jeff bent over and scrutinized the display case. Sherman pointed out the damage around the lock and showed how the case couldn't be properly secured without repair.

"I think he got in through an unlocked window upstairs, then picked and pried at the display-case lock until he was able to foul it enough where it could be opened. I had a Colt House Revolver, bullets, and some large Bowie knives in there that he apparently stole. I think he held one of those very knives up to my throat last night." Sherman demonstrated by placing a finger horizontally across his neck.

"So he's definitely armed *and* dangerous," said Jeff. "I don't know about you, Sherm, but I think it's best if we fight fire *with* fire. We need to get our hands on some guns ourselves…for protection."

Sherman immediately noted that Jeff had abbreviated his name. It had been a long time since anyone had called him Sherm. In fact, the only people who had ever called him Sherm were some of his closest friends in the army back during the war. At first he didn't understand how or why, but hearing Jeff casually refer to him as Sherm made him feel very comfortable and at ease. Somehow the simple one-syllable moniker invoked a sense of trust he had not felt since his fighting days. It was a strange feeling not readily explained, but he privately acknowledged and valued it.

Sherman answered, "I'll handle that Monday when I go into Portland. I need cartridges for the Henry, and I might look into buying a revolver or two. Hopefully I'll find the sheriff, who'll start up an investigation right away. I don't want to take the law into my own hands and I especially don't want to have to shoot someone…even if it is someone who wants to kill me."

"Ain't nothing wrong with protecting yourself with deadly force when the situation calls for it, Sherman," Jeff said colorlessly. "I'll kill any man who tries to kill me—it's that simple."

"Yeah," said Sherman, a bit on edge. "Let's hope it doesn't come to that."

"Why don't you go back to the house and make sure it's locked up tight before bedding down for the night. Here's your key back. Go ahead…lock me in and I'll keep a hawk's eye and an owl's ear on things from my bedroom window. I'll stay awake as long as I can and will holler out if there's any fracas."

"Thanks, Jeff. You hold onto the key for now. Lock *yourself* in. I don't want you to feel like a prisoner barred from the outside, especially if trouble's lurking around here somewhere."

Sherman got up and started for the door. Before exiting, he stopped to turn and look at Jeff.

"Your suit is on the counter. Sunday services start at nine o'clock tomorrow. Be ready before then and I'll come get you. This'll be a good opportunity to introduce you to the congregation and other members of the community. That'll be good since you'll be waiting on a lot of them at the store in the future."

Sherman hesitated again and struggled to get out what he wanted to say next.

"I really didn't want to bring you or anyone else into this ugly predicament of mine, but I sincerely appreciate your help. In return, I'll endeavor to help you any way I can. The bond between soldiers runs deep. Thank you, Jeff Parlin."

Parlin nodded his head affirmatively and rose stiffly as if standing at attention. He grinned and snapped Sherman a quick salute that the former sergeant returned with one of his own. The young storeowner then grabbed the candlestick and walked out the door. From the window, Jeff watched the glowing candle flame float through the darkness across the yard until it entered the house, where it was joined by additional and much brighter sources of illumination. Parlin then locked the door and lit his own candle before retreating upstairs.

+++

An hour passed before Jeff noticed the last bit of light extinguished from Sherman's bedroom window. He surmised that his new friend had finally gone to sleep. Parlin stealthily gazed out his own window, keeping an eye on whatever might be coming. The candle burned very dimly and he kept it hidden in the corner on the floor so as not to reveal his silhouette in the window. The thick clouds had finally moved out, revealing an infinite number of sparkling stars and some shimmering moonlight that made it easier to see any potential movement on the ground. After keeping watch for some time, Parlin eventually tired and turned his attention elsewhere. He sat on the floor near the candle after retrieving his rolled-up blanket. He paused a moment; then, as removing a newborn baby's swaddling cloth, and with the greatest of care, he unfurled the blanket, exposing what lay hidden inside.

"That's right," he muttered, "I'll kill any man who tries to kill me."

Parlin paused and reflected a moment on what lay before him. There was no mistaking what it was—even to the casual observer—but this odd-looking combination of blue steel and checkered walnut was curious, rare, and frightful looking. Parlin held it up. It was a .42-caliber cap-and-ball LeMat revolver.

What made this particular handgun so intriguing was its bulky design, its nine-shot cylinder, and most notably, its separate centralized smooth-bore barrel that functioned as a lethal close-range twenty-gauge shotgun. It was unwieldy, and its southern design more resembled a small cannon than a traditional revolver made by Colt or Remington. Even more astounding was the fact that it was fully loaded and could be discharged at any moment.

Parlin checked the gun over until his superfluous concerns about its readiness were satisfied. Even then he still felt restive and struggled to sit down on the bed. He cradled the LeMat and watched the already dim light from the candle grow weaker until the melted wax overwhelmed the wick, reducing the flame to nothing more than a wisp of smoke. In an instant, the room was enshrouded in darkness.

+++

The next morning the sun steadily rose over the clear eastern horizon. Sherman barely slept. Though extremely tired, he was eager to rise and start the day. He bathed, shaved, and dressed in his good blue suit that he normally reserved for church. He prepared some breakfast and tended his animals. Upon quick inspection, all seemed safe and sound with no indication of foul play. Satisfied, Sherman brought food over to the store and was surprised to find Jeff dressed and ready for services.

"Morning, Jeff. Glad you're up and ready to go. I brought you over a little breakfast," said Sherman, handing him a bowl of fresh berries and a cup of coffee.

"Good morning, Sherm," replied Jeff while sipping his coffee. "Any problems last night?"

"No. Didn't sleep much, but all seemed quiet. You?"

"Naw, nothing happened. I kept watch for as long as I could keep my eyes open. Didn't see nothin' or nobody."

"Glad to hear it," said Sherman. "I wasn't in the mood for any more trouble last night."

"You'll feel better after you talk to the sheriff," said Jeff.

Wanting to change the subject, Sherman said, "I see that suit fits you pretty good."

"Yeah, I like it…and I think the Lord will too," said Jeff proudly. "Just need some proper shoes."

Sherman looked down at Jeff's dirty old boots and chuckled. "We can fix that. Go pick yourself out a pair of shoes. I might have a pair that's your size."

Sherman pointed to a shelf in the back that contained three pairs of men's black and brown leather shoes. They weren't fancy or expensive, but they were appropriate for church. Jeff wandered over and grabbed the pair nearest to him. He took off his boots and held the shoes against the soles of his feet. Satisfied they might fit, he pulled them on and tied them up without hesitation.

"I think we have a winner," said Jeff. "These'll do just fine."

"Good," replied Sherman. "Keep 'em. There's also a bag of clothing up in your room. It belonged to Danny Ricker. As far as I'm concerned you can pick through it and wear whatever you want that fits. It's yours now."

"I can see that I'm gonna need to do a heap of work around here to repay all your kindness, Sherm. I do appreciate it all," eagerly stated Jeff.

Just then both men heard the sound of the church bell ringing out. Sherman pulled out his gold pocket watch and clicked it open.

"Getting to be that time," he said. "We should head over to the church now. Services will be starting up soon."

Both men finished their breakfast, drank down their coffee, and walked out the door. Sherman led the way and Jeff followed. Soon other well-dressed churchgoers from the community and neighboring towns joined them, forming a small procession heading for the North Scarborough Community Church. Upon arrival, Sherman and Jeff funneled inside and sat down together in one of the rear pews. They watched the members of the congregation file by and take their seats. Soon the church bell stopped tolling and the conversation ceased as Pastor Morrell entered and took his place at the podium. He slipped on his glasses and opened his Bible.

"A very blessed good morning to one and all," said the pastor with a grand smile and a jovial disposition. "My warmest welcome to each and every one of you. May God bless us all on this glorious Sunday."

Sherman watched and listened as Pastor Morrell began to preach his sermon. He was much older than his wife Erin and his features couldn't hide the fact. He had a long, white, bushy beard and thick untamed gray hair that stuck up on top of his head and ran down the sides. His nose was pointed and his eyes were dark and deep-set, almost haunting. Sherman couldn't help but think that Pastor Morrell bore a strong resemblance to the former Secretary of the Navy, Gideon Welles. If not for his exceedingly good nature and pleasant attitude that was forever accompanied by a tremendous smile, one would think the pastor was kin to the sour-looking, stone-faced Welles.

Seated in the front were the pastor's wife and sons. Both her boys, who were impeccably dressed but inattentive and showed absolutely no enthusiasm for their father's oration, flanked their plump mother. Erin seemed oblivious to their rascally fidgeting and remained happily fixated on her husband's preaching. Sherman continued to gaze around the room, casually looking for people of interest—one in particular whom he hadn't spotted yet.

Seated near the front and by herself was Milly McClatchy. Deeply engrossed in the pastor's sermon, the old widow seemed oblivious to any and all goings-on among the congregation. She sat firm and upright with her wrinkled face fixated on Pastor Morrell. As the assembly rose to sing the first hymn, Sherman spotted Edwin and Reba McPhee a few rows in front and to his right. Over to his left and slightly behind were Hiram and Gertrude Lovell with their well-behaved children Josephine and Alexander. Sherman recognized several other faces of people who shopped in the store occasionally. Some were local while others he knew travelled from South Gorham or from other areas farther away. The song came to a close, followed by everyone sitting back down after a lengthy and soulful "Amen."

Toward the end of the sermon, Sherman was convinced he had spied every face within the congregation. Despondent, he hadn't discovered whom he was desperately trying to locate. He sighed ever so slightly and dipped his head in silent frustration.

Pastor Morrell snapped his Bible shut and made an announcement. "My dear friends, before we conclude today's services, I have some community news to share. First, this Friday, on our country's birthday, Edwin and Reba McPhee will be holding an Independence Day celebration at the Old Liberty Grange Hall. There will be music, dancing, decorations, a picnic, and a brief fireworks display in the evening. All are encouraged to attend and bring whatever food and drink is desired. As a special treat, the McPhees are opening up the museum portion of the grange, free of admission, to everyone, in homage to their new patriotic exhibit honoring the soldiers who have fought for our country in wars past. I have not seen the exhibits, but I'm told they're a wonderful tribute to our men in uniform who fought so bravely to keep this grand nation of ours free and intact. I hope to see you all there. Secondly, I would like to take the opportunity to introduce you to a blessed young lady whom Mrs. Morrell and I have graciously and enthusiastically welcomed into our home. She is a shining example of a beautiful young Christian, and the Lord has sent her to our fair community to help educate and mold our precious youth. Now some of you may have seen or met her already, but please rise and give a warm welcome to the new summer-session teacher at our esteemed Budwin School…the lovely Miss Sophie Curtis."

The entire assembly rose from their pews in unison and bathed the church in warm, inviting applause as Sophie emerged, seemingly from nowhere, and took her place next to Pastor Morrell's podium. She smiled graciously, waved ever so delicately, and happily embraced the crowd's kindly acknowledgement. She wore an attractive emerald-green dress and stylish little hat. Her cheeks swelled with a sweet rosy color as she became slightly embarrassed by all the unexpected attention. The blushing made her look all the more beautiful while her strawberry-blonde curls perfectly framed her face in such a way that it was hard for any man present to take his eyes off her—particularly Sherman Jackson.

"With that I'd like to conclude today's services and wish each and every one of you a pleasant afternoon. May God be with you," said Pastor Morrell. "For those who have the time and wish to remain with us a bit longer," he added, "Erin and I invite you to join us out back under the pleasing shade of our grand oak tree for some refreshments and enlightening conversation. We have coffee, tea, sweet cakes, and some wonderfully delicious pies all graciously prepared and provided by the dear Mrs. McClatchy. Please join us. It will take only a minute to set up."

The crowd was abuzz and many filed out of the church to partake in the refreshments. Sherman strained to keep his eyes on Sophie, but amid all the confusion, both she and the rest of the Morrell family managed to slip out the back, presumably to set up and serve Mrs. McClatchy's delectable baked goods. Sherman, anxious to converse with Sophie, spared no time in suggesting to Jeff that the two remain and partake in the pastor's post-services gathering.

"Jeff, we've got some time to spare. I don't normally open the store on Sunday unless there's a great need. That list of chores I gave you can wait a bit. Let's stay a while and mingle. I think it'd be good for you to meet some of the townsfolk," said Sherman.

"Yeah, sounds like a good idea," replied Jeff, who, like Sherman, had a particular individual in mind.

Outside it was very sunny and still uncomfortably warm as the noontime hour approached. Several of the church's congregation remained and were all too willing to cluster beneath the expansive branches and thick leaves of the ancient oak that towered above the church. Small tables had been brought outside and set up with cups, dishes, and silverware. As the churchgoers milled about and chatted, Pastor Morrell soon happily appeared, loaded with armfuls of cakes and pies. Trailing behind him in a line were his wife and sons, also carrying refreshments to place on the tables for people to enjoy.

Sherman watched as the goodies were set up. Soon people began slicing, pouring, and serving themselves with the fruits of the widow

McClatchy's labors. Sherman looked far and wide but saw no trace of Sophie. He feared she may have gone and resumed her preparatory duties at the Budwin School. He had to hide his initial displeasure with that thought as other residents of North Scarborough began to approach and greet him. The first were the pastor and his wife. Their sons, unbeknownst to them, had managed to slip away undetected to pursue more interesting and potentially illicit activities.

"Hello, Sherman Jackson! It's good to see you, my boy," cheerfully bellowed Pastor Morrell. "I hope you enjoyed today's sermon?"

"Why, yes," responded Sherman before half-heartedly adding, "It was very uplifting and inspirational."

"We're so glad you liked it," said Erin before popping a forkful of white cake into her mouth. "And who is this individual at your side, sir?"

"Oh, excuse me," apologized Sherman. "May I present Jeffrey Parlin. He's new to this area and is currently my new employee at the store. He's originally from Missouri and this is his first time seeing New England, from what I understand. He aspires to learn about the art of whaling and eventually to serve aboard a ship of that nature."

"Good to know you, son," said the pastor. "My blessings go out to you and your future endeavors."

"Oh my," said Erin. "Did you receive your deformity in the service of the Union?" asked Erin, staring at Jeff's missing right arm and shoulder.

"Yes, ma'am," replied Jeff. "I was wounded at the battle of Bentonville in North Carolina toward the very end of the war."

"You poor man. Is it painful not having an arm? Must you rely heavily on others to help you accomplish personal tasks? How are you able to…?"

"Come my dear," interrupted the pastor, not wishing to be embarrassed by his wife's questions. "We must see to the comfort of our other guests. Please excuse us, gentlemen."

The two walked away together. Before Sherman could say anything, his eyes locked with those of the widow McClatchy. The old woman approached, and Sherman could tell she had something on her mind.

"Good day, Sherman."

"Good day, Mrs. McClatchy."

"Who's this gentleman?" she asked brusquely.

"May I introduce Mr. Jeffrey Parlin. He's new to town and is currently in my employ at the store."

"Well, I see that you've wasted no time in replacing young Danny. I suppose an older one-armed crippled individual can do just as good of a job as a younger, fully able-bodied man," she fired off without tact or pity.

"Mr. Parlin is quite capable of completing the tasks I set for him at the store, and he is much more reliable than Mr. Ricker ever was," said Sherman in soft defiance of the widow's partiality toward Danny.

"I hope you're proud of your decision," she answered with a raised voice. "I haven't seen poor Danny in days and he might be in need of food and shelter! He's probably ashamed to show his face around here because of what you did to him!"

"He was not performing his duties and he was stealing from me, Mrs. McClatchy," replied Sherman sternly but in a controlled voice so as not to alert others of the conversation.

"I don't believe that!" cried out the old widow. Her voice, now noticeably loud, started to draw the attention of others. "Danny Ricker was a dear, sweet, boy who wouldn't steal or cause harm to anyone. He had nothing and nobody to care for him except me. Now he's gone…and God forgive you if anything bad happens to him, because it's your fault he left! Now, good day to you and your new friend, Mr. Jackson. I hope you two get everything that's coming to you. Regrettably, I don't think we'll be able to do business together anymore!"

The old woman stomped off in a huff as many others watched. Jeff stood in silence, not knowing what to say. Sherman sighed and turned away. He helped himself to a piece of strawberry pie and casually tried to divert the attention away from him.

"You don't seem to be in very good standing with old Milly," said a familiar voice from behind Sherman. "What did you do…tell her that one of her pies was rancid or something?"

Sherman turned around to see that his friend Hiram Lovell was standing there.

"Hello, Hiram. The widow and I have had a disagreement of late concerning Danny Ricker. It's nothing more than a difference of opinion," said Sherman weakly. "This is Jeff Parlin. He's new in town and is working for me."

"Hello, Jeff," said Hiram with a smile and a firm handshake. "My wife Gertrude and my kids Josephine and Alexander are over there talking to the pastor." He pointed in their direction. "I own and operate a dairy farm not far from here."

"Good to meet you, Hiram," said Jeff politely.

"Sherman, have you seen Silas recently?" asked Lovell.

"He came into the store a few days ago. I sold him a rifle. He's supposedly coming back soon. He told me about some trouble out in Gorham…some thefts he was investigating."

"Well, that's interesting," replied Hiram, scratching his brown muttonchop whiskers that extended far down to the corners of his mouth. "I've had some trouble out my way."

"What kind of trouble?"

"The other night one of my milking cows was led out into the pasture and slaughtered. Somebody slit her throat wide open with a large blade and deeply mutilated the carcass. Some cheese and butter was stolen, as well as some vegetables from my garden," said Hiram in a low voice. "There were also indications that the bastard got into the house. I never seen anything like it around here. I was hoping to catch Silas at services today and report it. I haven't even told Gertrude and the children about it…don't want to frighten them. Any trouble like that around your place?"

Jeff stood in absolute silence and Sherman paused before answering.

"No, can't say that there has been," Sherman said evasively. "At least not to that extreme," he added. "Erin Morrell and her sons were in the store recently. The boys admitted to causing some mischief in my vegetable garden, but that's all. I can't imagine they'd do something as dastardly as purposely killing a cow."

"I was talking to old Milly earlier, and she told me that her garden was missing some vegetables too. She also said that her well water tasted funny and made her vomit once during the night."

"Hmmm…extraordinary coincidence of events," said Sherman, unsure of how to react.

"Ayuh, looks to me like we have a serious problem brewing here. I can't afford to lose a cow so senselessly. I'm going to be on guard from now on and God help anyone who tries to disrupt my livelihood again. He'll be sorry. I guarantee you of that."

Sherman shook his head. He wanted to say more but held his tongue. He looked at Jeff, who stood calmly and said nothing.

"Do me a favor, Sherman. If you see Silas anytime soon, send him out my way. I'm hesitant to leave the wife and kids alone to make a trip out to Portland after what I saw was done to that cow," said Hiram. "I'm going to ask around some more and try to find out if anyone else has had trouble like this lately. Good to see you, Sherman, and nice to meet you, Jeff."

Hiram sauntered away, leaving Sherman and Jeff alone. The two looked awkwardly at each other and said nothing. Jeff walked off to procure himself a cup of coffee while Sherman finished his slice of pie. He began to feel really uneasy and decided that now was a good time to leave. Gawkily standing alone, Sherman plotted his escape route, then looked around for Jeff, who was now mingling on his own. Sherman spotted him chatting with the McPhees. He took one step in their direction but then abruptly stopped upon hearing some soft words from behind.

"Why, hello, Sherman. I was hoping to see you today."

A nervous twinge shot through Sherman's gut. He turned around and standing before him was the one sight that instantly made him forget about all other matters—good or bad.

"Hello, Sophie. I was looking for you earlier. I'm so glad *you* found *me*."

The two gazed at each other in a fashion that would have left no question in the eyes of a casual observer that they shared a mutual attraction.

"Are you enjoying the refreshments?" she asked.

"Oh, very much so," he replied. "But I'm especially enjoying your company at this particular moment."

Sophie blushed and happily looked away in embarrassment. Sherman couldn't help but sneak a glance at her beautiful figure while her face was turned.

"I was worried about you the other night, having to ride home in that awful storm. I pray you made it without much discomfort or exasperation?" she inquired.

"I was fine," he said confidently. "A little wet and windswept, but intact without incident or injury, I'm glad to report. I hope there was no damage to the Morrell farm or the schoolhouse?"

"No, thank goodness. All my hard work didn't wash away with the storm," she said, laughing. "I'm starting class tomorrow. It's very exciting! Olin and Wilbur Morrell will be there and so will Alexander and Josephine Lovell. I'm also expecting some younger children from South

Gorham. Their mother met with me early this morning and decided to enroll them at the last minute. They're a girl named Patricia and a boy named Andrew. I believe they're seven and eight years old respectively. I'm a little nervous."

"Don't be nervous. I know you'll be great, and if there's anything I can do to help, just ask," Sherman said willingly.

"Thank you, Sherman," Sophie said, drawing nearer to the man that had captivated her.

Sherman reached out to clasp her hand. Sophie responded in kind, but before the two touched, a voice interrupted them.

"This is a wonderful gathering. I'm glad we decided to stay for the good company and refreshments," said Jeff, his eyes locked on Sophie. Not waiting to be introduced, Parlin extended his hand to the young teacher and said, "I'm Jeff Parlin, a friend of Sherman. What might your name be, my dear?"

"My name is Sophie Curtis. It's a pleasure to meet you, Mr. Parlin."

"Sophie Curtis? What a lovely name."

"Yes it is," interjected Sherman. "Surely you couldn't have forgotten it after the pastor's introduction of Miss Curtis earlier during services?"

"You're quite right, Sherman," said Jeff, picking up on his friend's little jab. "Regardless, I'm very happy to meet you, Miss Curtis. The pleasure is most assuredly all mine."

With that, it was Jeff who reached out and clasped Sophie's right hand. He then brazenly and confidently drew it up to his lips, whereupon he delicately kissed then gently released it with a seductive wink of his eye. Surprised and a bit unsure of how to respond to Parlin's cavalier gesture of affection, Sophie took a step backward and tried to fabricate a pleasant smile.

"If you don't mind, Jeff, Miss Curtis and I would like to continue our conversation in private," said an outwardly calm but inwardly incensed Sherman. "Please take the key and return to the store. I need you to get started on that list of chores I gave you. Some may take longer than others and I think it would be a good idea to begin as early as possible. Here's the key. Instructions are on the list. I'll be along in a while to give you a hand."

"Of course, Sherm," said Jeff. "Miss Curtis, I bid you farewell—for now."

Parlin bowed to Sophie and walked off with the store key and list of chores.

"My, my, your friend is quite gallant," said Sophie, still feeling a bit uneasy.

"Yes, it certainly appears so," Sherman replied.

"Have you known each other a long time?"

"No, actually just a few days. He appeared on my doorstep the night of the storm. He's a drifter, from Missouri originally. He had no place to go and was miserably drenched and exhausted that night. I was obliged to shelter and feed him. He has no money at present. I thought it best to hire him to help me at the store…at least temporarily until he's earned enough cash to resume his travels."

"Oh, I see. Was he injured in the war?" Sophie asked timidly.

"Yes, from what he says, he took his wound while fighting in North Carolina toward the end of Sherman's famous march through the Deep South."

"Oh dear, that's certainly very unfortunate. He does seem to be in decent spirits for a man with only one arm, though. He must be quite strong and courageous."

Sherman dipped his head a bit after Sophie's last comment and said nothing.

"And you, sir," she continued, "Are quite noble and compassionate for offering to assist a stranger with such limited means. Your generosity and kindness are without measure, Sherman."

Sophie then reached over and touched Sherman's chin, lifting it up. Then, unexpectedly, she leaned over and kissed his cheek. The young man's spirits soared, buoyed by a euphoria that could only be catalyzed by the soft caress of a lovely woman. The tender gesture heartily emboldened Sherman to take Sophie by both hands and look squarely into her beautiful blue eyes.

"Sophie, would you do me the honor of escorting me to the Independence Day celebration on Friday? Provided, of course, that it doesn't interfere with any of your scholastic duties."

"Why, Sherman, I would be delighted to accompany you to the festivities this Friday. You may meet me at the schoolhouse at noontime, where I'll be ready to enjoy the rest of the day in your company."

"Excellent! You've made me very happy, Sophie. I look forward to our rendezvous and shall go through the week with a permanent grin on my face in anticipation."

"Wonderful. I should like to see that very much, Sherman. Now if you'll excuse me, I can see Mrs. Morrell waving in this direction. She must be in need of my assistance. Please forgive me. I must go now. I do indeed look forward to our next meeting! By the way, Mrs. Morrell speaks very highly of you."

"That's good to hear. Until our next meeting," said Sherman with a slight bow and a smile. The two parted ways, Sophie toward the pastor's wife and Sherman heading back to the store. As he walked down Settler Road, Sherman's thoughts turned to Jeff Parlin. The smile on his face quickly evaporated as he began to wonder about his new friend.

CHAPTER 7

Portland

Monday morning arrived without incident. Sherman awoke anxious to ride out to Portland and locate Sheriff Ridgeway. After hearing Hiram Lovell's gruesome tale, coupled with the widow McClatchy's recent misfortunes, Sherman was eager to do everything necessary to prevent further escalations of trouble. He locked up the house and went into the livery. He looked over both his Morgans and determined Skipper and Budley were in good spirits. There was every indication that Jeff had tended to them earlier, as buckets of water and feed were nearby. Sherman started to walk over to his Shire stallions when he stopped and took a closer look at Budley. His hooves were very muddy and there were some twigs and leaf fragments lodged in both his mane and tail. Skipper, by comparison, was clean of any mud or debris. The sight was curious and raised a question or two in Sherman's mind, but he was late and he had other more important matters weighing heavily on his thoughts.

Sherman harnessed his two bay Shire stallions and led them out of the livery. He attached his wagon to the horses and set the brake after guiding it out onto the road. He was now ready to journey into Portland. However, one last piece of business remained before his imminent departure. Sherman went into the store and was pleased to find Jeff busy stocking new inventory and tidying up the place. He had already completed every task on Sherman's list from Sunday and was now busy doing additional work to help prepare for the day's business. Sherman couldn't help but be thoroughly impressed. Never before had he seen such a hard-working and capable individual, despite his obvious physical limitations. He was certainly a fast learner and he followed direction without difficulty or complaint. He was doing a magnificent job and was earning his keep above and beyond what Sherman had anticipated.

"Damn, you accomplish more work with one arm than most men manage with two," Sherman trumpeted proudly.

"Much obliged, Sherm. Oh…before I forget, we had two early customers this morning. They bought some tools, rope, and a sack of coffee beans. I seen how you record sales in your ledger, so I went ahead, totaled 'em up, and sold 'em the goods. I wrote down the transaction like you do in your book there. The money is on the counter. Fortunately I didn't have to make change. I didn't want to overstep my bounds and have to get into your cashbox."

"Well, it wouldn't have mattered even if you did because it's empty…plus, you don't have the key. I've been making sure no cash is left in the store after business hours. Since this ugliness with Danny Ricker began, I don't want to take any chances. I keep all the money locked up in the house at night. I project how much I need in the store on a daily basis and bring that minimum amount with me each morning."

Sherman walked around in back of the counter and reached down underneath to retrieve the cashbox. It was purposely placed on a hidden little shelf out of plain view. He pulled a little brass key out of his pocket and opened the box, whereupon he proceeded to fill it with a paltry amount of United States Notes, state-issued banknotes, and coins, also produced from his pockets. It was far from a fortune, but it was all he estimated would be needed for the day.

"I'll leave this unlocked for now. I'm going into Portland to address my problem with the sheriff."

"*Our* problem," corrected Jeff.

"Okay, *our* problem," reluctantly conceded Sherman.

"If you're agreeable, Jeff, I'm going to leave you fully in charge of the store while I'm gone. From what little I've seen, you've proven that you're reliable and capable of handling business around here—at least in the short term. I'm confident I can trust you to manage things while I'm away. I hope I'm correct in my assumption?"

"You are indeed, Sherm. I know I can handle things around here. I've had some experience temporarily working in general stores in my travels. I failed to mention that earlier, but I do feel comfortable in places like this. Oh, also…I might add that I didn't spy any trouble last night. I kept watch again from my window. No sign of your Danny Ricker causing any mischief."

"That's good to hear. I want this problem dealt with as soon as possible. I'll be taking the stallions and the wagon. I anticipate doing some buying while in Portland and will most likely come back with a load of goods to sell. Depending on how long my errands take and the length of my meeting with the sheriff, I predict I'll return sometime tomorrow afternoon. Help yourself to the food in here. Feel free to fix your meals on the stove if necessary. Just keep a record of all you take so that I may properly record and manage the inventory. Keep an eye on the cashbox. You should have enough money but if for some reason you run out of change, you can accept credit. I don't think that will be necessary, though, as people around here tend to pay the exact amount for goods. Look after the animals and lock up the store each night. Here's the key. Don't worry about the house. It's sealed up tight."

"Good. I can handle it. Have a safe journey to Portland. I'll see you when you return. While you're absent, just remember what I said the other day. It's good to fight fire *with* fire. I think it best that you lay your hands on some guns for the both of us for protection. There's no telling what this crazy kid will do."

Sherman paused, then nodded his head slightly, indicating that he understood but wasn't exceptionally keen on the idea. He bid Jeff farewell, then mounted his wagon and proceeded down Settler Road in the direction of Portland. As the wagon lumbered along Sherman felt confident Jeff would handle business properly. He'd entrusted his property and very livelihood with a man he'd met just a few days earlier and seemed at peace with his decision; though he stopped short with his most precious possession—his house. Something deep down in his gut, some feeling Sherman couldn't readily distinguish, prevented him from allowing Parlin into his home. Whether it was a simple lack of trust or an instinctive suspicion buried deep within, something drove Sherman to keep Jeff at arm's length.

It was another sunny and warm day, but the heat was not as oppressive as it had been. Sherman guided his horses along steadily and in relative comfort. They weren't kicking up much dust, which pleased him. Occasionally he'd pass a man on horseback or someone walking along the road, but for the most part he journeyed alone, which gave him time to think.

One curious thought revisited his mind and caused him to ponder. Again he thought back to the day he had discovered the open window upstairs and the missing gun and knife from the display case. He now wondered why Danny hadn't stolen the cashbox. He knew where it was and certainly was aware of its daily contents. He could have easily made off with it. Sherman knew he had left a moderate amount of cash in the box that night. It wasn't until after the incident that he discreetly started bringing all the money into his home after closing. Why didn't Ricker take the money? Why did he leave his extra clothes? Why didn't he steal any other items of value, for that matter? Perhaps there wasn't time, or maybe he lost his nerve. It was possible that someone or something spooked him and he made a hasty exit for fear of getting caught.

Then again, there was the question of the Morrell boys' possible involvement in the crime. Could they have been the sole thieves? They wouldn't have known the location of the cashbox; therefore, they couldn't have readily stolen it. They would have had to search for it, which would have taken time—time needed to crack open the display-case lock. Being young boys, it would have been easy for them to have lost their nerve and hustled away after they secured their primary prizes. The fear of getting caught and severely punished would have given them motivation to exit quickly and not risk taking anything else. Then there was the idea that the Morrell boys could have been working *with*, or were at least pawns of, Danny Ricker. He could have coerced them into doing his dirty work for him. But if he was the ringleader, he could've told them about the hidden money and instructed them to grab it.

There were no clear answers, but Sherman began to consider seriously that the Morrell boys could very well have been the sole criminals involved with the store theft. However, that didn't explain the personal attack Sherman suffered, or Hiram Lovell's mutilated cow. Though he never got a look at his attacker, Sherman knew without a doubt that he had been knocked down and subdued by a full-grown man with powerful muscles, unlike the thin fifteen-year-old Olin Morrell. And as much as he tried to conceive it, Sherman just couldn't accept that Olin was deranged enough to arbitrarily slaughter and mutilate a cow for no apparent reason other than pure wickedness. He felt that type of unbalanced behavior wasn't in Wilbur Morrell's constitution either. However, he could envision Ricker performing such a gory task, especially under the heavy influence of alcohol.

The more Sherman thought about his problems, the more he simply desired to find Sheriff Ridgeway and compare notes. Was Danny

Ricker responsible for the original trouble the sheriff spoke of in Gorham? Had he solved the crime and was now looking to arrest him? Had the sheriff linked him to other crimes leading back to North Scarborough? Questions abounded, and he hoped to find answers…soon.

The coastal city of Portland was long considered one of Maine's precious jewels, not only by its own residents but also by many who visited there. The origin of the former state capital dated all the way back to 1632, when two white settlers named George Cleeve and Richard Tucker established homesteads on the eastern edge of a peninsula soon to be called Falmouth Neck—and over time, Portland. They and their families prospered, and soon other settlers followed. A number of years later the thriving location caught the greedy eye of the powerful Massachusetts Bay Colony. Its leaders wasted no time in annexing the vast northern territory and claiming full control and jurisdiction over its newly acquired land—a province called Maine. The English leaders of the Massachusetts Bay Colony saw the area as rich in natural resources, particularly white pine timber from which tall ship masts could be harvested and fashioned. They also saw the southwestern province as strategically important to their defense against the French and Indians, long considered a growing threat.

Present-day Portland, Maine, was reincorporated as Falmouth, Massachusetts, in the year 1718 by the Massachusetts General Court. The city continued to prosper, grow, and modernize until 1775. Throughout that turbulent year, the rising intolerance of British rule had fanned the flames of rebellion among the thirteen colonies, and it wasn't long before conflict reached the shores of Maine. On October 18, Royal Navy Lieutenant Henry Mowat, in command of a small British flotilla of vessels tasked with suppressing rebellious activity and authorized to bombard key colonial seaports, launched a day-long torrent of naval gunfire against Falmouth, effectively reducing the town to ashes. Hundreds of families were displaced just before the onset of winter and many suffered further from out-of-town looters who took advantage of their neighbors' misfortunes. The destruction of Falmouth at the hands of the Royal Navy served as a key catalyst in the decision by the colonies to wage a war of independence against British rule.

Mulling over some of Portland's past events from colonial times, Sherman was reminded of some of its more fascinating and recent history. He thought back to the war and remembered learning about the daring capture of the U.S. revenue cutter *Caleb Cushing* by Confederate raiders in 1863. At that time, Confederate activity in Maine and other northern states was limited primarily to spy operations, small acts of sabotage, and the occasional raid, which oftentimes resulted in theft and the disruption of shipping. The fact that there were no major engagements between Union and Confederate forces on Maine soil during the entire war gave the local population a false sense of security. That feeling of safety would be shattered when the captured fishing schooner *Archer* out of Southport, commanded by Confederate raider Lieutenant Charles Read, quietly slipped past Fort Preble, Fort Scammell, and the incomplete Fort Gorges, easily entering Portland Harbor. They dropped anchor between Fort Gorges on Hog Island Ledge and the foot of Munjoy Hill. Disguised as fishermen, the raiders rowed out to their secondary target, the hundred-foot cutter *Caleb Cushing*, after determining that their primary target, the steamer *Chesapeake*, was unattainable because of the time it would take to fire up her boilers and bring the engine up to steam. The *Caleb Cushing* was anchored toward the middle of Portland's inner harbor. The armed Confederates quickly swarmed the cutter and overpowered its skeleton crew—the result of shore leave, which the majority of the ship's officers and sailors were enjoying. To make matters more confusing, the *Caleb Cushing* was waiting for its new captain to arrive. Her previous commander, Captain George Clark, had unexpectedly suffered a severe heart attack and died. Lieutenant Dudley Davenport, ironically a southerner from Savannah, Georgia, was the ship's new temporary commander.

Once the crew was turned out of their hammocks and put into submission, Lieutenant Read ordered his men to get underway. His plan was to link up with the *Archer* and slip away with his prize. If the three forts fired on him while making his escape, he'd return to the inner harbor and use the *Caleb Cushing*'s guns—a thirty-two pounder located amidships and a twelve-pounder on the gallant forecastle—to shell the city and also pummel the two new nearby gunboats—U.S.S. *Agawam* and U.S.S. *Poutoosac*—awaiting engines and conveniently tied up at Franklin Wharf. He'd then make his escape by bypassing the main shipping channel and the forts that protected it. Instead of running the gauntlet of fire the three forts would undeniably unleash, Read would plot a course taking him through Hussey Sound Passage to the far side of Peaks and Hog Island, far away and out of sight of the menacing guns on Forts Preble, Scammell, and Gorges. He'd then flee to open water where he'd be free to continue his raiding of Yankee merchant shipping.

Unfortunately for the wily Confederate naval lieutenant, his escape was not successful. Preparing the *Caleb Cushing* to sail proved harder than expected. She was aground and wouldn't budge once the sails were hoisted. Some of the raiders quickly rowed out to another smaller vessel anchored in front of the *Caleb Cushing* and fastened a line connecting the two ships. With nothing but brute force, Read and his men heaved on the line until the *Caleb Cushing* was pulled into deeper water. Another obstacle hindering their escape was the wind, which had died down considerably. Again, Read's men were forced into their small boats and strained to tow their prize out of the inner harbor. In the process, they were observed by the steamer *Forest City* returning from Boston around four o'clock in the morning. Upon making port, those aboard the *Forest City* informed Jedediah Jewett, the port's customs collector, that the *Caleb Cushing* had put to sea. Immediately suspecting the cutter had been stolen by Lieutenant Davenport—the present commander with southern roots—Jewett wasted no time sounding the alarm.

Soon, with the backing of Mayor Jacob McLellan, the *Forest City* and the *Chesapeake* were ordered to pursue. With the help of the steam tug *Tiger*, the *Chesapeake* took on soldiers from the swiftly alerted 7th Maine Volunteers rushed up from Fort Abraham Lincoln just a few miles away. Another small steamer named the *Casco* transported men and arms of the 17th Maine Infantry from Fort Preble to the *Forest City*, which was unable to dock directly at the fort. Within a short time, both vessels were underway and in pursuit of the *Caleb Cushing*.

It wasn't long before the steamers had the fleeing cutter in their sights. Lieutenant Read knew he couldn't outrun his pursuers. He realized his only option was to put up a fight in hopes of damaging the vessels or intimidating them enough that they'd be forced to break off. He ordered the thirty-two pounder, located amidships, swung as far aft as possible. As soon as the gun was ready, he pulled the lanyard and sent a shot in the direction of the steamers. The *Forest City* wasn't hit, but her captain was spooked enough to halt the pursuit. The *Chesapeake*, trailing behind *Forest City*, continued on toward the defiant cutter. The *Caleb Cushing* continued firing on the *Chesapeake* but registered no hits. The *Chesapeake* timidly fired an experimental shot but also was unsuccessful at hitting its target.

The two steamers eventually regrouped and decided it was best to ram the fleeing cutter. The task was put to the *Chesapeake*. Unbeknownst to Captain John Liscomb of the *Forest City* and Mayor McLellan, with U.S. Naval Inspector William F. Leighton in joint command of the *Chesapeake*, the raiders aboard the *Caleb Cushing* had been unable to locate the vast stores of powder and shot needed to fight off the steamers. They had scoured the ship and questioned the imprisoned crew to no avail. Cleverly, Lieutenant Davenport did not disclose the existence of the ship's hidden ammunition chamber next to the captain's cabin. He also refused to reveal the shot locker's whereabouts and skillfully denied Read the keys that would gain him entry to the ship's powder magazine. All these factors contributed to the swift exhaustion of the scarce ammunition available on deck. Soon the raiders were scrounging for anything that could serve as an adequate projectile, but their efforts proved to be in vain.

As the two steamers, loaded with both armed soldiers and civilians, bore down on the now defenseless cutter, Lieutenant Read knew his outnumbered and outgunned crew of raiders was no match for what was coming should he be boarded. In a final act of southern defiance, he ordered his prize torched. After quickly setting fire to the *Caleb Cushing*, Read put himself, his men, and the prisoners off separately in small boats. He ordered his men to discard their small arms and quickly hoisted a white flag of surrender. The *Forest City* picked up Read and his men upon noticing the spreading fire aboard the doomed cutter. They were subdued, searched, and taken into custody. The unarmed *Archer* made its own attempt to flee but was identified and captured intact before it could get away.

The Confederates had more than one hundred thousand dollars in bonds in their possession, of which they were promptly relieved. The Rebel pirates were taken ashore and held at Fort Preble amid public outcry. They were swiftly transferred to Fort Warren in Boston Harbor to prevent riots by angered Portlanders.

The *Caleb Cushing* was left to burn after it was decided she couldn't be saved. Fear of her powder magazine blowing the burning vessel sky-high was enough to keep both the *Forest City* and the *Chesapeake* well clear, though both vessels remained on the scene to watch the inevitable obliteration before returning to dock. Eventually the flames reached the powder stores and the *Caleb Cushing* went up in a magnificent display of fiery destructive force. The cutter was no more.

Reminiscing about the famous maritime incidents helped Sherman pass the time as he rumbled toward Portland. As the day grew old and morning turned into afternoon, Sherman's wagon eventually reached the coast. He could see seagulls wheeling in the sky above him and detected the distinct smell of the salty air as it flowed into his nostrils. Soon the great city was upon him and he carefully navigated his horse-drawn wagon in the direction of busy Congress Street. The city looked different from what Sherman remembered seeing years earlier. The vibrant, bustling crowds of people out and about conducting business and or engaged in their daily routines looked the same, but the landscape and the buildings looked very different.

Portland was now a city built not of wood, but rather of red brick and stone of Victorian-influenced design. Its streets were broader, its newly established water supply piped from Sebago Lake was cleaner and healthier, and its governmental, mercantile, and residential sections more clearly defined. With the arrival of the Atlantic and St. Lawrence Railroad, and the completion of the tracks in 1853, Portland became a foremost rail link in New England. Soon it was connected to major Canadian cities such as Montreal, which promoted growth both physically and economically.

Alongside its growing rail service, Portland also had a burgeoning shipping industry, particularly in the passenger steamship business. Portland-based steamers began regular routes ferrying people to and from coastal cities such as Boston and New York. With the increased rail and maritime commerce, city officials recognized the need to expand Portland's old, cramped, and increasingly insufficient waterfront to accommodate the growing business windfall. The creation of a new waterfront thoroughfare, fittingly named Commercial Street, began. Using landfill from nearby Munjoy and Bramhall Hills, engineers literally expanded the waterfront outward to the sea, creating the new street in the process. When completed, this innovative and very broad road made from cobblestones was constructed with railroad tracks and rail spurs leading into newer and larger commercial buildings near the docks. Rail links were connected and expanded, shipping routes were mapped out and more clearly defined, and the new waterfront exploded with profitable industry. Portland was now cemented as a "city on the grow."

Portland's rising prosperity suffered a major setback in the summer of 1866. On Independence Day, the city suffered the greatest fire in the history of the country, until Chicago burned in 1871. A fire that started in a boathouse on Commercial Street rapidly spread, engulfing the eastern portion of the city in flames. It burned for approximately fifteen hours, causing massive devastation to the mostly wooden buildings before eventually relenting. A shortage of water from cisterns, wells, and other depleted sources, and a general unpreparedness for such a swift-moving calamity, insured the city's doom. The Portland Fire Department was overwhelmed and unable to effectively combat the flames due to myriad problems, primarily the deficiency of water. Other problems included extremely hot and dry weather conditions and steam-engine fire-fighting equipment that malfunctioned or was itself damaged by the blaze.

Eventually the conflagration burned itself out once its source of fuel was exhausted. Remarkably the fire only caused two deaths, but also took with it countless homes and buildings and displaced thousands of families. Once the air finally cleared, the citizens of Portland stood tall and were dedicated to rebuilding the city in a fashion that would deter this kind of catastrophe from ever happening again. What rose from the ashes were newer and stronger buildings made from brick and stone, broader and tidier streets, and an abundant water supply piped in from pristine Sebago Lake. All these improvements would contribute to the city flourishing again, and were the cause of what Sherman Jackson was seeing unfold before his eyes now.

Sherman had several stops to make. He needed to visit Sheriff Ridgeway's office in the administrative section of town on Congress Street. He'd then travel to nearby Exchange Street to shop and pick up personal necessities among its wide range of retail stores and merchants. He'd finish his day in Portland by meeting with wholesalers, brokers, and other vendors to secure goods for resale in his own store. It was much later in the afternoon than he preferred, but after several minor delays, including an extended and very late lunch, Sherman's wagon finally pulled up in front of Sheriff Ridgeway's office. To his dismay, he found the office dark, quiet, empty, and locked.

"Damn it all," uttered Sherman.

Displeased and frustrated that the sheriff was not around, Sherman began randomly asking people in the street if anyone knew his whereabouts.

"Pardon me, but is anyone aware of the sheriff's current business? Would anyone possibly know if he's in town or where I might locate him?"

Several people stopped to hear Sherman's questions, which he repeated several times, yet no one was able to assist him. His queries were met with confused faces, innocent but unhelpful head nods, and negative responses. He felt compelled to smile and tip his hat graciously despite not getting any answers and being no better off. Not wanting to waste any more time, Sherman directed his horses and wagon to nearby Exchange Street. He was now very anxious to find cartridges for the Henry. He stopped just outside a familiar storefront. The place was called Chester & Co's. Sherman knew the owner and had done business with him before. The hardware store made of solid red brick, nestled amid large banks, brokerage houses, and various office buildings, sold a modest variety of general merchandise such as shovels, axes, picks, tools, saddles, satchels, oil lamps, rope, fishing gear, lobster traps, dynamite, gunpowder, and an assortment of firearms and ammunition.

"Sherman Jackson! Haven't seen you in a dog's age," boomed a deep voice as the young man entered the store.

"Hello, Chet," replied Sherman upon spying the bespectacled, chubby, bald-headed owner partially hidden behind the counter.

"Doing your own dirty work today? Where's that kid—ahh... umm...what's his name—Ricker, who you always send in here to rob me?" asked Chet playfully.

"He's no longer in my employ. Had to dismiss him. We had some problems that couldn't be reconciled."

"Oh, I see. Can't say that I blame you. I never liked dealing with him either. He was always so gloomy and irritable...never wanted to cooperate neither. Always found myself doing more of his work than him! He never wanted to sign any papers and always complained when it came time to load up your wagon. Laziest son of a bitch I ever met, for his age. Good riddance, I say!"

"Ayuh, he's caused me too much grief lately. It was time to part ways," said Sherman, wanting to change the subject.

"So what brings you in? I wasn't expecting to do business with Jackson's General Store for at least another month," Chet said.

"Personal business," replied Sherman. "I need to lay my hands on some .44 rim-fire cartridges for a rifle I got back at the house. Do you have any in stock?"

"Sure do. I got several boxes. How many do you need?"

"Gimme three boxes. That'll do for now."

"Looking to do some hunting, Sherman? Trying to up your profits by selling more smoked meat? Venison perhaps? Would certainly be unfortunate if a big fat buck wandered onto your property and you had no bullets to shoot at it. What type of rifle you got?"

"I got a Henry."

"Oh, fancy that. I haven't seen too many of those. Call the new models Winchesters now, don't they? They're nice from what I hear. You can shoot all day and never have to reload," Chet said with a chuckle that made him turn away and cough. When he recovered he turned back to Sherman and said, "Where in hell did you ever get a Henry? Order it for your store and then decide to keep it once you figured out them poor farmers out in Scarborough ain't got no money to afford a gun like that?"

"Naw, it was a gift from my parents. I was supposed to get it during the fighting back in '63 or '64…but there were problems. Parents didn't know where to ship it…other things like that," said Sherman, his voice trailing off.

"Well," said Chet, "let me get your cartridges for you." He went out back and returned with three boxes of bullets.

"How much do I owe you?" asked Sherman as he reached for his billfold.

"Oh just take 'em, Sherman," Chet replied with a wave of his hand. "Next time I'm up your way you can pay me back with something of equal value from your store…*plus* a free pie of my choice from that old lady who makes 'em for you. Deal?"

"Deal," answered Sherman, shrewdly knowing that he wasn't going to end up on the short end of this business contract since it was unlikely that Mrs. McClatchy would ever bake him another pie again. "Thanks, Chet. By the way, what kind of pistols are you carrying now?"

"I have assorted models. Are you looking to buy a pistol too?"

"Yes, I'm in the market for a reliable revolver. Do you have one that would pair nicely with the Henry—something that would take the same .44-caliber load? I don't want to mess with a cap-and-ball gun. Powder is useless when it gets wet. I learned that lesson fast during the war."

"As a matter of fact, I have just what you need," said Chet, reaching under the counter. He pulled out a box and opened it. "This is the Smith & Wesson Model 3 single-action revolver. It's a top break-action gun that can take .44-caliber rim-fire cartridges, same as your Henry. It's quite the modern piece of hand-gunnery if you ask me, Sherman. I've sold quite a few to many officers and some enlisted boys out at Fort Preble. It's very popular among military men, which I know you can appreciate."

Chet held the gun up for Sherman so he could demonstrate how to load and unload the weapon.

"Just pull the hammer back a bit, release this top latch here, and then the whole business just swings open. The extractor pops up and ejects all six cartridges simultaneously. You don't even need to dig 'em out. They eject on their own. Just be careful they don't hit you in the face or pop you in the eye," quipped Chet.

Sherman took the gun to get a feel for it. He aimed it several times, then practiced working the top latch to break the gun open for reloading. It felt comfortable in his hand and he instantly took to it. He felt anxious to purchase the revolver and decided it might be a good gun to carry and sell in his own store.

"Whaddya asking for it, Chet?" said Sherman, pretending to appear uninterested.

"I been selling 'em for forty dollars," answered Chet as he pulled out a handkerchief and mopped his sweaty brow.

"Forty dollars...for a revolver? I've sold rifles at that price," exclaimed Sherman.

"Simple economics. There's a high demand for this particular item in this vicinity. The supply is limited so I can charge a higher premium and get my asking price without difficulty. Forty dollars, Sherman—not negotiable. That's where I stand, and…uh…no credit accepted on this item either, sorry."

"For Christ's sake, Chet. What's a man gotta do to get a break around here? It hasn't been a great month at my store, you know. My numbers are flat at best. How about a little help, businessman to businessman?"

"Sherman, that's my last one. I can't order 'em fast enough. Once it's gone, it'll be weeks before I get a new shipment. In fact, I know a man who wants it now and will meet my price. He just hasn't been around to buy it yet. Why don't you just order some for your store? You might get a better deal that way. In fact, why don't you order your cartridges and sell them at your store too? Why buy 'em from me?"

"I don't sell many guns. I have a few on hand but I end up sitting on 'em for years sometimes. Not much of a market for firearms in my town. Don't make sense for a rural area like Scarborough. You'd think I'd be selling rifles left and right—cartridge models *and* muzzle loaders— but for some reason I don't. Everybody in my town is too tightfisted to spend money on a new gun. Wouldn't surprise me if the townsfolk still use rusty old Revolutionary-era flintlocks handed down to them by their grandpappies or something like that. Anything to save a few pennies."

Sherman was now fidgeting and clearly irritated. It was obvious that there was a lot on the Scarborough man's mind. Unbeknownst to the owner of the hardware store, Sherman hadn't accomplished much on his visit to Portland and the day was waning fast, as was his patience. The firm price of the revolver wasn't helping matters.

"I came here, Chet, because I need a gun and ammunition now. I can't wait."

Just then, Sherman made a rash decision.

"Here's your forty dollars…and gimme a receipt," he said begrudgingly as he handed Chet the cash in greenbacks from his billfold.

"You're not in any trouble, are you?" asked Chet, hesitating.

"No," replied Sherman tersely. "I just need a gun—maybe even two."

"Another revolver?"

Sherman paused and wished he hadn't said what he did. His mind worked quickly. He was certain he didn't have enough extra notes to pay for another gun and he was now looking at spending the night in Portland, which would require money for supper and lodgings. He needed store supplies, too, and the wholesalers on Commercial Street were not known for selling their goods cheaply.

"No, never mind. I just need this one revolver and the cartridges."

"Okay. Take the presentation box too," said Chet as he scribbled out a receipt and placed it in his buyer's hand. Sherman put the gun back in the box and tucked it under his arm. He put the three boxes of cartridges in his suit's pockets.

"Will there be anything else?" asked Chet with concern, trying to ignore his customer's displeasure with the sale price.

"No, that's all I need." He followed up his statement with a forced, "Thank you."

"Glad to be of service," replied Chet with a slight bow.

"I'll be back in a couple weeks and will pick up some supplies from you then. I know you have some items I'll be needing."

"Good to hear that, Sherman. We always seem to do good business together," said Chet in an attempt to alleviate any strain he may have inadvertently heaped on his professional relationship with Sherman.

Sherman took three steps to the door, then stopped and turned to face his friend again. He got the hint and adjusted his attitude. He knew there would be plenty of future opportunities to regain the financial advantage over his fellow businessman. He just needed to be smart and, above all, patient. He also had a question he needed to ask.

"Chet, you haven't seen Silas lately, have you?" he inquired coyly.

"Not lately. Last time he was around here was well over a week ago. He was looking to buy a rifle but claimed he couldn't afford one from me after I showed him several models. He said my prices were way too high, so I told him what I told you—supply and demand. He didn't take kindly to that, so he left empty-handed."

"Imagine that," Sherman remarked sarcastically. "He didn't say where he was going or when he'd be back, did he?"

"Matter of fact, he did say something about some trouble out in Gorham he was preparing to investigate—some thefts or something that had folks riled up. Didn't say when he'd be back. He seems to spend more time out in the country than here. Don't know why he doesn't just move his office out your way. Might save him a heap of extra traveling if you ask me."

"Thanks. Give my regards to your wife and family," said Sherman as he turned back to the door.

"Sherman Jackson!" cried out Chet, waddling out from behind the counter. "Are you sure you're not in any trouble? Something I can help you with, maybe?"

"It's fine," he replied. "No trouble. I have to go now before the crooks down on Commercial Street close up shop. I'd like to get down there posthaste so as not to deprive them of their ordained duty of relieving me of the meager amount of money left in my pocket. They have the honor of finishing the fleecing you so brilliantly started today," he said with a caustic smile and a quick wink.

"Take care of yourself, Mr. Jackson."

"Always do. Good day to you, sir."

Sherman left the store. Before mounting his wagon he busily called on several additional retail establishments, plus numerous transient street peddlers with handcarts that lined the crowded thoroughfares linking up with Congress Street. He walked swiftly, but kept a sharp eye open for intriguing novelties that could be easily resold in his own store. He made his way to Market Square, where he stopped to witness several chatty and cheerful young ladies decorating windows and entryways with colorful bunting, twisty streamers, and numerous American flags all exploding in vibrant hues of red, white, and blue. Portland was making its own Independence Day preparations, and Sherman wondered what was in store for festivities on the fourth. He didn't ponder it long. He clicked open his pocket watch and was mortified at how late it was getting. He hurried back to Exchange Street with only a few small purchases that accompanied his boxed revolver. He loaded the items into his wagon and climbed aboard himself.

"Hyah!" he called out with a snap of the reins. Phineas and Lucky each gave a quick snort and then trotted down toward Commercial Street. Their hooves made a distinguishing clopping sound that resonated sharply with each impact against the cobblestoned roadway. Sherman found a good location to park his wagon, then made his way to the waterfront where several ships were docked and unloading cargo. His sights were set on both Union and Widgery wharves. He knew he'd find wholesalers there who would be willing to sell him goods straight off the boat.

Sherman walked up and down the piers. He greeted several men he had done business with before. He was primarily looking for goods that were hard to obtain. He wanted southern tobacco, high-proof distilled spirits, cotton, and textiles. He longed for interesting and exotic spices from international locations such as India, and more refined personal products like perfume and health tonics from Europe. At the bottom of his list were everyday staples such as sugar, flour, grains, and molasses. He would take whatever he could get—and could afford.

Sherman placed his orders and gave instructions to the wholesalers to cart the purchased items over to his wagon. His goods were selected and wheeled to a central location on Union Wharf. As he waited for all his merchandise to be gathered, Sherman strolled down the wharf to look at the sea. He loved the ocean and regretted not spending more time near it. The cool, steady breeze was refreshing and crisp. The slow, undulating movement of the sea-green water was soothing and hypnotic as it lapped against the sides of the docked vessels. He had never visited any of the islands of Casco Bay, but had a secret and adventurous yearning to do so. The image of peace and tranquility driven by the notion of freedom and mastery of one's destiny fueled Sherman's fervent desire to escape to the sea. It was not to be, however, for now he was firmly tethered to the land—specifically Jackson's General Store.

"Everything's gathered up and accounted for, Mr. Jackson," said a gamy seaman pointing to the small mound of sacks, barrels, and crates of goods.

"Very well. Thank you, my good man. I've made arrangements with Mr. Burnham, the wholesaler over there, to have my goods carted over to my wagon just across the way," said Sherman, pointing to his horses. "Would you be so good as to transport them over? I shall not require you to load the items onto my wagon, but if you're so inclined, I would be most grateful."

The man didn't answer. He simply rolled his eyes and walked away in the direction of a nearby cart. He commandeered some help and began moving Sherman's goods over to the wagon. Sherman walked over to Mr. Burnham and proceeded to fill out the appropriate paperwork needed to legally take possession of his new merchandise. After scrawling out his signature on multiple forms, he finally reached for his billfold and coin purse. He counted out what remained of his greenbacks and then sifted through his coins to produce the money necessary to finalize the purchase. When finished, he was a bit distraught upon seeing only one ten-dollar gold eagle coin remaining in his possession. It was all the money he had, as he was sure there wasn't any more in the house back home. It would have to do, as it was now certain he'd have to spend the night in Portland. He hoped Jeff and the store had a busy day.

Sherman bid Mr. Burnham goodbye, then assisted the dockworkers with loading his wagon. The sun was setting fast and he was anxious to find lodgings for the night. He knew of an inn toward the west end of town that was easy to get to and had reasonable prices, plus the necessary accommodations to suit all his needs. He pointed his horses in the right direction and wasted no time getting underway. The wagon, now weighed down with supplies, rumbled along a little more slowly, but Sherman was confident he'd reach his destination before nightfall.

After a short journey, Sherman saw the inn just down the road. It was conveniently lit up with gaslights. Outside over the door hung a thick, wooden oval sign, carved with blue and white painted lettering that read, "The Old Portside Inn." He brought his wagon to a halt, secured the brake, and walked inside.

"Good evening, sir. May I be of some assistance to you?" asked the innkeeper at the front desk.

"Yes, good evening to you as well. I am in need of a room for one night," said Sherman.

"Very well, sir. Let me just check my register and verify what rooms are available. Just one moment, please."

The innkeeper was a razor-thin man with a brown handlebar moustache and matching brown hair heavily slicked with a fragrant pomade and parted in the center. He wore a pince-nez and a gray suit and tie over a white shirt. His fingers glided down the page of the register and stopped at the first empty space he saw.

"Ah yes, we have just one room available this evening. Interesting...I thought for certain we had more. Well, we can accommodate you. Shall I put you down for the night?"

"Yes, please do."

"Excellent, sir. Now if you would just be so kind as to inscribe your name in this empty space right here, we can get you settled."

The innkeeper spun his register around so that Sherman could sign his name with the pen and ink provided. He then wheeled the book back around and blew on the signature to help dry the ink.

"Do you have any luggage with you, Mr. Jackson?"

"No; however, I do have two horses pulling my wagon filled with recently purchased goods. I trust you still have suitable accommodations to protect and shelter my property?"

"We do indeed, sir. There's a stable behind the inn where your horses and goods will be kept for the evening. I have a man who will tend to both their protection and well-being. Of course, I must charge a bit extra for the service, but I assure you that it's worth it. Your animals will be well cared for."

"I understand and agree," said Sherman. "What is the total charge for my stay?"

"Tonight's lodging, which includes supper plus the care of your animals and property, comes to…four dollars, Mr. Jackson."

"Very well. Allow me to pay you in advance."

Sherman reached into his coin purse and laid his last scrap of gold on the desk.

"Thank you. Allow me to get your change and arrange for your wagon to be brought out back. Is that it I see out front?"

"Yes, indeed."

"Excellent. Here is your key. The room is upstairs. It's the last door on the right. My name is Mr. Webster Stratton, and if there's anything I can do for you this evening, please don't hesitate to call on me. Dinner will be served in our dining room in just a few short minutes, so I advise you to get settled quickly and come join the other guests. Tonight we will be having lobster and assorted vegetables."

"Lobster?"

"Yes, lobster."

"Perhaps the chef has a nice cut of beef or lamb prepared as well?"

"I don't believe so, sir, but I can check. Is there a problem with the lobster?"

"I never cared for it. My father used to call lobster the 'cockroach of the sea.' We never ate it much, and when we did it was awful no matter how you prepared it. My mother used to cook it to death but it never improved the taste."

"Well, our chef is trying a new method of preparing it. What we have was just caught and brought in this evening. The chef is going to cook it under cover of hot steam, and live so that it doesn't have a chance to deteriorate and go rancid. He feels it will produce a better and more succulent dish."

"Hmmm…Well, in that case I'm both intrigued and inclined to try it. Thank you. I must retrieve a few things from my wagon and prepare for supper. Please excuse me, Mr. Stratton, and thank you for your hospitality."

Sherman tipped his hat and went outside to retrieve his new revolver. He watched as the innkeeper's attendant brought the horses and wagon out back to the stable. When satisfied they were in good hands, Sherman rushed to his room and spruced up the best he could for supper. The dining room was small and intimate. A bevy of candles provided the room's only illumination. There were five guests on hand to dine— two young couples and an older gentleman who was alone like Sherman. Everyone sat at the same table, exchanged pleasantries, and engaged in small talk until the food was served.

Placed before the hungry guests was a large silver platter of hot, steaming, red lobsters and cooked vegetables next to a basket of bread. After a minute's hesitation, the server helped crack open the lobster shells, making it easier for everyone to get at the meat. Wine and beer was poured, to everyone's delight, and it wasn't long before everyone had settled into their meal.

Sherman, reluctant to take a bite of the salty crustacean, finally succumbed and placed some claw meat into his mouth. Immediately he was surprised at the pleasant texture and unexpected sweetness of the meat. As he chewed, he couldn't help but begin to savor each bit that slid down his throat. He found himself reaching for more. He sprinkled a pinch of salt on his next bite and even dabbed a little fresh butter on successive morsels. He smiled as he ate. This was the first time in his life he had ever enjoyed a lobster and hoped it wouldn't be his last.

At the conclusion of dinner, Sherman bid everyone goodnight and returned to his room. It was simply furnished with nothing more than a single bed, one upholstered chair, and a bureau with a mirror. There was also a small writing desk and a rickety wooden chair. One oil lamp provided the only source of light in the room. A small window was located on the back wall. Sherman looked out into the darkness and could see the stars and the moonlight shimmer off the rippling waters of the harbor. It was a peaceful sight Sherman wished he could take with him back to Scarborough.

The tired young man eventually pulled himself away from the window and got ready for bed. He used the chamber pot, then covered and pushed it as far from himself as he could. He lay above the covers on his back with his hands tucked behind his head. He was very weary but restless nonetheless. His thoughts were on the store. He wondered if it had been wise to leave Jeff in charge. He wondered if Jeff could handle it, or if he had even tried. As much as he didn't want to think about it, he pondered the idea of Parlin robbing him blind and taking off the second his wagon rolled out of sight for Portland. The idea put a knot in his lobster-gorged stomach.

Next, his mind shifted to Danny Ricker. He wondered if he had caused any more mischief or if his house was safe. Would Jeff be able to protect it? Would he be able to detect any trouble in time? Where was Sheriff Ridgeway? And would he be able to offer the protection Sherman needed? Questions…so many questions and precious few answered plagued his thoughts. Tomorrow would be Tuesday. Maybe Silas would show his face a day earlier than expected. This business was bound to get worse before it got any better. Sherman grimaced at the thought of more trouble. It led him to get up and open his gun case. He handled his new revolver with care. He examined it and practiced the process of loading and then unloading it. For some reason he started to question why he had bought it. He forced himself to put it away and go to bed. Too many hostile thoughts swamped his head and he swiftly deduced that fatigue was impairing his better judgment. He cleared his mind of question and allowed his thoughts to settle on something much more pleasant and soothing. In time he slipped off to sleep with flowery visions of Sophie Curtis happily lingering in his dreams.

CHAPTER 8

Ridgeway's Resurgence

With Portland far behind him and Scarborough in front, Sherman's wagon continued to roll forward at a decent pace. It was now Tuesday, July 1, and it was late in the afternoon. Sherman was happy and somewhat relieved he'd be home soon. His mind feverishly leapt back and forth as a whirlwind of thoughts swirled through his head. He wondered about the state of his store and his house, Jeff Parlin, Danny Ricker, the Morrell boys, the whereabouts of Sheriff Ridgeway, Sophie Curtis, and an assortment of other smaller issues. He'd have some answers very soon as his horses turned onto Settler Road.

It wasn't long before his house and the store were in sight. He parked the wagon next to the ramp and platform in front of the barn, then unlocked the large door and slid it open. He didn't commence to unload the wagon, but rather kept going across the barn and then through the door that led to the sheltered walkway into the house. He had only one item under his arm—his new revolver. Starting with the kitchen he looked through each room to see if it was exactly as he'd left it. When he reached his bedroom he put the revolver case on his nightstand next to the bed. He did the same with the three boxes of bullets in his coat pockets. Nothing in the house seemed disturbed or out of place. Satisfied, he made his way over to the store.

"Ah, the head proprietor of this fine establishment has safely returned," trumpeted a self-assured Jeff Parlin upon witnessing Sherman's entrance into the store. "No worse for the wear I hope?"

"I'm a little dingy and tired. I could use some clean clothes, a nap, and a shave. But besides that I'm in pretty good shape. How's everything here? Did you run into any trouble while I was away? Or more specifically, did any trouble run into you?"

"I'd say things flowed pretty smoothly while you were gone. No trouble to speak of. Nothing happened that I felt I couldn't handle. We did great from a business standpoint. Just take a gander at the sales ledger and feast your eyes on this."

Sherman walked behind the counter and ran his fingers down the pages of the ledger. He was pleasantly surprised to see numerous entries listed in Jeff's hardly legible handwriting. Meticulously recorded were customers' names, what they purchased, and the amount they paid. Jeff showed Sherman the cashbox that was nearly filled with both greenbacks and coins.

"This is great, Jeff," said Sherman with a smile. "Looks like we took in at least enough to partially if not fully cover what I spent on new purchases yesterday. The store looks neat and clean and well stocked. I'm impressed at your abilities to quickly adapt to new surroundings and job duties."

"I've had to in order to survive. When you've moved around as much as I have, you have to learn to adjust to new places rapidly. It ain't easy when you're crippled like me. But like I told you earlier, I'm a 'jack of all trades.' I'm a survivor, too. Nothin' will stop me once I put my mind to something."

"I can see that. That's an honorable quality to be very proud of. Come help me unload the wagon and get everything coordinated before it starts to get dark."

Jeff followed Sherman out to the wagon whereupon both men began unloading and storing the new lot of goods in the barn. Again Sherman was impressed by Jeff's work ethic, demonstrated by his vigor and enthusiasm to go after the heavier and more cumbersome sacks and barrels first. In no time they were finished. Sherman tidied up the paperwork and secured the barn door.

"Hey Jeff, why don't you park the wagon out back and unhitch the horses? Put 'em in the livery and give 'em feed and water. Also, bring out the Morgans and let them wander freely about the pasture for a bit. They probably could use some exercise."

"No need to worry about that, Sherm. I rented both out for a few hours to a nice couple passing through town this morning. They returned 'em about an hour before you got back. They've been well run, fed, watered, and sheltered for the night. I'll just take care of these stallions for ya."

"You're amazing, Jeff. Thank you. Meet me back in the store when you're done."

Sherman walked back to the store and began to do some light inventory work before closing up for the night. He emptied the cashbox and stuffed his billfold and pockets with most of the money. Thirty minutes later Jeff appeared. He was sweaty, tired, and looked as if he'd had enough work for one day.

"Sit down before you fall down, my friend," said Sherman as he pointed Jeff to the nearest stool. "I'm just going to finish up this paperwork and then we'll close up early tonight. We're both pretty tired and I don't expect any more customers. Looks quiet out there. Why don't you go upstairs and get cleaned up? When you're ready...come over to the house and I'll fix us some supper."

For some reason Sherman was still not completely comfortable inviting Jeff into his home. However, he was pleased with his work, he had done an admirable job minding the store, he was sympathetic and willing to help Sherman with his problems, and Parlin really hadn't given him a bona fide reason to distrust him aside from simply not knowing him well or for long. Still, something didn't sit right with Sherman and he couldn't put his finger on it. That's what bothered him the most. Perhaps he had been too guarded of late, and that was impairing his character judgment. Regardless of how he felt, he knew there was much to be discussed between the two and it was better to have a conversation outside of the store and free from working hours. He felt Jeff had earned some trust.

"I should like that very much, Sherm. I'll go make myself a bit more presentable. Excuse me," he said as he made his way up to his room.

A few minutes later Sherman finished his work and went over to the house. He went into the kitchen and cut up several fresh vegetables and berries. He brought in a loaf of bread he had purchased in Portland as well as some smoked pork that he heated up in the freshly lit stove. Soon there was a knock on the front door.

"Do come in," he said upon opening the door and finding Jeff standing there. "Please feel comfortable to look around or simply have a seat in the parlor here. Dinner will be ready in just a moment. I'm going to set the table. Excuse me."

Jeff nodded and wandered into the parlor. He gazed about the room, taking in the surroundings and its contents. He admired the plush furniture and spent long minutes scrutinizing the oil paintings and family portraits that decorated the walls. Next he was drawn to the numerous tintypes of Sherman and his relatives sitting on tabletops and shelves. He quietly picked several up and examined each very closely. He took care to put them back in the exact position he had found them. Next he was lured to the fireplace mantel, specifically the Henry rifle mounted above it. His eyes seductively ran up and down the gun while he imagined what it would feel like to have both arms and be capable of firing shot after shot in rapid succession.

"Now that's power," he uttered. "That's *real* power."

Sherman was busy between setting the table in the dining room and putting the finishing touches on the food he had prepared in the kitchen. Soon everything was in place, and he was about to call out to Jeff when he heard a soft and simple melody begin to flow from the piano in the parlor. The notes were soothing and pleasant to the ear in their simplicity. Sherman was instantly reminded of his past and wasted no time investigating the source of the sweet sound. Though he knew whom it was, for a fragment of a second he hoped to find his mother sitting at the piano bench, happily playing as she had so often done many years ago.

"Do you play?" asked Sherman.

Jeff took his hand off the keys and turned around.

"No," he answered. "I was just fiddling with it. I hope you don't mind."

"Not at all. It sounded quite nice, actually. My mother used to play for us…for my father and me, that is."

"A piano's an instrument for a man with two hands, unfortunately. I doubt I could make a living traveling the world and playing for royalty with just one arm. However, maybe I could be one of P.T. Barnum's freakish circus attractions. I could be the 'Wondrous One-Armed Piano Wonder.' That is, of course, if I knew how to play—which I don't. I ain't exactly a virtuoso. Yes, there's a lot of things I wish I could do if I just had my right arm back," he said, casually glancing back at the Henry.

"I can understand that, Jeff. I think you do pretty good with what you have now, though."

A moment of awkward silence ensued before Sherman said, "Join me in the dining room. Our dinner is ready."

The two men went to the dining room table where they ate heartily. There was little conversation during the meal. When they did speak, the topics revolved around insignificant and superficial matters. When the meal was finished, both men withdrew to the parlor where each sat down in one of the leather chairs facing the fireplace. Sherman produced two cigars and handed one to Jeff. He then reached for the nearby set of glasses and bottle of Old Crow bourbon whiskey that permanently rested on the small table between the chairs. He poured Jeff a drink, then one for himself.

"Thank you," said Jeff. "Would you mind helping with this?" He held up his cigar.

"Not at all," replied Sherman, striking a match to light it after Jeff bit off the end. The tip smoked and glowed after the successful uniting of tobacco and flame. Jeff pulled back and sat comfortably in the chair, puffing away. Sherman took a sip of his whiskey before igniting his own cigar.

"Nothing compares to good southern tobacco," Jeff said. "Anything else is an abomination and an insult to the gentleman smoker."

Jeff's tone was neither discerningly scolding nor complimentary. Sherman couldn't readily determine if his guest was happily content with his cigar or indirectly implying that he loathed it. But Sherman wasn't interested in discussing cigars. Turns out, neither was Jeff Parlin.

"So did you have any luck in Portland? Did you find the sheriff?" asked Jeff.

"No," said Sherman, adding, "His office was empty and all locked up. My guess is that he's traveling, taking care of other official business. With luck we'll see him tomorrow. He owes me money."

"Did you, uh…did you buy any guns?"

"No," lied Sherman directly and without hesitation. "I got cartridges for the Henry but couldn't obtain the pistols I was looking for. My dealer didn't have any in stock. I put one on order though. He'll notify me when it comes in. Meantime we'll just have to settle for the rifle. I don't anticipate using it, nor do I really want to. I'd like to keep it right where it is. The sheriff needs to sort out this business. We shouldn't try to take the law into our own hands. The more I've thought about this, the more I desire a nonviolent solution."

"I don't disagree with you, Sherm, but you might be thinking a bit too optimistically about the situation. It don't hurt to be prepared to defend oneself at all times. We don't know what this Ricker kid is capable of doing. You can be a helluva lot more persuasive in a confrontation with a few rough words and a gun than just a few rough words—that's my experience."

"I don't want to shoot anybody. I don't want to be tried for murder and sentenced to life in jail—or worse, hanged. We're not in uniform anymore and this isn't the frontier. There are stiff penalties for killing a man. I'm not sure I'm prepared to tangle with those particular sorts of serious consequences."

"Having killed a man, I'd say that it's better to take your chances with a judge and jury than the alternative. What good is it if you're dead? You got no chance, and no choice for that matter, when you're the one that's been killed."

"I see your point, Jeff. I'll defend my life and my property; I just don't wish to kill anymore. I saw enough bloodshed in three years of fighting to fill up an entire lifetime."

"Sometimes life just ain't that simple, Sherm. Sometimes killing is all you got if you want to stay alive yourself. Things might be different here in Maine, but where I come from back in Missouri, a man had to be harsh and remorseless if he wanted to remain among the living. There was no law or even lawmen it seemed, only chaos and unthinkable suffering. I learned quickly that being opposite the business end of a gun barrel was often the best way to resolve a quarrel—and I had my share of quarrels, Sherman, and I'm still here."

Sherman was unsure how to respond. He looked at Jeff, who set his cigar down so he could take a swig of his whiskey. Once the glass was drained, he put the cigar back in his mouth and poured himself another shot. A chill seemed to go down his spine as he shuddered for a second or too. Sherman noticed the visible tremble and wondered if Jeff's words had inadvertently dredged up violent and unpleasant memories of his own frightening experiences from the past—war-related or otherwise.

"Never get used to the cold up here," said Jeff. "Ain't like home where the nights are nice and sultry. Whiskey helps take the chill off. Hope you don't mind me taking another shot?"

Sherman was a bit surprised at Parlin's statement. Though the sun had set and the temperature was noticeably cooler and less humid, it was hardly cold or even chilly by Sherman's estimation. In fact, he found himself reaching for a handkerchief to wipe the perspiration from his brow. He didn't believe Missouri to be a tremendously hot state, but he didn't know for certain as he had never traveled there. It made him wonder.

"No, help yourself to all you want," said Sherman in reference to the whiskey. "If you're uncomfortable, I don't mind building a small fire."

"Yes, that would be just fine. A fire would take the chill off."

What chill? Sherman silently asked in his mind as he got up and put some kindling into the fireplace. *It must be seventy-five degrees Fahrenheit outside,* he thought.

Sherman stepped out and returned a minute later with some wood gathered from the barn. With the strike of a match he set the kindling alight and watched the fire slowly build in strength. Parlin was increasingly drawn to it while Sherman sat as far back from it as he could without appearing put off by it. He lit a three-branched candelabrum and placed it on the piano for some additional light, as it was getting late and growing darker outside. The fire grew to a small but steady blaze. Sherman was careful not to load it up with large, heavy pieces of wood.

The two men continued to smoke and drink. Sherman offered some minor details of his trip to Portland and Jeff in return shared select stories of some of the people he'd attended in the store and the items he'd sold them while Sherman was away. Suddenly, and without warning, Sherman leapt out of his chair and raced to the window.

"What is it, Sherm?"

Sherman threw open the window and stuck his head out.

"Silas!" he shouted. "Over here! Come over to the house."

Within a few seconds the muffled sound of a horse's hooves impacting the road in front of the house was heard. Sherman hurried to the front door and opened it wide.

"Tie him up in front of the store, Silas, then please come in here. We have much to discuss."

Ridgeway tended to his horse, then walked back over to the house where Sherman was still waiting in the doorway.

"Christ Almighty, Sherman. I got your ten dollars right here. You don't need to accost me for it. You should be happy I'm here a day early with it," said Silas.

"Never mind that. Just come inside if you will. I need to talk to you about another more urgent matter."

"Fine by me, but I can't stay long."

Sherman led the sheriff into the parlor. Jeff rose out of his seat as the two men came into view.

"Silas, may I introduce Jeffrey Parlin. He's my new assistant at the store. Jeff, this is Sheriff Silas Ridgeway."

The two men greeted each other and shook hands. Sherman poured the sheriff a drink and said, "Please have a seat." Jeff sat back down too while Sherman stood in front of the fire facing them like an actor about to put on a performance.

"You look pretty tense, Sherman. What's this all about? Have you decided to raise the price on that Spencer you sold me?" asked Silas.

"No. I've got a problem that I need your help with."

"Oh, what's that?"

"Silas, before I get into it, do you mind if I ask you about the problems you were investigating in Gorham? You told me last week that there had been some trouble out there—some thefts?"

"Yeah," replied Silas. "Some barns were broken into and some livestock was stolen. Found a pig's head not far from the farm where he was reported stolen. God awful mess, I tell ya."

"Did you discover who the perpetrator was? Were any arrests made?"

"No, unfortunately. There were no eyewitnesses. I'm not even absolutely sure it was a man. It's possible that a bear or other wild animal might be the culprit. It's remote, but I have to entertain all possibilities."

"Are you going back out there? Are there other leads you're following? How are you planning to deal with this problem?" anxiously asked Sherman.

"There's not much I can do at the moment, Sherman," replied Silas. "I've interviewed as many people as I could find who knew about the crimes and I've documented everything I could. Apart from that, there's not much else I can do. I can't endlessly patrol the area in blind hopes of catching who or what it is in the act. I was planning on riding back to Portland tonight, but it's too late for that now. I'll probably just ride back to Gorham and spend the night there. Maybe I can find out something more in the morning. Why are you so interested, Sherman? Are you afraid you might fall victim to similar circumstances?"

Sherman sighed and dipped his head. He leaned against the mantel and summoned up the courage to finally reveal his problem to the sheriff.

"I'm afraid I might have already fallen victim, Silas. I think I know who may be committing these crimes. I can't speak with certainty about what's happened out in Gorham, but I can say that some similar occurrences have just recently transpired here in Scarborough."

"Exactly what's happened here, Sherman?" Silas asked gravely.

"Last week after you left the store, I fired Danny Ricker. Aside from being lazy and neglectful of his duties, I discovered that he had been stealing from me for quite a long period of time. We got into a confrontation that turned into a physical altercation. He pulled a pocketknife on me. We struggled and I managed to ward him off. He ran away, but not before verbally threatening me with harm. The next day I discovered a Bowie knife and revolver had been taken from my store's display case. I went upstairs and saw that a window was open and a ladder was on the ground outside. I'm quite sure it was Danny who used it to steal from me yet again. Now's he armed, dangerous, and not of sound mind, in my estimation."

"Is that all, or is there more?" asked Silas.

"I'm afraid there *is* more. The other night I was attacked while walking to the store. The assailant knocked me down and held a blade to my throat. He then threatened me in much the same manner as Danny had during our last untimely meeting."

"Was it in fact Ricker who attacked you?" Silas asked.

"I didn't see who it was and he whispered when he spoke. I couldn't recognize his voice. I was a bit dazed as you can imagine, but I know it was him. It had to be."

"You *know* it was him?"

"Why, yes, Silas. Who else could it have been after all that's transpired?"

"I don't know, Sherman. What I do know is that there's a big difference between *knowing* somebody committed a crime and *seeing* somebody commit a crime. Do you understand me? You didn't actually *see* Danny Ricker assault you so you can't say with complete confidence that it was him. Correct?"

"I suppose…."

"Look, I'm not saying it wasn't him," interrupted Silas, "but you have to be objective and focus on the facts. I believe in all likelihood that it was him based on what you've told me, but we can't just assume it. We need hard evidence. Is that all? Have you told me everything?"

"There's just one more thing. I spoke with Hiram Lovell the other day. You'll want to speak with him too. One of his cows was found mutilated. He was looking for you so he could report it. In my humble view, Silas, I submit that Danny Ricker is responsible for all the recent thefts, wrongdoings, and animal butchery suffered by select citizens of Gorham and Scarborough. That of course includes myself."

"You sound a bit like a prosecuting attorney, Sherman. Maybe you missed your true calling in life," said Silas with a snicker. "I'll talk to Hiram tomorrow. Maybe it's best I stick around here until we can locate Danny for questioning. If it is in fact him that's causing all this mischief, I wonder why he's not going after you and your property exclusively? If he's enraged with you for firing him, why go to the trouble of lashing out at others, I wonder?"

"He's deranged, Silas. He belongs in a sanitarium. Perhaps he feels that if he hurts others it will wound me even more—wound me and cripple my business, possibly? He called you a son of a bitch and spoke disparagingly of this community. I don't think he cares who he hurts or even why. I do think he'll come back for me, though. I think he'll try to rob me and perhaps even kill me. He's disgruntled. I had a knife and gun stolen from me in a way that fits Danny's knowledge of the store and his type of behavior. I was assaulted, threatened, and several other people in the area have had their property butchered or stolen. It all fits, Silas—it all makes sense."

"I see your point, Sherman, but let's not start accusing anybody just yet. I think it's best to keep this entire matter quiet for now. Don't mention your quarrel with Ricker to anyone. People could start blaming you for all that's happened thus far. Folks could say you're the one responsible for unleashing this wave of violence and misfortune; and then they'd come after you with pitchforks and a hanging noose just as quickly as Danny Ricker. Let me start a new investigation, which will give me time to try to locate our prime suspect. I'll try to linger around your place undetected in the evenings. If he comes around here, it'll most likely be at night. We stand a better chance at catching him then. I'll keep a low profile so as not to scare him off. You got any protection of your own?"

"Just that Henry," said Sherman as his eyes looked to the mantel.

"Keep it handy. I don't want you to have to use it, but I won't discourage it if you feel your life's in danger. I'll back you with all the powers at my disposal should you have to explain to a judge why you killed a man. Fair enough?"

"Sounds good to me, Sheriff."

"You," said Silas as he rose to his feet and looked at Parlin. "You been awful quiet. Is there anything you want to contribute to this conversation?"

"Only that I understand all that's been discussed and am willing to help out my friend in any way I can," replied Parlin.

"What I've said to Sherman applies to you as well, Mister. Keep quiet about this business until you hear back from me. Don't go flapping your jaws to anyone. I don't want people to panic. That's the last thing we need."

"It won't be a problem, Sheriff," said Jeff.

"Good. Sherman, I'll be in touch. Oh, here's your weekly payment for the Spencer."

Silas doled out ten dollars in gold coins and handed them over to Sherman.

"Thank you, Sheriff. I hope you don't have to break in that Spencer anytime soon."

"Yeah. Me either. Good evening to you gentlemen. I have a friend who can put me up for the night in Gorham. Don't want to keep her waiting. I'll be nearby in the morning if you need me."

Sherman escorted Silas to the door and let him out. The sheriff mounted his horse and rode off into the night in the direction of South Gorham.

"Now there goes a man with a purpose," said Jeff as he joined Sherman in the doorway. "Guess he's pretty anxious for a clean bed to gallop off at such a speed in the dark. Must know exactly where he's going and exactly how to get there to risk breaking his neck in a fall at night."

"Yeah, he knows where he's going. He's been there many times before…only his wife and kids don't know about it."

"How's that?" asked Jeff.

"Silas occasionally has illicit relations with a young woman in Gorham. I met her once a year or two ago. She's quite attractive and lives alone. She spoke to me like they had been married for years. Silas denies seeing her but he ain't real good at keeping secrets, and he loves to brag about his sexual conquests, especially when he's drunk."

"You said he's married, though."

"Yeah, he's married, but that never stopped him from straying. His poor wife is back in Portland with the kids—two girls—and they don't ever see him much. He prefers the freedom and thrill his job affords him. He doesn't like to be tied down. He craves adventure and the company of loose women. That's probably why he's hardly ever in his office."

"Sounds like a typical rotten Yankee scoundrel to me," said Jeff.

"Well, he's no angel, I'll admit that, but he does his job very well and we need his help."

"He doesn't set a very decent or moral example for a lawman does he?"

"Like I said, he does his job."

"I suppose he does. Let's hope he can provide a solution to our problem," said Jeff, unconvinced.

The chimes in the longcase clock rang out, signaling that it was now ten o'clock.

"Gettin' late. I suppose I should lock up the store and think about going to bed. I assume we have a lot of work to do tomorrow?"

"Yes, I need to make another list. If you're awake and out and about early in the morning, you can take care of the animals before opening the store. Be sure to lock up tight. Hopefully we won't have any problems now that the sheriff is around," said Sherman.

"Will do. I'll see you in the morning. Thanks for the cigar and whiskey."

"Good night, Jeff."

Parlin exited the house and began walking back to the store with a single candle to light the way. Halfway there he stopped. He looked at the store first, then gazed back at Sherman's house, and then slowly directed his stare toward the livery. A full minute elapsed before he resumed his course back to the store. Once inside, he locked the door and crept up to his bedroom.

┽┼┼

The sun rose slowly the next morning as its rays of light gently fanned out through Sherman's bedroom window. It was now Wednesday, July 2. Sherman dressed quickly and made his way over to the store without eating breakfast. He was again happily surprised to see Jeff was already awake and had everything in order and ready for business.

"No trouble?" asked Sherman.

"None."

"Good, let's open up for business."

The store was busy throughout the morning as several customers made purchases in preparation for the fast-approaching holiday. As noontime drew near, Sherman's thoughts drifted from work to a more inspiring and pleasurable idea. He gathered up some food and placed it in a basket. He took off his apron and tidied himself up before telling Jeff, "I'm going out for lunch. I trust you to keep things under control here until I return. Help yourself to some lunch of your own when you have time. Just record what you take."

"Certainly. You can count on me. I'll see you when you get back," said Jeff.

Sherman made a direct line for the Budwin schoolhouse. Upon arrival he peeked in one of the windows. Inside he saw Sophie comfortably seated on a chair facing two lonely students at their desks. She was reading from a book while her pupils—Hiram Lovell's children—listened and took notes. A moment passed before Sophie noticed Sherman at the window. She smiled instantly at the sight of him and quickly finished up what she was reading. She waved for him to enter the classroom.

"Alexander, Josephine, why don't we break for lunch and a short recess. Go out and stretch your legs as you enjoy your lunch, but please stay close by. I'll expect you to return promptly when I ring my bell. Understood?"

"Yes, Miss Curtis," the children answered in unison.

"Good. Now, off you go."

The kids got up and raced outside.

"They seem quite spirited. I would say that they must be overflowing with knowledge and positive energy that could only be imparted by a teacher with such extraordinary skills. How are you this fine day, Miss Curtis?"

"Very well, indeed, Mr. Jackson. It's a lovely surprise to see you before our Friday engagement."

"I couldn't wait for Friday. I wanted to see you today. I hope it's not inconvenient?"

"Not at all. Your timing was perfect, actually."

"I brought us some lunch. Would you like to join me under a nice shady tree and partake in some food and conversation?"

"That sounds lovely. Please lead the way." Sophie beamed a beautiful smile that melted Sherman's heart.

The young woman took his arm and Sherman escorted her outside to the nearest tree with ample shade. The two sat down and lunched on fresh fruits and vegetables, bread, and thin-sliced smoked ham. Sherman had also brought a bottle of wine that Sophie politely refused, not wanting the smell of alcohol on her breath while teaching.

"Are the Lovell children your only students?" asked Sherman.

"Not officially," replied Sophie. "The Morrell children are supposed to be in my class as well, but I've had a hard time getting them to school. They have disappeared each morning after leaving the house and have not been seen again until it's time for supper. I've not informed the pastor or his wife of their truancy yet. I want to give them another chance since school just started. I'm afraid their parents are blissfully unaware of the boys' whereabouts most of the day. I fear they may find mischievous activities more appealing than worshiping in church or learning in school. If their malingering continues, however, I will be forced to confront them in the presence of their parents. I can't set a good example for others if I come across as tolerant of poor attendance in the classroom."

"I agree completely, Sophie. Olin and Wilbur are both a bit misguided and lack discipline from their parents, whom I fear are too lenient with the kids' upbringing. They will be a handful, but I'm sure that they can be properly controlled and taught respect. I have no doubt a woman of your drive and educational integrity will prevail in steering them onto the right path."

"That's sweet of you to say, Sherman. I hope you're right."

"I know I am. How are Alexander and Josephine doing?"

"They're model students. They're well behaved and very motivated to learn. I couldn't ask for better pupils. Today I was reading Shakespeare, which they really seem to enjoy. Overall it's been a good first few days of school. My only regret is that I don't have a larger class, and one with younger kids. I was very much hoping to teach to smaller children. I had a nice curriculum all planned out for little ones. Those two young children from South Gorham I told you about, Patricia and Andrew, never showed up."

"Well, perhaps you'll get some other late arrivals to your class. It's still early and it's possible some families didn't get the word that school is open here in North Scarborough."

"You could be right, Sherman. Maybe I need to be a bit more patient."

Sophie smiled again and looked deep into Sherman's eyes. He was undeniably taken with her. Her very essence was intoxicating in the warmest and most desirable manner a woman could possess. Sherman was attracted to her wholesome external loveliness—she was unquestionably an extremely pretty young woman—but he found himself engrossed by every word that she spoke. He felt as if he could talk with her for hours and never become bored or disinterested in anything she said. Her company was so soothing and enjoyable that Sherman found himself reluctant even to consider that their little picnic would eventually have to end.

They talked, laughed, and got to know each other better until Sophie realized she must ring the bell and return to her classroom. Sherman helped the young beauty to her feet. He escorted her back to the school where she loudly rang her brass wooden-handled hand bell and called out to the Lovell kids to return.

Before Sherman bid his friend farewell he said, "Sophie, if you trust me, I'd love to see you again this evening and take you on a little mischievous, yet harmless adventure. It requires a bit of cunning and dash and perhaps a little trickery on your part, but it truly is harmless and is something I think you'll enjoy. Whaddya say? Do you trust me?"

Sophie hesitated before answering. As a young lady and a teacher, she knew it was best to avoid situations that might put her in a bad or embarrassing light with the community. All her instincts told her to politely refuse Sherman's offer. Yet she didn't. She too was smitten by his charm and handsome face. She sensed honesty and a decency within him that was very appealing to her. She did trust him and longed to spend more time with him. She felt curiously excited and physically aroused when he was near. She wondered if he felt the same way. Her attraction to him was growing like a fire out of control and suddenly she felt perfectly at ease in saying, "Yes, I trust you, Sherman, and I want to see you tonight. Let's be daring and mischievous like a couple of little imps. What does your adventure entail?"

"I want to surprise you, my dear. All you need to do is sneak out of the pastor's house just before midnight tonight. I'll fetch you on my horse and we'll go for a short ride to our destination. I promise that neither our journey nor our goal will be dangerous or break any laws. It will, however, be daring and a bit naughty. Most importantly, it will be enjoyable. You have my word on that. Are you game, Sophie?"

"I'm game," she replied with a smile and an excited little giggle.

"Marvelous! I'll be waiting for you tonight."

Sherman took her by both hands and pulled her close. He moved in slowly to kiss her but abruptly stopped at the sound of running feet fast approaching the school. A second later the Lovell kids ran into view and hurried by the young couple as they raced to their seats. Sherman and Sophie laughed, then said goodbye. Their romance had to wait as she temporarily returned to being a teacher while he had to resume his duties as a storeowner. Both looked forward to their nighttime escapade.

Sherman got back to the store where he found Jeff neatly stacking canned goods.

"It takes immeasurable skill to do this right with just one arm," said Jeff proudly.

Sherman put his apron back on and replied, "I imagine it takes immeasurable skill to do just about anything with one arm. I commend you, sir. You've managed to get along with your 'hindrance' remarkably well."

"Why, thank you, sir. You seem to be in quite the good mood now," said Jeff, noticing Sherman's broad smile and extra zip in his step. "I assume you had more than just a tasty lunch?"

"I did indeed. I had the pleasure of enjoying my midday meal with the lovely Sophie Curtis. Help yourself to whatever's left in the picnic basket. I think there's still some untouched food in there," said Sherman.

"She's that girl from church, right?"

"Yes, the very one."

"I'd steer clear of her, Sherman," said Jeff directly.

"Why is that?"

"Because I think she's got her sights on other men and I don't believe she's as pure as she would have you believe."

"And just what do you base these accusations on?" asked Sherman in a slightly agitated tone. "You've only met her once."

"No, she came in the store while you were in Portland. She was quite chatty and flirtatious with me. She said I reminded her of many other dashing young men she had spent time with in Boston. She even went so far as to ask me to meet up with her some evening and have a drink. I was certainly intrigued and flattered; she is a beautiful young woman. However, I restrained myself and suggested we first get to know one another a bit better in a more respectable manner. I thought it best if we took a stroll down by the stream or maybe went for a horseback ride together on a sunny day. She seemed quite agreeable, yet I couldn't help but notice a bit of deviousness in her, like she had many secrets just waiting to be exposed—among other things."

"That's quite enough, Mr. Parlin! I won't have you speak about Miss Curtis in such a disreputable manner regardless of what she may or may not have told you! I don't appreciate such slanderous talk in my store!"

"My apologies, Mr. Jackson," said Parlin with a peculiar cadence that instantly piqued Sherman's attention. "I meant no disrespect. However, as your friend I believe it's my duty to inform and protect you from those who might do you harm either physically or emotionally. You're too good for her, in my opinion. I, on the other hand, just might be what she needs."

"Jeff, I need you to tend to the garden and bring in some fresh vegetables. When you're done with that, please inventory what we're running low on in the supply room and replenish it with fresh provisions from the barn. Then come back and see me. On your way, please, sir."

"Right away, Sherm." Jeff strolled out the front door with a basket in his hand.

Sherman was infuriated and tried everything in his power to remain calm. For the first time, he felt genuine rage toward the man who had just recently entered his life. Despite all the good things he had done and the trust he had earned, this assassination of Sophie's character was inexcusable. Furthermore, his apparent interest in her, notwithstanding all he claimed was at fault with her personality, was all the more puzzling. Sherman didn't know what bothered him more; the fact that Parlin had a romantic interest in Sophie, or the fact that what he said about her might actually be true. Just then the front door swung open.

"Silas," said the surprised storekeeper.

"Afternoon, Sherman. I thought I'd stop by and check in on you."

"I appreciate that. Did you find out anything useful today?"

"A few things. Do you have any water? I'm parched."

"Yeah, over there in the barrel. Help yourself to a dipperful."

"Much obliged," said Silas. He scooped out some water and drank it down in long swallows. "Ah, that's good. I needed that."

"What did you find out?"

"I went and saw Hiram this morning. He told me about what had happened. Unfortunately, it's happened again. He lost another cow. Found her all cut up about a half-mile from his dairy. He's fuming mad and bent on finding out who did it. It was all I could do to stop him from going out and taking the law into his own hands."

"Inconceivable," Sherman uttered. "Anything else?"

"Yes, the widow McClatchy seems to be very ill. I visited her too. She's white as a sheet. She kept mumbling on about how odd her water tastes, and…."

"And what?" asked Sherman.

"Well, she must be touched with some form of illness that's causing her to perceive unnatural things, I reckon. She kept going on about seeing some horrible ghostly figure on horseback galloping through the countryside, shrieking out a bloodcurdling yell and brandishing a torch. Says she's seen him more than once and only at night. She's convinced he's real and is terrified to leave her home. After what I saw today, I doubt she has the strength."

"Has anyone summoned a doctor to help her?"

"I'm going to ride out to Oak Hill when I leave here. There's a doctor I know there who'll come out and examine her. I doubt there's much he'll be able to do, though. I think the widow is just a victim of her own agedness. Her old mind is frail and playing tricks on her. Nothin'll cure that."

"Perhaps not. It's so strange. I saw her last Sunday and she seemed fine. Hiram told me that he overheard her complaining about her water, but other than that, she appeared to be her old self. Perhaps her well is contaminated with some unnatural substance that is causing her malady, thus forcing her to imagine this unholy vision of a ghost rider?"

"Could be, Sherman. I ain't a doctor, but if I had to offer a diagnosis, I'd say she was just plum loony. They get that way when they get old."

"Maybe, but you'll get the doctor out here right away won't you, Silas?"

"As soon as I leave, Sherman."

"Did you find out anything about Danny Ricker and his whereabouts?"

"Nobody's seen him for at least a week. You fired him the day I came in asking about the rifle, correct?"

"Yeah, that was a week ago today," recalled Sherman. "Anything else? Any other disturbances reported?"

"Well, the widow's vegetable garden looked pretty heavily pilfered. And now that you ask, I spoke with Erin Morrell, who was quite distraught about someone or something that had apparently trampled all the geraniums she had recently planted in front of the church. How about you, Sherman? Have you experienced any more trouble since the night you were knocked down? Has your property been vandalized in any way since then?"

"No, thank God. Everything's in order."

"Your friend helps you look after the place, I assume?"

"Yes, Mr. Parlin has dutifully volunteered to assist in helping me look after my property and my own neck. In return I provide him with food and a place to stay free of charge. Very soon I'm going to reward him further by offering him a steady wage here at the store."

"Sounds like a good arrangement. I hope he hasn't been any trouble to you?"

"On the contrary, he's been an excellent addition and a stellar replacement for Danny Ricker. He does more with just one arm than Danny ever did with two."

"Good to hear. I'll be around more often to check on you, Sherman. I'm gonna stay in the area until I start to get some answers or find Ricker for questioning."

"Not going back to Portland?"

"No, it's better if I keep a high-profile presence around here. It might calm things down, too. I think people are starting to get antsy. I can feel it."

"Where are you gonna stay?"

Silas paused, then answered, "My friend in Gorham will provide accommodations for me as needed."

Not being able to resist, Sherman asked, "How's the wife and kids, Silas? They must miss you something fierce when you're away for so long."

"Rose understands the sacrifices a man must make in my line of work. She supports my decisions…and me. My job requirements are not an issue of contention between us."

"I see. Well, good to hear. Be sure and tell Rose and the girls I said hello the next time you see them."

"Will do. I'm headed for Oak Hill now. Take care of yourself and let me know if anything out of the ordinary happens. Remember, keep quiet about Ricker. This is a delicate situation, as I see it, and I don't want people shooting off sparks around a powder keg. Understand?"

"No problem, Silas. I understand completely. I'd like this business to end with a fizzle and not an explosion."

"Good. I'll be in touch."

Sherman watched as Silas mounted his horse and rode off. He was relieved that the sheriff was informed and on top of matters, but deep down he wondered if he'd be able to stop Danny Ricker before something truly disastrous or even deadly occurred. His thoughts shifted back to Sophie. Unpleasant questions piled up in his head and he wondered if the night's planned rendezvous would be the *start* of something wonderful or simply the *end*.

CHAPTER 9

Independence Day

Sherman's eyes snapped open in a sea of darkness. He panicked for a brief moment as he groped for his bedside candle and a match. A sigh of relief burst from his body upon lighting the taper and clicking open his gold pocket watch. It was only eleven o'clock. Thank God he hadn't overslept. Regardless, there was no time to lose. He dressed hurriedly in his brown suit, having already washed and shaved before going to bed. He crept down the stairs quietly as if his house were filled with sleeping guests or imaginary family members whom he wished not to disturb. Once outside, he was happy the skies were clear and filled with shimmering stars and bright moonlight that would enable him to navigate more easily through the darkness of the night.

On his way to the livery he glanced up toward Parlin's window. It was completely dark and he assumed Jeff was sound asleep. Inside the stable, Sherman lit an oil lamp and dialed back the wick so it burned low and gave off just enough light to see. He turned to face his horses and was shocked at what he saw. His primary riding horse, Skipper, was gone! Budley was in his proper place, as were his stallions Phineas and Lucky, but Skipper was nowhere to be seen. There was no sign that he had broken loose, and his saddle and bridle were also gone.

"That son of a bitch Ricker," said Sherman. "He finally got to me and grabbed one of my horses." A dozen thoughts raced through Sherman's mind. He was inclined to saddle up and go looking for his stolen horse with grit, determination, and his Henry rifle. He thought about riding off to find the sheriff, and he even contemplated waking Jeff so the two of them could hunt together. But it was late, and despite the moonlight, it would be very difficult at night to find a horse and rider who had a head start, and with no idea in which direction to search. The risk was too great, and Sherman thought better of racing out blindly unprepared into a potentially deadly situation. He came to realize that there was very little that could be done until dawn. As much as he wanted to act, and as distracted as his mind was, he decided to focus on the task at hand. His thoughts settled back on Sophie, who would be waiting for him alone in the dark. As eager as he was to see her and fulfill his surprise, his thoughts toward her were tarnished by what Jeff had told him earlier. Whether completely true or pure fantasy, the simple fact that Parlin had obvious designs on Sophie left a bitter taste in Sherman's mouth. He put all the unpleasantness, uncertainty, and danger out of his mind as he saddled up Budley and snuffed out the light.

"Git up," he commanded. In an instant he was out of the livery and trotting slowly down the moonlit road that led to the Morrell farm. The night was eerily quiet and Sherman found himself constantly checking behind himself to see if he was being observed or followed. All looked clear, but he couldn't shake the unmistakable feeling of being watched. At one point he stopped entirely and listened hard for evidence of a pursuing presence; again he detected nothing. He spurred Budley on, causing the horse to trot at a quicker pace. Navigating at night was a challenge, but soon Sherman found himself nearing his destination.

As he approached the pastor's house he noticed a speck of light on the front porch. The light grew in intensity and appeared to rise up and float in the air the closer he got to it. He pulled the reins tight and brought Budley to a halt. Standing on the porch holding a small candlestick was Sophie. Sherman could see her smile in the dim light. She wore a little blue dress and matching bonnet.

"My goodness. Am I glad to see you," Sophie whispered as Sherman helped her up onto the horse. "I was quite nervous I'd be discovered. Everyone's asleep, but I feared one of the boys might wake and find me out here after raiding the kitchen for a late-night snack. I'm also a little frightened of the dark. My courage was waning fast until you arrived."

"You're safe now, my dear. Let us be off for a little nighttime fun. Git up, Budley."

Sophie held on to Sherman tight as the two trotted off. He felt a rush of happiness and excitement as she snuggled up to him. For a moment all his worries thawed away. The two said little to each other during the journey, but when they reached their endpoint, the conversation picked up.

"The grange hall? Is this our destination this evening?" asked Sophie.

"Yes it is," grinned Sherman. "Once inside I think you'll see why I brought you here tonight."

Sherman tied Budley securely to a tree out of sight and motioned for Sophie to walk up to the front door. As she did, he went around to the side and stepped on a large tree stump that gave him access to an unlocked window. He climbed inside. Sophie waited patiently, unaware of where Sherman was or what he was doing. She turned around and quietly called out his name, thinking he was still outside. Suddenly the front door eased open. Sophie turned around to see Sherman standing in the doorway bathed in a soft glow of light emanating from inside. A look of surprise crept across her face, followed by a broad smile that was more illuminating than the numerous burning candles Sherman had lit throughout the room. She stepped inside while he closed the door behind her. The windows were shuttered so as not to let any light escape and attract unwanted attention. The two stood side by side and gazed upon the room in private splendor.

"Do the McPhees know we're here?" asked Sophie.

"No. There's no fun or thrill in having permission. I heard they finished decorating this afternoon and I thought that a special someone like you ought to be the first to see the fruits of their patriotic labors," beamed Sherman.

"What a thoughtful notion. It's beautiful!"

"And that's not all, my dear. After we're done monopolizing all the romantic majesty this floor has to offer, we'll then continue our tour and explore the upstairs where an even bigger surprise awaits."

"I can hardly wait!"

Sherman and Sophie strolled arm in arm throughout the immaculately decorated first floor of the Old Liberty Grange Hall. The grand ballroom was filled with an impressive array of fragrant native wildflowers expertly cut and arranged in artistic vases set upon linen-covered tabletops and shelves decorated with red, white, and blue bunting. Colorful paper streamers hung from the ceiling and the walls to create a stunning interlaced web of patriotic artistry. American flags of all shapes, sizes, and styles from throughout the young country's history were unfurled and prominently draped over furniture or protruding from the walls on makeshift flagpoles. Elaborate oil paintings of influential American leaders of the past, such as Washington, Jefferson, Madison, and of course Lincoln, were hung on display around a central portrait of President Ulysses S. Grant. An impressive white banner filled with inspiring words and phrases of freedom, independence, and heroic sacrifice in the name of American liberty stretched from wall to wall. Chairs were set up in rows flanking the dance floor while the stage at the head of the room was set for a string quartet. A long buffet table neatly stacked with dishes, glasses, and silverware was ready to accommodate a hungry crowd of people. All seemed ready and in place for the Independence Day celebration.

"It's such an inspiring and impressive display of work," said Sophie. "It all looks so beautiful in the soft candlelight. What a patriotically romantic picture. A talented artist would be challenged to capture its essence on canvas."

"I would agree," replied Sherman. "But we're not done yet. Please join me upstairs. I think you'll enjoy what we find up there just as much as what we've seen down here."

"Lead the way," she said enthusiastically.

The two carefully made their way upstairs through the darkness. Once inside the room, Sherman used a burning candle to light additional candles he had set up earlier. Slowly, the room took on the same magical glow as the ballroom downstairs. Sophie put her hand over her mouth and looked on in amazement as Sherman smiled and motioned with outstretched arms at the various displays surrounding them.

"I've never seen this astonishing collection before," said Sophie. "I've never been up here. Regrettably, I've only seen the downstairs once and it didn't look half as impressive as it does now. What is this room? A museum of sorts?"

"Yes," responded Sherman. "The McPhees are dedicated to honoring and remembering those who have sacrificed so much in the creation and preservation of our great country. It started with a personal display of artifacts, letters, and other objects relating to their son Charles, who was lost during the war. The personal tribute grew into an all-encompassing acknowledgment of the soldiers and civilians who fought and suffered to make this country what it is today. The collection of items has expanded over the years, turning this part of the grange into a magnificent place of tribute, remembrance, and honor to so many who've lost so much. I've been here before, but never have I seen such a stunning display of personal effects, war-related artifacts, and documented research. The McPhees have turned into very talented historians and their work should be praised by all fortunate enough to see it."

"What a remarkable accomplishment and a wonderful gift to the community. The scars of war don't heal easily, but we must never forget those who paid the ultimate price for our freedom and the freedom of those forced here in chains."

"Do you come from an abolitionist family?" asked Sherman.

"Yes," she answered. "My parents were staunch abolitionists who fought to keep northern Negroes free and help unchain those enslaved in the South. They were huge supporters of Lincoln's 13th Amendment and were overjoyed when it passed through the House of Representatives in 1865."

"I remember hearing the news in the field. Many soldiers cheered, applauded, and danced about like they were drunk. It was a historic day, I remember. Unfortunately, I wasn't feeling very well and spent most of it in my tent. I had a stomach ailment of sorts that didn't allow me to stand without great pain. I got over it quickly though, thank goodness. Shall we take a few moments and look over these fine exhibits? There are artifacts and personal information here that dates all the way back to the revolutionary days when our country was fledgling and struggling for survival before it was even given a proper chance to flourish."

"Indeed, I should be very anxious to read and fully grasp some of this remarkable information," said Sophie eagerly.

The two meandered around the room together, arm in arm like an old married couple. The room was decorated similarly to the downstairs and both took care not to disturb or accidentally damage anything. There was a lot to read and study. Old uniforms adorned with colorful medals, grainy pictures of soldiers in the field, letters written home, small arms and field equipment of all sorts, musical instruments, and personal items that seemed curiously out of place until examined closely with an imaginative mind.

Sophie took special interest in the focal point of the collection, which was the display about Charles McPhee. She read about his tour of duty with the 4th Maine Volunteer Infantry Regiment and closely examined several posed tintypes taken of him in uniform. He was an impressive-looking young man of average height and build with dark hair and a moustache. His expression in the photographs portrayed a very serious and attentive disposition, yet Sophie wondered if a more merry and lighthearted young man was hidden beneath the dark uniform he wore. She was sure there was.

"Is there any information about the regiment you fought with, Sherman?"

"Actually there's surprisingly little about the 20th Maine outside of the exploits of our commander, Joshua Chamberlain," answered Sherman. "There's some written information over here about his command at Gettysburg and being present at Appomattox during the surrender, but not much else."

"Why is that?" asked Sophie curiously.

"I'm not sure. I guess the McPhees haven't had much contact with veterans of the 20th."

"Why don't you contribute your recollections? I'm sure they'd love to add your oral history and war-related tangibles to this magnificent collection."

"Actually, Reba McPhee asked me about that very topic last week."

"Wonderful! Are you going to make a contribution and add to the distinction of your old regiment?"

Sherman didn't answer right way. Sophie sensed that the question might have been a bit indelicate.

"It's difficult thinking back to those days," confessed Sherman. "Most of the time I just want to forget about that ugly chapter of my life. I saw so much death and destruction that it's hard to recall the bravery and heroic triumphs of my fellow soldiers in battle. I want to contribute to a very noble and worthy memorial such as this, I really do, but it's hard for me. I have mixed feelings I can't readily explain. I see a glorious room such as this and it fills me with pride and honor to know I was a direct part of the effort that saved this country from being ripped apart at the seams. But another part of me is filled with grief and despair when I see the various regimental flags, the empty uniforms, the marching drums, the tintypes, and the neatly stacked weapons all quietly displayed and missing the most integral part—the soldiers who used them. I wonder where those men are now…and I know deep in my heart that most of them are gone—forever."

Sherman's head dipped as his mind began to fill with despairingly weighted thoughts of soldiers and friends long since perished in the cruelty of war. Sophie, sensing his anguish, turned to him and placed her delicate hand on his cheek. Her soothing touch provided relief to his aching heart that thumped anew with explosive vigor and passionate vitality. She turned to him and removed her bonnet, letting it drop to the floor, liberating her strawberry-blonde curls hitherto imprisoned beneath. Her beautiful hair now draped sweetly over her shoulders in a sumptuously alluring fashion. Their eyes locked as the two drew closer. Together they felt a smoldering passion growing inside that threatened to erupt into an uncontrollable fiery blaze that would utterly consume them both. They lustfully embraced it, and neither tried to fight it.

"Touch me," said Sophie. "I want you to touch me."

She spoke with a confidence and determination that sharply contrasted with every shred of suitable feminine etiquette, social decorum, and religious upbringing she had been boundlessly indoctrinated with since she was a little girl. Sherman, with a twinge of nervousness coursing up and down his spine, was astounded at Sophie's sexual aggressiveness. She took his hands and seductively placed them on her breasts. As they leaned in to kiss, he could tell she was a woman who knew what she wanted and had no fear of going after it. That thought reiterated itself the harder they kissed and caressed one another. Suppressed feelings of passion and desire that had been locked away and buried deep within Sherman's soul slowly began to break free. His heart pounded relentlessly as a rush of impassioned, adrenaline-fueled energy surged through every artery in his body. He felt as if he had the strength of ten men and the sexual drive of a mighty bull. He couldn't ever remember feeling so virile and electrified in all his life. The strange part was that deep down, he knew his charged feelings weren't an exclusive result of simple lust. Even though they had known each other for just a short time, Sherman felt something much deeper and more meaningful. He hoped Sophie felt the same way. His fears were quickly put to rest with three simple words.

"I love you," she said with unmistakable honesty and a sincerity Sherman had never heard before from a woman. It was the sweetest, truest, most heartfelt sentiment ever conveyed to him. He felt exactly the same way and didn't hesitate to express it.

"I love you, too," he said confidently as he swept Sophie off the floor and into his arms. "Come, let's leave this room of honor and remembrance and go downstairs into more festive surroundings."

"What a wonderful idea," she replied softly before kissing him again.

Sherman carried his new love delicately down the stairs and placed her gingerly on the dance floor. Ignoring every social principle she knew, the lovely young woman playfully stretched out on the floor and watched Sherman with a yearning eye and a seductive posture. Wanting to provide a bit of comfort, he walked over to a narrow closet door, which he had seen Reba McPhee open many times in the past. Inside were several garments, but more importantly, there was a large folded quilt in the pattern of various American flags that Reba had stitched together. It was a lovely patriotic piece, but Sherman was more interested in its softness than anything else. He snatched it up and was happily surprised to find two rectangular-shaped pillows of the same design underneath it. He grabbed those as well and turned back toward Sophie.

Her shoes were already off and strewn across the floor while her dress was noticeably looser as she lay there waiting for him. He neatly spread out the quilt and pillows, making an impromptu little bed. For a moment, he stood over Sophie, who rose up and faced him. Feeling the need to express some form of chivalry, Sherman said, "I didn't plan this. It wasn't my intention to bring you here and…."

"Shhh," said Sophie. "I know. It's okay. I want this and I want you."

As soon as the last word exited her mouth, her undone dress slipped off and fell to the floor, revealing her long silken undergarments and a tight corset.

"Can you help me with this?" she asked while slowly turning around.

Sherman reached up and began undoing the corset laces until the rigid garment released Sophie's torso from its taut and unforgiving grip.

"Oh, that feels so much better," she sang out while stretching her arms high in the air and twirling about like a gleeful ballerina. "Now I think it's your turn, Mr. Jackson."

Without pause, Sherman took off his suit jacket and vest. But before he could get to his shirt buttons, Sophie was already at his suspenders, then his trousers, and finally his undergarments and shoes. Sherman hastily undid his buttons and threw off his shirt. The last pieces of clothing to be stripped were Sophie's lower undergarments, which she gave Sherman the pleasure of gently disrobing. In the romantic glow of flickering candlelight stood the fully undraped forms of a man and a woman about to give themselves fully to one another.

With as much charisma and savvy as he could muster, Sherman pulled Sophie close and gently draped her neck with soft, warm kisses. They embraced and fell on each other with unbridled desire. Sophie showed no timidity and was not afraid to assert to Sherman how she wanted to be made love to. The young man happily obliged and was aroused yet somewhat surprised by his lover's sensual tenacity. He climbed on top and drove forth his rigid masculinity with ever-increasing penetrative thrusts of sexual pleasure. She moaned low with delight as she closed her eyes and spread her legs wider, enjoying every erogenous sensation he gave her. They switched positions over and over again, sometimes smoothly, and sometimes with embarrassingly painful awkwardness which was swiftly remedied with a playful giggle or a goofy smile.

In the final act of their first sexual encounter, Sophie climbed on top of Sherman and gently eased his hard lower extremity inside her. She breathed heavily and rhythmically rose and fell, gradually building up momentum. Her moans grew louder in unison with each feminine thrust as she neared the point of climax. Sherman was rapidly approaching his carnal apex as well and knew he would erupt with ecstasy at any moment. Sophie let out one last unrestrained moan, which triggered Sherman's involuntary response. He squeezed her supple bare breasts and let out a voluminous cry of delight upon the release. Both climaxed together and instantly embraced in a long kiss immediately followed by a deep, intimate hug. A thin film of perspiration covered both bodies and glistened in the candlelight. Minutes passed. Neither said anything. They lay there in silence, just happy to be in one another's arms.

Sophie made the first move and indicated she wished to crawl under the quilt rather than lie on top of it. Sherman accommodated her and soon both were snug under the blanket with their heads resting on the pillows. At first they whispered adoring thoughts to each other, but then a deep sense of relaxing fatigue set in, and both were induced to fall asleep. As the candles burned down, the room grew darker and darker. Before either could prevent it, the two lovers dropped off into a deep slumber.

As Sherman slept he began to dream. Lucid images and sounds of Jeff Parlin filled his mind. In his dream, Sherman was back at the store listening to Jeff describe Sophie's loose and unladylike behavior. In the dream, the descriptions were far more intense and graphic. Parlin spoke boldly, as if the right to Sophie's hand were a contest between the two men that he had already won. He boasted that she was his and that he'd had her many times in several different places, including Sherman's own bed. The next image that flashed through the dozing man's mind was Sophie herself. Only now, she didn't appear sweet, innocent, and proper. Instead, she looked dirty and ragged, wicked almost, like an unscrupulous prostitute who only longed for money and didn't care what it took to get it. The last vision Sherman saw was Parlin and Sophie laughing maliciously before she leapt up and wrapped her legs around his waist. Sherman, powerless to speak or act, stood and watched helplessly until he was overcome with grief. He snapped awake!

The room was very dark now. Only a few candles remained alight and they were dimming fast. For a moment Sherman didn't know where he was. As he shook off his sleep-induced lethargy, he looked over at Sophie, who was still snoozing soundly next to him. He quietly got up and reached into his vest pocket to retrieve his watch. He opened it and squinted in the dim light. It was three o'clock in the morning. He clicked it shut and looked again at Sophie. He felt restless and unnerved. The vivid dream replayed over and over in his mind and he couldn't shake the uneasy feeling now churning in the base of his gut. He slid back under the quilt. As he did, Sophie stirred and turned toward him. Her eyes flickered open and she smiled as his face came into focus. Sherman tried to smile back at her but couldn't. Immediately sensing something was amiss, Sophie said, "What is it? What's wrong?"

"I had a bad dream," he said.

"Oh, what kind of bad dream?"

Sherman hesitated. He tried to think of something that might throw Sophie off the scent but couldn't. Deep down he wanted to address the matter before the relationship went any further.

"It was about Parlin. Jeff Parlin and you."

"What do you mean, Sherman? What about him and me?"

"Sophie…have you spent time with Jeff? Have you flirted with him or in any way indicated that you like him? He said things to me earlier—things I couldn't believe and didn't want to believe were true."

"That's a rather unusual and rude question to ask, especially after what just happened between us," said Sophie firmly.

"It's not my intention to offer offense; quite the contrary. It's just that he said things about you that were disheartening and unbelievable."

"What, Sherman? What did he say? Tell me now."

"He told me that you were in the store the day I was away in Portland. He said you flirted with him and suggested the two of you should get together and have a drink. He made it sound as if you had no scruples and desired nothing more than a good time as you had done so often in the past with several other men."

Stunned at what she had just heard, a tear began to roll down Sophie's cheek. She got up and quickly began to dress herself. Unsure of what to say or do next, Sherman reached for his trousers and pulled them on. Sophie kept her back to Sherman as she got dressed. The silence became deafening and he couldn't stand it anymore.

"Sophie…."

"And what do you believe?" she snapped. "What am I, some sort of a plaything? Something for you and your friend's disgusting amusement? Am I not a woman with thoughts and feelings…and morals? I can't believe for a second you'd even consider something so horrible. I am truly hurt and offended at the very thought of it, Mr. Jackson!"

"I don't believe it, Sophie," said Sherman grabbing her arm and turning her to face him. "I couldn't believe it then and I certainly can't believe it now. I guess I was angry, and worst of all—jealous. I wanted to punch him in the face and kick him out of my store for good after hearing it. I wanted to force him to appear in front of you and apologize for even thinking of such a disgusting notion and defaming your character. If we were in different times I would have called him out and demanded a duel with pistols at ten paces. Deep down I knew what he was saying was pure rubbish, but I guess I just couldn't cope with the thought of him having designs on you. That day after church when I introduced you, I could tell quite plainly that he desired you, and that enraged me. Jealousy will make a man say and do inane things. I know better now. I love you, dearly. I'm sorry I ever allowed such drivel to make me think you are anything else than what you truly are, which is a lovely, intelligent, kind, and blessed woman. I mean that sincerely."

Sophie began to weep softly, then threw herself into Sherman's arms. The two held each other in a loving embrace. Sherman whispered sweet sentiments of comfort while Sophie slowly composed herself. The two kissed again and gave each other reassuring glances while they both finished getting fully dressed. The two sat down at one of the brightly decorated tables.

"Sherman, what I'm about to say will sting a little, but hear me out. I did visit the store while you were in Portland. I was unaware you were away. I wanted to see you because you are all I ever think about. When I dismissed my class I went straight to your store hoping to find you. Instead I found Mr. Parlin, who seemed all too delighted to see me. He looked at me lustfully and his words were not spoken cleanly; they just seemed to ooze and drip from his mouth as if he were drunken. I tried to engage in polite conversation, simple things, like where I was from and my family, but he kept shifting the topic back to himself and other inappropriate things—things you would not discuss in front of a lady. I felt uncomfortable and offended at his strange words; moreover, his dialect seemed quite odd to me. I have never heard an accent like his before. It's labored and inconsistent. I thought it to be quite peculiar. When I'd had enough, I made an excuse to leave. But before I left, he told me you were away and probably would be for several days. He also mentioned that the brothels in Portland were always quite busy this time of year. I said nothing at that point and simply left. I had no desire to be in his company ever again after that unpleasant encounter. It was very obvious to me that day that he had the notion to court me—and goodness knows what else."

"I knew it. I knew he lied. He wants you and obviously doesn't want us to be together."

"Sherman, I have a very bad feeling about him. Though I've only met him twice, I can't help but feel that there's something very unstable about him. He's a liar, we've determined that, but I can't help but think there's more. A woman can sense these things about a man that other men may not. He's a drifter and he could be dangerous. We really don't know much about him. I refuse to be in his presence alone again."

"I understand your concern, but let's not get too ruffled. I will assuredly confront him about his inappropriate behavior toward you. If it requires disciplinary measures, then rest assured I will take them. If he refuses to acknowledge his defamation of your character, and will not bring himself to offer you a thorough and sincere apology, then I will release him from my employ and suggest he leave town forever."

"I sense you're reluctant to rid him from our lives, despite what he said. I'm not sure how to take that, Sherman."

"I'm furious at what he said, but I don't wish to condemn him outright without first giving him a chance to make up for it. He's crippled, a war veteran, he's suffered a hard life in a state torn apart by outright murder and horrific bloodshed, and his customs and manners are undeniably different from ours. He's from Independence, Missouri, and maybe not accustomed to New England etiquette. What he said was definitely wrong, but perhaps it was a misunderstanding due to cultural ignorance."

"Perhaps, Sherman, but I caution you against that line of thinking. I feel that Mr. Parlin is a lot more intelligent than you may be giving him credit for."

"He's been a tremendous help to me at the store. I would be in serious trouble if he hadn't come into my employ. I was skeptical at first, but he's done a lot to earn my trust. He's helped me with other problems as well," said Sherman, his voice trailing off. He had no desire to talk about his problems with Danny Ricker to Sophie…or anyone else, for that matter.

"Stay wary, Sherman. Don't let your good judgment be clouded. That's my advice, my love. It's not just what he said to me, it's more than that. It's something deeper I can't explain. By the way, what part of the army did he fight with?"

"I think your womanly instincts may be getting the better of you, my dear. However, I shall heed your advice. As far as Jeff's war involvement, he told me he was part of the XV Corps, 1st Division, 3rd Brigade. He fought with the 32nd Missouri Infantry Regiment—yeah, that's what he told me. I remember it clearly. But we mustn't dwell on that now. We must put everything back in order around here and leave no trace of our visit, lest someone take offense at our pre-celebration activities."

"I couldn't agree more. It's so early in the morning and I fear I will be in no condition to properly conduct class once the sun is up and the day has begun."

"With a little luck, I'll have you home without much delay. Perhaps you'll be able to sleep a few short hours before rushing off to school."

"Let us hope. Now, let's remove all signs of tonight's pleasurable encounter and be on our way. I hope the pastor and his wife are heavy sleepers."

"Amen to that," said Sherman.

The two straightened up and removed all signs that they had been there. The spent candles were removed and disposed of and the wax cleaned up. The last thing Sherman did was open all the shutters to allow what little moonlight remained to shine in. Satisfied that everything was in order, Sherman carefully escorted Sophie through the darkness to the front door.

"Okay, I'm going to let you out and then lock the door from the inside. I'll then crawl out the window and meet you on the front steps," said Sherman.

"You didn't steal one of the McPhees' keys to the door, did you?" asked Sophie nervously.

"Certainly not. I got in through the unlocked window and then opened the door using this."

Sherman reached into his pocket and produced a woman's hairpin that was bent and twisted in an abnormal fashion.

"One might say I have my own key," he quipped.

"Indeed," said Sophie with a little grin.

She slipped out the door. Sherman stuck his makeshift key into the keyhole and worked it around until he heard a click indicating it was locked. He then hurried to the window and ducked through it, making sure to close it securely. He hustled over to the tree where Budley was tied and quickly freed the horse. He then led him by the reins to the front of the grange hall where Sophie was waiting for him.

"I feel a bit of a chill," she said as she rubbed her shoulders and arms.

"Let's get you home and warmed up. Shall we make our exit, my dear?" he asked, preparing to help her up onto the horse.

"Yes, let's be…."

Sophie paused before finishing her sentence. She looked up Settler Road. Her gaze became eerily transfixed on something unusual-looking off in the distance. Sherman shifted his attention away from readying the horse to looking at what had caught his lover's notice.

"What is that?" asked Sophie, gripping her man's arm tight. Sherman strained to see the unusual form in the pale moonlight. It was partially obscured by shadow and difficult to see with the naked eye. Try as he might, his brain couldn't positively construct and identify the obscure form off in the distance. It was definitely large, but even more so, imposing and scary as it did not move or make a sound, even as Sherman was certain it was watching them.

"Sherman, I'm frightened," declared Sophie as she clung to him even harder. "What is that monstrous-looking thing over there lurking in the shadows?"

"Not to worry, my dear. It's probably just a large bull moose who's taken a wrong turn and wandered into town. It seems to be quite stoic, I must admit."

"I want to leave now. Can we mount up and be on our way, please?" Sophie asked with fear on her breath.

Just then Budley began to snort and whicker. Just as he did, the same sound faintly emanated from the mysterious entity down the road. It was a sound Sherman was familiar with as he had heard it many times. To Sophie's dismay, he took several steps in the direction of the large, unidentified shape. As he did, it moved, and that was when he discovered what they were dealing with. It was a man on horseback!

"You, there! Come forward and be seen at once!" commanded Sherman as he continued to step closer. Just then the horse whinnied and reared. As it did, Sherman tried to make out whoever was atop it. But it was too dark and the mysterious rider appeared to be covered by some type of baggy sack-like shirt and what appeared to be a hood or mask of sorts. The rider turned the horse around and galloped off into the night toward South Gorham. Sherman quickly stepped back to Sophie.

"Who was that?" she asked. "What do you suppose he was doing and why?"

"I don't know," replied Sherman. "It's obvious that he didn't want anything to do with us. Maybe a stranger or simply someone who had gotten lost and was spooked."

"Please, I don't want to be out here any longer. I'm frightened and I want to go home. Please, let's be off," she implored.

Sherman wasted no time and helped her onto the horse. To Budley's dismay, he climbed aboard too and pointed the Morgan in the direction of the Morrell farm. Soon they were under way, but at very slow pace. Sophie clung to Sherman and trembled almost uncontrollably. He was unsure if it was due to the early morning chill or from fear of what had just happened. He pondered as they rode and couldn't help but think he had just encountered Danny Ricker atop his stolen horse. He was utterly certain of it. But beyond theft, what more had he been up to? The answer presented itself as he navigated down the road directly leading to the Morrell farm. Both looked up and saw a speck of light in the distance. It grew larger the closer they got and soon became horribly unmistakable. The Morrell house was on fire!

"My God, look, Sherman!" shrieked Sophie.

"Hyah," he yelled, giving Budley the spurs. The horse bolted forward toward the house. As they approached, they saw Thaddeus, Erin, and Wilbur rush out the front door in a panic. Sherman brought the horse up alongside and leapt off.

"Wilbur," called out Sherman. "Rush to the well and start bringing up as many buckets of water as you can carry. We'll start a bucket brigade and douse these flames before the whole house is destroyed. How many buckets do you have?"

"Five, Mr. Jackson," the young boy replied.

"Get running! I'll join you in a second! Thaddeus, you'll be the second part of the chain, Erin you're the third in line, and I'll be the last link. Sophie, after I toss the water, you need to run the empty buckets back down to Wilbur at the well. Can you do that?"

"Yes, everybody get into line," she said.

"Wait a minute," cried out Erin hysterically in Sophie's direction. "Where's Olin? And where have you been? Why are you with Mr. Jackson at such a ridiculous hour and not in bed? Lord in Heaven, what's going on here?"

Both Sophie and Sherman ignored the frantic woman's questions. Sherman raced toward the well to assist Wilbur, who was filling buckets. He grabbed two and hustled up to the corner of the house. Sophie pleaded with Erin to get into line and not panic. Sherman tossed the water onto the flames and handed the empty bucket to Sophie, who scurried off back to the well. Wilbur handed the next bucket to his father, who then relayed it to the sobbing Erin, who gave it to Sherman. The young man attacked the flames, hoping to knock down the fire at its weakest point. The flames were heavily entrenched at the base of one corner of the house and were steadily licking their way up the side, but they had not reached the roof yet, so there was still hope—if only they could get enough water on it in time. It was a deadly race. Little by little the buckets continued to work their way up through the line to the house. Sherman concentrated on killing the blaze by dousing the base and not allowing the flames to spread out of control. Each time he dropped an empty bucket, a fresh one was handed to him. After a few minutes, it appeared as if the blaze was beginning to be brought under control. The buckets kept coming, and the water rained down to smother the flames. Like a dutiful soldier, Sophie ran back and forth with the empties for Wilbur to fill. Through much hard work and struggle, the fire was finally brought under control.

"That's it," shouted an exhausted Sherman. "We have it licked."

Smoke and specks of glowing embers rose through the charred hole in the side of the house that Sherman estimated was at least ten feet wide and eight feet high. He could see right inside the household to the personal items and furniture the fire had damaged. The Morrell family pitifully gathered around the damaged area of their home and looked on in shock and disbelief.

"How did this happen? Why has the Lord chosen to test us in such a way?" lamented Pastor Thaddeus.

"Olin!" cried out Erin. She waddled her plump frame over to the missing older Morrell son, who had miraculously and silently appeared, seemingly out of nowhere. Erin hugged him while praising the Lord and sobbing uncontrollably.

"What happened?" Olin asked innocently.

"The house caught fire," answered Erin, fighting back her tears. "Where were you?" she demanded, adding, "I looked in your room and your bed was empty. Willy was sound asleep. Where were you? Where was my Ollie?"

"I was restless and unable to sleep, mother," the boy replied. "I decided to go for a walk. I thought the early-morning air might do me some good. I crept out quietly so as not to wake anyone. I wasn't planning on being gone long."

Olin looked over in Wilbur's direction. The younger brother was staring intently at him. He stood frozen in place and appeared as if he wanted to say something. Olin shot his brother a subtle but stern look that effectively made Willy dip his head and keep his mouth closed.

"How did this happen? Sherman, I thank God you were here to take charge and assist us, but I can't understand why you were out and about on our land at such an odd hour of the morning. Do you have any knowledge concerning the cause of this dastardly conflagration?" asked the pastor.

Before Sherman could answer, Erin spoke up and said, "He rode up with Sophie on the back of his horse. They were out together. Our dear, sweet maiden was…oh my goodness…I fear I may faint!"

Sophie stepped forward and said, "Sherman took me to the grange hall last night to show me the holiday decorations and celebratory preparations before anyone else. He thought it would be a nice gesture and a wonderful surprise. I accepted his invitation and was pleased with all he showed me. He was the perfect gentlemen and did not persuade me to do anything against my will or God's. It was all very innocent and I'm sorry if the odd timing of it worried you; that wasn't my intention. I would think the Lord would praise Mr. Jackson for taking the occasion to share a little joy and hospitality with a new friend who's still a bit of a stranger around these parts."

"Indeed," replied a huffing and indignant Erin. She fanned herself excessively and tried not to faint, with a little help from her sons who stood behind her and offered her something to lean on.

"Enough of that matter for the moment," said the pastor. "Sherman, I want to know if you know anything about this fire. Did you see anything or anyone?"

"No, Thaddeus, but it does look suspicious. To me it appears like it was deliberately set by someone," Sherman speculated.

"Agreed," replied the pastor. "But who would perpetrate such a devilish task? Why would someone want to harm my family?"

Sherman hesitated and looked away. He then answered, "I don't know, sir. Perhaps the Lord will give us the answer in due course and help bring the architect of this crime to justice. I would seek out Sheriff Ridgeway as soon as possible and report this. I know he's been nearby lately. Perhaps he'll be out this way in a few hours."

"Amen. In the meantime I'm going to be a good shepherd and look after my flock. Erin, the damage is far from catastrophic. We will stay here and decide the best course of action after the sun rises. Take the boys in and put them to bed. Sophie as well, please. I'm going to stand watch out here until I feel there's no danger lurking. Sherman, I suggest you go home—and thank you again," said the pastor. "On your way, sir."

Sherman looked at Sophie who looked back at him as Erin motioned for her and the boys to go inside. He gave her a reassuring nod and then mounted Budley. The early-morning hours were waning fast and soon the sun would be rising. He knew it was best to get home quickly. He spurred his horse and trotted away, leaving Thaddeus to stand guard armed with nothing more than a Bible tucked away under his robe.

As Sherman made the trek back home, he was astounded at how perfectly the night had begun and how terribly the early morning had ended. He wondered if he'd find his own home blanketed in flames upon arrival. To his relief, the sun gradually made its first appearance just as the store came into view. Everything looked quiet. He rode up to the house and was happy to see it standing untouched.

"C'mon, Budley, let's get you to bed," said a very dirty and tired Sherman.

He rode up to the livery and dismounted. He led Budley inside and was taken aback by what he saw in the early-morning light.

"Skipper!"

Tied up in his usual spot was his prized Morgan, Skipper.

"What kind of a thief steals your horse and then returns him? Why would Ricker bring him back, unsaddle him, and tie him up?" Sherman whispered. He inspected Skipper for any clues that might reveal his thief. Apart from some twigs and leaves in his mane, and mud on his hooves, there was nothing even the brightest Pinkerton could detect that would reveal the identity of the thief. Sherman tied up Budley and checked on his two stallions as well. He did everything he could to insure they were securely bound. He then staggered out of the stable and looked up at Jeff's window. All was quiet. The exhausted young man made his way inside his house and promptly went to sleep. It was all he could do.

✜

Thursday, July 3, was a sunny morning and quite warm. Sherman slept later than he'd expected. He was more worn out than he had realized. He hurriedly cleaned himself up, put on fresh clothes, and fixed coffee and warm oatmeal, which he brought over to the store. Upon arrival he again found Jeff working hard and taking care of the necessary daily chores that needed to be accomplished in order for the store to run smoothly.

"There you are," said Jeff, stocking some canned foods. "I was beginning to wonder if you were all right. I was gonna give you another twenty minutes before I went up to the house and checked on you. Did you sleep okay?" Jeff asked while Sherman handed him his coffee.

"Yes, fine," said Sherman. "I don't know why I was so lazy this morning. Just couldn't get going. Have some oatmeal."

"Thank you, don't mind if I do."

"Busy this morning?"

"The usual, a few customers here and there."

"Any trouble last night? See anything out of the ordinary concerning our problem? Assuming you were awake, of course."

"No, nothin'. I was powerful tired and turned in earlier than usual. I watched from my window for a little while just after dark, but didn't see nothin' or nobody."

"Good. Let's hope the sheriff is on top of matters. Maybe he's already got Ricker in custody."

"Maybe," said Parlin.

"Let's eat up quick and get to work. There's usually a rush on certain supplies the day before a major holiday," said Sherman.

The two worked throughout the day in a normal routine while customers came and went. All of them were folks Sherman didn't recognize, and he assumed they were people traveling from neighboring towns needing supplies for the holiday. All in all, it seemed to be a typical day. There was no sign of the sheriff and no mention of the McPhees' fire. Sherman wondered about Sophie and if she was at school. He decided not to tell Jeff about his previous night's encounter with her or his involvement battling the house fire. He even made it a point not to mention the mysterious horseman or even the strange circumstances involving the disappearance and then reappearance of Skipper. The story involving the exchange between Sophie and Jeff angered Sherman to no end, and Jeff's lies put a dent in the fragile foundation of trust built between the two men, as far as Sherman was concerned. The young storekeeper had growing apprehensions about his new friend, but he wasn't going to bluntly denounce him. He needed some answers first and he thought Jeff had at least earned the benefit of the doubt. Perhaps there was a great misunderstanding that could be cleared up with a mature and intelligent conversation.

"Hey, Jeff," called out Sherman.

"Yeah, Sherm," was the reply from the supply room.

"Why don't you come over to the house again this evening. I'll make supper and we can talk some more. I was thinking we could go over your salary. I think it's time to start paying you some money for all the hard work and time you've put in around here. How's that sound?"

"Sounds damn fine, Sherm. Count me in!"

For the rest of the day the store was very busy. Neither Sherman nor Jeff could relax for very long as there always seemed to be a customer wanting something. It pleased Sherman immensely that the store was doing well, but it also frustrated him, as he had no opportunity to slip out and visit Sophie at the schoolhouse. He wanted to know how she was and if the McPhees had any new information on who caused their fire. He was also hoping to find Silas and learn what new developments he had uncovered. It was not to be, however. The store was too busy and Sherman couldn't get away. Eventually it started to get dark and Sherman hung the "Closed" sign in the window. He counted the money brought in over the course of the day and was ecstatic at the total. He pocketed the cash and said to Jeff, "Get everything squared away here for me. I'm going to start supper. Should be ready when you come over."

Jeff nodded and Sherman walked over to the house. He prepared some smoked beef and vegetables for dinner. The table had been set and the food plated just as Jeff knocked on the door. The two sat and pleasantly ate their meals while engaging in light conversation. When they were finished and everything was put away, they again adjourned to the parlor and sank into the chairs facing the fireplace with whiskey and cigars. Sherman again built a low-burning fire to appease his guest despite the July heat. Once he felt Jeff was comfortable and happy, he was ready to begin a new and more serious conversation.

"We had a great day. We brought in a lot of holiday revenue. Best I've seen in years, actually," Sherman boasted.

"Never understood Independence Day," grumbled Jeff. "It's a meaningless holiday, if you ask me. Never had any use for it. It was never extremely popular in the South, even before the war. Don't know why people make such a big uproar about it, especially now when the country is still so divided."

"Don't you think a holiday like Independence Day helps serve the cause of bringing the country together? I think it's quite meaningful. It celebrates the birth of our nation, our independence from England and such," said Sherman.

Jeff swallowed his whiskey in one big gulp and reached for the bottle. He poured himself another glass and said, "Do you think southern folks give a shit about the birth of the United States? To them, Independence Day is nothing more than a grim reminder of the triumph of the country that shattered *their* independence. The South had its own country, the Confederate States of America, and all they wanted was the right to choose their own destiny just like the colonials did back before the Revolutionary War. They formed the Confederacy and went to war to protect a way of life they held dear and believed in completely, only to see it obliterated, scattered to the wind. Unlike in 1783, the foreign power won and the revolutionaries lost. The United States prevailed and imposed its will on the South. Any good southerner has not and will not ever celebrate Independence Day. To a southerner, there's no such holiday."

Jeff took another long drink of whiskey. He was well ahead of Sherman, who hadn't even finished a quarter of his first glass yet.

"I'll say one thing further: if President Grant had any intelligence at all, he would ban Independence Day celebrations, particularly by those Federal troops still garrisoning southern states. By allowing such celebrations in territories that are still hostile, he's courting the threat of a whole new round of bloodshed and insurgency by the locals.

"Am I to understand that you're not a supporter of the president?" asked Sherman dryly.

"That man is an overrated, incompetent ass who couldn't pour piss out of a boot with the instructions written on the heel!" fired Jeff after finishing another glass of whiskey that he replenished immediately. "He was reckless on the battlefield and a drunk! He never outgeneraled anyone. He was victorious because he always had superior numbers, well fed and equipped troops, and more armaments. If General Lee had the resources and the numbers Grant had, we'd all be whistling Dixie now. How that son of a bitch got to be president is a textbook study of the complete ignorance and incompetence of the American voter. To date, there is no other president I loathe more than 'Useless' S. Grant. Oh, just a minute, Sherm. I stand corrected. There is one, or more accurately, there *was* one tyrant worse than our current chief executive."

"And who would that be?" asked Sherman, knowing full well what he was about to hear from the partially intoxicated man seated next to him.

"Lincoln!" he bellowed. "There has never been a guiltier president than Abraham Lincoln! No other tyrant in history brought more misery on his people in such a short period of time than that corrupt, lying, son-of-a-bitching huckster, Abe Lincoln!"

"Would it be safe to assume that you're a Democrat?" asked Sherman with a bit of a sarcastic tone and a slight grin that he hoped would add a little levity to the conversation and calm Jeff down a bit.

"Damn right," he replied after taking yet another swig. "My family might have been pro-Union and anti-slavery, but we all reviled Lincoln. He brought so much grief to so many people—good people who deserved better than his abhorrent politics."

"Interesting," replied Sherman simply, with no intention of escalating the conversation by revealing his family's Republican Party affiliation or their fervent support of the assassinated former president. Though he wished not to provoke Jeff any further, he was intrigued by the words spilling from his whiskey-soaked mouth. Moreover, he couldn't help but notice a shift in his odd accent the more intoxicated he became. At first it was subtle and not easily recognized, but the more whiskey that was introduced to his innards, the more his drawl sounded more remarkably and undeniably southern. Out of sheer curiosity, and in reference to Jeff's apparent aversion to President Grant, Sherman decided to ask Jeff a question regarding another famous figure from the war—one with whom Jeff was well acquainted.

"Your distaste for our current president is clear, sir. From what you've said regarding his command and how he conducted the war, it's also clear that you have no respect for Grant as a general, either. But what about his dear friend Bill Sherman? He was your boss, as Grant was mine. You fought with General Sherman. What think you of him?"

Parlin paused and took another drink. He looked like a man who was struggling with what to say next. The alcohol wasn't helping matters as Sherman patiently awaited his reply.

"Uncle Billy was a good leader," he said monotonously. "He was a fighter who believed in making hard war. He made tough decisions and stood by his actions, like a man does. He tore through the South like a banshee or some unstoppable monster. Everyone feared him. He laid waste to whatever town, city, or Reb force was foolish enough to get in his way. He cut a swath of destruction from Atlanta to the coast unlike anything we ever dreamed. Total annihilation…total annihilation. But he did what had to be done. He was a man who loved the South but knew he had to destroy it. That must eat away at him every day of his life. Cursed is Sherman, a cursed man. I feel sorry for him."

Sherman listened intently while puffing on his cigar. He wasn't sure what to make of Parlin's answer to his question about the fiery general who terrorized the South in 1864, but the one thing that was clear was that his one-armed friend was now inebriated—and it was really beginning to show.

"You know what's funny," Jeff slurred. "Your name is Sherman Jackson. You're named after a Union general and a Confederate general. You'd fit right in if you lived in Missouri. You could say you were either Yankee or Reb depending on who knocked on your door. I wonder what ol' Stonewall himself would say to that? He was a fighter…he woulda licked ol' Uncle Billy if he lived to have the chance."

Jeff snickered and sat back in his chair with a fresh glass of whiskey. Sherman had never seen him act this way before and was curious to see what would come next. He decided not to ask any more questions, and just let Jeff do all the talking.

"The food around these parts is awful, Sherm, you know that? Can't never get biscuits and white gravy. Ain't no grits, good greens, or good barbecued meats. And nobody around here knows how to properly cook a pig. I'd give my one good arm to have a fresh peach or some pecan pie, or even some sweet tea. God only knows how you folks survive up here. In the South, before the war, families were cordial and respected one another. People knew their place in society. It was elegant and chivalrous. Glorious plantations dotted the landscape bursting with fields of white cotton and tobacco. Beautiful and virtuous southern belles wearing sophisticated and fashionable dresses attended elegant parties and cotillions. It was marvelous…just marvelous, I say. Don't see anything like that up here. That way of life is gone, courtesy of the Union Army."

"An army we both fought with. An army that saved the country and helped eradicate slavery," stated Sherman.

"Ha! The South's economy is dependent on slaves. You remove their slaves, you destroy their way of life and possibly their very existence. Ain't nothin' President Grant can say or do that will change that. All he cares about is keepin' the South under his boot heel. I 'spect he'll be forced to commit endless numbers of troops to keep order down there. Before you know it, the South will be in full rebellion again and there'll be another war. I wonder if it was all worth it."

"Worth what, precisely?"

"Worth all the destruction and death of a noble civilization to free a bunch of ignorant Negroes," said Parlin.

"I suppose time will tell, Jeff. Unchaining the Negro and setting him free was necessary and just. Our country wouldn't have survived torn apart as it was."

"It would have survived. The Union and the Confederacy could have survived side by side, but we fucked it all up!"

Parlin drank another shot and slumped back in his chair. His eyes were glassy and his eyelids appeared heavy as they slowly sank downward.

"Let's change the subject, Jeff. Let's talk about your salary," said Sherman.

There was no response. It was obvious Jeff was too drunk to carry on a normal conversation. Sherman gave up and sat quietly, pondering everything he had just heard. He wondered if Jeff struggled with identity issues. He clearly seemed to have sympathies toward the old antebellum South, and coming from a deep-rooted, divided border state like Missouri, maybe it had been torturous for him to don a Union uniform and help destroy a part of the country he admired. Maybe he always had conflicting views and loyalties concerning the issues that drove the North and the South to war. Or maybe he was just drunk and unable to think and speak clearly about how he really felt.

Sherman got up and extinguished his cigar. He looked closely at Jeff, who was nearly unconscious in his chair. He shook the lifeless man's arm but there was no response. He was disappointed he had lost the opportunity to discuss with Jeff what was really on his mind—the man's previous encounter with Sophie—but he also realized that he had learned a bit more about Jeff's character by listening to his politics. Still, there were more questions and discussions that needed to be had before the Sophie issue was fully resolved.

Sherman lifted Jeff's limp body out of the chair and carried him over to the store. With great effort, Sherman conveyed him up the stairs and put him in bed. By now Jeff was fully unconscious and snoring up a storm. Sherman wondered if losing a major body part such as an arm or a leg made a man more easily intoxicated. He didn't think too hard about it. Instead he took the keys and locked up the store. He wandered over to the barn and checked his horses, which were safe and secure. He checked his chicken coop and then the garden. All appeared in order.

He knew he'd have no lookout tonight, so Sherman went inside determined not to let one of his horses be stolen again. He went upstairs and into his bedroom. He puttered around, found what he was looking for, and retreated back downstairs to the parlor where, for the first time ever, he pulled the Henry rifle off its perch above the mantel. He checked the gun over before sliding up the spring-loaded tab and locking it in place with a simple twist of the barrel tip. He then slid thirteen .44 rimfire cartridges down the tube, fully loading the gun.

"Now, let's see what this evening brings us for excitement," he muttered. He let the house get dark and set himself up in a chair next to the rear kitchen window that looked out onto the livery, garden, and chicken coop. "Come on in, Mr. Ricker, and we'll settle this business tonight, once and for all."

An hour or two passed. Unsuspectingly, Sherman fell victim to boredom fueled by inactivity and dropped off into a deep sleep. He slumped back in his chair, carelessly allowing the Henry to drop onto the floor. As he slept he was oblivious to all that was happening and all that could be happening just outside his locked door. Though he slept deeply, his slumber wasn't entirely peaceful. Visions of burning houses, unabated vandalism, slaughtered animals, stolen property, and enraged citizens clogged his dreams while filling his mind with worrisome thoughts of fear and desperation unlike anything he had felt since being under fire during the war.

He woke at dawn. It took several minutes for him to realize where he was and what was going on. Soon his early-morning weariness began to subside and the visions of slumbering fantasy were slowly replaced by the tangibles of reality. He picked up the Henry and looked out the window. Nothing seemed amiss at first glance, which pleased him, yet he was angry with himself for falling asleep so quickly. He got himself cleaned up and changed into a fresh suit, and then fixed a small breakfast. As he ate he wondered if Parlin had sobered up yet. When finished he took his rifle into the parlor and put it back in its place over the mantel. It was now July 4—Independence Day—the country's birthday. Sherman anxiously thought about the day's festivities and how he'd enjoy them with Sophie. He wondered if the Morrells held any ill will toward him after discovering his and Sophie's late-night rendezvous. He also wondered if they'd try to prevent further encounters.

Sherman put that ugly thought out of his mind and made his way over to the store. Settler Road was quiet and not yet bustling with activity. Sherman walked alone and paused only a minute to watch the sun rise over the eastern horizon. He stepped up to the front door and tried the knob—it was still locked. Fumbling with his keys, he eventually unlocked the door and let himself in. Unlike mornings before, this time the store had not been properly tended and was clearly not ready to open for business. Much needed to be done, and Jeff hadn't tackled the early-morning prep work as he had done so efficiently in days past. Sherman put on his apron and started to get things in order. After a while his curiosity got the better of him and he found himself quietly creeping up the stairs. He looked into Jeff's room and saw him on the bed in a tangled mass of blankets and sheets.

Sherman cautiously stepped in. The room was in disarray as drawers were open, clothing was scattered on the floor, and the desk looked as if someone had rifled through it. Sherman picked up a knocked-over chair and set it upright. As he did, he caught sight of something that immediately captured his full attention. An object was partially sticking out of a blanket under Jeff's bed. Sherman knelt down for a better look. He reached out and snatched the object. As soon as he pulled it into his line of sight, he knew what it was.

"I'll be damned," he muttered. "I haven't seen one of these in a while."

Sherman held in his right hand Jeff's loaded LeMat revolver. He looked it over closely and remembered taking similar weapons off captured Confederate officers just prior to war's end. He was careful how he handled it after noticing it was loaded. His mind started to work feverishly as he wondered why Jeff had the gun and why he had never mentioned it. Then another thought entered his head—a more frightening notion. He looked at the window and saw that it was open. He then looked closely at Jeff. For an instant, the cluttered room, the open window, and the mysterious gun led Sherman to believe that Jeff might have been assaulted in his sleep last night.

Sherman dropped the gun back on the floor and looked for signs that Jeff was still alive. He hadn't stirred one bit since Sherman entered the room. Thoughts raced through the storeowner's mind of Ricker climbing in through the window during the night and attacking Jeff—thinking he was Sherman—and ransacking the room before dropping his gun in the dark and fleeing. Immediately he looked for blood and listened for a heartbeat. To his relief, he found one but not the other. Parlin was breathing and simply in a deep sleep.

"Jeff…Jeff," said Sherman while gently shaking his right leg. "Jeff… wake up."

Parlin snorted out some breath and slowly came back to life.

"You all right, Jeff?"

"That you, Sherm?"

"Yeah, of course it is. Are you okay?"

"I been better. That whiskey of yours sure do pack a wallop. My head just won't stop spinning."

"Can you sit up?"

"Yeah, just gimme…just gimme a second or two whilst I shake out the cobwebs."

With great effort, Jeff sat up and sluggishly rubbed his head with his eyes closed. After a minute passed he became more responsive.

"What happened? This room looks like it was robbed or something," asked Sherman.

"I don't know, Sherm. I was drunk…I can't remember what happened. I probably messed up the place before passing out last night. How'd I get up here? Last thing I remember is being in your parlor."

"I brought you here last night. I figured you'd stay right in bed, but I guess you had other plans that called for some redecorating."

"Is the store okay? I didn't mess up the store, did I?"

"No, the store's fine. Your nocturnal activities seemed to be confined to just this room. Maybe you were walking in your sleep or something? I've seen it with other men before, you know."

"Who knows," replied Jeff as he dipped his head and rubbed it hard with both hands. As he looked down, he saw the exposed LeMat lying on the floor at his feet. Surreptitiously he kicked a loose blanket over it.

"Are you going to be able to work today?"

"I may need some more rest, Sherm. My head is pounding and

right now it's taking all my strength just to sit upright. I may sleep a bit longer if you're agreeable. I'll sleep this off and be more useful later. What time is it now?"

"It's just after seven in the morning. You stay here and recover. I'll handle the store today. I'm gonna close up early since it's a holiday. I have plans tonight with Sophie Curtis. You just rest up and don't worry about doing anything until you feel better."

"Yeah, okay," said Jeff insipidly as he labored to lie back down. As soon as his head hit the pillow, he was out. Sherman covered him in blankets, making sure not to disturb the hidden pistol. He would address that matter later if Jeff continued to hide its existence. Regrettably, it became yet another source of concern for Sherman.

He went downstairs and continued readying the store for the day's business, though he suspected that he'd have only a few customers if any. At quarter of eight, he went to hang the "Open" sign in the window. As he did, he noticed some people all walking in the same direction. He didn't give it any thought until he opened the door and stepped outside to tie it open. He looked up Settler Road in the direction of the Budwin School. There was a small crowd congregated around the flagpole. Thinking the tiny mass of people milling about in front of the schoolhouse looked odd, Sherman instantly had thoughts of Sophie and hustled over to see if anything was wrong.

He walked up to the schoolhouse ignoring the mass of people and immediately looked inside. The room was empty. He hurried back to the buzzing crowd. It didn't take long to figure out what the commotion was all about. Everyone's gaze was fixated skyward and up the flagpole. Sherman looked up too and was appalled at what he saw.

"Who ran up that abomination?" he asked in a troubled and authoritative voice. His question was answered by numerous replies of mixed uncertainty and disbelief. Sherman turned around and looked down Settler Road. In the distance he spied Sophie walking toward the school, hand in hand with Josephine and Alexander Lovell. As they approached, Sherman could see the growing look of concern on her face. She let go of the kids' hands and told them to ignore the crowd and go straight into the classroom, which they did faithfully and obediently.

"Miss, do you know anything about this?" asked an old farmer. Before Sophie could answer, the young teacher was assailed by similar questions from others in the crowd. Sherman immediately stood by her side and came to her defense.

"Now, just wait a minute, everyone!" he bellowed. "I'm positive Miss Curtis knows nothing about this."

"About what, Sherman? What's going on here? Who are all these people?" Sophie timidly asked, as if fearing she had done something terribly wrong.

"They're mostly farmers who live on the outskirts of Scarborough. They're most likely here to partake in the festivities later," Sherman whispered in her ear. "I'm sure as they passed the school this morning, they saw that."

Sophie looked up and gasped at what she saw. Flying high and fluttering ominously in the breeze was a large and vibrantly colored Confederate battle flag! The highly visible "Southern Cross" looked flawlessly new, as if it was sewn yesterday. Two rows of thirteen perfectly aligned white stars sat atop two crossed bars of blue that rested on a solid red base. Sherman had seen this flag many times, as it was used by the Confederate Army of Northern Virginia—Lee's army—with which the 20th Maine had seemed endlessly engaged during the later battles of the war.

"Oh my goodness," said Sophie. "Where did that come from? What happened to my American flag? Surely everyone doesn't think I raised this flag!" she asked loudly so the crowd could here.

"Of course they don't," replied Sherman in an equally raised voice. "This is just a highly inappropriate practical joke concocted by an immature and unpatriotic miscreant who should be disciplined severely by the law. Does anyone know if the sheriff has seen this yet?"

"Don't think so," said the old farmer.

"Well, we'll be sure to report it. Please, everyone just go about your business. Miss Curtis and I will take down this repugnant eyesore."

"Cut it up and distribute the rags to every outhouse in the area. That's what I'd do," said the farmer before walking away.

Gradually the small crowd dispersed, leaving Sherman and Sophie the task of taking down the morbid reminder of the turbulent days of struggle with the old Confederacy.

"You better go and start your class. I'll take the flag down," said Sherman.

"This is just awful! Why would someone do such a thing…and on Independence Day?" bemoaned Sophie.

"It's like I said," Sherman answered, "It's a tasteless prank. I'll go back to the store and get you a new United States flag."

"Thank you, dear. This is all very distressing."

"I'm very sorry. I'll get this taken care of right away," assured Sherman. "Sophie...what happened after I left the other night?"

"Well, the pastor and his wife were not pleased that I had snuck away at nighttime to meet with a gentleman suitor. They expressed their displeasure and reminded me of their house rules and the rules of the Lord, which I must abide by if I'm to remain under their roof. I convinced them that our meeting was innocent and that you're a decent and a respectable gentleman. They agreed and did not forbid me to see you.

"Personally, I think they need to spend more energy on disciplinary measures involving their two boys and not focus on me. Those boys have their parents completely fooled. I can't get them to attend class. They lie to their parents constantly concerning their daily whereabouts and their activities. The pastor and Erin don't doubt a single word they utter and trust them implicitly. I fear that if I step forward and try to reveal the truth about their truancy from school and their other dishonest behaviors, the pastor and his wife will simply not believe me and become irritated and distrustful of my word. Their discovery of the recent activities between us may have reinforced that point and lowered their expectations and opinion of my character."

"I doubt it's that serious. They're very trusting and forgiving souls. A few dedicated church visits will certainly cleanse your soul in their eyes, trust me. You didn't tell them about our...well, you know...our...."

"Of course not, Sherman. What kind of lady speaks openly about such things? I'm surprised that even crossed your mind."

"You're right. My apologies. What about the fire and the house?"

"Pastor Morrell asked us not to speak of it. He hasn't seen the sheriff, nor has he told a single soul about it...that is, unless you include multiple prayers to the Lord. If the house sustains further damage or becomes uninhabitable for any reason, the pastor said we'd move into the church temporarily. He plans to make a public announcement about the entire incident on Sunday during services. He thought church would be the best venue to disclose the unfortunate events of that morning to our neighbors."

"Perhaps you're right. Did you discover any clue as to what caused the fire?"

"No, I'm afraid the pastor's detective skills are sorely lacking. To compound problems, his trust and faith in the good nature of people is excessively abundant, and that does not bode well when trying to identify something or someone who has done you harm."

"I agree. Perhaps when the sheriff is notified and starts an investigation, we'll have better success identifying the culprit," Sherman stated with a trailing voice and broken eye contact.

"Miss Curtis, are we going to have class today?"

Sophie and Sherman turned around to find Josephine Lovell standing there in the doorway. Before Sophie could answer the young girl's question, Josephine looked up and pointed down the road.

"Look, there's Daddy with Sheriff Ridgeway."

Riding side by side on horseback were Hiram Lovell and the sheriff. The two seemed to be discussing some unpleasant matter, as Lovell appeared animated and unsettled in the saddle. Just then an ear-piercing shriek shattered the morning calm. Lovell and Ridgeway wheeled their horses around and galloped off in the direction of the Old Liberty Grange. Without saying a word, Sherman and Sophie instinctively and hastily followed suit on foot, unaware that both Lovell kids were right behind them.

Soon everyone on Settler Road in the vicinity of the grange hall began to gather around the front steps. Many had just seen the peculiar flag at the Budwin School and were now fixated on what was happening at the grange. As Sherman and Sophie made their way to the front of the building, Reba McPhee came rushing out and collapsed to her knees, sobbing, on the front steps. She was met by both Lovell and Ridgeway, who had quickly dismounted their horses and ran up to discover what was the matter.

"Why?" she cried out. "In God's name, why?" Reba looked inconsolable and buried her face in her hands as she wept. Ridgeway repeatedly asked her what was wrong. The troubled woman did not answer and only continued to cry loudly. Some of the other women in the crowd came up the steps and tried to calm her down. As they did, Lovell and Ridgeway stood up and slowly entered the grange. Sherman immediately took Sophie by the hand and led her up the steps. Both wanted to see inside.

"What in hell?" voiced Ridgeway upon laying eyes on sheer desecration.

"Goddammit," shouted Lovell as he kicked a knocked-over chair in anger and frustration.

"My God," said Sherman while Sophie let out a small cry and covered her mouth. Tears welled up in her eyes as she was unable to find any words to express her mounting grief.

What lay before the shocked foursome was a scene of unspeakable ruin. The once lavishly decorated first floor was now a wasteland of shredded decorations, trampled and scattered flower fragments, upended and smashed furniture, broken glass, gouged walls, and a floor littered with nearly unrecognizable refuse. The stage was smeared with filth and mud emanating a foul odor that was easily identified as animal excrement. Nothing in the once grand ballroom remained intact. All the American flags had been taken down and dredged through a load of muddy filth and then left to decay in an unholy pile. Every picture on the wall had been removed and destroyed while every dish and glass on the buffet table had been smashed and reduced to hazardous shards strewn across the room.

"This is the most heinous display of unmitigated vandalism I've ever seen," said Sherman after catching a wary eye from Ridgeway.

"It only gets worse," came a voice from across the room.

Everyone looked up to find Edwin McPhee standing lugubriously at the base of the stairs. He slowly turned and walked up. The others followed until all five were on the second floor. Everyone stood on the precipice of shock and fear at what unfolded before their eyes.

"What kind of disturbed individual could conceive and perform such a devious and unholy act of destruction and degradation?" desperately implored Edwin. "What have my dear wife and I done to deserve this?"

Edwin pointed around the room at the shattered remnants of artifacts scattered everywhere. Irreplaceable books, letters, uniforms, guns, musical instruments, pictures, and everything else the McPhees had collected and held dear was now severely damaged or destroyed. What was even more disturbing was what hung from the ceiling over a pile of shredded U.S. flags.

"That's the second symbol of dishonor I've seen elevated today," said Sherman.

"What do you mean?" responded Ridgeway.

"Someone ran up a Confederate flag on the schoolhouse flagpole. It was discovered this morning."

Everyone stood in stunned silence for a brief moment while examining the Confederate battle flag that closely resembled the one Sherman had seen earlier. Just then, voices were heard downstairs. All five went down to investigate. The crowd that had gathered outside was now inside investigating the destruction. Hiram Lovell was discouraged to see his kids among them.

"Miss Curtis, I would appreciate it if you would escort my children back to school and execute your lesson plan for the day. I have no wish for them to see this," sternly ordered Hiram.

"Of course, Mr. Lovell. Alexander, Josephine, come with me now, please," said Sophie, trying to hold back her emotions. She looked over at Sherman, who shot her a reassuring glance. She nodded and left the grange, saying, "Children, let's go and take down the silly flag that some prankster put up on our flagpole. Shall we?"

By now the small crowd was visibly angry and bothered by what they had seen. Several people began asking questions. Led by the distraught McPhees, the crowd quickly surrounded Sheriff Ridgeway and demanded answers. Sherman stayed cautiously back and silently out of the way.

"Who's responsible for this sordid business?" shouted the same old farmer who had commented about the flag at the school earlier.

"What's happening here?" shouted another voice.

"Are we in any danger?" yet another man called out.

"What are you going to do about this horrible affair, Sheriff?" cried out Reba McPhee.

"Everybody just stay calm," ordered Ridgeway, his voice raised. "I know some of you have reported recent troubles with vandalism and theft. I'm going to find who did this, but I need information first. I'm going to call an emergency town meeting here tonight at six o'clock. Spread the word to everyone in the North Scarborough community and other adjoining areas who wish to attend. At the meeting I'll listen to everyone's grievances and document all recent offenses. Maybe after some discussion, we can identify some suspects, establish some kind of pattern...maybe even get a confession out of somebody. For now, I reckon we ought to cancel all public Independence Day celebrations, especially after what's happened here. I want everyone to leave now and just go about your business or go home. But make sure you tell everyone you see about the meeting. Let's have a good turnout. That's all. Go on now."

The grumbling crowd gradually started to exit. Soon the only people that remained were the McPhees, Hiram Lovell, Sherman, and the sheriff.

"I'm not losing anymore livestock," Hiram muttered to Sheriff Ridgeway. "My wife is scared senseless, my kids are asking too many questions, and my business is suffering immensely. If I see or hear anything that even resembles a threat to my family or my property, I'm gonna shoot first and not stop until I have a corpse."

"I'd be careful who I said that to," replied Ridgeway. "Some folks might take that the wrong way. I don't care what you think you're protecting, outright murder is a crime no matter how you look at it...least it is in my eyes."

"Ayuh, I hear you. But I'm gonna have justice, Silas. Understand that. I will have compensation one way or another, whether the law helps me or not."

With that, Hiram stomped out of the grange and hurriedly rode off.

"Has Mr. Lovell been the victim of recent wrongdoing also?" politely asked Edwin as he held a quiet but still distraught Reba in his arms.

"Unfortunately, yes," said the sheriff. "I'm afraid we're going to hear a lot more complaints this evening. Edwin, can you do your best to tidy up the first floor here? All we need is some space to line up chairs. I'll use the stage to address the crowd."

"Is that all, Sheriff?" suddenly spouted Reba sarcastically. "Can we leave the shit right where it is or should I get down on my hands and knees and clean that up too? Perhaps we should allow it to remain as evidence? Maybe someone can identify the cow it came from by the smell."

Silas sighed and calmly answered, "Anything you can do to make tonight's meeting go more smoothly would be appreciated, Mrs. McPhee."

"Of course, Sheriff. I will do my part for the betterment of the community...again!"

"You're not the only one who's suffered, Mrs. McPhee. You're not the only victim here," said Silas.

"Perhaps not, Sheriff, but I certainly feel like it. Tell me, have you had to scrub shit off the floor of Jackson's General Store lately?" asked Reba, turning to face Sherman.

"No, Mrs. McPhee," he said sheepishly.

"Reba!" scolded Edwin.

"I didn't think so!" she said in reference to Sherman's reply, ignoring her husband. "Now, if you gentlemen will excuse me, I'm going to try to salvage some shred of my dear son's memory from the appalling rubble upstairs. Perhaps if I'm successful, then I'll find strength enough to take care of matters down here. For now I'm content with letting this place stink!"

After turning to walk away from everyone, Reba paused a moment, then spun back to them and said, "We worked so hard to bring to this community a building that served a useful, an entertaining, and an honorable purpose. And this is the thanks we get for all our hard work and dedication. Whoever did this should be hanged, Silas. They should be hanged! Our holiday has been ruined and possibly tarnished forever. We don't deserve this. That's all I have to say."

Reba McPhee started to weep again as she climbed the stairs in an effort to put back together what had been cruelly torn asunder. Her thoughts were with her departed son Charles. She wept for him, and directed all her remaining strength to preserving his memory. Nothing else mattered to her.

"I'll see to it that everything is cleaned up for the meeting tonight, Sheriff. Can't guarantee the place will be without blemish, but we'll do our best," declared Edwin. "Can't blame her really," he added. "She worked extremely hard. We both did. If you'll excuse me, I'm going up to give her a hand."

Edwin retreated up the stairs leaving Silas and Sherman by themselves.

"We need to talk," said the sheriff, clutching Sherman's arm and pulling him into a corner. "This can't be contained anymore. It's affected too many people and caused too much damage. I think you should speak at the meeting tonight and divulge everything that transpired between you and Danny Ricker. After you've revealed everything you know, including your own recent troubles, I'll declare Ricker a prime suspect. Maybe someone knows his whereabouts."

"And what happens if people start directly blaming me for all that's occurred? What if I'm vilified and it's my neck the townspeople demand stretched and not Ricker's?"

"There's no reason to think that will happen. You haven't committed any crimes and I'll stand by your side if things start to get edgy. I think stating the truth is the best course of action," said Silas. "The townspeople will respect your honesty and integrity. I'm sure of it."

"But people might get angry that I didn't come forward right away, that I didn't warn of a potentially unstable and enraged individual who openly spoke of contempt for this community...and me," cautioned Sherman. "I think I saw him the other night on horseback. Silas...have you been out to the Morrell Farm lately?"

"No, just the Lovells'. Why?"

"You'll find out tonight at the meeting," said Sherman. "The pastor has had some recent trouble. Best if he tells you though."

"Fine. Any reason I should go out there now, Sherman?"

"No, Silas, just wait until tonight. Trust me."

"Okay, I'm going to patrol the area and see what other problems have arisen. I'll stay close by and try and spread the word about the meeting. Find me if you run into any more trouble. Inform everyone who comes into your store about the assembly tonight. I don't care if they're just visiting from Bangor, tell them what's going on. Be there at six o'clock, not a minute after."

"I understand, Silas. You can count on me."

"Good. Now let's get going. I can't take the stench in here any longer."

The two men exited the grange. Silas mounted his horse and rode off while Sherman walked back to the store. He was still determined to lock up early, though he was certain his plans with Sophie were all but shattered, much like the innards of the grange hall. He decided he would go over to the school before class let out and tell her about the emergency meeting. He would also deliver and run up a new U.S. flag.

Sherman entered the store and was relieved to find it empty and not full of customers demanding service and wondering where the absent storekeeper was. In the same moment, he was selfishly hoping that in the time he'd been gone, Jeff had made a miraculous recovery and was ready to resume his duties. It became readily apparent that was not the case. Sherman could tell Jeff was still upstairs asleep by the sounds of his heavy breathing and the creak of the bed as he stirred. He decided to leave him be. When the time came, he would wake him and bring him along to the meeting.

The rest of the morning went by without incident. Sherman attended his store duties and spent much time observing the eerie absence of any holiday merriment through his window. Settler Road was unusually quiet. Occasionally he'd hear the random pop of a lone firecracker after detonation, but nothing else. There was no music or patriotic singing to be heard, and there was no smell of baking cakes, pies, or any other type of food in the air. The atmosphere surrounding the town seemed very glum and depressing. Obviously the news of the atrocious crime inflicted upon the grange hall had spread and put a serious damper on people's disposition. He was sure that many were sad and disappointed, but many others were simply afraid.

Sherman looked at his pocket watch and decided it was time to lock up and connect with Sophie before she went home. He gathered a new American flag from his inventory in the storage room. As he made his way back to the front counter, he was pleasantly surprised to see Sophie standing there waiting for him.

"Hello, Sherman. I closed down the school for the rest of the afternoon and let the Lovell kids go home. In spite of what's happened today, it's still a holiday, so I thought it best to send them along."

"I was just coming to see you. I was bringing you this."

Sherman handed Sophie the new flag.

"What's happening, Sherman?" she asked with an unsteady twinge of fear in her voice. "Why would someone despoil the grange hall in such a repulsive manner? Why would someone attack and defile such an innocent place where children gather—my schoolhouse? I took that Confederate flag down as quickly as I could. I placed it in the stove and burned it to ashes. I never want to see another one again. I keep asking myself why this is happening. After seeing that mysterious-looking man on horseback the other morning, I'm becoming very frightened. I keep wondering who he was and why he was there—and if he intends to do us harm. Do you think that man was responsible for what happened this morning?"

Sherman wanted to confide in his lover and tell her all about Danny Ricker. He felt he owed it to her and thought she'd understand, and could possibly help. But he was unsure of himself and afraid of what to tell her. He realized he was rapidly becoming terrified by the thought of what he was going to say later at the meeting. His stomach began to churn. For the moment, all he could do was answer her last question.

"I think the man we saw could be responsible, though I still have no idea as to his identity," he calmly stated. "There's a meeting tonight at the grange hall at six o'clock. I'll be there, and I think you should encourage Thaddeus and Erin to come. The boys should go, too. We're going to discuss what's been happening around here recently. It will be a good opportunity for the pastor to speak and inform the townsfolk of the Morrell family's misfortune."

Sherman drew Sophie close to him and mournfully expressed his regret that their upcoming romantic holiday date had been reduced to a stuffy and frightful emergency town meeting.

"I'm so sorry our plans have been unexpectedly altered this evening. I was so looking forward to the party, some dancing, good food, and a brilliant fireworks display later tonight. It seems all that has been ruined," he said.

"It is tragic, and I grieve for those who put so much hard work in preparation. I especially grieve for those now unable to participate in the scheduled festivities. But we both can take a bit of selfish solace in the fact that we were fortunate enough to have a special moment together amid all that splendor before it was destroyed. I shall keep that special memory in my heart forever."

Both were able to produce tiny smiles before hugging one another. Sherman was about to kiss his love when suddenly he heard a voice from above.

"Hope I ain't interrupting you two? I heard voices down here and decided it was time to get up and see what's what."

Sherman and Sophie pulled apart from their embrace and saw Jeff emerge from the staircase. He was cleaned up and he had changed into an outfit that made him look less disheveled.

"Why, hello, Miss Curtis. It's so nice to see you again. Have you come back to pay me a visit this fine afternoon?" asked Parlin with an arrogant smile and a lustful tone that caused Sophie instinctively to take a step backward.

Before she could answer, Sherman stepped between the two, effectively cutting off Parlin's inappropriate advance. He spoke up, saying rather brashly, "Miss Curtis stopped by to pick up this new flag. She also came to see me concerning other matters of a more personal nature."

"Oh, I see," responded Parlin cockily. He sidestepped the pair and ducked behind the counter, all the while never taking his gaze off Sophie.

"I should be going now," Sophie said abruptly. "I'll see you tonight, Sherman. I'll bring money to pay for the flag."

"Goodbye for now," he answered. "Safe journey home."

With that, the young woman hurriedly left the store, letting the door bang shut behind her.

"You see that? You see that puckish little twinkle in her eye? She's a pistol, Sherm. She's got a feistiness that's just raring to burst out from under that old schoolmarm dress of hers...and I know I'm the man to help her find it. I'm now certain of it. There's most assuredly something of a sexually inquisitive nature about her. I can just feel it...boy, can I feel it. You must sense it too, Sherm?"

Sherman boiled with anger and balled up his fists as if he were about to take a swing at Parlin. The disrespectful and ungentlemanly words spewing from his associate's lips triggered a jealous rage that was almost uncontrollable—almost.

Keeping his emotions in check, Sherman calmly but directly said, "As I've stated before, Jeff, I don't appreciate your vulgar insinuations concerning Miss Curtis. I happen to think she is a remarkably upstanding young lady who in no way matches the reprehensible character in which you describe her! She is not sexually charged or promiscuous in any manner, and I find it very hard to believe a single thing you've said about her, including the overly flirtatious conversation you claim to have had the day I was in Portland. I say this again, sir, I cannot and will not allow such demeaning comments about Miss Curtis to be spoken in my store!"

Sherman spoke from his heart in defense of his lover, but deep down he wondered if Parlin had a point. Sherman thought back to the other night at the grange hall. He had never known a woman to be so sexually aggressive in his whole life.

"You're sweet on her, aren't you? You're under the delusion that she's all prim and proper...a true lady. I'm telling ya, she ain't, Sherm. I know what she is. I've seen her type before. You'd be better off steering clear of that train wreck. She ain't the type you fall in love with and marry. She'll ruin you...I know."

"Sophie is my sweetheart, Jeff! I have courted her of late and I intend to keep courting her! I would appreciate it if you'd stay out of our business!"

"That ain't the way she described it to me, Sherm. I didn't mention it earlier, but now seems like a good time. She told me that she was only being polite to you and had no intention of starting any kind of relationship. She likes your store—probably your money, too. I bet she'd do anything to get a little piece of it. She told me other things while you were in Portland, but I'll respect your order and not say what they were. I wouldn't want to bruise your delicate sensibilities," said Jeff condescendingly.

"You're a goddamn liar," fired back Sherman. "You'll say anything, 'cause you want her for yourself. I forbid it! Don't talk to her again!"

"Now wait just a damn minute, Sherman," said Jeff heatedly. "No one calls me a liar! I may be your employee, but you have no right to dictate to me who I can or cannot speak to or whom I can or cannot court. You say she's one way; I say she's another. I also say let her choose the better man. Now, you can fire me and ban me from this store, but I ain't gonna go away. I'll still find the means to see her, and the only thing that will happen from my termination will be that your store will suffer and decline for it—and you'll end up in Ricker's sights all the faster without my help and protection."

Sherman was speechless. He couldn't find any appropriate words to launch back at his employee, whose help he did want and need in many ways.

"I'm not your enemy, Sherman, and I don't want to be. Let's just simmer down before one or both of us says something we truly don't mean. If Sophie sincerely wants to be with you and not me, I'll respect that and back off. If she truly has no interest in having a little fun with me, then I won't stand in *your* way. I'll step aside like a gentleman and will still consider myself your friend and faithful employee."

"Have a little fun with you? You make it sound as if you have no intention of engaging in a true courtship with her," speculated Sherman.

Jeff laughed and said, "I don't. I want to have *fun* with her. Like I said before, she ain't the marrying type…but she's good for other things, that's a certainty."

"You're disgusting!"

"And you still need my help. Why don't we end this useless conversation and carry on like gentlemen. I will not bring up Sophie ever again. The fate of who she intends to spend time with is entirely in her hands. Regardless of what happens, Sherman, remember what I said. I ain't a liar. I seen many women just like her during the war—masters of manipulation and deception. You're a decent man and I'd hate for you to get swept up in the arms of a tainted woman just out to get the better of you," Jeff spouted while extending his hand to shake.

"Very well. I leave it to her good senses to make the right decision," replied Sherman as he took Jeff's hand and shook it. "We'll speak of this no more."

"Understood," said Jeff as he walked to the window and looked out. "It's dead out there. I could care less about this stupid holiday, but I thought there'd be more activity than this. What time does the grange hall celebration start?"

Sherman sighed and said, "We're closing up early. Right now, as a matter of fact. A lot's happened today that you're unaware of. Why don't we go over to the house and I'll explain it over an early supper. It's not good news, unfortunately."

"Ricker?" asked Jeff tersely.

"Most assuredly."

"Damn."

CHAPTER 10

The Town Meeting

Sherman paced back and forth in front of the parlor fireplace while Jeff sat in his usual chair watching and listening. The whiskey was there, but this night he ignored the bottle entirely, as if pretending it were invisible. He puffed heavily on a cigar instead and listened as Sherman described in detail all that had happened at the Budwin School and the Old Liberty Grange Hall. He finished his talk by telling Jeff about the emergency meeting at six.

"Good," expounded Jeff as he tugged at his beard. "The issue will be out in the open now. There'll be active support from the community. Everybody will be watching out for Danny Ricker, making it impossible for him to hide. Somebody will catch him off-guard and bring him to justice…one way or the other."

"I wish it were that simple," said Sherman pensively.

"Isn't it?"

"I fear nothing's that simple."

"You think everyone to whom Ricker's done harm will somehow transfer blame onto you?" asked Jeff.

"That notion had crossed my mind. I must be truthful about the matter when I address the assembly. Lying can only negatively impact the situation. Besides, I've already divulged most everything to Sheriff Ridgeway. I'm the source of the problem. Everything, it seems, points directly to me."

"Maybe. And just maybe smart folks around here won't see it that way at all."

"Perhaps. I suppose we should be on our way now. The meeting is going to start soon," said Sherman impatiently.

The two men got up and started walking toward the grange hall. They joined a grumbling procession of people anxious to find resolution. Men and women climbed the steps of the grange and entered the meeting room. Sherman looked over the chamber and was astonished at how clean it now was. There was little trace that anything had been amiss earlier. The room was well lit and rows of chairs, lined up perfectly, faced the stage. A wooden podium was placed at the top of the stage where Ridgeway would address the crowd. The once-pungent smell of animal dung was now gone, and every damaged item had been cleverly hidden or removed. The room was now ready to accommodate a group in an official-type setting. However, despite the obvious hard work the McPhees had employed to turn the lower level of the grange from a total disaster to a functioning meeting place, Sherman was saddened as he was one of the only people in the room who knew what it looked like a day earlier—a magnificently decorated ballroom bursting with patriotism.

People milled about until Sheriff Ridgeway entered the hall. He promptly made his way up to the podium and gestured for everyone to take their seats. Just then Sherman saw Sophie enter the room, followed closely by the entire Morrell family. They sat down just a row or two behind Sherman and Parlin. Sophie gave Sherman a nervous wink. He in return shot her a little smile while Parlin pretended to ignore the two.

The buzz of conversation quickly died down as people took to their chairs. In attendance were several farmers from all over Scarborough, a few residents of South Gorham, and all the folks who lived in the immediate area, which included Hiram Lovell and his family, Edwin and Reba McPhee, Milly McClatchy, and of course the Morrells. Ridgeway cleared his throat and began to speak.

"For those who don't know me, I'm the sheriff of Cumberland County, Silas Ridgeway. We have a lot to cover here this evening so I'm going to get right down to business. There's been a series of crimes over the past several days that not only have been an unlawful nuisance, but also have the potential of becoming life threatening. Today, a despicable crime was committed on these very premises. An unknown criminal perpetrated an unspeakable act of vandalism and national sacrilege."

"Our grange hall and museum were destroyed today," shouted Reba McPhee as she rose from her seat and faced the crowd. "We had planned a beautiful Independence Day celebration to be shared by all. Edwin and I worked for weeks in advance preparing the perfect setting for folks to mingle, sing, dance, eat, and enjoy everything the holiday has to offer. We had everything ready just in time, too. But instead of being blessed by having the pleasure of seeing the townsfolk enjoy themselves in the splendid environment we created, an environment not only for amusement but also for remembrance, we were shocked to discover our property obliterated in unspeakable ways! There was a Confederate flag hanging from our rafters! Now who would do such an indescribably wicked thing on our nation's birthday?"

The crowd buzzed with discussion until a soft voice spoke up from the rear of the room.

"A similar Confederate flag was run up the school's flagpole earlier today as well. My name is Sophie Curtis and I'm the summer-session teacher at the Budwin School. I'm new to this area, but I've never seen such a disrespectful act carried out at an innocent place of learning where children gather. It's disgraceful and must stop."

The crowd buzzed until Ridgeway put his hand up, signaling he wanted quiet.

"Last week I started investigating reports of thefts and slaughtered livestock in South Gorham. I see some of the victims in the crowd here tonight. A few days ago, some of the same types of crimes were reported here in North Scarborough. I think they could all be connected somehow."

"You're damn right they're connected! No doubt in my mind," boomed Hiram Lovell as he got up from his chair. The crowd turned to face the irate dairy farmer.

"Over the past few days I've lost three cows, two pigs, and had my barn burgled. My dairy business is suffering and my family is scared to leave the house. Not only were my animals killed, they were butchered! Mutilated in a grotesque fashion. I can't believe the same crimes committed in South Gorham aren't related to what's happened here. They can't be random. They're cold, calculated acts of butchery by the same lunatic—I'm sure of it. I'll tell ya'll something else, I ain't gonna stand for it no more!"

As soon as Hiram sat down, Pastor Morrell rose from his chair. Unlike the others, he wasn't content with shouting from his seat. He gracefully walked to the podium and started his invocation as if he was in his church leading a Sunday sermon.

"My friends, my family suffered a horrible malady early yesterday morning. Our house caught fire under very suspicious circumstances.

By God's good grace, my family was uninjured and the Devil's blaze was contained before it reduced all we hold sacred to ashes. We are not a vengeful people and I have a very forgiving heart, but this crime against my family cannot go unrecognized or unpunished. I pray that if anyone has information concerning the culprit of this terrible act, may he step forward and help expedite God's justice upon the guilty. In reference to the guilty, whether he sits among us now or not, I say, may he be forgiven in the eyes of the Lord. Amen."

Pastor Morrell bowed his head and benevolently strolled back to his seat. Once again the crowd buzzed with heated discussion. Voices rang out randomly.

"Someone stole from my garden," said one farmer.

"I had some chickens taken right out of the coop. Broke the lock and everything," stated another farmer.

"Someone painted 'The South shall have its revenge' on the side of my barn," said yet another disgruntled agrarian.

"What are you gonna do about this, Sheriff?" one man demanded.

"Do you suspect anyone?" another shouted.

"There is someone who we believe might be responsible," said Ridgeway as he fixed his gaze squarely on Sherman. The young store-owner froze in his chair as a deep chill ran down his spine.

"Mr. Sherman Jackson is familiar to you all, I think. He's the owner of Jackson's General Store and he holds information that might shed some light on what we're dealing with here. I've asked him to speak tonight. Mr. Jackson, would you please come up to the podium and address the assembly?"

Sherman reluctantly rose from his seat and made his way up front. Ridgeway stepped aside and Sherman stepped up to the podium. He wasn't exactly sure what he was going to say or how he truly wanted to express his thoughts. After a minute of hesitation followed by a deep breath, the young man began his oration.

"Last week I had an altercation with my former employee. Most of you know him, but for those who don't, his name is Danny Ricker. I discovered he had been stealing from me and not performing his duties to my satisfaction. I was left with no other course of action, and I terminated his employment. Mr. Ricker became quite perturbed and hostile, going so far as to attack me with a knife when I refused to pay him the money he felt he had earned. I escaped the incident unharmed, but Mr. Ricker ran off vowing he would get back at me. I believe Danny Ricker is the cause of all the criminal activity that's been reported lately."

"That's a lie!" screamed out an old, frail voice that struggled to be heard. "Sweet, young Danny would never commit any crimes or acts of violence, certainly none described in the manner here tonight. He's as innocent as a newly born babe. He had nothing in this world and no one to care for him except me. You robbed him of any chance of bettering himself when you fired him! Danny was a kind and hardworking young man. He never showed anything but gratitude for the love and support I gave him. I can't imagine he ever showed any animosity toward you or a single soul in this town. I find your story to be reckless and quite untrue, Mr. Jackson."

Sherman was astonished to see the widow McClatchy standing by her chair defending the boy he knew had taken full advantage of her. Milly was feeble looking and haggard. Her voice was weak, but she continued to rail at him with as much energy as she could muster.

"I know the cause of all the problems around here," confidently declared the old widow, "and it has nothing to do with my dear, innocent, Danny."

The crowd hushed to a dead silence as all eyes focused on the old woman, whose unkempt appearance more resembled a deranged witch than an aged, sane, Christian woman.

"I've seen the culprit. I've seen him riding across the countryside at night! He wreaks havoc wherever he goes and sows fear and unrest among the unfortunate souls he encounters. He wears ghostly robes and a hood to conceal his identity. I've heard him howl and wail this ungodly sound as he gallops along, sometimes with a bright torch in his hand. He's come to my house many a night in terrifying form. His shrieks rattle the very foundation of my soul and I find myself crawling under the bed to hide from this menacing specter. At first I thought he was just a man, but now I know he's a ghost—a dreadful apparition spawned by that cursed place of evil next to Pyne's Cemetery!"

The crowd starting buzzing again in hushed conversation at the mention of Pyne's Cemetery. Most everyone knew of it and its unholy reputation. The story of the murders that occurred years earlier at the now-deserted home of Sam Lester was infamous. That was the evil place of which Milly spoke.

"The specter rides back to that dreadful place of the dead every night. I'm sure of it. I wouldn't be surprised if it was the ghost of Sam Lester himself that's terrorizing this community. I'd stake what few remaining years I have left on it. Sam was a misunderstood man too, like my Danny. But instead of offering him help, this community shunned him, forcing him to go insane and do what he did. Now he's come back for his revenge! Mark my words!"

The crowd's astonishment gently turned to sporadic grins and chuckles at the widow's outlandish claims. Milly slumped down into her seat and appeared particularly ill. A gray pallor crept across her face, causing some people seated near her to rush to her side.

"Take me home. I wish to go home and retire to my bed. I feel the burning return to my stomach and I must rest before I become too dizzy and unable to stand," said the weakened woman.

"Would someone please help Mrs. McClatchy home?" requested Silas.

"We will. Our farm is not far from hers," volunteered two good Samaritans who gently lifted the widow from her seat and helped her out the door.

The crowd again mostly chuckled and snickered at the widow's remarks; however, a few stayed remarkably silent and visibly concerned.

"Notwithstanding Milly McClatchy's boogeyman stories, does anyone else have anything to say or report?" asked Silas as Sherman started to make his way back to his seat.

"I'd like to ask Mr. Jackson a question or two," said a stranger he didn't recognize. Sherman returned to the podium.

"So I understand correctly, you think this Danny Ricker fella is causing trouble because you owe him money? Why don't you just pay him, for Christ's sake, and maybe I can salvage what's left of my tore-up fence and dug-up garden."

"I don't know that it's him. I haven't seen him commit any of these crimes, but he's threatened me with my life and he's definitely dangerous," answered Sherman.

"Are you sure it's him that did the threatening?" asked the man curiously.

"What do you mean," replied Sherman.

"I mean that I saw that man run out of your store last week. He run up Settler Road like shot from a gun. What I saw next was *you* standing in your doorway all deranged-looking and holding an axe!"

"It's true, I saw it too," said a woman who spoke up from the crowd.

"He attacked me. I was defending myself," Sherman responded.

"Ha! Looked like he was unarmed and scared out of his mind. You, on the other hand, looked like a determined killer ready to lop his head off," the accusing man said.

"He had a knife…uh…a pocketknife that he…he…."

"A pocketknife!" bellowed the man. "He had a pocketknife and you had an axe? What fool carrying a pocketknife would attack a man with an axe? Makes no sense, mister."

The crowd started to get antsy as Sherman started to perspire. He wanted to sit down quickly but wasn't given the chance as another man stood up and started to question him. To his surprise, it was his friend Hiram Lovell.

"Sherman, I've heard a lot of folks here talk about what they've lost in the past few days. What I saw happen here in the grange this morning was cruel and tragic. I'm curious—what exactly have you suffered? Your store, your house, and your property—they all look pretty pristine to me. If Danny Ricker is in fact our man, and he's got a major quarrel with you as you claim, why hasn't he killed your horses or looted your store, or burned your house down for that matter? The way I see it, everybody in here is paying for your debt owed to him!"

"I had a revolver and a Bowie knife stolen from my display cabinet just after I fired Ricker. I'm…I'm…I'm positive it was him," said Sherman unconvincingly. "Someone used a ladder to come through an open window on the second floor of my store. The case was forced into and the items stolen. It had to have been him."

"But you don't know for certain?" asked Hiram. "Was anything else stolen? Did he steal any of your cash that you keep on hand under the counter?"

"Well, no…no, he didn't, as a matter of fact," reluctantly answered Sherman.

"That don't add up. You claim he wants money from you and yet he didn't take it when he had the chance? He didn't take anything else? You have a lot of valuable goods on hand. He could have really cleaned you out. Why didn't he? Instead he's cleaning us out!" thundered Hiram.

Sherman thought feverishly to come up with a reply. Unwittingly, he blurted out, "He stole my Morgan, Skipper."

"You saw him do this?" asked Hiram.

"No…but I noticed he was gone from my livery late the other night."

"Are you sure he didn't just get away from you and wander off?"

"No, I'm positive he didn't wander off. He was stolen. I'm sure of it," Sherman insisted.

"What makes you so sure? What evidence is there that he was taken?" asked Hiram like a prosecuting attorney cross-examining a witness on the stand.

"Because he was brought back and tied up proper," said Sherman, instantly regretting his answer.

Some people in the crowd laughed while others shook their heads in disbelief. Hiram didn't relent and kept pressuring Sherman.

"What kind of thief steals property and then returns it—especially one who allegedly has a deep quarrel with you? Sherman, that really makes no sense, and I for one don't want to hear another word from your mouth. Maybe you ought to go see Mrs. McClatchy and compare ghost stories!"

The crowd erupted with laughter while Sherman, stunned and ashamed, returned to his seat. As he sat down he looked at Parlin, who offered no comfort or counsel. Sherman watched as the sheriff returned to the podium and wondered why he had remained silent and didn't defend him in any way. He put his head down as he felt every eyeball in the room was now glaring at him.

"Ahh, unless anyone else wants to speak out about our problem or has any additional information they'd like to share, I'll conclude by saying that I plan to remain in the area and conduct an ongoing investigation until we get a break in this case or the culprit is apprehended or killed. In the meantime, I urge everyone to stay on guard and vigilant. Talk to and help one another. Eventually we'll catch this fiend," said Silas.

"What if we don't?" boldly asked a woman as she stood up. "What if he can't be caught? I've seen the ghost rider, too, and I know others here have as well and just won't admit it! I don't know about the rest of you, but I don't plan to go anywhere near the old Lester house or Pyne's Cemetery for as long as I live!"

The crowd grew deathly silent and people started to look at one another with trepidation. Eventually the crowd rose from their seats and began to filter out the front door. Many had worried expressions chiseled on their faces.

Sherman remained seated. He wanted everyone to leave before him. Even Silas filed out without saying a word.

"Are you ready to head back, Sherm?" asked Jeff.

"No, I don't feel like moving at the moment."

"Okay, well…I'm going to go back to my room now. I'm still a little woozy and could turn in early. I got the key. I'll lock up tight before bed."

Jeff stood up and started to make his way to the door. Halfway there he stopped and said, "Nothin's changed Sherman. I am still gonna look out for ya. Soldiers don't abandon their old brothers-in-arms." With that he walked away, but not before casting a lusty smile in Sophie's direction.

"Mr. Jackson, my wife and I are going upstairs to continue cleaning. When we come back down, we'd like for you not to be here," said Edwin McPhee. "For a long time I've desired to have a display of artifacts and an oral history of the 20th Maine. It seems I'll have to wait for it a little longer now…and I don't believe I want you to be the primary contributor anymore."

Sherman never looked up and didn't see Edwin walk away. The last thing he heard was, "You go ahead, I'll be along in a short while. Just remember what he helped us save the other morning before passing judgment." It was the voice of Sophie telling the Morrells to go home without her. A moment later Sherman felt a warm hand caress his.

"Why didn't you tell me about any of this?" she asked, sitting down next to him.

"I'm not sure. I didn't know what to tell you and I didn't want to frighten you, or anybody else for that matter. I had no idea a simple quarrel with a lowly employee could turn into such a catastrophe."

Sophie continued to caress his hand and then asked, "What was all that talk about Pyne's Cemetery, and who was Sam Lester?"

Sherman sighed and answered, "Sam Lester was the undertaker of Pyne's Cemetery, which is not far from here. His house was right next to the graveyard. Many years ago he went insane and allegedly murdered his wife and two children in a very brutal fashion. My father and a group of men went there and discovered a grisly scene of death unlike anything they had ever come across before. Lester's wife and children were killed, but there was no sign of Sam. He was nowhere to be found. Sheriff Ridgeway concluded that he committed the crimes, but it was never proven and he was never found. Sam Lester just disappeared and has never resurfaced. Everyone around here assumes he's dead and has been for a long time, but no one knows for sure. His house has been deserted for years because no one wants to buy it after learning what happened there. Both it and the cemetery have been neglected for several years and many old folks around these parts believe the Lester house is haunted. Nobody speaks of it and as far as I know, nobody ever goes up there."

"Could...could it have been this Lester fellow we saw on the horse the other morning?" asked Sophie with a chill.

"I don't know," replied Sherman looking right into her eyes. "It makes me wonder if Danny Ricker is causing all these problems, or something far worse. From what my father told me, Sam Lester was certifiably insane and a probable murderer. If ever I imagined a twisted man wicked enough to commit such evil deeds upon innocent people, it would be Sam Lester. I shudder to think he's still alive and roaming freely. What a terrible thought, indeed."

"What are we going to do?" asked Sophie meekly.

"What can we do except as the sheriff says and stay vigilant and on guard? I have Jeff helping me mind the store and protect my property."

"I wouldn't trust him with one Indian-head cent. I believe him to be a lowly scoundrel and not a gentleman," she scoffed.

"He desires to be with you...and I told him that we were a couple and that his earlier remarks were deplorable and would not be tolerated. I confronted him with stern language, which should put an end to the matter," Sherman said innocently without volunteering any additional information regarding his earlier discussion with Jeff about Sophie.

"I feel uneasy in his company. I feel as if something is terribly out of place whenever he's around. I can't explain it."

"It's okay. He won't bother you anymore. If he does, he'll have hell to pay from me," Sherman said confidently. "Now, let's get you home safely. I hope the pastor has made plans to repair his home?"

"He has indeed. He knows a carpenter in Portland to whom he's sent word in a letter. As long as it remains warm without any substantial rainfall, we should be fine. The roof, thankfully, was not damaged."

"Fires are extremely hazardous in rural communities like this. Unlike big cities such as Boston, or even Portland, we don't have organized fire departments. If a house catches fire, and there isn't sufficient help or water to battle the flames, then there's virtually no chance of saving it. We were lucky that your fire was caught early and quickly contained. Maybe it would be safer if you all moved into the church. I'd feel...."

"Don't say anymore. I'm frightened enough as it is."

"I'm sorry. Let's get going before it starts to get dark." Sherman paused, then added, "This place sure looks different from just a day ago." Sophie blushed a little and smiled. She took Sherman's arm and the two walked off in the direction of the Morrell farm.

Later that evening, Silas Ridgeway found himself patrolling an area just outside South Gorham. He trotted along on horseback looking for signs of anything out of the ordinary, no matter how insignificant. The skies darkened as the sun set, and the tired sheriff anxiously pointed his mount in the direction of his mistress's house just a mile or two away. His thoughts selfishly turned from those of duty and concern for the endangered community to those of personal indulgence and lust. His mistress, a simple washerwoman who made her living by doing laundry, was named Ophelia Norris and was not without controversy in her own right. The young and attractive woman had been married earlier in life to a much older man who had made a small fortune in Maine's winter ice-harvesting industry. A few years earlier Ophelia's husband had been found dead in their South Gorham home under suspicious circumstances. The cause of death was eventually ruled a heart attack and the young widow was cleared of any potential wrongdoing. She became the sole heiress of her husband's fortune and rapidly drove the business into the ground before being forced to sell it outright at a huge loss. Subsequently she squandered nearly all of her inherited wealth and was reduced to near poverty, retaining only her house and working a meager job to sustain herself. Ophelia was known as Ridgeway's mistress by a select few in the area. Those same few wondered if he used her like a prostitute or if the two were actually in love. It mattered little. Such gossip was frowned upon—especially when it involved a law-enforcement official with power over the average citizen.

Silas picked up the pace as thoughts of a hot meal, a bath, a rub-down, and a night of spirited sex entered his mind. As a smug little smile crept across his face, the sheriff's content world of lustful self-indulgence instantly came to a crashing halt as a gunshot ripped clean through his left shoulder.

"Son of a bitch," he cried in pain. He reached for his Spencer and drew it out of its leather case strapped to the saddle, just as another shot rang out, forcing him to jump off the horse and roll away into a roadside ditch for cover. Silas readied the Spencer and carefully poked his head up to get a glimpse of his attacker. From out of the woods across the narrow road emerged a form pointing a pistol right at him. In the waning daylight, Silas recognized who he was up against. The man was dirty and ragged. His face was unshaven and his hair a bushy mess. He was lean and hungry, and faced the wounded sheriff with an evil look of determination in his eyes. It was Danny Ricker!

"I ain't gonna be hunted by the law or anybody else," proclaimed Danny in a raspy voice. "I heard what you all said at that meeting in the grange. I was there, hidden outside beneath an open window! Sherman Jackson was there, too, spouting off his big mouth, saying all kinds of lies about me. I'm gonna get that son of a bitch. As God is my witness, I'm gonna get him and everything he owes me—and everything that shithole of a town owes me, too! And God help anyone who gets in my way! I'll line 'em up right next to you, Sheriff!"

As Ricker continued to rant, it became clear to Ridgeway that he was deranged and mad beyond all help. He put his pain aside and summoned all his strength to raise the Spencer into firing position as blood oozed down his stricken shoulder. He hurriedly squeezed off a shot before Ricker could train his pistol on him. The bullet failed to hit its target but succeeded in forcing Ricker to dash for cover. Silas painfully recycled his rifle and desperately scanned the edge of the woods looking for his adversary, who had disappeared.

"Give it up, Danny!" foolishly called out Silas. "You can't win! Everyone knows you're causing all these problems and you'll be brought to justice…at the end of a rope!"

"Lies! Goddamned lies started by that bastard Jackson!" yelled Ricker before firing another shot that whizzed by Ridgeway's head. The sheriff fired blindly in the direction of Ricker's voice. He squeezed off a shot, then another, not knowing if he'd hit his intended target. His head started to spin as the rapid loss of blood from his injured shoulder numbed his body and dulled his senses. His hands started to shake and soon he found it difficult to grip or raise the rifle.

"Put down your gun and give up," yelled Ridgeway in one last feeble attempt to defuse the situation and save his own life. "Give up... just give up...put down...put down your gun," ordered the sheriff, on the verge of slipping unconscious in a rising pool of his own blood. He slumped forward, then rolled onto his back as the Spencer tumbled out of his hands. He breathed heavily and used his right hand to try to plug the hole in his left shoulder, preventing further blood loss. It was all in vain. The last image, forever burned into the dying sheriff's eyeballs, was that of Danny Ricker's Colt House Revolver being aimed point-blank at his forehead. In one bloody and blinding flash, the sheriff was no more.

Ricker sneered at the corpse that lay before him. He went through the fallen sheriff's pockets, hoping to find items of value. He came up with a few coins, a pocketknife, some additional Spencer cartridges, and an old watch. He plucked the sheriff's badge off his vest and added it to his small collection of stolen goods. Last, he took off the sheriff's hat and put it on his own head. He wore it like a trophy and likened himself to a hunter who had just removed the prized rack of antlers from freshly killed game. Eventually his warped mind came to its senses. The murderer dragged the body into the woods and covered it fully with dirt and brush until he was satisfied no one would find it. He then went back to the scene of the crime and collected the Spencer before mounting the deceased sheriff's horse. He spurred the animal and galloped off just as the last remnants of day shifted over to night and the countryside was enshrouded in darkness.

CHAPTER 11

Descent into Bedlam

Sherman wasn't sleeping anymore. Occasionally his mind and body would be so overwhelmed with fatigue that he would fall unconscious while in bed, but he wasn't truly sleeping. Thoughts of all that had happened and all that could happen constantly raced through his mind and deprived him of rest. As dawn broke, the tired young man emerged from the tangled mess of sheets and blankets and wasted no time in cleaning up and dressing himself.

It was now Saturday, July 5. Before Sherman could begin his routine morning inspections, there was a knock on his door. To his surprise, standing before him was Pastor Morrell, his wife Erin, and Sophie. At first, Sherman was sure the good pastor and his wife were on a righteous mission to sit down and discuss his sinful rendezvous with Sophie two nights earlier. He wondered what she might have told them in some conscience-clearing session. Immediately after that thought, another more disturbing one popped into his head. What if there had been more trouble at the Morrell farm? What if they had come to accuse or prosecute him in some manner? He was afraid to ask and simply stood in the doorway like a fool and said nothing.

"Good morning, Mr. Jackson," piped up the pastor.

"Good morning, Thaddeus," replied Sherman, followed by, "Good morning, Erin and Miss Curtis. Delighted to see you all."

Sophie smiled but Erin did not. The corpulent wife of the pastor stood and scowled, saying nothing while she fanned herself with a gloved hand.

"I'm sorry to trouble you at this early hour," the pastor said, "but Erin, Miss Curtis, and I are in need of your wagon and the marvelous stallions that pull it. We're off to Portland this morning to see about procuring the services of a carpenter who might be able to repair the damage inflicted on our house. We may need to purchase and transport certain building materials back with us, and your wagon would be best suited for the job. Might I ask how much it will cost to rent them for a maximum of two days?"

"Of course, Thaddeus," said Sherman, relieved that the matter related to business. "Please allow me to fetch your conveyance from my livery. Feel free to step inside and make yourself comfortable in the parlor as you wait. I'll only be a few minutes."

"Thank you kindly, Mr. Jackson. Ladies, shall we retire inside for but a moment?" asked the pastor while showing the women into Sherman's home. Erin walked in with her nose stuck up in the air while Sophie shot Sherman a little smile. Sherman winked at her, then walked out back to the livery, which he was happy to see hadn't been destroyed or robbed in the middle of the night. As he entered, he subtly glanced up at Parlin's window. He had felt that he was being watched, and sure enough, he was. He paid it no mind and harnessed his stallions. He led Phineas and Lucky to the loading dock by the barn where he parked his wagon. Within minutes they were hitched up and ready. He attached feedbags to both of them before returning to the house. They needed to be fed before the journey to Portland.

Sherman entered the parlor to find his three guests sitting comfortably and waiting. He resisted all urges to address Sophie first and went straight to Thaddeus.

"Okay, Thaddeus, I typically charge a dollar a day for the use of my horses and wagon. There are additional charges that would apply upon return if my property is damaged in any way. Typically, I collect my fee in advance, but in your case I'll collect payment after service has been satisfactorily rendered."

"Humph!" was the sound that escaped Erin's lips. Sherman looked at her. The woman's nose was still held high and she refused to return his glance. Clearly she was unhappy with him. He wondered if it was because of his unapproved date with Sophie, his recent admission of his indirect involvement with the town's troubles, or a combination of the two.

"Nonsense, my son. I shall pay you up front and in full. The price is fair and the equipment in fine working order I'm sure. Here are your greenbacks. Do you require a signed contract?"

"No, sir. Not for you. Your word is all I need," said Sherman.

"We would like a receipt, please, Mr. Jackson," chimed in Erin in an uppity tone.

"Of course, Mrs. Morrell. I will get you one immediately."

Sherman retreated to his office and scribbled out a receipt. He gave it to the pastor and led everyone outside to their waiting transport. He took off the feedbags and helped Erin and Sophie aboard. The pastor climbed up himself and promptly took the reins.

"If you don't mind my asking, sir," said Sherman, "but where are your sons? Surely they would wish to accompany you on your journey?"

"Indeed they would, Mr. Jackson," said the pastor, "but to my pleasant surprise, Olin requested to remain behind so he could look after our battered home. He so wants to right the wrong imposed on us and he feels he needs to do everything he can to help. He offered to continue the cleanup and to take care of everything at the church while we're gone. He even offered to help write up a new sermon for me that will appeal to the town's generous spirit and promote unity and justice during these difficult days. I couldn't be more proud of him. Wilbur volunteered to be his faithful servant by remaining at his side and catering to his needs. Such selfless acts by my two boys."

"Indeed. Will you be back to conduct Sunday morning services?"

"Alas, no, Sherman. We hope to return Sunday afternoon. The church will be closed tomorrow, but I plan on doing a double service next Sunday," said Thaddeus.

"Nice to hear. All my best for your journey ahead. I hope your endeavors are successful. I'm sure they will be."

"God be with you, Mr. Jackson," said Thaddeus with a smile.

"And with you, sir," he replied as the wagon got underway.

"I'll see you soon," mouthed Sophie in an inaudible tone.

Sherman nodded and waved goodbye as he watched the wagon rumble down Settler Road and eventually out of sight. He then made his way over to the store.

"Rental?" asked Jeff from behind the counter as Sherman entered.

"Yeah, the pastor has some business in Portland."

"Probably going to buy a gun," Jeff remarked in a snarky tone.

"I highly doubt that," fired back Sherman. "Are we ready for business today, Mr. Parlin? That's my main and only concern at this moment."

"I got a few more things to take care of, but we're ready to open. I could use a cup of coffee, though, and maybe some bacon and an egg or two," said Jeff.

Sherman got the hint and went back to the house to make some breakfast. He returned a bit later and the two ate in near silence. There was growing tension between the men and it was obvious. What wasn't obvious to Sherman was the immediate source of the discontent. Was Jeff finally beginning to side with other townsfolk and starting to place blame for all that had happened squarely on Sherman? Was Jeff's initial gratitude and adventurous loyalty to his employer wavering? Or was it something else—something deeper? Had the uneasy Sophie situation finally become impossible for both men to mask?

The two went about the day awkwardly. They spoke only when necessary and tried to stay out of each other's way. Virtually nobody came into the store and those that did left quickly without purchasing anything. There was definitely a feeling of resentfulness and anxiety in the air. This was the beginning of something that Sherman dreaded. His reputation as a reliable merchant, and more importantly, a good citizen was now in jeopardy. If people truly believed he was the root cause of the entire community's recent problems, it could have serious repercussions on his business as well as his personal and civic standing within North Scarborough. In short, it could ruin him. The thought pained him like a slow-turning knife embedded in his gut. He tried not to dwell on the excruciating notion; yet he couldn't help but concede that all forms of potential resolution to the town's ongoing nightmare seemed to lead directly back to him. He was the key, whether he wanted to accept it or not.

As the day started to wind down, Sherman stood by the big display window and watched two chickadees playfully chase each other up and down the street. As the two birds flew away out of sight, Sherman decided that he didn't wish to be alone during the evening. He felt it best to be in someone else's company. It would make him feel more secure, but it would also help reassure him that the world wasn't totally against him.

"Hey, Jeff?"

"Yeah?"

"Let's have dinner in my dining room. I'd like to talk about a few things with you."

"Well…if that's what you want. I won't deprive you of the opportunity of cooking and serving me my supper. That was the arrangement, wasn't it?"

Sherman picked up on Jeff's subtle sarcasm, which he found irksome. Instead of ignoring it, however, he acknowledged and used it.

"A regular paying salary is one topic I want to discuss with you. Maybe this time, you'll be more receptive to the matter by being less inebriated…like the last time."

Jeff let loose a fake chuckle and shook his head.

"You go start dinner, Sherm. I'll close the place up and be over in a short while. Just make sure you don't burn nothing."

"Don't worry, I won't," replied Sherman, before emptying out his cashbox and stuffing the money in his pocket.

Jeff went to the storage room while Sherman exited through the front door. He stopped at his chicken coop and slaughtered one of his birds that he intended to put in a pot and serve for dinner. He wasted no time and went right to work in the kitchen. An hour passed before the familiar knock on the door came. It was another forty-five minutes before dinner was served. The conversation was light and often meaningless. When the two men adjourned to the parlor for their customary cigars and whiskey, it was readily apparent to Sherman that Jeff had little interest in engaging in any topic of discussion. He appeared distant and aloof, not even showing the least bit of courtesy for the generous amounts of alcohol and tobacco graciously provided. He didn't even request a fire.

There was discussion, but it was terse and often fragmented. Sherman avoided the obvious contentious and distressing subjects—most deliberately the topic of Sophie—but still got little response or enthusiasm from his clearly indifferent guest. There was talk of salary. Sherman offered Parlin regular pay for his good work plus other benefits he thought were fair and deserved. That got a slight reaction from him, but nothing Sherman construed as being either impressed or grateful.

At last, Jeff got fidgety and just stood up and excused himself without explanation. Sherman let him out and watched him walk back to the store. After a while, Sherman went upstairs and slipped into the sewing room. He peeked out the window that faced the store's guest room window and watched for any sign of activity. He took care to stay concealed and not draw any attention to himself. He was anxious to see but not be seen. As it grew dark, Sherman saw candlelight in the window, but nothing else. As it got later, the light eventually went out. Tired, with a massive headache, the storeowner withdrew to his own bedroom, certain he would have no posted lookout tonight from Jackson's General Store. He went to bed, but not before locking himself in, the Henry propped up against the wall in easy reach.

╫

Several miles to the northeast, Sophie sat at a desk in her Portland hotel room. In an adjacent room, she could hear the faint snoring that indicated her pious guardians—the Morrells—were fast asleep. Under dim lamplight, she pored over pages of notes and lists she had written down from various reference books and other sources while visiting the Portland Athenaeum. She had spent a good portion of the day there while the pastor sought out his carpenter and Erin went shopping. Feigning the need to do some scholastic research for her incomplete Monday lesson plan, Sophie diligently went to work accumulating information on a pressing matter that she felt required her immediate and undivided attention.

The young woman went about her research meticulously and professionally. Her appearance mirrored her approach. Her strawberry-blonde hair, normally loose and draped down over her shoulders, was now bound up in a tight bun atop her head. She sat up straight in her chair and wielded her pencil across the pages as proficiently as if she were Shakespeare crafting a new masterpiece. With each mark her pencil scratched onto the paper came an ever-deepening expression of concern. Her eyes jumped back and forth between lists of information she had compiled earlier and new ones she was now creating. What she was expecting to find was not there. What she thought would be obvious wasn't. And what was supposed to make sense didn't. Her puzzlement flourished as her earlier worry now shifted into the realm of dread. She eventually reached a point of conclusion and then carefully gathered up all her material and placed it into a small leather satchel.

It was now very late and Sophie was extremely weary. She slowly undressed herself, then slipped into her nightgown. She crawled into bed longing for Sherman's warmth and his inviting touch. She thought back to the night they made love and tried to perfectly reconstruct and replay every delightful sensation over and over in her mind until her body tingled with pleasure. The impure thoughts were but a brief distraction from what was really worrying her; however, she reached a point where she could fight it no longer and surrendered to sleep.

+++

Back in North Scarborough, Sherman tossed and turned in his bed. He had fallen asleep earlier but had been tortured with nightmares that eventually wrenched him back into a state of semi-consciousness. He groggily sat up and lit a candle so he could see the time on his pocket watch. It was nearly two o'clock in the morning. He moaned slightly and rubbed his forehead, desperately wanting to escape back into a long and peaceful slumber. Something inside told him that wasn't going to happen, and it wasn't long before he heard a peculiar commotion coming from outside.

"Now what's happening?" he mumbled as he went to the window. To his astonishment several men on horseback galloped up Settler Road. They were followed by a horse-drawn wagon carrying many other people. Straggling behind were others rushing past on foot and yelling, "Fire! Fire!"

Sherman got dressed quickly and raced down the stairs and out his front door. He stopped the first person who crossed his path and asked, "Where's the fire?"

"Up the road that way," said a farmer Sherman recognized as someone who lived a few miles away. The man pointed at a fiery blaze, clearly visible through the trees, and not far away. Instantly Sherman knew what was burning—the widow McClatchy's house!

"C'mon! We need all the help we can get," said the farmer as he rushed off.

Sherman ran to the livery and mounted Skipper. He galloped up the road and into the forest, picking up the wide trail that led to the widow's house. In less than a minute he arrived at the raging inferno that had engulfed Milly McClatchy's home. The fire was all-consuming and there wasn't a single part of the house that wasn't encased in bright orange flames. Even those who had arrived earlier had ceased attacking the blaze and dropped their buckets and shovels as they realized their efforts were in vain. Sherman dismounted Skipper and joined the small crowd as they watched the burning structure start to collapse.

"Where's the old widow?" a voice bellowed out from the darkness. "Has anybody seen her?" another asked.

"She was sickly. Does anyone know if she got out?"

Slowly the small crowd began to realize that Milly had been incapable of doing much for herself over the past few days, and it was highly likely she was in bed when the fire broke out, and thus was trapped inside—and now dead. Some of the men got sick at the thought and vomited. Others bowed their heads and prayed. Sherman stood in stunned silence.

A thunderous crack soon rang out and the whole flaming structure shifted to the left and collapsed under the weight of the heavy roof. Horses whinnied and the men took cover as fiery debris shot out in all directions. Just then, amidst all the chaos and confusion, Sherman and several others looked up and saw a frightening sight. Just down the trail was the mysteriously robed and hooded figure on horseback brandishing a flaming torch. He let loose a blood-curdling shriek that struck terror in all who were in earshot. The horse reared and swung around as the shadowy horseman galloped off.

"The ghost rider! The widow McClatchy wasn't crazy! He does exist!" cried a terrified voice from the crowd.

"He must be stalking us one by one," said another man. "He's the ghost of Sam Lester and he's taking his vengeance on this town! He's out to destroy us all, then drag our corpses to rot in that condemned pit of evil—Pyne's Cemetery!"

The crowd was aghast and buzzed with indecision and fear. Sherman, fearing what he was about to say, bravely kept his wits about him, insisting on staying sensible and not giving in to the supernatural. He stepped forward and addressed the crowd as the widow's home continued to burn furiously behind him.

"People! Be reasonable! We're not being attacked by a rancorous ghost. That's just a man under those white robes—just a man trying to instill fear and rip this community apart."

"What man, Sherman? Sam Lester? Your Danny Ricker perhaps," vehemently shouted a farmer Sherman recognized from the grange hall meeting. A few others gathered next to him. "Ghost or no ghost, I feel you're responsible for this ongoing debacle, Sherman Jackson. And you'd better do something about it, right quick."

The other men nodded as the crowd was decidedly turning against the besieged storeowner.

"It might be Danny Ricker. He's a drunkard and mentally disturbed. He's capable of attacking anyone for any reason. But let's have faith in Sheriff Ridgeway. I'm sure the law will come to our rescue and that justice will ultimately be served on the guilty party executing these dastardly deeds."

"Like murder, Sherman! If you haven't noticed, there's a murdered body being charred to ashes in that inferno behind you," yelled an unknown voice from the darkness. "How many people need to die and how much property needs to be destroyed before you realize this is all your fault?"

"We don't have conclusive proof of who's behind all this! When the culprit is identified, then we'll determine if fault needs to be assessed onto other people—namely me—but not before!"

"I'd start watching my back if I were you, Sherman…especially since your property ain't been touched…yet!" said the farmer, implying that the Jackson household and the store could be targeted at any time, and not strictly by a white-robed ghost rider.

Suddenly another fiery glow erupted from the direction of Settler Road.

"Look!" shouted a farmer.

Everyone turned in the direction of the disturbance with fear and dismay. Sherman's heart sank as he mounted Skipper and realized that the location of the new blaze could very easily be his own home or the store! He couldn't know for certain until he got closer. He spurred Skipper and galloped off. The other men mounted their horses or piled into the wagon and followed his lead. Sherman madly rode as fast as Skipper could carry him until he reached Settler Road and closed in on the freshly burning building. As he approached it, he began to realize that it was not one of his properties that was ablaze, but rather the Budwin School!

"There's a well just beyond those trees! Let's get some water on this fire before the whole building is destroyed!" yelled Sherman to the other men arriving on the scene. But it was too late; the small one-room schoolhouse didn't stand a chance. The fire had spread too rapidly and the old building couldn't withstand the torturous blaze. The roof collapsed before the first bucket of water could be scooped from the nearby well. The tired and dumbfounded men watched in shocked amazement and fear at what was happening. Some were entranced by the fire while others kept a wary ear open, expecting to hear the shriek of the ghost rider pierce through the early morning air again. Sherman glanced up at the flagpole and to his horror, another Confederate flag hung limply from the apex, untouched by the flames, appearing to mock whoever gazed upon it.

"Is anybody armed?" shouted Sherman angrily. "He can't be far. Let's get some torches and ride the bastard down! I'm gonna get my rifle and I'm going out looking for the son of a bitch. If we fan out in all directions, we'll find him and put an end to this tonight!"

Just then the distinctive shriek of the ghost rider ripped through the darkness. The men looked up and saw the white-robed rider tearing along at full gallop up Settler Road. His torch was gone, but a far more menacing instrument of fear—a pistol—replaced it!

"Get down!" shouted Sherman. Suddenly the air was filled with gunfire as the mad rider fired shots in all directions before galloping out of sight. The men scattered to avoid the shots or to chase down their spooked horses. Rattled beyond comprehension, Sherman looked down Settler Road and curiously focused his eyes on a small orange glow coming from a window of the church. Suddenly the window exploded and flames leapt outward, licking their way up the side!

"The church!" hollered out Sherman. "Quickly! We can save it!"

The men swiftly unloaded several buckets from the wagon and formed a bucket brigade originating from the nearby well behind the church. Sherman was at the head of the line and mechanically dumped water through the window onto the flames. The men worked feverishly. Some left the line and battled the blaze from inside the church with buckets of water. The two-pronged attack began to pay off as the flames gradually retreated and the spread was contained. After only a few minutes, the fire was out and the church was saved with only a burned-out window, some damage to the side of the building, and a charred section of floor on the inside. The smoke hung heavy in the air, but it was of little consequence compared to what could have happened. Several men collapsed on the ground and coughed violently, trying to expel the life-choking smoke from their lungs. Others felt dizzy and completely spent—like Sherman. All dreaded what would happen next.

"We can still go after him," Sherman said feebly but bravely. "We saw the direction he headed in and we can still ride him down."

"Ride him down? To hell with that, Jackson. I ain't ridin' nowhere but home," said the ornery farmer who had first confronted Sherman.

"What? Are you afraid of the ghost? To my knowledge, ghosts don't carry pistols, shoot at people, and set houses on fire. Men do that!" proclaimed Sherman.

"We ain't in any goddamned shape to go chasing a man or a ghost in the dark right now," fired back the farmer. "We're exhausted, disoriented, and we got no guns. And for all I know, that bastard could be circling back and headed for my farm right now. Damned if I'm not going home immediately to protect what's mine! You hear that, boys? Let's go before all our homes are burned to cinders! To hell with you, Jackson!"

One by one the small crowd of men mounted their horses and fearfully rode off in all directions. Those without horses simply staggered off into the night. Soon Sherman was alone with only his faithful mount Skipper at his side. The Budwin School had been reduced to a flaming pile of rubble that burned brightly while the distinct scorching glow of the McClatchy home could still be seen through the woods and far off in the distance. Neither posed a threat of spreading and would simply burn out in time.

Sherman led Skipper back to the livery. Part of him wanted to go after the ghost rider, but the other part knew it would be a fruitless act. He'd wait until morning and ride out to find Silas in South Gorham. He'd pry him away from his mistress and ask to be deputized. Then together they'd hunt down this fiend, no matter how long it took. That was the plan, but for now he needed rest.

Before he entered the house, Sherman stopped and gazed over at the store, now partially lit by the light of the burning school. Something compelled him to go in. Astonishingly, the door was unlocked. Sherman crept inside and quietly made his way upstairs. He entered the spare room and found Jeff missing. By the orange light coming in from the fire outside, Sherman looked around the room. He didn't know what he was searching for or why Jeff was nowhere to be found. He only knew that if there was a clue in the room, he needed to find it. He went through the bureau, the desk, and even the bookcase but found nothing out of the ordinary. The LeMat was nowhere to be seen and that worried him. Jeff

Parlin had arrived with nothing, and there wasn't anything of Sherman's missing. After putting things back exactly as he had found them, Sherman staggered down the stairs and left the store, purposely leaving the door unlocked as Jeff apparently had. He returned to his bedroom and crumpled onto his bed. It was now just after four in the morning and the sun would be coming up soon. Sherman instantly fell asleep face-down on the pillow, his body cutting diagonally across the bed. Morning, and all its renewed turmoil, would be upon him soon.

✛✛✛

The demons continued to chase him until his eyes snapped open. He had been having more nightmares and was gratefully relieved to be awake. The amount of bright sunshine pouring in through his bedroom window caused him some distress, as he knew he had badly overslept. But what time was it?

"My God, it's nearly ten o'clock," he lamented as he poured water into a basin and prepared to wash and shave the filth from his face and neck. When finished he spared no time changing his clothes and rushed out the front door and over to the store. The door was still unlocked and there was no sign of Jeff. Sherman went upstairs only to find the room still empty and just like he'd left it hours earlier. "Where is that son of a bitch?" he muttered.

He heard the sound of people milling about outside. Some sounded wistful while others were clearly afraid. Some expressed anger and disbelief about what had happened. Sherman hung the "Closed" sign in his window and locked up the store. He saw a small crowd of men, women, and children dressed in their Sunday church clothes gathered around the charred remains of the schoolhouse. They hushed as he started to approach them. He stopped halfway and could see nobody had removed the Confederate flag that was defiantly waving in the wind atop the flagpole. He decided it was best not to talk to anybody and simply get his gun, mount Skipper, and ride out to South Gorham and Ophelia Norris's house, where he hoped Silas still was. As he turned back toward his house, he looked down Settler Road and saw his horses and wagon parked in front of the church. Immediately he hustled over, as he was shocked to see it.

Sitting atop the wagon were Olin and Wilbur. It was filled with lumber, paint, and assorted hardware all procured from the carpenter Thaddeus had met with in Portland. The boys watched Sherman approach and stood up when he reached the wagon.

"Boys, where are your parents and Miss Curtis?" he asked.

Olin said nothing and looked away. Wilbur eventually spoke up. "They're inside, Mr. Jackson. Papa is quite grief-stricken and Mama is not well either. She's fainted twice, I'm afraid."

"Sherman, what's going on?" cried a voice from the church entrance. Sophie ran out and embraced him. "How did this happen?" she pleaded.

"The fire was set early this morning, just like it was at the Morrell farm," said Sherman pulling Sophie aside. "I was here, and so were a group of farmers from the outskirts of the community. We fought the blaze and put it out before the whole church burned down. It was deliberately set…by the man everyone is calling the 'ghost rider.' He was who was haunting old Milly McClatchy, but he's definitely not a ghost. He's a man with a gun and a penchant for committing arson."

"Were you injured? Has the sheriff caught this horrible man? Do you know if it is indeed Danny Ricker?" asked Sophie anxiously.

"I'm afraid the answer is no to all your questions, my dear," Sherman answered gravely. "What are you doing back so soon? I didn't expect your return until late this evening at the very earliest."

"The pastor was uneasy about canceling today's services. He came to the conclusion very early this morning that God would be unhappy with him if he let a Sunday go by without worship, so he insisted we rush back so he could give his sermon. We just arrived not ten minutes ago. Our only stop was to pick up the boys at the house and bring them here. And look at what we discovered. God help us all."

"Then you don't know about the rest? You haven't heard about what else happened?"

"Why, no. Is there more foulness afoot?"

"I'm afraid there is, my darling…and it's none too pleasant. You'd better come with me now."

"All right. We should alert Thaddeus and Erin first."

The two climbed the steps and entered the church to find Erin sprawled out on a pew and the Pastor kneeling beside her, fanning her face.

"Pastor Thaddeus, Mr. Jackson and I must see to some business immediately. We'll return upon its completion," said Sophie.

The pastor said nothing and continued to look after his insentient wife.

"Sir, I see you still have need of my horses and wagon, loaded up as it is. Please keep them for as long as necessary today. I'll send my assistant out to your farm tomorrow to retrieve them. I…I am deeply sorry for your continued troubles," said Sherman.

"The Lord doth test me, Mr. Jackson, but I am a resilient man able to withstand all forms of evil. I pray you're able to stand up to the test when God decides it's your turn to run the gauntlet. I fear his wrath on you will be much more severe. Leave us now…both of you. I wish to look after my wife in peace and solitude. There will be no sermon today. I appreciate your generosity concerning your rented property, Mr. Jackson. Rest assured your stallions will be looked after and your wagon ready for retrieval tomorrow. I will await your man and will compensate you fairly. Now please go. I wish to pray now…alone."

Sophie and Sherman said nothing and slowly backed away and exited the church. Sherman addressed the small crowd. "There are no services today, everyone. You can all go on home. Please direct the sheriff this way if you come across him in your travels."

The people eventually started on their way, but not before one of the men spoke up and said, "God help you, Jackson. Old lady McClatchy will haunt your conscience forever, you bastard."

Sherman ignored the crude remark and led Sophie up the road. A minute or two passed before they realized Olin and Wilbur, who were understandably curious of what was going on, were following them. It didn't take long for Sophie to figure it out. She broke down and started to weep at the sight of the smoldering pile of charred wood and glass that was once the Budwin School.

"Why? Why is this happening? What kind of monster gains pleasure from destroying innocent and sacred institutions such as churches and schools? And what does that confounded symbol have to do with all this?" she asked loudly while looking up at the flag.

"I wish I had solid answers to all your questions, Sophie. At best I can only offer speculation and flawed theory, which doesn't really help, I'm afraid. I feel I'm the biggest part in this ugly business and yet I feel just as much in the dark as anyone else."

Olin looked up at the flag and seemed mesmerized by it. No one took notice except Wilbur who stared at him timidly. Eventually Olin came out of his odd trance and stepped onto a large chunk of smoldering wood with one foot. As he did, his pant leg hiked up, revealing a large knife strapped to his ankle. As Sherman hugged the weeping Sophie, he caught sight of the exposed pommel and handle and made a startling discovery. It was the stolen Bowie knife from his burgled display case!

"Ollie, my boy, step forward for a moment if you please," said Sherman politely. Olin turned in Sherman's direction and took two steps toward him. "I noticed you have a nice-looking knife strapped to your ankle. May I see it?"

Olin hesitated at first, then slowly reached down and pulled up his pant leg. He gripped the knife by its protruding handle and carefully pulled it from its sheath. The knife was so long it appeared to run up the entire length of the boy's calf. Once free, Olin held up the blade but did not offer to place it in Sherman's hand for closer inspection. Regardless, Sherman saw that it was in fact one of his stolen Bowie knives.

"Ollie, where'd you get that knife?" Sherman asked calmly and without accusation.

"Found it," the fifteen-year-old replied with a touch of indignation on his tongue.

"That's a really pristine-looking knife. I'd swear it was new. Someone would have to have been very careless and not too bright to lose something that nice and that big."

"Maybe," answered Olin.

"Where did you find it?"

"In a field."

"Which field?"

"Can't remember. I think it was one out in Gorham," Olin said with growing defiance.

"You can't remember which field, Ollie? Do you intend to keep it? A proper young man would be trying to return it to its rightful owner."

"I found it. I'm going to keep it. It's mine," answered Olin with clear disdain for Sherman's questions.

Unable to tolerate the boy's lack of respect and apparent dishonesty any further, Sherman threw down the gauntlet.

"Olin," he said, now purposely addressing him by his proper name, "that Bowie knife belongs to me. It was stolen from my store several days ago and I'd like it back. Now."

"Look, I said I found it. It's mine! I ain't a thief," fired back Olin as he slipped the knife back into its sheath.

"I wasn't implying that you stole it, Olin. I am merely stating that it *is* stolen property—*my* stolen property—and I'd like it back."

"No. The knife belongs to me, and not you or anybody else is going to take what's mine—and if anyone tries, they're gonna get hurt!"

"Ollie," said Sophie in a very surprised tone. "Why, you apologize to Mr. Jackson this instant."

"Like hell I will. He's got some nerve calling me a thief!"

"Boy, if I was your daddy I'd give you a good whipping for talking like that!" asserted Sherman.

"You ain't my daddy, and I ain't gotta listen to another damn word you say!"

"Olin! You apologize immediately or I'll tell your parents of this dishonest, disrespectful, and ungodly behavior. Plus I'll also inform them of your absenteeism from school," declared Sophie.

"Go ahead, Sophie. Who will they believe? Their own precious flesh and blood who can do no wrong in their eyes, or some sinning whore who sneaks off in the middle of the night to fuck the town's storeowner in the grange hall?"

Sophie and Sherman stood in stunned silence as Olin snickered and trotted off into the woods.

"How does he…."

"I don't know," interrupted Sherman. "You're sure you didn't…."

"Of course not! We've been over this already. I didn't tell a soul what happened in the grange that night. I only told Thaddeus and Erin that we privately viewed the decorations. That's all! You don't suppose he was there, do you? Hidden inside?" she asked in horror.

"I can't be sure, but he was definitely out and about that morning. Remember when we arrived back at the farm? He showed up out of nowhere when we finished putting out the fire."

"My God," said Sophie as she covered her face with her hands. "What can we do?"

The young schoolteacher angrily ran to the flagpole and lowered the Southern Cross. She ripped it from the ropes and threw it onto the ground before stomping on it in a crying rage. Sherman rushed to her side to try to console her.

"Miss Curtis?"

Both Sophie and Sherman looked down at young Wilbur Morrell, who was quietly lingering after the swift departure of his older brother. Both became further distressed, wondering what kind of blackmail the younger Morrell brother would threaten them with after being privy to their conversation.

"Yes, Wilbur?" said Sophie, fearing the worst and trying to compose herself.

The thirteen-year-old began to cry. He stood there blubbering until Sophie went to him and put her hand on his cheek.

"What's wrong, Willy?" she asked, sensing a deep pain within the young boy.

"Miss Curtis…Mr. Jackson…I have something I need to tell you both but I'm scared to say it," said Willy between tears. "I just can't hold it inside anymore. I don't want to be bad. I don't want to cause trouble. I don't want anyone to die like Mrs. McClatchy!" he wailed, crumpling to the ground in a pool of tears.

Sophie looked confused and Sherman said, "Come with me. Let's all go to my house and then we can talk. Come, Willy, don't be afraid."

Sherman helped the boy up and carefully walked him over to his house with Sophie in close pursuit. The three adjourned to the parlor. Sherman fetched Willy a glass of water to help calm him down.

"Breathe slowly and deeply, Willy. You're safe here. Just relax and tell us what's bothering you," Sherman said reassuringly.

"Olin didn't find that knife like he said. He made me steal it for him," said a trembling Wilbur. "We snuck out during the night and put a ladder up to your window. I thought Olin would go, but he made me climb up and open the window. He then told me to go down into the store and pick open the display case lock so I could steal the pistol and one knife. I did what I was told and scurried out the same way I came in. I didn't want to do it! I really didn't!" plead Wilbur.

"What happened next, Willy? And where's the gun?" asked Sherman, his arms crossed as he stood in front of the fireplace.

"We ran into the woods. At some point Olin dropped the pistol and lost it altogether. He was so mad…and afraid."

"Why was he afraid?" asked Sophie.

"He was afraid of angering the man."

"What man?" asked Sherman.

Willy started to get uncomfortable and looked as if he didn't want to say any more. Sophie leaned over from her chair and caressed his hand with a calming touch that only a caring woman could provide. She soothed his nerves and the boy bravely went on.

"About two weeks ago, or maybe longer—I can't remember—Olin and I snuck out at night. He wanted to have some fun and cause a little mischief. He always found a way to convince me to go along with him. I knew what we were doing was wrong, but I liked the thrill. It made me feel alive inside. Anyway…we stole some vegetables from your garden, tore up some farmer's fence, and camped out in a clearing in the woods somewhere between North Scarborough and South Gorham. We built a little fire and munched on the stolen vegetables. After a while we started hearing noises. We went silent and huddled close to the fire. Then out of nowhere appeared the ghost rider! This frightening presence atop a horse trotted up the trail to our camp. He dismounted and walked over to us. We were both paralyzed with fear and couldn't move! He was covered from head to toe in these long, flowing white robes that concealed his arms and legs. His face was hidden behind a gruesome-looking hood that demonized his appearance and instantly struck fear into our hearts. There were eyeholes and a mouth hole cut out, but that was all."

"Did he speak to you, Willy?" Sherman inquired.

"Yes. He sat down and told us not to be afraid and that he wasn't going to harm us. He then asked if we wanted to learn about a special club that gave power, influence, and wealth to all its members. I didn't say anything, but Olin spoke up and insisted on hearing more. The ghost rider handed us each a gold coin and wrapped candies from under his robe. He said that all members of his club—a 'special fraternal order,' he called it—received such luxuries with membership. He asked if we wanted to join. I was too afraid to say anything, but Olin said yes. The ghost rider said that membership came with a small price and that certain tasks had to be accomplished first before joining. However, he reminded us that once in the club, we would have power that transcended all law and recognized authority of the land. We would be like crusading knights, free to dispense justice in any fashion and acquire wealth and influence unlike anything we had ever experienced. All we had to do was come back to that same location each night and wait for him to assign us these initiation tasks. Once completed, we'd be in the special fraternal order."

"What was the name of this 'order,' Willy?" Sherman asked.

"The ghost rider said that all details would be revealed to us once we were accepted."

"Do you have any idea who this ghost rider is? When he spoke to you, did you recognize his voice? Did he sound like Danny Ricker?"

"No, I don't know who he is. His identity is a mystery to me and I don't think Olin knows who he is either. If he does, he won't say."

"What about his voice? Is it one you recognize?"

"He only spoke to us in disguised whispers. He never raised his voice. I have no idea who he is. I only know that he terrifies me and I want nothing more to do with him."

"Did you have further dealings with him?"

"Yes. Olin made us go back time and time again. I didn't want to, but he made me go. I even tried to get him in trouble by telling our parents he had stolen from your garden, but they never punished him and he roughed me up in order to keep me quiet. Mama told you he confessed to her and Papa. He didn't. They knew nothing of the vegetable thefts until I told them. That's when she forced him to apologize to you."

"I understand, Willy. Tell me more about the ghost rider and my stolen gun and knife."

"The night of the theft, we met the ghost rider in our usual spot. He told Olin he wanted us to sneak into your store and steal a knife and pistol from your locked display case. He told us we'd be rewarded handsomely if we could do it without being caught. I wanted no part of it, but Olin made me do it. He told me the ghost rider would be angry and come after me if I didn't do what he wanted. I was so terrified that I went along with everything. As I said earlier, Olin forced me to commit the actual robbery. When we returned to our camp, the ghost rider was waiting. Olin told him that *I* dropped and lost the gun, but *he* got the knife. He rewarded Olin by letting him keep the knife. He admonished me and told me not to disappoint him again. My own brother turned on me. After the robbery, I told Olin I didn't want to steal anymore. I told him I was through sneaking off at night and I didn't want to see the ghost rider ever again. I wanted no part of his special club. Olin became furious with me and said he'd kill me if I ever told anybody about what was happening. Every night he goes out to meet the ghost rider. He's obsessed with him. Now all these terrible things have happened—fires…slaughtered livestock…I don't…."

Willy broke down and started to cry again. He was clearly overwhelmed and very frightened. He started to shake, which prompted Sophie to take the boy in her arms and gently try to rock away his fears.

"It's okay, Willy," said Sherman. You've done the right thing by coming forward and telling us what you know. That was very brave and worthy of a young Christian. Here's what I want you to do now. I want you to go back to the church and stay close to your mother and father. Don't tell them anything; in fact, pretend as if you haven't told us anything either. Don't say or do anything that will raise your brother's suspicions. I don't want you getting hurt by him any further. When the time is right, Miss Curtis and I will confront your parents and Olin…only we'll have the sheriff with us. He'll decide what disciplinary measures will need to be taken. That fact that Olin has my knife is enough reason for us to bring the sheriff in. Also, if we all confront him at once, maybe we can get him to reveal more details about the ghost rider and where we can catch him. Do you understand, Willy?"

"Yes, I understand, Mr. Jackson, but be careful. I think Olin has the Devil in him now."

"No, he's just being manipulated by one. With some luck we can turn him away from this demonic influence and put him back onto the path of righteousness. Now go back to the church. Keep your parents close and remember not to say anything about what we've discussed. Clear?"

"Yes, sir. Thank you, Mr. Jackson."

"Willy, I'll be watching after you, too. You're not alone anymore," Sophie said with a big hug.

Willy smiled and wiped the tears from his eyes. He took a big breath and walked out the front door.

"What else has happened, Sherman? Is there more I don't know about?"

Sherman sighed and answered, "Last night not only was the schoolhouse burned and the church damaged, but Milly McClatchy's house burned to the ground and most assuredly killed her."

"Oh my God," Sophie gasped. "Do you think…."

"We saw the ghost rider there, and by the church," Sherman interrupted. "Nobody gave chase. They were all too tired, too confused, or just plain selfish and cowardly."

"Will this madness never end? What are we going to do? How can we protect Wilbur? I doubt Thaddeus and Erin would ever believe anything we said against their eldest son—especially after they learned of our unchaperoned rendezvous," said Sophie.

"I'm going to ride out to South Gorham tomorrow and find the sheriff. I know where he stays on nights he doesn't go home. I'll tell him about what's happened here, particularly what happened to Mrs. McClatchy and what Willy told us about Olin. Together we'll ride the back trails between here and South Gorham. I have a hunch of what routes the ghost rider is using at night. Maybe we can pick up some clues as to his movement and identity. Then we'll go out to the old Lester house next to Pyne's Cemetery. I've always believed that evil places attract evil men. If I was a lunatic like Sam Lester or highly disturbed like Danny Ricker, that's where I'd go if I didn't want anyone to find me."

"Dear God, Sherman, please be careful, and don't go at night, I beg you."

"I've avoided that house ever since I first came home from the war back in '65. I listened to all the rumors and ghost stories and never felt it was worth investigating. Now, after all that's happened, I feel differently. I'll keep the store closed today. Maybe I'll get Jeff to go out there with me and the sheriff…three men are better than two."

Sophie's mood went from bad to worse upon hearing Sherman mention Jeff Parlin. He saw it in her face and asked what was wrong.

"Sherman, I think you need to seriously consider removing Jeff Parlin from your life…for good," said Sophie as Sherman sat down next to her.

"Why?" he asked.

"While I was in Portland, I took it upon myself to do some research on Jeff. I remembered what you told me about his past and particularly about his war involvement. I looked up the Army of the Tennessee and the units that fought within it. I found the XV Corps, 1st Division, 3rd Brigade…but there was no 32nd Missouri Infantry Regiment. Every source I could find lists no record of that unit. It's as if it never existed.

I'm convinced it never did. I then went through countless pages of lists of men who served in other Missouri regiments and I couldn't find one single Parlin. I went so far as to go through every name listed with the Army of the Tennessee—nothing. I came across a list of wounded combatants from the battle of Bentonville, North Carolina; again, there was no record of a Union soldier named Jeffrey Parlin taking an injury there. The last thing I checked were census lists of property owners from Independence, Missouri. As you probably can guess, I couldn't find one landowner from Independence surnamed Parlin. He's a liar, Sherman. I don't know what his intentions are, but I don't trust him and neither should you."

"He's acted strangely on occasion, and we've had some odd conversations that have left me doubting many things. He's got a pistol in his possession, which he's never mentioned, all the while claiming that he's defenseless and that I should arm him. What's even more peculiar is that he's missing right now. He wasn't in his bed last night or this morning. I haven't a clue where he is at this exact moment. He could have snuck away and simply left town for good. Maybe he fell prey to the ghost rider? God only knows," said Sherman.

"He's trouble. I know it…I feel it. Though I've only had scarce few brief encounters with him, each one left a lasting impression of creepiness and distrust that I can't articulate. He repulses me in ways I don't clearly understand. I should have pity on him for being crippled as he is, and his vagabond situation, but I don't. I wish he would just drift right on out of town and never come back," said Sophie.

"I can't argue your womanly instincts. You clearly have a keen feminine insight that I'll never possess or even understand. I don't dispute that his actions and manners have been both odd and disrespectful at times, but he hasn't committed any crimes and he's been a tremendous help to me while in my employ. I admit he should be scrutinized closely; however, I can't just persecute and cast him off without hard evidence of a crime or a malicious act."

"I would think that his inappropriate advances toward me would be reason enough, Sherman," said Sophie as she abruptly stood up in a huff.

"Perhaps you're right," he replied meekly. "Perhaps my reasons for keeping him around are not sound, practical, or even desirable. Perhaps

I've become selfish, lazy, and even scared. With all that's happened recently, maybe I've lost focus on things I should be paying extra attention too."

Sherman looked at Sophie and took her by the hands. He searched for forgiveness and reassurance deep within the pools of her blue eyes. Fortunately his quest was brief as the young woman unlocked her heart and soul, channeling her compassion, understanding, and sympathy through her eyes and into his. The two leaned in and kissed.

Just then there came a knock at the front door. Sherman looked out the open window and was slightly taken aback. Standing outside his door was Jeffrey Parlin. Sherman looked at Sophie with a curious eye, then went to open the door.

"Jeff, come in," said Sherman.

The one-armed man entered the house and made his way into the parlor with Sherman close behind. His appearance was slightly disheveled and his face was smudged. Initially he looked tired, but upon seeing Sophie present in the room, his spirits lifted and his swagger returned with confident vigor.

"Why, hello, Miss Curtis. Might I say what an unconquerable pleasure it is to see you. You are as lovely as a magnolia in full bloom," chivalrously gushed Parlin.

"Hello, Mr. Parlin," returned Sophie monotonously and without any hint of genuine warmth in her voice. Before Sherman could open his mouth, Sophie promptly said, "Sherman I must go now. I have a great deal of unpleasant business to attend to now with the schoolhouse and the church being in the tragic state they're in. I don't believe the full impact of what's happened has struck me yet. I fear how the force and shock of it all will affect me once it truly settles in."

"My dear, Miss Curtis, may I say that I am stunned and dismayed at what has happened. On my way here I could see that the schoolhouse is no more. Why, it's nothing but a pile of charred rubble. What on earth caused such a calamity?" Jeff asked, his voice dripping with theatrical sympathy.

Reluctantly, Sophie turned to face him. Every fiber in her being wanted to lash out at the brazen man who she was convinced had lied about many things and had acted inappropriately toward her on every occasion they had met. However, she restrained herself and opted for a more subtle yet decisive response.

"Mr. Parlin, the schoolhouse was malevolently and deliberately set ablaze by a repugnant scoundrel of such low character and esteem, that he should be immediately castrated upon capture without the benefit of trial or jury. To think that one could orchestrate and execute such a vile act of cowardly destruction against an innocent institution such as education, leads me to think that not only is the perpetrator a spineless, pusillanimous, degenerate louse, but also a selfish, ignorant, impotent example of a man. I hope the guilty party and all those associated with him are brought to swift justice. I also pray that justice is meted out appropriately and in the manner I've expressed."

"Why, Miss Curtis, your passion concerning this matter is quite profound. I must say that it stimulates my senses in ways I dare not express openly," said Jeff cunningly. He added, "I do believe the culprit will be apprehended and punished accordingly. Do not fret about that. In the meantime, if there's anything I can do to ease your suffering, don't hesitate to call on me. I'll be here, ready and willing."

Thoroughly disgusted, Sophie looked to Sherman, then said, "I hope you remember what we've discussed and act on it accordingly." She then headed out the door, but not before saying, "Good day, gentlemen."

Before Parlin could offer up another crass comment, Sherman brusquely asked, "Where have you been?"

"What do you mean? And what exactly has happened around here?"

"I mean just what I said," answered Sherman, adding, "Where have you been? The store was unlocked and you weren't in your bed this morning."

Not waiting for an invitation, Jeff sat down in his usual spot in front of the fireplace and didn't hesitate to pour himself a drink. Sherman stood before him and crossed his arms, waiting for a response.

"I woke at dawn's first light," said Jeff. "I couldn't sleep. I have a lot on my mind and my restlessness and wandering nature often get the best of me. I went for a walk in the woods to contemplate my next move. I'm not sure I desire to remain here much longer. I'm starting to grow weary of this place, its problems, and of you, Sherman."

Knowing full well he had just caught Jeff in another lie, Sherman probed forward carefully.

"This is sudden," said Sherman. "What's brought this on? I thought we were friends and that we agreed to help each other, especially through this dangerous time. What's the matter? You no longer feel compelled to help a fellow soldier in need? Or have you just finally realized that it's me that Sophie wants and not you?"

"Ha! Don't flatter yourself, Sherman," Jeff said confidently after taking a swig of whiskey. "Why don't you tell me what's going on around here first? What happened to the schoolhouse, and the church, for that matter?"

"The schoolhouse was set ablaze early this morning, as was the church; however, that's not the worst of it. Milly McClatchy's house burned to the ground with her in it! Several farmers raced up Settler Road to fight the blaze. All the commotion and shouting woke me up. I mounted my horse and joined them. Surely you must have been woken by the sounds of the same turmoil as I? Particularly if you had trouble sleeping."

"No, I heard nothing. I slept until dawn; otherwise, I would have rushed to help, naturally," said Jeff without looking Sherman in the face.

"Well, when you left this morning for your walk, you must have seen the smoldering schoolhouse and the damaged church? I assume you must have investigated both?"

"I was groggy and confused when I left. I didn't exit the store through the front door. I went out the back through the storage room. I didn't go near the street. I walked through the meadow and down to the stream by the back edge of your property. After stopping to look at your little funeral plot with the two headstones, I slipped through the split-rail fence and wandered off through the woods. I didn't see anything. I came directly here after finding the store closed."

"I understand. And after seeing the latest acts of destruction, you've decided you want no part of this place anymore? You're afraid of Danny Ricker or whoever else may be causing all this trouble and you want to leave? Do you remember saying to me, 'soldiers don't abandon their old brothers-in-arms,' the other day?"

"I ain't a soldier anymore…and neither are you," snarled Jeff. " I'm just a man trying to eke out a decent living while traveling from place to place. I can't be tied down anywhere, and lately I've come to realize my physical limitations. I frequently overcome them, but I'm not invulnerable and I sure as hell don't intend to wind up killed by some disgruntled fool who's out to settle a score with my employer. What's worse is that the whole town's turned against you. Won't be long before they turn against me, too. I'll simply be judged guilty by association! I'd rather not be around when that time comes."

Sherman stood fast and remained motionless with his arms crossed as he looked down at Jeff. Wild thoughts went through his mind, including one that sent a chill up his spine and a twinge of fear through his stomach. Was the man sitting before him now the ghost rider? Was he the shadowy one Sherman had seen on horseback hidden behind ghostly robes and a hood? The theory was a curious one in which several pieces of the puzzle seem to fit; however, Sherman sharply dismissed it as he quickly deduced that the ghost rider had been seen brandishing a torch while riding at full gallop. Though not entirely impossible, it was highly improbable Parlin could control a horse at full gallop without his one arm and hand holding the reins. He would most assuredly fall off at the speed the horse had maintained and would never be able to maneuver and turn it with the precision Sherman had witnessed…let alone do it all while carrying a lit torch or firing a pistol. Sherman promptly swept the thought from his mind as he distinctly recalled seeing the ghost rider with two arms. He switched his thoughts to another topic.

"We never cease to be soldiers," preached Sherman. "We may put away our uniforms, our medals, and our guns, but the soldier in us lives on, even when we're not at war or taking orders from a barking general. That bond of brotherhood that's forged in battle is never lost or forgotten in time of need, even after the battle has ended and we find ourselves back in civilian clothes years later."

Jeff sat stone-faced and was visibly uninterested in what Sherman was saying. He crossed his legs and sat back in the chair while continuing to sip his whiskey. He never made eye contact with his employer.

"There was a time when my regiment was heavily engaged at the battle of Spotsylvania Courthouse in Virginia. I remember looking across the field at a thick line of Rebel fire that felled many of my comrades positioned around me. We were getting pummeled and our own line was near collapse. A friend of mine got shot through the leg and dropped to the ground in unbearable pain. He was bleeding so fast his face started to turn white in a matter of seconds. I quickly got a tourniquet around his wound and was able to stop the accursed stream of blood draining from his body. He looked up at me and begged me not to leave him no matter what happened. Amidst all the chaos, bloodshed, and insufferable fighting still unfolding around my battered regiment, I swore I wouldn't leave him…and I didn't. Even as the bullets whizzed by my head and the threat of charging Confederates loomed, I stood fast and remained by my comrade until the Rebels were driven off and help arrived. Later I learned I had saved my friend's life. I could have easily continued fighting and let him die, but something compelled me to do what I did, and I'm proud of it. Surely you must have had a similar experience with your regiment. What was it again…the 39th Missouri? That's what you told me, right?"

"Yeah," said Parlin, adding, "And the 39th was the toughest outfit ever to come out of Missouri. I helped many of my brothers in arms and sacrificed much. Don't preach to me about brotherhood."

"Tell me more about your regiment—the 39th Missouri. I'd like to hear more about it," said Sherman as he sat down and poured himself a whiskey. "Maybe we can swap some war stories and then discuss your issues a bit more. You're a tremendous help to me at the store and I'd like to keep you around a bit longer despite all that's happened," said Sherman.

Jeff reluctantly nodded and took another drink. At the moment he seemed in no hurry to go anywhere. Sherman started by talking about his old regiment and its movements throughout the war. He spoke of skirmishes, full battles, and smaller events in the army that shaped his military life. He didn't hesitate to throw out very precise dates of when certain actions occurred and he made it a point to speak of less relevant day-to-day happenings between major engagements. He described what the V Corps divisional flag looked like as well as other insignia associated with his regiment and the Army of the Potomac. When finished he peppered in some very pro-Union sentiments and then began to ask Jeff questions about his army life.

Sherman was clever. He took in everything Parlin said and committed it to memory. He asked about certain precise subjects such as the names of officers and commanders of the 39th Missouri. He asked if the 39th had a particular song or emblem it identified with. He asked questions about the XV Corps and the Army of the Tennessee in general and pretended to be enthralled with anything said about General Sherman or his famous March to the Sea campaign.

At first, Parlin's answers were clear and concise with little to no hesitation or pause for reflection. However, as Sherman probed deeper, asking specific questions that often tied in with ones asked earlier, Parlin began to falter. He began to waver and appear indecisive when asked about common things that Sherman felt most every Union soldier knew or would easily recollect with little thought. Parlin would state a fact about some element of his unit or his army experience, only to correct himself or claim something entirely different at a later point. Sherman instantly identified the holes in his story that seemed to grow deeper by the minute. Even when the talk shifted to his home and the years of harsh life in Independence, Missouri, the timeline of events was still hazy and often hard to follow. The very description of his family seemed to slightly change every time they came up.

Sherman noticed other peculiar things during their conversation. Parlin would constantly refer to the events surrounding General Sherman's March to the Sea and eventual swing northward. They had discussed it briefly once before, but this time Parlin spoke in broader terms and often mentioned events that were not very personal, but widely known by the general population. He spoke of the capture of Savannah, Georgia, the burning of Columbia, South Carolina, and the destruction inflicted by Sherman's troops as they tore through the South. He mentioned the suffering of the southern people and often referred to them as helpless victims who didn't deserve to have their way of life ripped apart. He never praised his regiment, or any part of Sherman's army, for that matter. He never talked about bravery, duty, honor, discipline, or the hardships faced by the men in blue fighting their way through hostile territory. His sentiments always took a sympathetic view toward the South's suffering, and a hostile one toward the arrogance and proclaimed tyranny of Lincoln.

Then there was talk of the countless numbers of Negro refugees who had been liberated by Sherman's men and followed the army wherever it went. Parlin talked of the freed slaves as if they were filthy rotten parasites that clung to and sucked the life out of the Union soldiers who had driven off their masters and given them liberty. He spoke about them scornfully and without any sense of pity toward their plight. It was apparent he took no satisfaction in freeing slaves, and his attitude suggested he preferred them kept in bondage rather than happily walking down the road next to him—then or even now.

Parlin's affection for the old antebellum South was clear, as was the fact that he had lied repeatedly about many things concerning his military service—or lack thereof. Sherman was convinced Sophie's research and suspicions were dead on. The very fact that Parlin never acknowledged or corrected Sherman's mistake after repeatedly referring to his regiment as the 39th and not the 32nd, as Jeff had originally told him, was reason enough to seriously doubt he'd ever served under Sherman—or even in the Union Army at all.

Sherman was uncertain what it all meant. Were the lies, coupled with his missing arm, just a convenient means to generate sympathy among caregivers and prospective employers as he drifted from place to place? Did he actually lose his arm in battle, or by some other misfortunate accident? Was he just a skilled con artist or something much worse? Most importantly, what were his true intentions, and just how dangerous was he?

As time went by, Sherman shifted the topic of conversation so as not to appear as if he was purposely trying to catch Jeff in a lie and expose his duplicitous tales. He never challenged him and simply took his words as truth. He was cordial, agreeable, and hospitable to a fault. He had no desire to anger his guest or give him reason to leave unexpectedly. All talk of the store and its future plans included Jeff, as well as anything to do with rebuilding and healing the community in its time of need.

Sherman further placated Parlin by fixing him a hearty lunch and by keeping the whiskey flowing freely. He wanted to project the illusion that he desperately needed Parlin to stay and continue working for him. In reality, he was more than willing to see the drifter walk out of his life—the sooner the better. If Jeff wanted to leave, Sherman wouldn't stop him. However, he couldn't make it look as if he *wanted* him to go. In the meantime, Sherman's little ruse seemed to be working as Parlin temporarily ceased all discussion of leaving right away.

"I assume the store will remain closed all day?" asked Jeff.

"Yes, I think it's best, with all that's happened. Perhaps we should concentrate our efforts on helping clean up. We should start with the schoolhouse."

"Of course. I bet Sophie would like that very much," Jeff said with a hint of sarcasm.

Sherman ignored the remark and further stated, "My wagon is currently still rented out to the Morrells. I'll need you to go and retrieve it tomorrow. You should also collect the rental fee from the pastor. In the meantime, we can use my Morgans to help clean up. We'll fit them with long harnesses and small carts to carry away the debris. I have two in the barn that will do the job nicely."

"Very well. Let's get started."

The two men led Skipper and Budley over to the barn, where they harnessed them to Sherman's two carts. They then led them over to the site of the burned-down Budwin School. Armed with shovels, picks, and steel rakes taken from the store, the two started to attack the blackened mass of charred wood, iron, and broken glass. Looking down the road, Sherman could see that his wagon was no longer parked in front of the church. He could only deduce that the Morrells and Sophie had taken it home and started the process of unloading it. Settler Road was again unusually quiet. Though normally the case on a Sunday afternoon, this day seemed eerily peaceful and a bit unsettling as if a thousand eyes were watching them.

The hours slipped by while the two labored on. Sherman did most of the clearing and loading while Jeff drove away with the refuse and discarded it into a natural depression on Sherman's property. They said little to one another and simply concentrated on the job at hand. In time the work was done, with only the final task of removing the twisted mass of chimney metal and the stove from the site. The two struggled immensely but finally managed to load the heavy iron onto the carts. They drove the horses over to the disposal area and dumped the metal. When that task was finished, they returned the carts to the barn and the horses to the livery. It was late and starting to get dark now.

"Wait," said Sherman. "We need to do one more thing before we retire for the evening." He walked back to the site of the schoolhouse with Jeff curiously in tow. He stopped at the flagpole where the Confederate battle flag still hung flaccidly. He untied the ropes holding it aloft and quickly lowered the old symbol of the Confederacy. He let it drop to the ground, then pulled a bundle of matches from his pocket.

"Stop!" cried out Jeff as Sherman struck a match to life. "Have you no sense of military honor or decency—even for a simple symbol representing those who tried to give birth to a new nation?"

"I see this flag as a symbol of defiance, treason, suffering, and death. It has no place here. The Confederacy is no more. It represents nothing and should be destroyed."

"It won't be burned to ashes. I won't allow it. It deserves as much respect as the United States flag!"

Sherman blew out the match and watched as a defiant Parlin knelt down and carefully folded up the Stars and Bars into a neat square.

"I'll hold onto this until it can be disposed of properly! For one who speaks so freely about his soldierly service to this country, you have much to learn about military etiquette and respect for vanquished foes. You never know, Sherman—they might come back to haunt you some-day!"

Sherman stood in place and said nothing. Jeff glared at him for a moment as he tucked the flag into his shirt. He then said, "I'm tired, dirty, and I'm hungry. I wish to clean up before dining this evening. I should like to wash up in the house and relax a bit before supper. After I've been fed I'll render a decision concerning my future here, but not before. Is that agreeable to you, Sherman?"

"Most agreeable, Jeff," Sherman said while holding back his growing irritation with a man he felt was getting way too comfortable challeng-ing his authority and abusing his hospitality regardless of any prior agree-ments they had made. "Let us retire inside and I'll start preparing supper. I'll fetch some fresh water from the well and heat it up for washing."

The two went inside after Sherman retrieved the water. Both took time to clean themselves up before Sherman went to work in the kitchen while Jeff relaxed in the parlor. In time, a simple meal of smoked pork, baked beans, and garden vegetables was ready. Sherman even produced a bottle of wine to go with dinner. The two took their time and dined slowly without saying much. When the meal was finished it was dark outside. Sherman lit a few oil lamps that gave off low ambient light in the kitchen, the hallway, and the parlor. He then proceeded to clear away the remains of dinner.

"I need a moment to organize my thoughts and smoke a mediocre cigar. I know where I can do both," said Jeff as he haughtily stood up from the table and walked down the hallway to the parlor.

Sherman finished his work in the kitchen, then joined Parlin in the parlor. Jeff stood by the piano and puffed away on a freshly lit cigar. He had helped himself to what remained of the whiskey and had brazenly built a small fire. All these things showed a blatant lack of respect and annoyed Sherman to no end.

"You know, Sherm," started Jeff, "we're different, you and I. To be honest, I thought I'd be content here for a while, but lately I've considered moving on. I'm not sure our agreement is a sound one anymore…and honestly, I'm tired of feeling unsafe and insecure in a community that has largely turned against you. I think it's best if you compensate me fairly and let me go on my way. I don't wish to be entangled in your problems any further. This I've decided."

"And what do you figure is fair compensation?" Sherman asked, knowing he was about to be hit with a demand for a ridiculous sum of money or goods from a clever con man who undoubtedly had vast experience in these sorts of dealings.

Suddenly a bright glow pierced the darkness through the front window. Sherman looked outside, then instantly turned and raced upstairs. Parlin walked over to the window and took a look for himself. His eyes grew wide with fear while only one word escaped his lips.

"Shit," he muttered.

Sherman hurriedly stomped back down the stairs, his Henry rifle in hand. He threw open the front door and rushed outside. Not sure of what was going to happen next, Parlin reluctantly followed him out. Sherman held up his gun in plain sight as a large torch-bearing mob began to form a semicircle in front of him. Parlin picked up a nearby shovel and wielded it in an aggressive fashion. The two stood side by side and waited for what was to happen next.

"This business has gone far enough, Sherman!" bellowed the voice of Hiram Lovell from the crowd. "We're tired of paying the price for your mistakes, your problems, and your unpaid debts! My barn was burned to the ground last night, as were several others in Scarborough and Gorham. My business is ruined and all my animals are dead! I had to send my wife and kids away to Portland because they're terrified of what could happen next. All I have left is my house and I damn sure am not going to lose that! I will not become a victim of your demons like Milly McClatchy. Everyone here has lost something or suffered a tragedy these past few days—everyone except you. Your store is still standing, your house is untouched, and your animals all alive and well. That strikes me as pretty damn peculiar. The sheriff is nowhere to be found, and I think it's time you paid your debt!"

Several members of the crowd starting moving toward the store with torches held high. It was clear what they planned to do and Sherman was not about to let his livelihood go up in smoke. He aimed his rifle and fired a shot into the air. The crowd abruptly froze in their tracks. Sherman worked the Henry's lever action and quickly chambered a fresh round.

"This is a Henry rifle," he announced with authority. "With this in hand I can fire all week, so I advise you not to test me! I *will* protect what's mine and deal with the consequences later! You have no right to threaten me! I haven't committed a single act of malice against any of you! How dare you hold me responsible for crimes I didn't commit?"

As Sherman spoke he recognized several members of the crowd that included not only Hiram Lovell, but also Edwin and Reba McPhee, numerous farmers from the outskirts of town including ones he had quarreled with earlier, and, most shockingly, Pastor Thaddeus Morrell and his wife Erin!

"You're the crux of the problem, whether you want to accept it or not," yelled Hiram. "You claimed to have had a confrontation with Danny Ricker. You were witnessed holding an axe while he ran out of your store and off into the woods. Regardless of who was truly at fault, it's clear to me that someone is seeking some form of sick revenge against this town and others. You're the only one who seems to have any clue what's happening, and in my book, that makes you responsible. You're also the only one with all his resources and possessions still intact. If Ricker is causing all this destruction, then he's your problem and I suggest you find a way to resolve it right quick! Rifle or no rifle, Sherman, if anyone here loses so much as another chicken, I guarantee you will pay for it in a manner similar to what befell the widow McClatchy!"

"I say we make him pay now!" boomed a voice from the crowd. "Ain't no store clerk and a cripple gonna stop us! He ain't got the balls to shoot! Let's loot his store, then burn everything he's got left to the ground!"

Sherman aimed his rifle again, only this time he pointed it directly at the crowd. His hands were steady but his insides shuddered with fear and indecision similar to what he had felt on the battlefield just prior to a bloody engagement. Parlin stood fast and used his one arm to menacingly point his shovel at anyone who looked to be an immediate threat.

"I'm going to say this just once, and whatever happens afterwards, happens," shouted Sherman. "This is a good community, filled with decent and law-abiding citizens. We've been tested—like Job—and though many have lost much, we can't allow ourselves to descend into anarchy! I appeal to your good nature and sense of self-decency. You don't want to do this. You don't want to lower yourselves to the level of criminal arsonists by destroying my home and my livelihood any more than I want to shoot a single soul out here tonight. Be reasonable and rational before it's too late. Go home. Look after your families and your livestock. The enemy is somewhere out there, not here. Please, everyone; don't make this harder than it already is. I'm putting my gun down now. My friend is going to drop his shovel. Please go on your way peacefully."

Sherman placed the Henry on the ground and motioned for Jeff to drop his shovel, which he did with reluctance. The crowd began to buzz with numerous conversations and a few of the people started to walk away. But not Hiram Lovell.

"That ain't good enough, Sherman! The problem is still out there! Whether it's a man or a ghost, I want it dealt with and I want to know how you plan to do it," yelled Lovell.

"Tomorrow I plan to ride out to South Gorham and locate Sheriff Ridgeway. Together we'll track down this ghost rider and reveal his true identity. He'll be taken into custody…or, if necessary, killed. I will not rest until Danny Ricker is located. I'm positive that once he's found and incarcerated, the ghost rider will simply vanish forever."

"You better be dogged in your pursuit of this fiend, Sherman," replied Lovell, "because if he ain't caught soon, or if any more destruction is wrought on this area, I guarantee there will be retribution against you in some unpleasant form or another. I'm not a patient man and I will not tolerate any more of this. I'll take matters into my own hands, as I'm sure everyone else here will as well. Woe betides you and your one-armed friend if that happens, Sherman. Mark my words."

The angry mob grumbled in agreement with Lovell's words and gradually began to disperse. Sherman picked up the Henry and stood tall, showing no sign of weakness or fear lest the mob change its mind and decide to turn on him in a moment of desperation. When the crowd finally and completely disappeared from sight, Sherman looked over at Parlin, who glared at him and said nothing. Sherman didn't waste his breath as his angry employee marched over to the store and closed the door behind him with a bang. Sherman was sure he would leave that night once he was certain he could get away undetected. He didn't care anymore. He would stay awake long enough to insure Parlin didn't steal one of his horses and gallop off with half the contents of his store, but beyond that, there was little else to do except prepare for the next day's hunt. He went inside, sat in the dim light of the parlor, drank some wine, and looked out the window with his loaded rifle within arm's reach.

CHAPTER 12

Hunting the Ghost Rider

Dawn broke, bringing with it another clear and hot day. The sun started to creep through the front window of the Jackson home, gradually climbing its way up Sherman's neck. As the beam of light eventually overtook his closed eyes, his face started to scrunch up until his shield of unconsciousness was shattered by the sun's unyielding assault. He snapped awake and clumsily slid from his chair onto the floor. After taking a minute to realize where he was and what was happening, he got up, took his rifle in hand, and hurried out the door, dreading what he would find at the store.

The door was unlocked and Sherman pushed it open. He carefully perused the display floor looking for any signs of deliberate pilferage. After careful inspection, he concluded that his inventory was sound and untouched since yesterday morning. He directed his attention to the stairs and quietly made his way up. Not surprisingly, Jeff was gone. There was no sign of him or any of his meager possessions. The room was a mess, but everything seemed to be there including several articles of Ricker's old clothes scattered across the floor. Sherman lowered his gun and went back downstairs. As he reached the last step, it hit him. He rushed to the display case and saw that his one remaining Bowie knife was gone! The lock had been forced open and the knife taken. Sherman then remembered he had left money stashed away in the cashbox below the counter. He reached down and set it atop the display case. His fears were realized after opening it and finding not a single cent remaining.

"That son of a bitch," proclaimed Sherman as he raced outside to the livery. To his relief, both Skipper and Budley were still there. "Well, if the cost of getting rid of Jeff Parlin is a few dollars and a knife, then I happily pay it," he said as he saddled up Skipper and attached a leather rifle case into which he slid the Henry. He led Skipper outside to the front of the store, which he locked up securely before mounting his horse. He gazed down Settler Road and noticed his horses and wagon were again parked in front of the church. His thoughts turned to Sophie and he decided to investigate in hopes she was there.

The wagon had been unloaded and his stallions were in good shape. Keeping in mind that Thaddeus and Erin had been a part of the crowd that threatened to burn down his house and store, Sherman entered the house of worship cautiously.

"Is anyone here?" he called out. He heard footsteps from behind closed doors in the front of the church. The doors opened and out stepped Sophie and Wilbur, much to Sherman's relief.

"Oh, Sherman, I'm so glad to see you. I heard what happened last night and I was so afraid for you," said Sophie as she raced into his arms. "I was shocked and dismayed to hear that the Morrells participated and couldn't bear their company a minute further. I insisted on taking Willy with me and used the excuse of returning your wagon to get out of their house. Imagine, a family that serves God acting in this vengeful way toward you. It's beyond unacceptable behavior! I wouldn't have known anything about it had it not been for Erin's big mouth this morning."

"Sir, Olin wasn't in his bed last night. I don't know exactly where he was, but I'm sure he met up with the ghost rider at some point," chimed in Wilbur.

"I understand, Willy. Give Miss Curtis and I a moment of privacy, please. Go outside and look after my horses and wagon."

Willy nodded and went outside.

"Parlin's gone," said Sherman. "Probably for good. I'm heading out to South Gorham now to find the sheriff. We're going to hunt down Danny Ricker and put an end to all this. After we hit all the back trails, my intention is to thoroughly investigate Pyne's Cemetery and the old Lester house. I just have this suspicion that both locations play a part in all this madness."

"Oh, Sherman, do you truly believe this is the best course of action? I fear for your safety."

"It's the only course of action. If something isn't done right away, I fear the whole state could burn, to say nothing about what will happen to this community."

"Please be careful," she pleaded.

"I will. The sheriff will be with me. I've survived many a danger in battle and don't intend to be brought down by a deranged kid. Well, I have to go. Do me a favor and please return my horses and wagon to my livery. Also, watch after yourself and Wilbur. This whole community is on edge and there's no telling what could happen. Find someplace safe and hunker down, I beg you. I'll find you after this whole sordid business is concluded."

The two lovers embraced and kissed passionately. Sophie watched as Sherman exited the church and mounted Skipper. He gave Wilbur a sharp salute, then trotted off toward South Gorham. He knew exactly where he needed to go first. He only hoped what he needed to find was still there.

Skipper trotted along at an even clip and soon North Scarborough gave way to South Gorham. Sherman sat tall in the saddle and kept a vigilant watch in all directions. He had always held the U.S. Cavalry in high regard during the war and often wondered how he would have fared as a mounted cavalryman and not a marching infantryman. Cavalrymen were always called upon to probe enemy territory and report enemy troop movements, among other duties. As a result of these dangerous responsibilities, they were often involved in accidental clashes with superior numbers of enemy forces. This compelled them to acquire an uncanny knack for observation and alertness unlike anything the typical infantryman had. Sherman tried to mimic these important qualities. They were essential for a good hunter to exhibit, but more importantly, they could help save his life.

As the green and gold countryside unfolded before him, Sherman peered down the road and through the pine trees looking for the trail that led to Ophelia Norris's house. In time, and with a little backtracking, he found it. The trail was just wide enough for a horse and carriage to squeeze down. As he neared the spot where he was sure the house was located, he began to smell smoke in the air. Soon after, he heard the faint sounds of a woman whimpering.

"Whoa," Skipper. Sherman dismounted his horse and pulled out his rifle at the sight of the young Ophelia, dirty and disheveled, her hands covering her sobbing face, and her house completely destroyed by fire behind her.

"Who are you?" the frightened woman asked through her tears, seeing Sherman cautiously approach.

"My name's Jackson. I'm a friend of Sheriff Silas Ridgeway. I thought I might find him here. Do you know where he is?"

"I don't know what you're talking about. There's nobody here by that name," she blurted out.

"What happened here?" Sherman asked.

"What do you think happened here?" she replied hysterically. "My house burned down!"

"How did it happen? And when?" Sherman asked calmly.

"Last night while I was asleep. I don't know what caused it. I only know that I was lucky to get out with my life. The fire destroyed my house, my barn, and killed or scattered all my animals! I have no money, no possessions, no food, and no family to help me! I'll be dead before the first autumn frost blankets the ground."

"I'm sorry for your troubles. I'm looking for the man that did this. He's torched many properties back in North Scarborough and needs to be stopped, which is why I need you to tell me where Silas is now," Sherman demanded.

"I don't know you, sir," fired back Ophelia. "How dare you make demands of me? I have no acquaintance with the sheriff."

"Bullshit," said Sherman impatiently. "Your name is Ophelia Norris. We met a year or two ago and you all but acted like you were Silas's wife. Now, it's well known by many from York to Bangor that you're his mistress and that he comes out here regularly. I've been told that personally from his own drunken mouth. Now if you insist on remaining in danger and you want to risk more destruction by this lunatic that's roaming freely right now, by all means, continue denying your acquaintance with the sheriff!"

Ophelia, haggard-looking and stunned at what she just heard, meekly replied, "I don't know where he is. I was expecting him last night and he never showed up. Then this happened."

"You have no idea where he might be now?"

"No. He could be home with his wife and kids by now, for all I know," she said despondently and with a trace of resentment.

"Get on the back of my horse. I'm going to take you into town. Hurry now, I don't have a lot of time."

Ophelia agreed and climbed aboard Skipper with help from Sherman. The two rode off and didn't stop until they arrived in Gorham. Sherman found a boarding house and dropped Ophelia off.

"Here's some money for food and a night's lodging. Explain what happened to whoever will listen and try to whip up some support. I have to go find Silas and try to stop these arsonist crimes," Sherman said as he pointed his whickering horse in a new direction.

"Thank you…and good luck," Ophelia said as Sherman galloped off.

"What now?" Sherman muttered. He had no idea where Silas was and knew the entire day could be wasted searching for him. His patience started to wane and his blood began to boil. He was tired of waiting. He was tired of passivity. Most importantly he was tired of feeling helpless and victimized. Something needed to be done and it needed to be done now, with or without help. He made a decision right then and there. He would ride directly to the place he felt in his heart was the spawning source of all the area's ills. It was a place he knew well, but hadn't laid eyes on in years. He remembered what his father told him, and he remembered what the crazed Milly McClatchy said days earlier during the church meeting. Summoning up all the courage he could muster, Sherman turned his horse in the direction of Pyne's Cemetery.

Using his memory and all his navigational skills, Sherman struggled to find the trail that ultimately led to his forbidding destination. He stopped and backtracked more than once, often dismounting to examine the ground more closely. It was as if the earth had deliberately swallowed up all signs leading to that dreadful place. Eventually Sherman discovered a very faint trail.

"This has to be it. C'mon Skipper, hyah," he called out with a snap of the reins. A narrow path, barely visible, cut through a thick and seemingly endless expanse of pine, oak, and maple trees. Sherman cautiously maneuvered his horse through the tangled morass of extended tree limbs and ground overgrowth that obscured the indistinct route and hindered their progress. In time the path widened, and it wasn't long before he could spy a clearing up ahead.

"This is it," he muttered. Skipper stepped out into a small meadow of thick grass and thorny brush. The ground gradually sloped upward as they proceeded forward. At the peak, the ground leveled off, and the weatherworn headstones of many graves dotted the landscape. Even more daunting was what sat adjacent. Sherman's eyes locked on the dark and insidious structure that was the Lester house. Its color was a pale gray that gave it a weathered and almost ghostly look. Most of the windows were broken and the wood appeared to be rotting away in several spots. The roof looked dangerously insecure with an unhealthy sag in the middle. Sherman could hear an unsettling whistle as the breeze blew through the house. The sound was chilling and caused him to shudder with a sense of uneasiness he hadn't felt in a long time. The place appeared downright sinister and he could only imagine the potential horrors that lay in wait inside.

Sherman rode Skipper up to the edge of the cemetery. He calmly dismounted and slid the Henry from its leather case. With rifle at the ready, he cautiously investigated the abandoned burial ground. The cemetery was overgrown with thick weeds and debris consisting mainly of dead leaves and broken tree branches. The granite headstones were heavily weathered, while many of the names etched on them had eroded away, rendering them unreadable. Many headstones were covered in a furry green moss and several others were damaged or sticking out of the ground at an improper acute angle.

The cemetery no longer represented a holy and peaceful place of rest and remembrance; it was now an eerie and unhallowed ground of neglect and disrespect for those buried there. As uneasy as Sherman felt standing among the deserted remnants of the deceased, he found the thought of approaching the Lester house much more difficult. He hesitated, fearing what unknown evils lurked inside waiting for him. He gathered the strength to tie Skipper to a nearby tree, then guardedly approached the infamous residence. At first he circled the house's perimeter, closely examining the outside and looking for signs that someone had recently been there. He pointed the Henry up at the second-floor windows as if he expected some sniper to appear and try to kill him. When satisfied there was nothing more to pursue on the outside, his thoughts reluctantly turned to going inside. He made his way to the front steps.

Each tiny step he took brought him closer until he reached the first rotten stair leading up to the front door. He took a deep breath and stepped up. The wooden boards beneath cracked and creaked under the strain of his weight, but didn't give way. Sherman walked across the porch and up to the door. Strangely, he was tempted to knock, as if he expected someone to answer and invite him in. He quickly regained his senses and pushed the door open with great effort.

"Lord in Heaven," he proclaimed as his eyes surveyed the abhorrent mess before him. He covered his nose as the stench of black mold, which seemed to cover everything in sight, hung in the air. He stood in the living room. Remnants of broken furniture, glass, and assorted personal items littered the floor. There were dark circular stains on the walls and the floorboards, leading Sherman to wonder if they were splatters of blood. The thought sent a shock up his spine and he moved on to the kitchen. There he found much the same type of disarray. Filthy broken dishes and glasses littered the floor. Snapped long-handled wooden spoons and disfigured metal knives and forks caked in rust were strewn everywhere. A metal cooking pot, covered in some indescribable residue, lay upended in a corner.

Sherman turned around and exited the kitchen. He made his way to the staircase and stopped before going up. All the horrors of his father's story of what had been discovered there years ago crashed through his mind and body, causing severe apprehension and revulsion. He had seen death in many forms on the battlefield, but the sheer evil of the murders described to him were incomprehensible. Oddly enough, he shuddered with a morbid curiosity that willed him up the stairs.

It felt darker and colder upstairs. Sherman gripped the Henry tight and held it at the ready. The same dark stains were evident in the hallway at the top of the stairs and Sherman wondered if he was now viewing the exact spots where the Lester girls had been so brutally slain. To his left was the master bedroom. Sherman was now visibly trembling as he peeked in and saw the ragged and decaying bed still present. Horrible visions of what his late father told him had happened there ran through his head. It was almost as if he could see the decapitated corpse of Muriel Lester lying there, the blankets soaked in a pool of blood. Unsure of what compelled him to do so, Sherman knelt down and looked under the bed. The head of Muriel Lester wasn't there, of course, but it might as well have been. Sherman's imagination got the better of him as gruesome images flashed through his mind. He bolted upright and rushed out of the room. He took deep breaths to calm himself as he felt faint. Unable to take any more, he eased his way down the stairs, almost tripping twice. He took a moment to compose himself and stepped back into the living room. He yearned to rush back outside into the bright sunlight, but hesitated upon glancing at the fireplace. Something caught his eye and he knelt down before it. He inhaled deeply, then used the barrel of the Henry to poke around at the charred bed of wood and ash. To his astonishment, he unearthed small, glowing red embers. Someone had been using the fireplace very recently!

"I'll be damned." He stared intently at the tiny, glimmering coals. Just then he heard a noise that prompted him to stand up quickly. He looked around and saw nothing. He clutched his gun and rested his finger on the trigger. He heard the muffled sound again and took three steps around a corner to discover a door. A surge of adrenaline pumped through his veins.

"It ends today," he murmured. "I got you now, Danny Ricker. I got you, you undeniable, rotten, son of a bitch."

Sherman raised the Henry and yanked open the door. He saw nothing but a stairway leading down into a sea of darkness. Before he could take another breath, something struck him on the side of his skull, sending him crashing to the floor, unconscious. The door slammed shut, leaving him sprawled out, helpless—completely unaware of what happened next.

Sherman slowly slipped back into consciousness. His head spun madly and ached with pain. He opened his eyes and saw nothing but his boots and the floor. He tried to move his feet but couldn't. He then tried to move his arms and discovered they were firmly tied behind his back. As the dizziness swirling in his head gradually began to subside, he slowly raised it until his eyes were level and locked on an alarming sight. Sitting in a chair directly across from him was Danny Ricker!

Sherman quickly realized his hands and feet were tied to his chair. Apparently he had been unconscious for several hours, as it was very dark now. The only light in the room emanated from a burning fire in the fireplace and a few scattered low-burning candles. He looked at Ricker, who sat facing him in front of the fire with the Henry trained on him. His clothes looked ragged, torn, and dirty. His face was grungy and unshaven. His hair stuck up in all directions and he had a wild, vengeful, yet disturbingly satisfied look in his eye.

"I told you I would get you, you bastard," Ricker said in a low and gravelly voice. "I told you that you'd see me again. I wasn't just gonna disappear without gettin' what's owed me. First I'm gonna take partial payment out of your ass! I'm gonna beat you bloody until you can't even see straight. Then I'm gonna whip you some more until you're unable to beg me to stop. And if you're still alive after that, I'm gonna string you up and cut you open, let you bleed to death real slow. And when you're finally dead, I'm gonna take or destroy everything you value and hold dear until there's no proof that Sherman Jackson ever existed! Or maybe, just maybe, I'll use this fine rifle here and blow a hole right through your gut so you'll die slow with a lot of pain! Fucking with me was a very bad idea, Sherman—and it's gonna cost you. It's really gonna cost you!"

"What makes you think you can just terrorize people and destroy everything they have? What gives you the right to commit random acts of arson and murder on such a wide scale? Don't you think people will demand retribution? Do you think you can escape justice and not be held accountable for your sinister deeds? What happens when the law catches up with you?" demanded Sherman.

"Ha! The law? There ain't no law around here no more! I told you that neither the law, nor anyone, for that matter, could help you! That damn fool sheriff ain't coming to your rescue. If he didn't spend so much time fucking that whore out in Gorham he would have been harder to find. Fortunately for me, I knew right where to ambush him. He can't help you or anybody else anymore," shouted Ricker as he pulled the sheriff's bloody badge out of his trousers pocket and flung it into Sherman's lap.

Sherman's heart sank at the sight of the bloodstained metal star now resting on his upper thigh. He felt there was no limit to Ricker's cruel and murderous ways. He knew time was short and he thought of Sophie. He prayed her path and Danny's would never cross. Unwilling to succumb without some small form of resistance, Sherman used the only weapon he had to stave off death and buy some time—his voice of reason.

"Danny...they'll come for you. Someone will come for you and stretch your neck at the end of a rope. If you give up now and let me go, I'll see to it that you get a fair trial," he said.

"What in hell makes you think I'd trust you?" Ricker responded while sticking the barrel of the Henry deep into Sherman's gut.

"Where are you gonna go? How can you hide forever? Eventually you'll be found and executed for your crimes," implored Sherman.

"Ain't nobody found me yet. Everyone's too petrified of runnin' into Sam Lester's ghost to come looking around this place. I could remain here forever if I chose too. However, once I've taken care of you and collected my small fortune from the soon-to-be ashes of your estate, I plan to travel down south. Lately I've come to sympathize with the plight of the common southerner and his struggles against the conquering invader who tore his way of life asunder forever back in 1865."

Sherman listened and looked into Ricker's deranged eyes. He could see the madness pulsating through his calculating and warped mind. At this point he realized Danny was capable of anything—no matter how horrific. He started to put all the pieces together. Everything was finally starting to make sense and fall into place. The vandalism, the thefts, the fires, the slaughtered animals, murder, and the Confederate symbolism—Ricker was responsible for it all—he had to be. There was just one puzzling piece that even Sherman couldn't bring himself to comprehend.

"So it *is* you. You're the ghost rider. Just answer me one thing, though. Why the old widow? Why did the only person in the entire community who showed you unrestrained kindness and generosity deserve to be so brutally murdered?" asked Sherman.

Ricker's facial expression went from that of a determined, psychotic killer to one of broad puzzlement. He stood up and repositioned the Henry's barrel from Sherman's gut to his forehead.

"What the fuck are you talking about?" he sternly inquired.

"Why did Milly McClatchy have to be burned alive? Why did you have to torch her house with her in it? Why did you indiscriminately slaughter the one woman who foolishly protected and nourished you?"

"No...she wasn't supposed to...goddamn him!" shouted Ricker as he drew back the rifle's hammer.

Sherman stiffened with fear as he waited for the shot that would end his life. Just then the front door burst open! Ricker wheeled around and pointed the Henry at the figure standing there. Sherman turned to look and was thoroughly shocked and confused at what he saw. Standing there, draped in a long white robe that covered his whole body, with his face hidden behind a hooded mask, was the ghost rider!

Ricker slowly lowered his gun and glared at the frightful figure who stepped forward into the light.

"Why are you here?" he asked. "You're not supposed to be back until dawn! And where's the food?"

The ghost rider stood silently and offered no response. After a moment, his left arm rose up from out of a long-sagging sleeve and an index finger pointed at Sherman.

"He's mine," proclaimed Ricker. "He came here, just as we predicted he would. Now I'll have my revenge!"

"No, that's not the plan," said the ghost rider in a deep, forced, disguised voice that Sherman couldn't identify.

"To hell with the fucking plan," roared Ricker. "I've waited for this opportunity. I demand satisfaction, and I'll have it, no matter what anybody says!"

Ricker pressed the rifle barrel back into Sherman's forehead and started to squeeze the trigger. Just then the ghost rider's exposed arm quickly disappeared under his robe and reappeared holding a pistol. In a quick flash the revolver fired. The bullet ripped from the barrel and struck Ricker in the side of his head. He toppled sideways and crashed against the fireplace mantel onto the floor. Sherman recoiled in shock as he looked down at the slain body, blood draining out of the bullet hole and pooling on the floor. Danny Ricker was no more!

Sherman jerked his head in the direction of the ghost rider, who had replaced the revolver in his left hand with a familiar-looking Bowie knife. He charged at Sherman and violently slashed at his ropes until they were cut free. Without saying a word, he pointed the large blade at Sherman and motioned for him to stand up and go to the stairway door. Sherman, wanting to lunge for the fallen Henry, decided against it and cautiously did as he was told.

"Open it," growled the ghost rider.

Sherman pulled open the door then looked back just as the ghost rider shoved him forward, sending him tumbling downward into the black abyss. The door slammed shut behind him, but not before his head knocked hard against a step and rendered him unconscious yet again. He was unaware the door had been locked and secured by a bracketed crossbar.

Sherman came to much faster this time. He sat up slowly and rubbed his head until the dizziness subsided. It took him a minute to realize the blows to his skull hadn't blinded him; he was just encased in a room of darkness. Bravely he reached out with both hands and groped around the floor for anything that could give him a clue to his surroundings or help him see. His first attempt was unsuccessful. It was then that he realized something, and quickly stuffed his right hand in his suit coat's inner pocket.

"Thank God," he said with relief as his fingers pulled out a miraculous little bundle of matches. "Praise the Lord for my renewed interest in cigars and whiskey."

He struck one of the matches to life. The tiny flickering torch provided just enough light for his eyes to quickly locate an oil lamp sitting on a nearby rounded end table against the wall. He hurried over to it just as the match burned out. Swiftly he struck a new one and carried the flame to the oil lamp's wick. Instantly the darkness was swept aside and the room was bathed in warm, glowing light. Still facing the wall, Sherman turned around to examine his surroundings.

"My God," he said, standing dumbfounded. His eyes slowly moved around the room, scanning everything from the floor, to the walls, up to the very ceiling. He moved carefully, taking everything in. He was overwhelmed at what he saw. He tried to articulate words, but they wouldn't come. Finally he gave up and sat down in a small wooden chair next to the lamp. He wanted to bury his head in his hands, but he couldn't...he couldn't stop gazing upon the sight that left him utterly speechless.

Surrounding Sherman on all sides was an overpowering display of relics and memorabilia from the old Confederacy. Draped down the walls alongside pictures of Jefferson Davis, Robert E. Lee, and Nathan Bedford Forrest were numerous Confederate battle and national flags of differing shapes, sizes, and configurations. Heroic southern slogans such as "The South Shall Rise from Ruin," and "Yankee Beware the Wrath of Rebel Vengeance" were scrawled out in strategic places on the walls in chalk, while a bloodied, tattered, gray uniform and slouch hat sat precariously displayed on a table next to an innocent piece of sheet music representing the tune of "Dixie." There were other things as well, but the powerful display of Confederate symbolism was all consuming. This underground crypt was not just a place of Sherman's detention; it was a Confederate shrine.

In a corner, Sherman shined the lamplight on a display of candles ringing a photograph of John Wilkes Booth and newspaper drawings of him assassinating Abraham Lincoln. The eerie display portrayed him as a hero and not the crazed, racist, melodramatic, entitled, and cowardly assassin he was. Sherman shook his head in disbelief. He stepped to the stairway and was about to go up when suddenly he eyed another eerie sight that made him stop and change direction. Hanging on a coat rack in the corner was a familiar-looking garment. Upon closer inspection, Sherman determined it was another set of the ghost rider's robe and hood. Beneath it was another small table displaying wooden crosses and curious literature. Sherman picked up a booklet and started to read through it. It was filled with pro-Confederate, pro-slavery, racist political and religious viewpoints. Suddenly Sherman got a scary notion. For the first time he finally grasped what the ghost rider truly was and what he represented. That thought echoed throughout his mind upon reading three ominous and identical letters stamped on the cover of a piece of anti-Negro literature—KKK.

"The Ku Klux Klan...of course," said Sherman. "How could I not have realized it sooner?"

Sherman had read about the rise of the KKK not long after the war ended. He understood it to be a southern terrorist insurgency group hell-bent on restoring the antebellum South by wreaking havoc with Federal reconstruction plans and terrorizing the newly freed Negro population. He knew of its founder, ex-Confederate General Nathan Bedford Forrest, and of the constant disruption, destruction, and murder it had caused in the Deep South over a period of several years. What he hadn't ever heard of, and what he found especially troubling, was Klan activity in the North—particularly as far north as Maine. He was certain that there were inhabitants of many northern states, including Maine, who had never heard of the KKK and would shudder in fear and ignorance at first sight of their ghoulish attire. This was most likely the case with the residents of North Scarborough and South Gorham.

"Why here and why now?" Sherman inquired. "It makes no sense. Why would the Klan try to assert influence in a place such as Maine?"

Several other questions sped through his mind but were quickly shoved aside as he focused on the immediate problem. He put down the lamp and hustled up the stairs. He tried the door only to discover it wouldn't open. He rammed it with his shoulder and kicked it like a mule to no avail. The door wouldn't budge. He went back down and scoured the room for anything he could find that he might be able to use to break the door down. Unfortunately he found nothing. Realizing he was trapped, he decided to sit and wait for whatever was next to come.

It wasn't long before he heard the sound of a galloping horse and then footsteps entering the house. He wondered if Skipper was all right. He quickly doused the oil lamp and hid in a corner. He hoped whoever was upstairs would foolishly come down in the dark looking for him. Then he would jump him. A few minutes went by. He stood hidden near the bottom of the stairs as the sound of the door being unbolted resonated through his ears. It swung open. Light from above beamed down into the darkness. There was a moment of pause as Sherman's heart raced in anticipation.

"Come out where I can see you," said a voice from above.

Sherman remained motionless and silent, still hoping to bait his jailer down the stairs.

"Show yourself, or I'll come down shooting in all directions. I'll bet that shiny rifle of yours could shoot all day. I'd love to test it out," said the voice.

Not wanting to risk being shot, Sherman stepped into the light at the bottom of the stairs. He looked up and saw the ghost rider standing there pointing his stolen Colt House Revolver at him.

"Come up here. Keep your hands raised where I can see them," said the ghost rider, still using his disguised voice. Sherman lifted his hands and slowly ascended the staircase. The ghost rider pointed Sherman down in the same chair in front of the burning fire where he had been bound earlier. Ricker's corpse still lay where it had fallen. It was a bloody mess that was now beginning to stink and attract flies. The ghost rider sat down in a chair and faced Sherman directly, his left hand still pointing the revolver at him.

"Who are you?" Sherman asked. "Why are you here, and why are you doing this? What right have you to terrorize this community?"

The ghost rider chuckled a bit, then slowly brought the barrel of the revolver up and under the base of his hood. With a sudden flick, the hood was flipped off and flung onto the floor. The revolver was quickly trained back onto Sherman as the storekeeper sat in disbelief at the newly revealed identity of his captor.

"Olin Morrell!" Sherman exclaimed. Sitting before him was the troubled fifteen-year-old son of the town's pastor. "Why? What brought you to this? How could you so easily be reduced to a shameless criminal and a murderer? Was it Danny Ricker that poisoned your soul and turned you away from all that's good and decent? He's the one that rode up to you and your brother in the woods that night and filled your head with lies and hateful Klan rhetoric, wasn't he? You took it as gospel...and look where it's led you. And now you've turned against your master, murdered him, and assumed his place. You're now the ghost rider, a deranged kid dressed in ghoulish Klan garb trying to sow hate and discontent into a peaceful community. You're part of a dying organization whose membership has been reduced from two to one. Regardless of what you do to me, the law will catch up with you eventually. Stop this madness now. I can help you. Put down the gun and let me take you out of here. I can speak on your behalf and swear you were manipulated by a deranged and devious influence in the form of Danny Ricker. The law will show you some leniency, I swear it."

"I'm not interested in anything you have to say, Mr. Jackson," said Olin, no longer disguising his voice. "I can do anything I want. I can take anything from anybody and never have to answer for it. I'm a member of a special fraternal order. I'm going to help resurrect the natural order of life and bring dignity and prosperity back to the Old South. It'll rise from the ashes and become a paradise on earth free from the tyranny of the oppressive United States and its blasphemous Constitution. The Negro will be put back in his cage and the southern states cleansed of all Federal and Republican political influences and oversight. All the carpetbaggers and scalawags will be lined up and executed by a newly resurrected Confederate Army, and all states south of the Mason-Dixon line will be free to determine their own destiny, so help me God! Our quest starts here. The North needs to experience the same suffering as the South endured during the war."

"Is that why you and Ricker took it upon yourselves to steal, vandalize, and murder? What do either of you know about the war or suffering? You were both young kids when the fighting broke out. What do you know about anything? I don't know where Ricker got his southern sympathies from, but he's poisoned your mind, Olin. The war is over. The Negro is free. And the North and South are reunited again as one country—the United States of America. And no matter what you've been told, no terrorizing rabble of ignorant fools dressed in bed sheets and calling themselves the Ku Klux Klan will ever change that."

"I ought to kill you right now, you godless sack of shit!" shouted Olin. "Goddamn Union soldier that you were, trampling all that was holy and just in the glorious South! I'm going to put a bullet through your head right now!"

Olin cocked the hammer and prepared to fire point-blank. Sherman closed his eyes. Just then the front door burst open.

"Stop! Boy, put down that pistol. How dare you even consider killing this man? That ain't the way we operate. You do as I say! And right now, I say get that decaying corpse out of here and bury him good in the cemetery. I don't care where. Just make sure he's buried in a spot where folks won't find him. Are we clear, young apprentice?"

"Yes, Grand Wizard," Olin obediently replied. He tucked his pistol away under his robe, grabbed Ricker's lifeless body by the legs, and hauled the body outside and out of sight. A long, narrow streak of blood was painted on the floor where the body was dragged.

Standing before Sherman was another figure wearing the same ghostly Klan garb. Unlike Olin's, his voice was distinctly southern. His accent was familiar to Sherman, as he had heard its like many times while the 20th Maine fought through the South. Sherman eyed the mystery man before him but remained silent. He was unsure of this person's intentions but knew deep down that they couldn't be good.

Curiously, the man turned around and dipped his head down. He reached up and pulled his hood off. He then reached under his robe and pulled out a revolver before slowly turning around to face his stunned captive.

"Surprise, surprise," said the man with a wide and sinister grin.

Sherman was incredulous and speechless. His body felt paralyzed and unable to move or do anything. The shock and confusion were overpowering. He'd been certain the man standing before him was the insane murderer from years past, Sam Lester. However, it wasn't Lester. In fact, the figure now standing before him with a LeMat revolver cocked and aimed in his direction was none other than Jeffrey Parlin!

"You," Sherman managed to squeak out feebly.

"You have no idea how long I've waited for this moment," Parlin said in a voice that no longer raised any curiosity as to its origin. His southern accent was clear and profound. He sat down in the chair facing Sherman, keeping the LeMat fiercely trained on him.

"Waited for what?" Sherman asked, adding, "You've stolen from me before. Now what? You're going to kill me, then loot my store and home before you burn them down in the name of southern justice? Is that it? Is that what you've been waiting for, Jeff?"

Parlin leaned in closer, allowing the firelight to better illuminate his face. He looked Sherman dead in the eyes and said, "You don't remember me, do you?"

Sherman didn't reply. A puzzled look crept across his face as he wondered what kind of game Parlin was playing with him.

"Yeah, I can see it in your eyes. You don't remember me. But I sure as hellfire remember you!"

"What are you talking about, Jeff?"

"I'm talking about a little town in Pennsylvania, Sherm. A place you and I visited ten years ago under much different circumstances! Oh, how I remember that place. I remember assembling at the base of that damned little rocky hill, the ground strewn with boulders and the men just itching for a fight. Alabamans and Texans, lean and hungry, waiting to be unleashed like a pack of ravenous dogs on the hunt. There was a sweet scent of victory in the air that day, just waiting to be bottled up and brought home by our triumphant soldiers in gray. The order was given and we charged, fighting our way up to smash through the inept defenders in blue who cowardly entrenched behind fat rocks and trees, safely firing into our advancing ranks. We charged time and again, trying desperately to smash through or flank that goddamn leftmost regiment that just wouldn't relent. Finally, after many of our boys lay dead or dying, we assembled again, only this time, before we could charge, we were met by a wave of blue sweeping down the hill. We were caught off guard. Many of us had no choice but to surrender, but I wouldn't have it. I hid behind a tree until some fool in blue crossed my path. Finally one came by. We fought until he figured he had me subdued. I fought back and nearly got away until the bastard struck me with his rifle butt and then drove his bayonet deep into my right shoulder!"

A bolt of shock violently raced up and down Sherman's spine. Gettysburg…he was talking about the battle fought for Little Round Top at Gettysburg. Suddenly Sherman was propelled back there, and the events of that bloody struggle vividly replayed in his mind. He thought about the end of the battle just after Chamberlain ordered the bayonet charge.

He remembered rounding up prisoners and his scrap with one in particular. Could it be? Was the man standing before him…?

"I suffered for hours with several other captured men. Eventually I was dragged to some Union field hospital where this inept and drunken surgeon looked at my shoulder, chloroformed me, then cut off my arm! I woke up in unbearable pain and shock after seeing what that butcher in blue did to me! Not long after, I was shipped out to a prisoner-of-war camp at Fort Delaware. For two long years I managed to stay alive, dodging typhoid fever, inflammation of the lungs, diarrhea, and smallpox. When the war ended, I was released and went home."

"Look…Jeff…I'm…."

"My name ain't Jeffrey Parlin, you damn fool! My name, my real name I'm proud to say, is Kyle Wilkinson. I'm not from Independence, Missouri, and I never fought for the Union Army under that vile, murderous son of a bitch, General Sherman! I'm from Tuskegee, Alabama, and I fought with the 15th Regiment Alabama Infantry—part of Robert E. Lee's Army of Northern Virginia. We squared off with the 20th Maine—your regiment—at Gettysburg back on July 2, 1863!"

"So that's why you're here now? Revenge?" inquired Sherman.

"It took me months to get home. When I finally arrived back at my family's cotton plantation, I was nothing but a filthy, lice-ridden skeleton! However, my personal appearance was nothing compared to the desolation of my ancestral home. The cotton fields had been burned; the slaves and field hands had run off; my family mansion gutted and my parents and sister dead! Despite all the family tragedy, despite the harassment of the local military garrison, despite the sneaky, underhanded, swindling carpetbaggers who tried to take my land, and despite every uppity nigger who rejoiced in their freedom and my misery, I persevered and held onto what was mine! One day, amidst all the toil and hardship, I decided the time had come to strike back at those who had caused me so much pain. I joined a fraternal organization of brotherhood that changed my life and gave me the means to protect what I love and destroy all those who sought to obliterate everything I held sacred."

"You became a member of a terror insurgency organization, one that threatened to tear apart the very fabric of the nation—the Ku Klux Klan," said Sherman.

"Tear apart your nation, not mine!" fired back Wilkinson. "The Klan fights to restore the South to what it once was—a bastion of chivalrous civilization ruled by democratic gentlemen and worked by legally owned slaves who know their place in society!"

"The Klan is weak and scattered now," said Sherman. "General Forrest formally disbanded it in 1869. The government has cracked down hard on it and the Union troops still garrisoning the South have vowed to stop its lynching and church-burning. I have read a lot about it in the newspaper over the years." He added, "You're part of a dying cause, just like the Confederacy."

"I am the Confederacy," preached Wilkinson. "I am the embodiment of all the customs, values, and traditions of the antebellum South! This town's inhabitants call me the 'ghost rider.' In a way, they're right. I am a ghostlike. I'm a living, breathing incarnation of every dead Confederate soldier who fought and was killed in the ongoing struggle for freedom against northern aggression! The battle rages to this day and will never end until the northern scourge is driven from the South forever! Our struggles might not be fought with mighty divisions of gray-uniformed troops massed on sprawling battlefields anymore, but they are certainly carried on by men...."

"Wrapped in bed sheets and silly-looking hooded masks," perilously interrupted Sherman, the LeMat still stuck in his face.

Wilkinson chuckled at Sherman's insolence. He stood up and started to pace back and forth.

"The day the Klan took me in as a member was the day I decided to take action against the one man I held most responsible for my personal loss and suffering. I vowed to find you, no matter how long it took, and destroy everything you held dear in your life before I killed you outright. When that fool Forrest disbanded the Klan, that's when I struck out on my own and headed north. It took time and money I didn't have, but eventually I made it here and learned everything I could about the 20th Maine and its soldiers. After endless nights of research, I found your name and picture in a military archive. I was then able to track down your family history and approximate whereabouts. I prayed you were still alive. When I arrived in Scarborough weeks ago, I wasn't sure you were here, but after I crossed paths with Danny Ricker one night, I got all the information and proof I needed. That night you foolishly let me into your life, you had no idea I had already set in motion a plan to destroy this town, turn everyone against you, and bring us both to this exact moment in time where I unreservedly and happily end your life!"

"You're the root cause of this? It was you behind all this death and destruction, not Ricker?" asked Sherman.

"Ricker was a puppet, Sherman. I used and controlled him to get to you. I found him here when I first arrived. He was angry and lost. He ranted about you endlessly. He told me all about you, your store, and all your possessions long before he had any clue I wanted to kill you. I furnished him with a sense of purpose. I showed him the glory of Klan membership and the rewards of punishing the people who supported the destruction of the South. He helped me do deeds I wouldn't have been able to achieve on my own—having just one arm, you see."

"So it was Ricker who started all the initial trouble out in South Gorham...trouble that eventually spread here," said Sherman.

"Oh, yes," answered Wilkinson. "Then he got foolish and arrogant. He decided to attack his employer one day. He could have killed you— and I couldn't allow that. Once you told the sheriff about suspecting him causing all the problems, I had to curtail his movements and keep him here, mostly, where no one dared look for him. Yes, he told me all about this house and Sam Lester long before the widow McClatchy rambled on about it at the grange hall meeting. I couldn't allow anyone to find him and bring him before your sheriff. He might have talked and revealed my true identity and intentions. That I couldn't have."

"It was you that knocked me down in the dark and held the knife to my throat that night, wasn't it? It wasn't Ricker, but you wanted me to think it was, right?"

"You're very clever, Sherm, and also very correct. It was I."

"Why Olin Morrell? You had your deranged lackey to do your bidding. Why bring an innocent boy into your sordid business?"

"Ricker was unreliable and not sound of mind. I couldn't trust him. He snuck away from here on occasion and dangerously exposed himself. I know this because he recently recovered your Colt House Revolver that young Willy Morrell dropped in the woods. Pity Willy didn't want to join my little club. I'll deal with him later. Ricker, on the other hand, thought he was doing good by killing the sheriff, but I had to remind him what a damn fool thing that was—with the butt of my revolver. Luckily I had decided earlier that I needed a fresh young mind to educate and mold—more importantly, to help do my bidding. Olin Morrell was just what I was looking for: young, rebellious, and in need of something to believe in. I gave him that something. He'll make a great Klan leader one day and will carry on the struggle indefinitely."

"So you made that fifteen-year-old boy into your pawn. You filled his head with hate and sent him off into the night to commit murder and arson—even against his own family!"

"His father doesn't preach good southern values; therefore, there's no use for him or his church. Both needed to be destroyed. The McPhees' grange hall was nothing more than a repugnant shrine showcasing the perverted relics of an army that brought tyranny and death onto a peaceful and civilized southern population. I arranged for a little pre-Independence Day remodel with proper exhibits of true heroism and righteous symbolism showcasing Confederate glory, not Union tyranny. As for Hiram Lovell, he reminds me of those greedy, loud-mouthed carpetbaggers I constantly fought against back home. Destroy their source of income and you destroy them."

"And the Budwin School? Why destroy that?" Sherman asked.

"Why not?" responded Wilkinson coldly. "If that bitch isn't intelligent enough to see that I'm a better man than you, then she deserves to have her little place of learnin' torched to ashes! And as for Milly Mc-Clatchy...well, according to Ricker she was a staunch Lincoln supporter during the war, and that just rubbed me the wrong way. I decided to toy with her and poison her well. In the end she had seen and said too much. She became dangerous and needed to be dealt with. I couldn't risk Ricker running back to her and revealing my identity. I had Olin take care of that matter."

"You're insane!" blurted out Sherman.

"No! I'm brilliant, because this whole area is in complete disarray and nobody has a single clue that I'm behind it. They are, however, enraged with you, and that makes your fast-approaching demise that much sweeter! Don't worry, though. I'll have taken your magnificent horses, which have already helped me many a time while you were sound asleep, and your valuables before I burn your house and store to the ground. You'll be dead before then! I told you long ago I'd remember you—Yankee!"

Sherman dipped his head. He didn't wish to look at Wilkinson anymore. He had been outmaneuvered and outwitted by this dangerous foe, and he felt his end was near. There was a pause of silence, and the front door opened again. Olin entered and approached his master.

"He's buried. The grave is shallow but nobody will ever find him, I guarantee it," the boy said.

"Good work, Olin. You obey well. That's an important quality for any upstanding Klansman. Now I have a new task for you to complete tonight. It's daunting, but it will show your mettle if completed successfully. I want you to ride out to the grange hall and burn it to the ground. Take the sheriff's horse and the Spencer. Kill anyone who tries to stop you. When you've accomplished that task, I want you to ride home. When you get there, I want you to kidnap Miss Curtis and bring her here. Again, if anyone, including your own family, tries to stop you, kill them. Remember, they're not righteous. They're loyal to the United States. Your father is a blasphemer who knows nothing of good southern worship. Your brother refused to join us and your mother humiliated you by making you apologize to this sorry sack of shit—remember when you told me that?"

"Yes, I will always do as ordered," replied Olin.

"What are you going to do with Sophie?" demanded Sherman.

"Miss Curtis is a young misguided flower. She is a maiden in need of rescuing from a despicable Yankee influence that has diseased her very soul. You are the white knight that will bring her here to my teachings of salvation. Together, Olin, you and I will show her the path of righteousness. She will become a model southern woman filled with virtue and respect. In time she will become the vessel that allows our cause to flourish and our family to grow. I will see to that personally. Now go. Bring that sweet magnolia to me, boy!"

"You're a despicable piece of southern trash, Wilkinson!" shouted Sherman. "Don't go near her, Olin! If you listen to this monster, you'll have nightmarish regrets for the rest of your life! Stop this now!"

"Olin," said Wilkinson, "Let's take Mr. Jackson downstairs."

The boy drew his Colt revolver and motioned for Sherman to head downstairs. Sherman raised his hands and complied. He walked down the steps and stood motionless as both Olin and Wilkinson followed him down.

"Tie him up tight to the chair," the one-armed man commanded as he held his LeMat on him.

Sherman sat down while Olin lashed his arms and legs to the chair.

"I hope you like my little shrine, Sherm," said Wilkinson. "I decorated it with mementoes from home and other places much more local. You'd be surprised how much Confederate memorabilia is hidden away in barns and houses around here—ripe for the taking."

Olin finished and signaled that Sherman was secure.

"Go now, Olin. Carry out your assignment and don't fail me. Since Sherman has so graciously provided me with his excellent mount, Skipper, I've decided to do a little late-night riding myself. I have one more task that needs to be carried out this evening. It won't take long and I'll meet you and Miss Curtis back here later. We'll have a regular party that will culminate in me putting a bullet through Mr. Jackson's head."

The two laughed and exited the basement, after which they secured the door with the crossbar. Sherman was again encased in total darkness as he heard the two gallop off. He desperately racked his mind trying to figure a way out. He twisted and wriggled his bound wrists, hoping to loosen the ropes enough that he might slip through them. His efforts were in vain, however, as Olin had tied his limbs firmly to the chair. He couldn't even harness enough leverage to snap the back of the chair or break its legs. The chair was too sturdy and he was too immobile. The struggle was useless. There was nothing he could do but wait.

Sherman's head dipped. He grew weary of staring into the darkness so he closed his eyes. He lamented his situation and thought about his parents. He knew he would be seeing them soon in a bittersweet reunion. He sighed heavily and asked God for forgiveness for all the pain and suffering he felt he had caused. The little prayer gave him some solace and prompted him to recall some of his favorite Bible verses. He spoke a few aloud and remembered the days as a child when he had all his favorites memorized and could recite them flawlessly on cue. It seemed like such a long time ago.

A half hour later, during a moment of quiet, Sherman's head bolted upright as his ears picked up the very faint thud of hooves impacting the ground. The sound grew nearer and Sherman was quickly able to determine that it was a single horse. He wondered if Wilkinson or Olin had returned for some unknown reason as neither had been gone long enough to complete their insidious tasks. He waited in silence and fear. Soon he heard the front door open, not with a bang, but with a slow, long-sounding creak. He listened intently as his heart pounded and sweat began to drip from his brow. He heard footsteps above him, but they were not the sounds of heavy boots impacting the floor, they sounded much different—softer.

Sherman's heart virtually leapt out of his chest when the next sound he heard was his own name called out in a sweet, quivering, female voice.

"Sophie!" he shouted with every ounce of breath his voice could command. "It's Sherman! I'm trapped downstairs! There's a door leading down! Follow my voice!"

The sound of the crossbar being lifted and the door swinging open filled Sherman's ears. Light poured down the stairs and Sherman looked up at what appeared to be a beautiful angel standing above him. With a lantern in her hand, Sophie rushed down to save her lover.

"My God, Sherman," she said, adding, "I can't believe you're here. Thank God I found you!"

Sophie struggled, trying to loosen the knots that bound Sherman's wrists.

"They're too tight, Sophie. Reach into my coat pocket and pull out the matches. Use them to carefully burn through the knots. Be careful though."

Sophie found the matches and sparked one to life. She began to burn through the ropes little by little, blowing out the flames before they grew too big.

"How did you find me?" asked Sherman.

"I got worried. I was so scared you would be hurt. When it got dark and I hadn't heard from you, I decided to go look for you. I feared you might be in trouble. I went to your house and you weren't there. After that, the first place I thought to look was here. Willy told me how to find this place. He wanted to come, too, but I wouldn't let him. I needed him to create a diversion and occupy his parents so I could slip away undetected. My God, Sherman, what is this place?" she asked, staring at all the Confederate symbolism surrounding them.

"We don't have much time," Sherman said. "I'm stunned you had the courage to find this horrible place at night. You're the bravest woman I know and you've saved my life. Parlin is the scoundrel behind all the crimes and destruction—only his name isn't Jeffrey Parlin and he's not a drifter from Missouri. You were right, Sophie. You were right to suspect him. He never served the Union Army and he has no roots in Missouri. His real name is Kyle Wilkinson and he was a Confederate soldier from Alabama. We fought at Gettysburg and I wounded him, which led to his capture and arm amputation. He survived and has spent years hunting me down so he can exact revenge upon me. What's worse is that he's a member of the Ku Klux Klan and actively trying to destroy this community—my community—in the same fashion as many in the South were destroyed during the war. He's insane, and he used both Danny Ricker and Olin to do his dirty work. They captured me and plan to kill me."

"Where are they now? Where's Sheriff Ridgeway?"

"The sheriff's dead. He was killed. Danny Ricker is dead now, too—Olin shot him on orders from Wilkinson. Both he and Olin rode off a while ago to kidnap you and burn down the grange hall. You didn't see them on your way out here, did you?"

"I saw no one. They may have taken a different route," said Sophie, finally burning through the rope that freed Sherman's hands.

"Thank God you didn't cross their path," Sherman said, untying his feet and legs from the chair. Soon he was free. He stood up and walked over to the Rebel uniform draped on the table he had seen earlier. He looked at it closely and remembered it as being the same one Wilkinson had worn the day they first fought. He then got an idea. Sherman struck a match and reignited the oil lamp. He took one last look at all the Confederate symbolism surrounding him and said, "They'll never use this house as a base for their wicked actions ever again. This is the end of this evil place."

With that, Sherman flung the oil lamp at the wall. The glass shattered, spreading oil and flame everywhere. Several flags ignited and burned quickly.

"We have to get out of here fast," he said, taking Sophie by the hand and rushing up the stairs. He glanced around the living room. He beamed with delight upon seeing the Henry still lying on the floor where Ricker had fallen.

"Thank God they didn't take it with them," he said as he picked up his prized gun. "C'mon, there's no time to lose. We have to get back to the Morrell farm and stop Olin before he murders his own family!"

With Sophie's lantern in hand, the two rushed outside. Sophie led Sherman to where she had tied up his horse.

"Am I glad to see you, Budley," he said, untying the Morgan. He helped Sophie aboard the animal and handed her the Henry and the lantern. He then climbed into the saddle himself. With help from the glowing lantern plus adequate moonlight, the two began to navigate their way back toward Settler Road. Sophie looked behind her and watched as flames began to lick through the windows of the old Lester house.

Sherman guided Budley along the trail until they were back on the main road. Then, without warning, shots rang out! Two bullets slammed into the horse's neck. The stricken animal reared and squealed in pain before toppling over and sending Sherman and Sophie tumbling to the ground. Sherman picked up the Henry and grabbed Sophie's hand. The two scrambled into a ditch, using the dead horse for cover. More shots were fired. Sherman saw the brief muzzle flashes and was able to determine the assailant's approximate position and distance. He cocked the Henry and fired a shot in his attacker's direction. Sophie covered her ears and kept her head down. More fire was returned from the mystery foe. Bullets slammed into Budley's slain carcass and ricocheted off nearby trees. Sherman worked the lever on the Henry and fired back several times at movement and sound, unsure whether he had hit his target. One final shot whizzed through the air, narrowly missing Sherman's head. Then a moment of silence ensued.

"I think he may be out," whispered Sherman.

"What are you going to do?" Sophie whispered back.

"Let him think I'm out too," he softly replied.

Sherman, captivated by the Henry's ability to seemingly fire endlessly without ever being reloaded, had lost count of just how many shots he had fired. Little did he realize, he was down to his final bullet. A moment passed and he saw a figure, silhouetted in the moonlight, stand up in the field across the road. The figure wobbled a bit and then drew a Bowie knife with his left hand. He let out a spine-chilling shriek and charged toward Sherman and Sophie!

"I will avenge you, General Pickett," screamed out the assailant as he charged forward with knife in hand. Sherman quickly rose up and aimed his rifle with precision. The final shot burst out of the barrel with a sharp crack and slammed into the chest of the charging attacker! He stopped instantly and crumpled to the ground, dead. Sophie retrieved and relit her lantern. With a crank of the lever, Sherman ejected the last spent round from his gun and soberly realized he was out of ammunition. The two rushed over to identify their attacker.

Soaked in blood lay a white-robed and masked body. Not knowing which of the two he had killed, Sherman pulled off the hood while Sophie shined the light in the corpse's face.

"My God," she said. "It's Olin."

Sherman took a few steps away and came across the empty Spencer rifle Olin was using.

"Goddamn shame it had to come to this," Sherman said mournfully. "He was so young and misguided. He could have been helped if put under the right guidance and influence."

"He was too far gone, Sherman. His mind was permanently distorted by the teachings of a southern radical. There was nothing you could have done. He would have killed us both. You saved us," said Sophie. "We'll come back for him later. Now we must get back and stop Wilkinson before he can do any more harm to the town. We must go!"

"You're right. It's not over yet," said Sherman. Just then he heard a horse snort. Sophie shined the lantern and saw the sheriff's horse tied to a nearby tree. They hurried over to it. Sherman tucked the Henry into the leather saddle case and the two climbed aboard. Once again they started off down Settler Road.

Soon they approached Sherman's house. To their horror, both the church and the grange hall were ablaze! In the distance, but out of sight, they could hear the chilling shrieks and whoops of Wilkinson.

"Why isn't anybody fighting the fires?" desperately asked Sophie.

"They're either unaware, afraid, or dead," replied Sherman. "Quickly," he said as he rode up to the store, "Go inside and lock yourself in. Here's the key. Hide upstairs in the spare room and stay there until I come for you."

"What about you?" she cried.

"I need to get more bullets from the house. Then I'm going to find and shoot Wilkinson. He can't be far and he doesn't know I'm free. Just stay hidden in the store. You'll be safe there."

"Be careful!" she exclaimed as she rushed inside, locking the door behind her. Sherman slapped the sheriff's horse from behind and watched it take off after retrieving the Henry. He then ran inside his house and raced upstairs. He lit the oil lamp in his bedroom and threw open his bedside table drawer. Inside was the Smith & Wesson Model 3 revolver. He broke open the action and was dismayed to find the gun empty. He then remembered he had taken the three boxes of cartridges down into the parlor where he first loaded the Henry.

"Damn," he muttered as he hurried down into the parlor. He tossed the rifle onto the sofa and found the cartridge boxes on the mantel. He quickly slammed the .44-caliber rim-fire bullets into the chamber and closed up the gun. He turned and faced the window. He recoiled in horror at the sight of a ghoulish face hauntingly staring in at him! It was Wilkinson! Sherman pointed the pistol and fired. The shot shattered the glass a second after the ghost rider ducked for cover. Sherman panicked and dashed out of the parlor, down the hall, and into the dining room. He heard Wilkinson shriek and holler outside. His cries sounded eerily familiar. Sherman finally recalled what it reminded him of—the Rebel Yell!

Suddenly the front door was violently kicked open! Wilkinson blindly fired a shot and leapt inside before Sherman realized what had happened. He ducked into the parlor and yelled, "I thought you didn't have a pistol, Sherm! You lied to me. You left me defenseless up in that room. What would have become of me if Danny Ricker decided to break in and assault me?" he asked in a deranged and twisted voice.

"You would have been just fine, you son of a bitch," fired back Sherman. "You would've just put a ball between his eyes with that LeMat you're carrying now!"

Wilkinson let out a sinister laugh and said, "I'm going to kill you with this LeMat, Sherm. You know what's great about this gun? It fires nine times before it needs reloading. Oh, and if there's a need for a tenth shot…well, there's a special surprise waiting for you then. I won't ruin it for you. I'll let you experience it when the time comes. Doubt I'll need any more than two shots to put you down for good, though, you Yankee cocksucker!"

Sherman looked down at his pistol. He was at a distinct disadvantage and he knew it. He had five shots left while Wilkinson had at least eight. There was no chance for reloading unless he could draw his adversary out of the parlor and get to the remaining bullets. He didn't fear Wilkinson using the Henry against him as he was sure he couldn't effectively load, cock, and fire the rifle with just one arm. The LeMat was a different story, however.

There were no candles or lamps burning in the house, save the bedroom upstairs, yet there was partial illumination coming in through the windows via moonlight and the raging church and grange hall fires down the road. It was barely light enough to see in the house, yet dark enough to easily hide.

"C'mon, Sherman, show me what you're made of," hollered Wilkinson. Just then two shots from the LeMat ripped past Sherman's head. He ducked down on the floor and threw a chair out in front of him for cover. He peeked out and got a glimpse of Wilkinson's hood. He took a shot at him and missed badly.

Wilkinson let out a quick laugh and said, "How'd you get out of my basement, Sherm? You're more resourceful than I gave you credit for. Stick your head out and let me end this fight, right quick."

Sherman, with four bullets remaining, knew he couldn't get a clear shot if he stayed where he was. He crawled on his belly into the kitchen as another shot from the LeMat tore through his pant leg, barely missing his flesh. In the kitchen he scrambled to his feet and opened the door that led out to the sheltered walkway connecting to the barn. As he did this, he heard heavy, fast-moving footsteps and deduced that Wilkinson had moved from the parlor, down the hallway, and was just around the corner from the dining room. Sherman hustled halfway down the walkway and looked back. He saw Wilkinson peeking around the corner. He waited for the Klansman to make his move first as Sherman knew he couldn't get his left arm out to fire without more fully exposing his body. The lack of a right arm prevented him from squeezing off a shot while covered from around the corner.

Wilkinson stepped out to fire. As he did, Sherman raised his pistol and shot at him. Again he missed, but not before causing his adversary to hit the deck and blindly fire another shot back at him without careful aim. Sherman ran down the rest of the walkway and into the barn. Again he heard footsteps behind him as he ran up to the sliding barn door. He turned and aimed at the doorway, hoping Wilkinson would foolishly expose himself in his hasty pursuit. Keeping his gun up and his eyes on the doorway, Sherman used his free hand to reach for the latch behind him and open the large sliding barn door. He got hold of it and tugged hard, but the door wouldn't slide open! He jerked harder and harder, but it wouldn't move. He took his eye off the walkway door for just a second when suddenly another shot from Wilkinson's LeMat rang out and grazed his left shoulder. Sherman fired back but missed as the bullet just smashed into the side of the doorframe. Finally, with a mighty heave, the barn door slid open just enough for Sherman to slip through. He fired one last covering shot before dashing outside. He now only had one bullet left.

The fires continued to rage down Settler Road. There was still no sign of another soul around anywhere. Unbeknownst to Sherman, Edwin and Reba McPhee had been asleep in the grange hall after a long day of cleanup convinced them both that they were too tired to travel home. Wilkinson had killed them when they tried to flee after the fire was set. He had surprised and stabbed both of them to death. Their corpses lay in the street. Hiram Lovell had fared no better. His house was also ablaze, his lifeless body lying in a nearby field. He too had fallen victim to the ghost rider.

Sherman wanted to flee into the open darkness and draw Wilkinson away from Sophie. However, he instantly realized there was little he could do with just one bullet and made the decision to run back into the house via the front door to get the Henry and his remaining cartridges, both still in the parlor. He raced to the front door. Another shot from Wilkinson, who emerged from the barn, whizzed by Sherman's ear. He got inside and raced into the parlor. He wisely ignored the Henry, figuring it would take too long to load. Instead he snatched a cartridge box and swiftly flipped open the revolver's action. But before he could reload, the front door burst open. Sherman lurched at the door and drove his shoulder into it, forcing it shut and sending Wilkinson toppling backward onto the ground. The box of cartridges fell out of Sherman's hand and hit the floor, sending the precious rounds rolling away in all directions, lost in the dark shadows. Another shot tore through the front door, barely missing Sherman's head. Instinctively, he turned and foolishly fled upstairs, unable to reload his pistol. He dashed up the steps as Wilkinson kicked in the front door in reckless, dogged pursuit.

In half a heartbeat, the hooded, one-armed Klansman cocked the LeMat, flipped up the unique striker on the hammer, and squeezed the trigger. An explosion of twenty-gauge shot erupted from the lower barrel and peppered Sherman's right shoulder. The shock of the blast propelled him forward, and he crumpled on his belly at the top of the staircase. His Smith & Wesson flew out of his hand and skidded across the floor, its action still open, and the one remaining bullet resting halfway out of the chamber.

Stunned at the unique sensation of being shot, Sherman slowly and painfully crawled toward his gun. In all his days of combat, he had never been hit and had never experienced the pain of a gunshot wound. It was a surreal feeling that he assumed was an immediate precursor to death. He felt weak and dazed, but something deep down inside him willed him to fight on and not give up! He reached for the gun.

"I just couldn't wait to reveal the surprise to ya, Sherm," sadistically said Wilkinson as he slowly climbed the stairs after his wounded prey. "What I love about this gun is that marvelous little shotgun feature. It's like two kinds of guns in one. What's even better is that I got two or three balls left in the chamber, too. Hell, I feel like I can fire all day without reloading! Good feeling to have when you got just one arm and it takes you twice as long to reload!"

Wilkinson reached the top of the stairs and found Sherman lying helplessly, still a good arm's length away from his pistol.

"I just got an idea." Wilkinson kicked Sherman in the gut, causing him to cry out in pain and cough up some blood. "I'm gonna do something I've dreamed about doing for many years now. Tonight I just wanted to shoot you dead. But now…I think you need to experience exactly what I experienced ten years ago!"

Wilkinson dropped his revolver and reached under his white robe. He pulled out one of Sherman's Bowie knives and held it up for the injured man to see.

"You wounded me in the shoulder all those years ago. Now I've wounded you in the same place. Your drunken field surgeons, armed with northern rage and Liston knives, took off my arm without so much as a second thought. Now I've got this here Bowie knife…and I'm going to slice off your arm! Then I'm going sit and watch as you experience, if only for a minute or two, what it's like not having a major body part. Then, just before you bleed to death and expire, I'm gonna slice off your balls and stuff 'em down your gullet until you choke!"

Sherman lay helpless. He was in severe pain, paralyzed with fear, and barely able to breathe. His eyes locked on the ghostly form standing over him with the large, imposing blade held up in position, ready to strike and rip through his defenseless body. This was it. This was the end. Sherman thought of his parents and how he'd be with them shortly.

"You're on your way now, Sherman Jackson! I'm gonna send you to hell!" shouted Wilkinson as he drew back the knife and prepared to plunge it deep into Sherman's bloody shoulder. "Don't worry about Sophie, neither. I'm gonna show that little girl what a real man can do… many times over, whether she likes it or not! Long live the South!"

Just then a tremendous screech echoed from behind. Out of nowhere, Sophie, armed with a metal poker from the fireplace, raced up the stairs and swung the iron for all she was worth. It crashed into Wilkinson's skull and sent him toppling over. With unrelenting fury, the young woman screamed and beat him repeatedly until blood started to seep through his white robe and hood. Satisfied she had killed him, Sophie dropped the iron and rushed to Sherman's side. She helped him sit up and regain his senses.

"Sherman! Sherman, are you all right?"

He coughed and cleared his throat. He waited a second or two for his head to clear and then said, "I'm okay. He got me with some sprayed shot in the shoulder, but I should be all right…I think," he added with pause. "Help me up, sweetheart. Help me to my feet. We need to get out of here."

Sophie wrapped her arms around Sherman's upper body and pulled hard. She strained but managed to get him up on one knee. She stood up, poised for one final tug that would get him onto his feet. A woozy Sherman looked up and his heart sank. Rising behind Sophie was the bloody and battered Klansman! Again he raised the Bowie knife and prepared to drive it deep into the back of young Sophie!

"Sophie, look out!" yelled Sherman. She turned around and screamed at the monstrous and murderous sight behind her. She trembled with fear as a dazed and bloody Wilkinson violently slashed downward. She leapt out of the way just before the knife crashed down into the floor.

Sherman dove onto the fallen Smith & Wesson, pushed the one remaining bullet into the chamber, and closed the action. He pointed the gun at Wilkinson, drew back the hammer, and fired. The gun clicked as the hammer dropped on an empty chamber. Wilkinson struggled to wrench the knife out of the floor. Sherman cocked the hammer back and fired again. The hammer struck yet another empty chamber! Wilkinson finally pulled the knife free and raised it over Sherman. He let out a final, terrifying Rebel Yell. Sherman cocked the pistol one last time. The cylinder rotated into place and he squeezed the trigger just as his nemesis thrust forward! This time the hammer dropped on the sole loaded chamber. The round exploded from the barrel and struck Wilkinson directly in the heart. The impact threw him backward and his body tumbled down the stairs. He crashed into the door where he came to a complete stop. He lay face up and finally dead.

"Sherman," cried Sophie as she hugged him.

Both got to their feet and looked down at the bloodied body illuminated by the raging fires outside.

"It's over. It's finally over," Sherman said, his voiced soaked with pain.

The two descended the stairs. Sherman knelt next to the body of Kyle Wilkinson and pulled off his hood. His eyes were still open, but all the feelings of hate and revenge—as well as his very life force—had finally been driven from his body—forever.

Sophie and Sherman stepped outside and embraced. They looked at the burning infernos that once were the North Scarborough Community Church and the Old Liberty Grange Hall. Each thought of all the destruction and death Kyle Wilkinson had wrought on their small community and each wondered if the nightmare was *truly* over.

⊹┼⊹

The next day, Sherman and Sophie stood over the desecrated headstones of both Anders and Julia Jackson. The grave markers had been toppled over and smashed. Sherman looked down in sadness as he felt that in a way, Wilkinson had gotten the last shot. He winced in pain and rubbed his injured shoulder.

"Come inside, dear," said Sophie. "We need to change the bandage and try to clean out more of that lead shot."

Sherman reluctantly nodded and the two retreated inside. He had the best nurse around, whether he knew it or not. In time, his body would heal, just as the town would heal.

CHAPTER 13

December 23, 1877

The snow fell softly and coated the ground like fine powdered sugar. A church bell rang out as several parishioners dressed in warm clothing scurried down the road so as not to be late for Sunday services. The church doors were open and soon the house of worship was filled. One of the last to enter was a couple that quietly sat down and held hands in a back pew. The crowd hushed as the pastor entered and stood at the podium.

"Dear friends, good morning, and a Merry Christmas to all. It is a blessing to see everyone present on this inspiring Sunday morning. Today, we're here not only to worship the Lord and his teachings, but we're here to celebrate the resurrection of our community, starting right here with the first service of the new North Scarborough Community Church. For those who are joining our congregation for the first time, I'm Pastor Thaddeus Morrell and I bid you welcome."

The audience applauded until the pastor raised his arms and called for silence.

"A few years ago, our community was stricken by a force of evil driven by a power in league with the very Devil himself. We all suffered greatly. Much valuable property was damaged or destroyed and many precious lives were taken from us, including my eldest son. We lost a lot, and the Lord tested our ability to stay righteous and holy in the face of the Devil's madness. Eventually, over several trying days, the Devil was cast out of North Scarborough and the healing began. Though the successful rebirth of our community can't be attributed to just one couple, I have to call your attention to two very special people who have been instrumental in getting us back on course. These two have been the driving force bringing hope and prosperity back to North Scarborough. Had it not been for their tireless fundraising and unmitigated generosity, we would not have this beautiful new house of worship that we are blessed with today. Also, we would not have the new schoolhouse or the new grange hall. Most importantly, we would not have the camaraderie and love that flourishes within our community. Not one family that was stricken by the Devil those few years ago has not been touched and helped in some fashion by the two blessed souls I speak of now. Before we begin our regular service today, I want to extend my personal thanks and blessings to Mr. and Mrs. Sherman Jackson."

Again the crowd broke out in applause as Sherman and Sophie, sitting quietly in the back, stood and acknowledged the kind sentiments. After a minute, they smiled and sat back down as Pastor Morrell began his sermon. Sherman looked around the room. Sitting up front he spied Erin and Wilbur. The wife of the pastor had grown more corpulent over the years and now was only seen wearing black. She had not applauded with the others in the congregation when the pastor praised the Jacksons. She often scowled at Sherman, viciously blaming him for the death of Olin. Deep down, Erin Morrell accused him for everything that happened those few hot and horrible weeks years ago and would never offer any forgiveness. The investigation and trial that followed the tragedy absolved Sherman of any wrongdoing and put all the blame on the dead Kyle Wilkinson. Sherman testified that Ricker admitted murdering Sheriff Ridgeway. He also stated that he witnessed Olin murder Ricker. With the help of Sophie's testimony, the judge ruled that the killing of Olin Morrell by Sherman was a clear act of self-defense, and he was not charged with murder. In time many forgave him, including the pastor.

Wilbur Morrell was now a strapping young seventeen-year-old and an asset to the community. He grew to be happy and helpful and didn't follow his brother's darker path. He was a regular employee at Sherman's store and a bigger help than either Danny Ricker or the man who claimed his name was Jeffrey Parlin had ever been. He was a stellar student and looked to attend college next year.

Gertrude Lovell sat in the middle with Josephine and Alexander, who were now seventeen and fifteen respectively. Gertrude had heavily mourned the loss of her husband and of all their possessions after the terror caused by the ghost rider. Sherman endeavored to help the Lovell family as best he could with several fundraisers and personal loans that allowed them to rebuild a modest house and start to get their dairy business back on track. Josephine and Alexander flourished under Sophie's private tutelage and were also model students and tremendous assets to the community.

Little could be done for the slain McPhees, but Sherman invested everything he had and managed to rebuild and own the Old Liberty Grange Hall. He maintained the McPhees' vision and filled it with collected artifacts, recorded oral testimonies, and other information pertaining to various American conflicts from the past. In time he had exceeded the McPhees' original collection. Also, there was a special area of the museum dedicated to their son Charles. With Sophie's help, Sherman researched Charles's past and put all his glorious exploits on display so that everyone who entered would not leave without knowing who Charles McPhee was. There was also a display that paid tribute to the 20th Maine. It became so widely known that the president of Bowdoin College and Sherman's old commander, Joshua Lawrence Chamberlain, paid the museum a special visit and personally thanked Sherman for his service and dedication to the old regiment. Under Sherman's ownership and management, the Old Liberty Grange Hall flourished and had a part-time staff that operated it during regular business hours.

The last major service Sherman provided to the community was the cleanup and care of Pyne's Cemetery. What remained of the Lester house was obliterated and the adjacent cemetery was cleaned up and no longer neglected. Sherman arranged for Hiram Lovell, Olin Morrell, the McPhees, and the remains of Milly McClatchy to be buried there. He also arranged for a special marker to be erected there in honor of Sheriff Silas Ridgeway, whose body was never found. The body of Kyle Wilkinson was transported to Portland, embalmed, and stored in the city morgue after its discovery by law enforcement officials. It was kept there throughout the trial. By a strange twist of fate, after exonerating Sherman of all wrongdoing, the judge ordered that the body of Wilkinson was Sherman's responsibility. Sherman had the body cremated, then disposed of the ashes in an unknown location. He didn't want Wilkinson associated with Pyne's cemetery or any other known place of rest. No longer was Pyne's a place to be feared. It soon became a place of peace, rest, and tranquility.

As for Jackson's General store, business flourished there as well. Sherman's good will toward the community was repaid to him with a healthy stream of customers and a prosperous business that had made him enough money to invest and thrive. A business he had known his whole life, and initially wanted no part of, was now booming and affording him luxuries he had never known.

Halfway through Pastor Morrell's sermon, Sherman looked at his wife and gave her a wink. She nodded and the two quietly slipped out of the church and happily strolled back home. It was still lightly snowing and the air was filled with beautiful swirling snowflakes that Sophie happily tried to catch on her tongue. The two arrived at the house, but before they went inside, they strolled out back. Sherman checked on Skipper, who was tied up in his usual spot in the livery. He then checked on the stallions, Phineas and Lucky. They were content too. The loss of Budley hadn't been forgotten, and Sherman thought of him often. Sherman took Sophie by the hand and escorted her to the oak tree by the stream. They both looked at the restored headstones of Anders and Julia. They each touched them and whispered a happy sentiment. A moment later they strolled back to the house.

Inside, the fire was burning heartily and the two sat down in the parlor together. The Henry rifle was mounted in its spot on the mantel above the fireplace. Sherman looked up at the magnificently decorated Christmas tree on display in the front window and all the colorfully wrapped presents that were tucked away beneath it. The light snowfall added the perfect Christmas backdrop. Sherman leaned over and kissed Sophie tenderly, then placed his hand on her midsection.

"How soon?" he whispered.

"It won't be much longer," she said with an impish grin. "Soon everyone will know."

Sherman kissed his pregnant wife again and then stood up.

"I know it's still early in the day, but can you play 'Silent Night'? It just seems fitting for some reason."

"Of course, my dear." Sophie sat down at the piano and started to play the sweet, serene holiday favorite. As she played, Sherman thought of traveling and taking her all over the world to see places he'd dreamed of visiting before the war. Life would be good from now on. There would be no more tragedy or horror. That was in the past and would stay buried there forever. He was determined of that.

As Sophie played, Sherman went to the window and watched the snowfall. His eyes wandered up Settler Road to the newly built Curtis

Memorial School. He looked at it with pride and dignity. As he sipped a little whiskey, his eyes were drawn to the flagpole. The wind suddenly picked up and Sherman let out a small gasp.

"No, it can't be," he said as he strained to get a better look at the flag pulsating in the cold December wind and snow. The harder he looked the more apparent it became. His eyes filled with the vision of the Confederate battle flag flying atop the pole!

"What's wrong, dear?" asked Sophie as she got up from the piano.

"Get your coat on. Come with me quickly, sweetheart," he responded.

Sherman took his wife by the hand and tugged her outside and up Settler Road to the school. They both stood under the flagpole and Sherman looked up in amazement. Sophie glanced up, too, unable to determine what was the matter.

"What is it, dear?" she asked in concern.

"I don't know," he replied with uncertainty. "I could have sworn I saw...."

"Saw what, Sherman?"

"Never mind. I must be a bit overtired or sipped some bad whiskey. My senses are playing a nasty trick on me. Don't be concerned, dear. Let's get back inside out of this cold," he said with a forced smile.

"Okay, my love. Perhaps you should lie down for a bit?"

"Yes, but only if you'll lie down with me," he quipped.

"Sherman, it's Sunday," she blushed.

"I know. Let's go home and get ready for the wonderful Christmas we're going to have. I do hope your family can make it here on time."

"They arrive by steamer in Portland tomorrow morning. If all goes well, they'll arrive here just in time for Christmas Eve wassailing," she said, stepping back toward the house. "Come, Sherman. I'm cold."

Sherman took three steps forward and then stopped. He turned and looked up at the flag one last time. Flapping in the wind was the national flag of the United States of America—the Stars and Stripes.

"And let nothing ever tear it down."

Acknowledgments

My sincere thanks to all my friends and family, long past and present who have provided me with inspiration and support throughout my life, and have contributed to the development of this book.

A special thanks to my Uncle Peter, who has shared many old photos and stories about the maternal side of my family's history. They were an integral part in the creation of this story.

Lastly I'd like to thank all the staff and other support personnel associated with Maine Author's Publishing. Their talented and professional organization is a shining example to the self-publishing industry.

 CHRISTOPHER MORIN was born, raised, and currently resides in Portland, Maine. He received a B.A. in Journalism from the University of Maine at Orono. He is a history enthusiast and has enjoyed creative writing ever since penning his first short story back in second grade. Along with this novel, he is also the author of *A Tale of Life & War* and *The Besieged*.